INFINITE STAKES

A Novel of the Battle of Britain

JOHN RHODES

 ROUNDEL HOUSE

Published by Roundel House, Wilmington, North Carolina
johnrhodesbooks.com

Edited and designed by Girl Friday Productions
www.girlfridayproductions.com

Cover design: Anna Curtis
Project management: Bethany Davis

Cover image credits: © Everett Collection Historical / Alamy Stock Photo, DavidSamperio, Laborant, Verina Marina Valerevna, Hudyma Natallia, Keith Tarrier

ISBN (paperback): 978-1-7353736-0-7
ISBN (ebook): 978-1-7353736-1-4

First edition

INFINITE
STAKES

With many thanks to Bunnie, Chris, Les, Maddee,
and Perry, for all their help and encouragement

The odds were great; our margins small; the stakes infinite.
—Winston Churchill, recalling 15 September 1940,
Battle of Britain Day

PART ONE

15 September 1940

0500 to 1300 Hours

ONE

Transcript of TV Interview of Dame Eleanor Shaux, 1 September 2010

Q: (To camera:) *Good evening. Welcome to the first of our special series commemorating the Battle of Britain, which occurred seventy years ago this summer, in 1940. As you know, 15 September is celebrated each year as Battle of Britain Day, which historians generally consider as the day that RAF Fighter Command defeated the Nazi Luftwaffe in the Second World War.*

We are very lucky to have Dame Eleanor Shaux, master emerita of St. Luke's College, Cambridge, to lead us through the process. At the outset of her distinguished career, Dame Eleanor was a WAAF officer— that used to be the Women's Auxiliary Air Force—in 11 Group, Fighter Command, during the Battle of Britain.

Dame Eleanor has agreed to help us put those momentous days in perspective as we look back through seventy years of history.

(To guest:) *Dame Eleanor, good evening, and thank you for being with us. It is seventy years since the Battle of Britain. Do you recall 15 September 1940, the first Battle of Britain Day?*

A: Good evening. Yes, indeed.

Q: I believe you were in the 11 Group control room that day, the room now known as the Battle of Britain Bunker?

A: Yes, I was.

(Deleted:

Q: Please give us longer answers, more descriptive answers, if you would. The audience wants to be able to visualize the experience, to see it through your eyes. Make it as real and personal as you can. Not just what happened, but how did it feel? Don't worry about making mistakes; we can edit them out later. Make it come alive!

A: Oh, sorry. Incidentally, it wasn't the first Battle of Britain Day, it was the actual day.

Q: Oh.

End of deletion.)

Q: Tell us about that day, if you would.

A: I will, but I have to clarify something you said in your introduction. The RAF never defeated the Luftwaffe—the Luftwaffe was still fighting on the day the war ended in 1945.

Q: I take your point that—

A: But, to address your question, the day started with a lot of commotion because Winston Churchill, the prime minister, came to visit 11 Group HQ in Uxbridge. It was the merest coincidence that it turned out to be such a pivotal day in the battle.

Everyone was pretending to carry on as if he wasn't there, but of course we were all a bit overwhelmed. I remember Park was really annoyed. He hated visitors—even Churchill, for whom he had great respect. Park wanted everyone to concentrate on the task at hand, without unnecessary distractions.

Q: Park? That's Sir Keith Park, the 11 Group commander at the time?

A: Yes. In those days, RAF Fighter Command was led by Stuffy Dowding. Fighter Command was divided into four main Groups, each responsible for defending a part of the British Isles. Under Park, 11 Group was responsible for defending London and southeastern England. He had seven squadrons of Spitfires and fourteen squadrons of Hurricanes available that day. There were ninety-two Spitfires and two hundred and eighteen Hurricanes when the day began.

Q: That's very precise of you, Dame Eleanor!

A: I'm a mathematician. I'm paid to be precise.

Q: Er . . . yes, indeed . . . um, quite so! Well, to help us understand the day, can you begin by giving us an idea of what the Battle of Britain was all about? What was its purpose, as it were? Why did it happen?

A: Yes, of course. World War II . . .

(Deleted:

Q: Dame Eleanor, please don't hesitate to ask for a break, or a rest, at any time. We can splice everything together afterwards. Just let me know if this is too much for you.

A: I may be over ninety, young man, but that doesn't mean I'm moribund. Besides, if I have a heart attack while we're doing this, it will undoubtedly improve the ratings for your show enormously, will it not?

End of deletion.)

A: World War II started in September 1939, and by the summer of 1940, Hitler had defeated almost all the nations of continental Europe, and he was preparing to invade Britain and thereby end all opposition to his Third Reich. He needed air superiority over southern England and the English Channel in order to protect his invasion fleet from the RAF.

The Battle of Britain began as a series of bombing attacks against 11 Group fighter stations, radar stations, and so on to force the RAF to retreat north of London and cede the southern skies to the Luftwaffe so that an invasion could take place across the English Channel under Luftwaffe aerial cover. Aircraft had quite limited endurances in those days, so geographic proximity to the Channel was key.

Every day the Germans sent hundreds of bombers to try to put the airfields out of commission, and RAF fighters tried to chase the bombers away and shoot them down if possible. The battle lasted from the middle of August 1940 until the middle of September.

Q: A month?

A: A month. It was a desperate struggle. The Germans lost over a thousand aircraft, and the RAF lost over six hundred—that's over fifty aircraft each day, day after day. It was aerial carnage unlike anything ever seen before or since.

Q: Fifty aircraft shot down every day for a month? That seems unbelievable.

A: Believe me, it happened. Throughout those five weeks, until the very end, the Luftwaffe was poised to win. The RAF was poised to lose—just one bad day, just one tactical mistake, one error of judgment by Park, away from defeat. But then on 15 September, as we now know, the pendulum swung.

Q: Please talk us through the day, Dame Eleanor. What actually happened, as you remember it? You're one of the few remaining witnesses who were there, at 11 Group. How did the day begin?

A: Well...

Eleanor's alarm clock dragged her from a dream of Johnnie—an all-enveloping dream as wickedly delightful as a warm bath lit by flickering candles and scented with rosewater—into a cold, lumpy, coarse-sheeted, narrow bed in a ramshackle WAAF barrack that smelled of inadequate bathroom facilities. It was as black as pitch; the electricity was switched off from midnight until six in the morning to preserve power, and her one grimy window was sealed with blackout material. She struggled into her unseen, shapeless uniform and felt her way to the bathroom at the end of the corridor. The plumbing offered a variety of muffled clunking noises but no running water.

As she attempted to brush her teeth, it occurred to her that it was possible—in fact, it was highly probable—that hell was not hot, as usually assumed, but cold, very cold. In which case it would always be 0500 in the morning, always be dark, and always have plumbing that doesn't function, and Johnnie would always be a trapped in a dream from which she had been dragged and thus excluded and denied.

Actually, she thought, the center, the very core of hell in Dante's *Inferno*, was solid ice—case proven!

At RAF Uxbridge, west of London, 11 Group headquarters consisted of Hillingdon House, a weary white stucco building dating back to the 1700s—somebody's hunting lodge, she'd heard—and an eclectic collection of buildings and barracks set in a small unkempt park. It wasn't a glamorous RAF station with fighters roaring in and out but rather a place to dump odd bits and pieces of administrative functions that didn't really fit into anything else; it had been a signals school, a convalescent center, and a way station for processing troops evacuated from Dunkirk. It now included an English-language school for pilots who had escaped from Hitler's attack on Poland. It had that shabby, uncared-for, run-down look that all government facilities seem to acquire.

Breakfast in the 11 Group officers' mess consisted of what might have once been pork sausages, now aged into fossilized remnants, accompanied by tea and toast. If RAF Uxbridge was destroyed by bombs, Eleanor thought, and many centuries passed, then future archaeologists examining the remains would conclude that everyone had died not from the effects of the bombing but from starvation given the appalling quality of RAF food.

The morning newspapers, tamed by threats of government censorship and editorial control, painted a picture of the air battle that she knew to be falsely optimistic—grossly optimistic. The papers' function, it seemed to Eleanor, was to pump out propaganda rather than actual news.

This was now thirty-something days since all hell had broken out over southern England on 12 August 1940. "The Battle of Britain," Churchill had named it. Every day since then, with only intermittent and short-lived interruptions caused by bad weather, Hitler's Luftwaffe air force had hurled itself at England. Droning bomber formations crossed the English Channel and advanced relentlessly across southern England, wave after wave, bearing death and destruction. Above the bombers, clouds of Messerschmitt Me 109 and Bf 110 fighters waited to howl down on any 11 Group fighters that rose to defy them.

Each day the skies above Kent and Surrey and over London were marked with a scribble-scrabble of contrails, drawn as if in white chalk against the blue sky by the hands of careless children. Every now and again a shattered aircraft or a random bomb or a broken airman would fall out of the sky. Southern England was becoming pockmarked—as though from some hideous disease—with craters dug by the detritus of war.

Hitler had conquered almost all of Europe—Belgium, Luxembourg, Holland, Denmark, Norway, France, Austria, Czechoslovakia, and Poland—in a matter of months. The remaining countries—Sweden, for example—survived by eking out a pallid neutrality. Meanwhile Italy and Russia, Hitler's allies, were picking off pieces of Europe around its edges—bits of Finland, Tunisia, and so on—like hyenas gnawing at a carcass.

The British army had been crushed by Hitler's Panzer divisions in France and Belgium. They had only been rescued from defeat and surrender at Dunkirk by the efforts of civilian sailors braving the cold waters of the Channel to bring the exhausted troops home. That was in June.

Eleanor remembered, to the exact second, the moment she received the telegram delivered by an elderly postman past retirement age to her flat in London—it was raining and the envelope was a little soggy and the glue on the flap was coming undone and the postman had a dripping nose—informing her that her husband, George, had been shot down in his Hurricane over Dunkirk and killed. She remembered, inexplicably guiltily, being saddened but not surprised.

Hitler had subsequently prepared an invasion fleet to cross the English Channel and conquer England, his last remaining enemy. He had stripped the rivers and canals of Holland and Germany of their commercial barges, and a fleet of more than two thousand large Rhine *péniches* and *Kampinenbarges*, capable of carrying at least 300 tons each, was amassed in ports from Bremerhaven in the north to Cherbourg in the south.

Thanks to the highly secret Ultra project breaking German military codes, the British were well aware of Hitler's intentions.

Operation Sea Lion—the invasion itself—was ready, but Hitler could only invade if he had control of the air over the Channel and southern England. Führer Directive No. 16, issued in July to launch the air war against England, instructed the Luftwaffe that the RAF was to be so "reduced morally and physically that it is unable to deliver any significant attack against the German crossing." Lest Hermann Göring, in command of the Luftwaffe, fail to grasp the point, Führer Directive No. 17 on 1 August told him "to overpower the English Air Force with all the forces at its command, in the shortest possible time."

Hence the endless bombing raids—blitzkrieg—to pave the way for his total victory.

It was the responsibility of 11 Group, Fighter Command, to defend southeastern England and drive the bombers and their escorting fighters away. Initially the Luftwaffe raids had focused on 11 Group's fighter stations. If the Luftwaffe could destroy the airfields, 11 Group would be forced to retreat northwards, away from the Channel and therefore away from Hitler's invasion fleet. More recently the raids had expanded into attacks on industrial areas—aircraft factories, docks, and railway stations, for example—and, inevitably, the civilian living areas around them.

Churchill had said, in one of his speeches, "Hitler knows he has to break us in this island or lose the war." Hitler had replied, in a speech of his own: "If one of us breaks, it won't be Nazi Germany."

Eleanor had observed these events unfolding as she stood beside Keith Park, 11 Group's commander, watching the big map in the Operations Room that displayed the ebb and flow of 11 Group and Luftwaffe aircraft as they fought for control of southern England. It was her responsibility to keep track of the statistics—the number of aircraft sent into battle by each side, the number shot down, and so on—so that Park had accurate information upon which to base his decisions.

Over the past few weeks, she had used these statistics as raw material for a mathematic model she painstakingly developed, a series of interrelated formulae that analyzed the balance of forces over England and even calculated the Luftwaffe's possible next steps. It had all been based on the work of the Princeton mathematician John von Neumann and his minimax theory of zero-sum games.

She had boiled the whole thing down to the elementary proposal that the key to winning was not to lose. Or, as Churchill or Hitler might say, not to break.

As Eleanor finished her breakfast and set aside the newspapers, a young RAF dispatch rider zigzagged his way through the half-empty dining tables and handed her a folder of operational reports. There had been bomber raids on several English cities throughout the night; unlike the newspapers, these official reports told a grim reality.

Bombing cities at night was a particularly cynical and cruel act of war, she thought; the raids were basically unstoppable because fighters could not find the bombers at night, and the bombers usually could not see where they were aiming and just dropped their loads, almost at random, often into heavily populated areas as civilians slept.

She flipped through the reports—she'd go back through them again later—and came to the only report that really, really mattered. The status report for 11 Group D Sector said that 339 Squadron, Johnnie's squadron, based at Hawkinge on the southern coast of Kent, was at full strength and listed as available. If the enemy came today—and, based on the weather forecast, they probably would—Johnnie would fly.

TWO

Q: Your husband, Johnnie, was a Spitfire fighter ace, of course, Dame Eleanor. Did he fly that day?

A: "Ace" is a cheap term invented by newspapers to sell newspapers and for the film industry to sell films. No one in Fighter Command in those days ever used that term. Johnnie, my husband, certainly did not consider himself to be an ace. Far from it.

Q: But it is a term that's often—

A: The Battle of Britain was not a video game, nor was it played wearing goggles in—what does one call it?—virtual reality. It was—how can I put it? It was the epitome of asymmetric warfare, a fight to the death between two very different sides with two very different objectives. It was unprecedented in the history of aerial warfare and remains unique to this day. Looking back in time, we see the pilots as heroes, as "the Few," as Churchill described them, but the pilots didn't think of themselves as heroes, or even as particularly brave . . .

Johnnie Shaux lay back in a battered armchair, feigning sleep as the rest of 339 Squadron went about their business around him. The sun wasn't out, but it was warm enough to sit outside in his heavy leather flying jacket. A few of the younger pilots were playing aerial golf with an old golf ball and a battered tennis racquet. The squadron's two flight commanders, Digby and Potter, were in deep conversation; they spent endless hours finding ways to improve 339's effectiveness and safety. Though Shaux was the squadron leader, he gave all the credit for 339's successes and survival to Diggers and Froggie Potter.

Only the ground crews tending the aircraft were working. They fought their own fierce battle against the Luftwaffe ground crews: the margin between victory and defeat in the air could well be the margin between a perfectly maintained airframe or a perfectly tuned engine versus an airframe or engine that was marginally less well maintained. The differences in performance between 11 Group's Spitfire Mk IIs and the Luftwaffe's Messerschmitt 109s were very slight, and the smallest weakness or mechanical failure could be decisive.

Shaux knew that the public assumed that the life of a fighter pilot, a Spitfire pilot, in this crucial pivot point of history, must be a life of nonstop, hectic action: vaulting into a Spitfire in one's dashing leather flying helmet, perhaps wearing an elegant long white silk scarf, as the illustrated papers portrayed it; roaring off into the cloud tops; engaging in a dramatic dogfight, wheeling and circling in a complex arabesque with the enemy, guns blazing; and then home to rearm and refuel and repeat—a life of glamor and glory, exemplifying noblesse oblige and derring-do.

In reality, it seemed to Shaux, the life of a Spitfire pilot was nothing of the sort. It was more accurately described as one of nonstop waiting. He would wait in the dispersal hut, possibly all day, for a telephone call from Sector that might command them to stand by. Then they would wait and perhaps be commanded to readiness, which meant waiting strapped into their aircraft instead of waiting in the hut. Finally, perhaps, after more waiting, they might be commanded into the air—but, then again, perhaps not.

Shaux knew from Eleanor's descriptions of the Operations Room in 11 Group headquarters that Keith Park, the Air Officer Commander of 11 Group, would study the plots of incoming Luftwaffe formations and decide whether and when to launch his fighter squadrons. The AOC, she had told him, was a counterpuncher, preserving his forces as long as possible, harrying the Germans with swift, scattered attacks rather than assembling large formations of Hurricanes and Spitfires and attacking en masse.

It made perfect sense to Shaux: the Luftwaffe had far more aircraft than the RAF, so counterpunching seemed exactly right. Eleanor had told Shaux that Generalfeldmarschall Kesselring, the Luftflotte II commander, Park's principal opponent, kept trying to trick Park into over-committing his forces. For the past month Park had resisted Kesselring's feints and, slowly but surely, had ground down Luftflotte II.

Eleanor, at Park's side, had used von Neumann's minimax theory of games to help Park develop a strategy for resisting the vastly superior Luftwaffe. Her theory was not to try to win but to try not to lose. Park had grasped the concept, as had his boss, Stuffy Dowding, the Fighter Command AOC-in-C. How simple and yet how profound. The greatest air battle in the history of mankind was now being fought on that principle: don't lose!

It was one of Digby's habits to make up mock Latin mottos. Shaux had been forced to learn Latin in school and still retained a smattering. Perhaps someone would adopt Eleanor's concept as a new RAF motto: *numquam perde.* Never lose . . .

A loud cry of "Fore!" and a crash of shattering glass snapped Shaux back to reality.

"I say, old chap, good shot!" someone yelled, and several of the pilots burst into applause. It transpired that the "hole" in aerial golf was the dispersal hut window.

The squadron flight sergeant erupted through the door, holding up a golf ball and clearly clutching at his dignity. "What's all this, then?" he demanded. "What's all this?"

"I think it was a birdie, Flight," Digby said, to a burst of laughter. "The A Flight dispersal hut window is a par four, and I believe that was his third shot."

Flight Sergeant Jenkins was not mollified.

"Well, Mr. Digby, be that as it may, be that as it may, whoever's responsible will have to pay for the repair out of his own pocket." He stared at the remnants of the window, shaking his head. "The station warrant officer will chew my balls off."

"It was me, Flight," said one of the new pilots who had arrived as replacements yesterday evening. Shaux thought his name was

Henderson. "How much is a window? I've haven't got much until pay-day, I'm afraid."

"Perhaps we can all contribute," Shaux said. "If everyone puts in something . . ."

"Absolutely," Digby said. "Good idea."

"Just a minute . . . just a minute . . . ," Jenkins said slowly, staring at the window and scratching the back of his head. "It was a birdie, you said, sir?"

"It was, Flight," said Digby.

"Well, on further reflection, that's a natural phenomenon," Jenkins said. "Birds fly into windows all the time. It can't be helped. It will have to be classified in the station records as an 'Breakages, Unavoidable, Other, Miscellaneous.'"

"Particularly at this time of year, Flight," Digby said. "It's all those baby birds that haven't fully mastered how to fly."

"Very true, sir. Very true." Jenkins nodded. "It's really very sad when you think about it, the cruelty of nature: all those tiny broken beaks, all that unfulfilled promise snuffed out in the twinkling of an eye. Very well. I'll report this to the SWO as a BUOM."

"Excuse me, Flight," said Henderson. "May I have my golf ball back?"

Shaux chuckled, stretched, and wandered out to his waiting Spitfire. The ground crews were fussing over it; two armorers had the inspection covers off the four machine guns in the port wing.

"Nothing wrong, sir; just checking for wear."

Shaux's Spitfire II, with the squadron code KN and his own identity letter, J, for KN-J—King Nuts Johnnie in the RAF's phonetic alphabet—looked a little weary, he thought. The riggers had patched and re-patched holes torn by cannon shells and machine gun bullets in the wings and fuselage. The tail had been replaced after an encounter with a 109, and the new paint didn't match the camouflage on the rest of the aircraft. The long, sleek nose that housed the magnificent twelve-cylinder, twenty-seven-liter Rolls-Royce Merlin Mk XII engine was scorched from a minor fire and streaked with a long line of black soot branded into the fuselage behind the exhaust manifolds. Definitely weary, Shaux thought; the Spit was fully twelve days old and beginning to show its age.

It was becoming a habit for pilots to paint little swastikas on their fuselages, just below the cockpit, to signify their combat victories. It was supposed to be like the notches on six-shooters in American Western cowboy films. The newspapers loved it. Shaux did not. He refused to allow it in 339: every swastika meant one or more dead Luftwaffe pilots and crewmen. Luftwaffe pilots were not the enemy in a traditional sense, as far as Shaux was concerned. They were just young men who had been swept up into a hideous war, just as Shaux and all of 339 had been, and were sent out to kill or be killed, like gladiators in ancient Rome.

Still, Shaux thought, a little worn and weary or not, the Spitfire remained the finest fighter in the sky. The Luftwaffe had two principal fighters, the single-engine Messerschmitt Me 109 and the twin-engine Messerschmitt Bf 110. The Spitfire had a performance edge—not much of an edge, but an edge nonetheless—over the 109 and was so superior to the 110 that the 110 often needed 109s to protect it.

The Spitfire was also superior to the Hawker Hurricane, 11 Group's main fighter, in Shaux's opinion. There were twice as many Hurricane squadrons as Spitfires in 11 Group. Park used Hurricanes to attack Luftwaffe bombers, whenever possible, and they did so with considerable success.

The Luftwaffe tended to send fighters in at high altitudes, at fifteen thousand to twenty-five thousand feet, to provide protective cover for their bombers, which usually flew at lower altitudes. This was the basis of Park's strategy: Spitfires would fly high to disrupt the 109s and prevent them from tracking along above the bombers, while Hurricanes jumped on the unprotected bombers down below. The Spitfires didn't need to shoot the 109s down; they just had to distract them so that the bombers flew on unescorted, into the gunsights of waiting Hurricanes.

The Germans were flying three types of bombers over England: Dornier 17s, Junkers 88s, and Heinkel 111s. Sometimes the Germans would send hundreds across the Channel at once, trying to overwhelm Park's defenses. They were described as *schnellbombers*—"fast bombers"—but they lumbered along at less than 250 miles per hour when fully loaded with a ton of bombs, 100 miles per hour slower than the fighters. They were very effective at delivering their lethal payloads when flying unopposed, but they were highly vulnerable when attacked by Hurricanes.

Shaux was always in awe of the rigid discipline that kept the German bomber crews flying in neat formations of ten or twenty or thirty aircraft towards their targets, even as Hurricanes surrounded and hacked away at them.

Shaux couldn't believe the Luftwaffe aircrews were all ardent Nazis, flying for the glory of the Aryan race, the honor of the Third Reich, or admiration of Adolf Hitler, the Führer, or any such nonsense. He was certain that they were simply young men, like the 11 Group pilots who opposed them; just finishing high school or in college, newly taught to fly and just trying to do the best they could to carry out the orders they had been given. One automatically obeyed adults as a child and teachers in school, because discipline was the backbone of society and a swift whack awaited any disobedience; now, similarly, one obeyed the senior officers who sent one into battle.

He strolled on past 339's other Spitfires. They all looked a bit battered, come to think of it. Well, they flew almost every day and often several times a day, and they were frequently outnumbered two to one or worse. The price of the privilege of flying a Spitfire, the finest aircraft ever made, was that one flew against 109s, which were almost as good and just as deadly.

He lit a cigarette and wondered what Eleanor was doing. She'd probably be in the 11 Group Operations Room or at her desk, working on her zero-sum model. It was ironic that she had a much better idea of what was going on over England than he did, and he was actually flying over England.

But far more importantly, tonight he had an overnight pass. A ground crew sergeant with access to a lorry had agreed to drive him up to London, and one of Eleanor's friends had lent Eleanor her flat near Harrods, and then they would both have exactly the same understanding of what was going on . . .

THREE

Q: The 11 Group Operations Room at Uxbridge is now preserved as a museum, the Battle of Britain Bunker, just as Churchill's War Rooms have been preserved in the basements and foundations of Whitehall in London. Have you been back to Uxbridge to see it?

A: No, I must admit I haven't. Goodness me. It all seems so long ago. I don't really know if I want to go back—perhaps I have too many memories . . .

Q: What was it like to work in that room back in 1940?

A: Looking back with the benefit of hindsight, I realize now that I was privileged to have a front-row seat at one of the greatest dramas in modern history. I can say that without exaggeration. But at the time it was just a place to work. It was noisy, dark, a bit smelly, a bit ramshackle, crowded, a bit claustrophobic . . .

Eleanor left the 11 Group headquarters building and crossed the lawn to the concrete entrance guarding the subterranean Operations Room. The grass was muddy and worn from constant use; it was typical of the whole makeshift command center that no one had thought to install a pathway. Long flights of roughly built stairs led downward to concrete tunnels festooned with communications wires and to the

11 Group Operations Room, the nerve center of England's resistance to the Luftwaffe's bomber swarms. Everything was painted in the yellowy-cream paint that seemed to be the standard color of British officialdom.

The Operations Room was dominated by a large table some twenty feet on a side. A huge map of southern England and northern France and Belgium was painted on it. WAAFs wearing telephone headsets pushed markers across the map to indicate the location of enemy aircraft formations and 11 Group defenders. Balconies overlooked the map table so that intelligence officers and controllers could see and assess the situation and direct RAF responses to Luftwaffe raids.

A large display on the far wall, known as the Tote Board, indicated the status of each squadron. Eleanor's eyes went automatically to 339. She saw that 339's status was "Available 30 Minutes." Johnnie would be waiting patiently, perhaps thinking about tonight—she was sure he was thinking about tonight.

It was tempting to think of the map table, with its markers advancing and retreating, ebbing and flowing, as the battle itself, but of course it was not. The real battle was being fought at fifteen thousand feet by pilots like Johnnie who were strapped into tiny cockpits in fighter aircraft and behind huge engines with a tank of explosive high-octane fuel just in front of the instrument panel, three feet from the pilot's face. The design of a Spitfire required weight to be concentrated forward with the center of gravity between the wing roots. This accounted for the superb balance of a Spit and its legendary agility, but also for the very high frequency with which Spitfire pilots were transformed into human torches and incinerated.

The pilots, she knew, had no idea of the battle as a whole. All they could see was their tiny section of the sky, their squadrons around them, and, occasionally, for just a few seconds at a time, the enemy appearing in their gunsights or bursting down upon them.

Eleanor saw that the map was almost empty. The WAAFs and controllers were at ease. It seemed the Luftwaffe were taking the day off or making a late start. A tiny premonition struck her. The days that the enemy sent really large formations usually started late, reaching a crescendo in the afternoon. It took time for Kesselring to get his forces all lined up at the right heights and in the right order . . . Might this be such a day? Eleanor accepted a cup of tea and began to review the last week of German activity, almost like a newsreel playing in her mind. Let's see . . .

There was a little rustle around the room as Park entered.

The man who commanded 11 Group, the man responsible for repelling the Luftwaffe and saving England, was Air Vice-Marshal Keith Park. He was a New Zealander who had been a distinguished fighter pilot in the 1914–18 war, the Great War, as it was called. He had been appointed to be the 11 Group AOC only in May; he'd had just two months to plan how to defend England before all hell broke loose.

The AOC looked exhausted, she thought. He'd lost weight in the last few weeks, and his cheeks had hollowed. His shoulders, usually so square and straight, like a Grenadier Guard on parade in front of Buckingham Palace, seemed to be drooping. It was as if, like Atlas, he was carrying the whole weight of the world on his shoulders. Well, she thought, as Churchill had said in one of his speeches, the whole weight of the *free* world.

A spider's web of lines radiated out from the corners of his eyes, etched by stress. She wondered if he could ever relax, have a good dinner and a glass of wine or whisky, and laugh at a comedy on the radio, or whether his mind was always on the map table, or in the cockpits with his pilots, or on the catalog of carnage her statistics gave him. When he slept, did he escape into oblivion, or was he haunted by dreams of falling bombs, falling aircraft, and falling men?

She resolved to stand up straight herself, and square her shoulders, and to eat more, regardless of how much the RAF diet disgusted her. Park needed her and, just as importantly—more so—so did Johnnie. Perhaps she should break the rules and buy real, unrationed food on the black market? She'd overheard two RAF clerks talking about a certain butcher's shop where you needed cash but not ration books. She wondered if Johnnie thought she was too thin. Perhaps he preferred plump, bouncy girls with well-rounded . . .

"Good morning, Eleanor," Park said, abruptly dragging her from her consideration of Johnnie's erotic preferences. "I hope it's quiet this morning. Churchill's coming to pay us a visit."

"He is? Mr. Churchill?"

"Indeed. I understand he wants to see how we do things firsthand, and I think he wants to talk to you again."

"Oh dear," Eleanor said, her heart sinking. "I hope not."

A week or two ago, when she had used her zero-sum model to predict a change in German tactics, a change towards bombing London, Churchill had summoned her to 10 Downing Street, the prime minister's official residence, in Westminster. He had decided, he told her, to establish a new intelligence unit, under her command, that would take over her mathematical model and develop it to study the war against Germany.

She had to admit she was flattered by his confidence and enthusiasm, but she really didn't want to do it. She didn't want to be the head of anything; she just wanted Johnnie.

After several false starts with other men, she had finally found Johnnie—a man she wanted and who wanted her. She realized that she had never really been in love before. She had assumed it would be happy and romantic, as Hollywood films showed it. She had never expected it to be painful, intensely demanding, all-consuming. Worse yet, she had fallen for a man who was engaged in a fight to the death, one in mortal danger every day.

Her deep-down, innermost insuppressible fear was that Johnnie was going to die, in which case she wanted his last days or weeks or months or whatever time he was given to be as wonderful as she could make them. They probably had no long-term future; today—tonight—was all that mattered.

In comparison, the thought of being put in charge of her own intelligence department to develop her own mathematical model, blessed by Churchill himself, was simply insignificant.

"Oh dear," she said again.

"Quite so, Eleanor. I agree," Park said. "Churchill's a great man. I admire him deeply. I just wish he would visit someone else. Anyway, that aside, how are we doing this morning?"

"We have ninety-two Spitfires available, sir, seven squadrons, and two hundred and eighteen Hurricanes in fourteen squadrons. In addition, 10 Group has a hundred and sixteen additional aircraft available to support us from the west of England, should we need them."

"And 12 Group?" Park asked. While Park enjoyed a warm relationship with the 10 Group AOC, Quinton Brand, his relationship with Trafford Leigh-Mallory, the 12 Group AOC, was frosty at best.

"They have approximately two hundred aircraft, as far as I can guess from what they tell us, sir." Eleanor sometimes suspected that Leigh-Mallory deliberately withheld information from Park. "They have the Duxford Wing available."

"Ah, yes, the Big Wing, five squadrons acting as one." Park smiled. A dispute over the use of multiple squadrons united in a single wing, favored by Leigh-Mallory, versus single squadrons or even single flights acting individually, favored by Park, was a major source of the acrimony between the two men.

"How about Luftflotte II, Eleanor?" Park asked. "I sometimes think we know more about the Luftwaffe than about 12 Group."

"I'm afraid so, sir." Eleanor smiled. "I estimate that Kesselring has approximately five hundred 109s, a hundred 110s, and five hundred bombers. The bombers are mostly 17s and 111s."

"I wonder if the day will ever dawn that Kesselring does *not* outnumber me." Park sighed. "I'm happy to compete with two hundred Hurricanes against five hundred bombers, and the 110s are less and less of a factor, but I'm not happy about one hundred Spitfires against five hundred 109s."

Those, thought Eleanor with a shudder, were the raw odds against Johnnie: five to one. Johnnie's Spitfire squadron was based at Hawkinge on the coast of Kent, less than thirty miles from France. There were 109s based at Caffiers, just south of Calais, led by Adolf Galland, Germany's greatest fighter pilot. Galland was only six minutes' flying time from Johnnie.

A telephone rang and Park turned away to answer it. She saw that her modeling team was waiting for her with the latest statistics and projections. Luftflotte II had lost half its bombers in the past month, Dornier 17s and Heinkel 111s. At some point they'd have to give up daylight bombing as simply too expensive.

That would mean that Hitler wouldn't be able to drive 11 Group away from southern England, which, in turn, meant that he wouldn't be able to invade across the Channel. Park would have done the impossible: defeated an enemy that everyone had thought was undefeatable.

But would Kesselring give up? Would Göring and Hitler permit him? It seemed hard to believe . . . Kesselring had a tendency to mount major raids after lulls . . . perhaps he'd try one more all-out attack . . . perhaps hundreds of aircraft, trying to swamp 11 Group . . . perhaps he'd try today.

Eleanor saw that Park was finishing a telephone call.

"Thank you," he said and replaced the receiver. "Churchill's on his way. Let's just hope for a quiet day."

They both glanced at the empty map table. Belgium and northern France, where the Luftflotte II airfields were located, were bare. Chain Home radar had not detected any moves by Kesselring. Galland was still on the ground: so far, so good. Several of the WAAFs were knitting, their needles clicking like well-tuned machinery. Eleanor had been taught to knit at school when she was eight or nine; the results had been lumpy and misshapen. Her mother had been appalled—at the school, not Eleanor. Only working-class girls knitted, it transpired, so Eleanor was taught embroidery instead. Johnnie had told her it was very cold in a Spitfire at altitude; it would have been nice to knit him a scarf. Perhaps she should get some fine linen for a handkerchief and embroider his initials, or even a silk scarf . . .

"What are we going to do with the prime minister, sir?" she asked.

"That's up to you, Eleanor." Park chuckled. "I'm appointing you his babysitter."

FOUR

Q: When did the first raids start that day?

A: I recall it was pretty quiet in the morning. The main excitement was an unexploded bomb they had to lift out of the crypt of St. Paul's Cathedral. They took it on a lorry through the streets of the East End until they could blow it up safely. Imagine a live, six-hundred-pound bomb on the back of a bumpy lorry driving down the Mile End Road! The police were telling everyone to open their windows to reduce the risk of flying glass in case it exploded prematurely.

Q: Hard to believe.

A: Churchill arrived at 11 Group in Uxbridge about eleven o'clock in the morning. He was in a huff. He had apparently forgotten that it was Mrs. Churchill's birthday, so he was in the doghouse, and to make matters worse, Park had to tell him he wasn't allowed to smoke cigars underground. He ended up in a hissy fit, glowering and chewing an unlit Havana.

Q: You knew him quite well, I believe. What was he like?

A: Well, I saw him often, but I don't know if I knew him well. In many ways he was like a child: willful, petulant, demanding, self-absorbed.

He was almost seventy, then, and I was only twenty-two. I know it's silly, but I always thought of myself as older and more mature.

Q: (Chuckles.)

A: On the other hand, he was overwhelming. He's often and correctly described as charismatic; he seemed to emanate a sort of primordial force, a sort of magnetism. Like him or loathe him—and there were plenty of people in both camps, then and throughout his life, before and since—you couldn't ignore him. It was almost as if he was a myth or a larger-than-life caricature of himself come to life, played by a skilled actor who could imitate his voice . . .

"Ah, Squadron Officer, we meet again," Churchill greeted her. "Let us hope for a quiet day. Let us hope there will be nothing to detain me in these grim caverns so that I might return to the upper atmosphere, where the sun shines and the breezes blow and I am permitted to smoke."

He shot a baleful glance at Park.

"Be that as it may," Churchill said, slumping in his chair and glaring up at her from beneath his eyebrows, "I have pondered our last conversation, Squadron Officer, in which you said that the key to winning is not losing. I know you do not mean a mere tautology. What, pray, do you mean?"

He had a way of making himself central and everyone else peripheral, she thought. It was not arrogance; it was just that he saw his own understanding as the most important, and she was being invited to make a contribution. Like the earth before Galileo and Copernicus, she thought, the universe revolved around him.

Eleanor took a deep breath.

"It means denying one's opponent the opportunity to win, sir. So, for example, one always takes the center space in a game of noughts and crosses because it halves the number of ways your opponent can win. It reduces the number of ways you can lose from eight ways to only four. It doesn't guarantee you'll win, but it makes it much less likely your opponent will beat you."

"But how does that apply to our present circumstances, pray tell me?" He shook his head in frustration.

Eleanor saw she had not explained anything.

"In order to win, sir, Kesselring, who commands Luftflotte II under Hermann Göring, must bomb RAF stations. He must put those RAF stations out of commission. Mr. Park is focusing on not letting the bombers through, thus denying Kesselring the opportunity to win. Thus, Mr. Park doesn't have to win in the sense of shooting down all the bombers; he just has to stop Kesselring from bombing RAF stations by chasing the bombers away."

"So we don't have to win?"

"Exactly, sir! We simply have to prevent Kesselring from winning."

Churchill frowned and Eleanor inwardly grimaced. He obviously thought she was simply playing with words!

"Well, be that as it may, Squadron Officer, let us move on." She couldn't tell if he had shrugged his shoulders or simply adjusted his posture. "Have you considered your new endeavor?"

When she had met Churchill at 10 Downing Street, he had been fascinated by her zero-sum model. She had taken the pioneering work on game theory done by the Princeton mathematician von Neumann, which he called minimax or zero-sum, and used it as the basis of her new mathematical model of asymmetrical warfare. The underlying proposition was that the key to winning a contest was not to lose. She had used that proposition to help Park develop 11 Group's strategies and to predict the Luftwaffe's counterstrategy.

Destroying 11 Group's RAF stations and Chain Home radar stations was fundamental to Hitler's ability to launch an invasion. But Eleanor had predicted that Hitler would stop bombing RAF stations, and start launching bombing attacks on London early in September—and indeed he had.

Churchill had been deeply impressed by her model and her prediction. He told her that he wanted her to apply her theory to the war against Germany as a whole. He wanted her to develop a strategic model that would analyze every move Hitler made, and predict its causes and consequences. This was to be her new endeavor.

Eleanor didn't want a new mission. She wanted to stay with Park. She wanted to luxuriate in her newfound love for Johnnie. She wanted a long break after the cumulative stress of the past few months.

She wanted someone else to take over her strategic model, her zero-sum analysis of the battle. Her team members had all been killed in bombing raids. She wanted time to grieve for them. She had been proud of her model, her accomplishment, but now it simply reminded her of the people, the companions, she had lost and how much she missed them. Their replacements just wouldn't be the same.

She secretly feared her model might be a stroke of luck that worked for the Battle of Britain—for a discrete competition between two finite, describable forces—but would not work for anything larger and more complicated, like, for example, Germany's alliance with Soviet Russia. She emphatically did not want to spend her days trying to put herself in Hitler's deranged shoes and guess his next moves, like some latter-day devil's advocate.

She didn't want to be sent off to some gloomy country house to be surrounded by tightly strung, self-absorbed mathematical geniuses with monstrous egos and poor habits of personal hygiene. She had been sent to Bletchley Park, where a coterie of young Cambridge mathematicians worked on German codes and cyphers, the highly secret Ultra project, to "get an idea of what her group would be like." She had been horrified.

She was, well . . . in her innermost heart, she was frightened of her model. She was frightened that it reduced warfare to a handful of formulae that were utterly devoid of humanity. Soldiers, sailors, and airmen would be pushed around like automata by mathematical formulae that might well be wrong but were certainly heartless. She was frightened by what the model could do—what it could be made to do—in the wrong hands. She was frightened it would consume her.

Worse yet, her model had been declared top secret. No one was allowed to talk about it for fear the Germans would develop a version of their own. Her office—her oversized closet—was now locked and guarded by a fierce-looking RAF policeman. She was being transferred into Military Intelligence, into a new group named MI6-3b. She was being drawn from the clear blue skies of 11 Group into a shadowy world of deception and equivocation, a world whose motto might as well be "The end justifies the means."

"Yes, Prime Minister," she answered, for, in truth, despite her misgivings, she had no choice but to do as he asked.

"I foresee that you will be very successful, Mrs. Rand," he said, as if sensing her concerns.

"How do you know, sir?"

"Because I understand a new organization is being prepared to harbor you, a new intelligence department, and they're all fighting over you," Churchill chuckled. "All of them! MI6 . . . RAF Intelligence . . . MI5 . . . the GC&CS chaps at Bletchley Park . . . NID in room 39 . . . even the War Office! They all want you! It is my experience that when civil servants and senior uniformed officers and other government officials compete for something, that something is considered important and valuable and, above all, powerful."

He shook his head. "But I will put a stop to that. I want you to be independent. I don't want you to be merely an item in someone else's agenda. I shall therefore give instructions that you will report to the cabinet secretary directly. If you wish to see me, speak to him."

He shot a spiteful look to Park.

"Doubtless you will be housed in some bleak country house: such are the ways of government. However, wherever it is, I will make it very clear to all concerned that smoking cigars will always be permitted and, indeed, encouraged."

Park grinned but did not reply, his eyes on the map table. Churchill followed his eyes. The map was still almost bare. The few markers scattered across it represented lone German aircraft on reconnaissance missions. There were no 11 Group aircraft airborne. The attendant WAAFs still sat around the table, knitting or writing letters. There was a subdued clatter of teacups on saucers.

"Tell me, Squadron Officer, what do you see when you look at the map?" Churchill asked. "How does the map transform itself into a set of formulae and columns of numbers in your mathematical construction?"

Eleanor paused. No one had ever asked her that. He might not understand the mathematics of probabilities, but he seemed to have an instinctive grasp of what was . . . she struggled to frame her thought . . . what was important, what was essential.

"The map is flat, two-dimensional, sir, just paint on the tabletop with the markers on it," she answered slowly. "But the actual battle is being waged in the skies in three dimensions—or, I should say, in four. Imagine, if you can, that the markers the WAAFs are pushing around could rise into the air and float at different altitudes. Imagine that the markers could move so that you could see them converging and diverging, climbing and descending.

"It is often said that Mr. Park and the AOC-in-C on our side and Kesselring and Göring on their side are playing chess. That's true, but they are playing chess in three dimensions. That's what I see. It's a mathematician's eye, I suppose. A nonmathematician sees numbers; a mathematician sees form and flow. I see a virtual three-dimensional space with aircraft moving within it, just as fish swim in a body of water. The flight of each aircraft can be described precisely by a mathematical function within the rules of calculus—a function derivative from, and obedient to, the laws of fluid dynamics. I see mathematical functions moving above the map, climbing, descending, turning, clashing; describing, with absolute precision, aircraft moving in the three-dimensional space above Kent and Surrey."

"That's fascinating, Mrs. Rand. I think I see exactly what you mean. You write a formula; I paint a tree. When I paint a tree, or an orchard, or a coppice, I'm not trying to make a hand-drawn photograph; I'm trying to capture the essence of the tree, the *tree-ness* of the tree."

Eleanor had heard that Churchill painted landscapes to relax. She wondered what they looked like.

"Anyway, to business," he continued, returning to the prosaic functions of government. "When you commence your new endeavor, the Cabinet Office will send you a summary of all the operational intelligence I have, perhaps every few days or more frequently if occasion warrants. You will respond by telling me what you think it means in terms of German intentions and objectives. You will also, and this is most important, tell me if you think their plans will succeed or fail and why. I shall ask you not only about specific tactics but also about strategies at a more general level. You must not under any circumstances communicate with anyone but the Cabinet Office unless I so instruct. You must . . ."

A phone rang shrilly, and then another, and another. The controllers jerked to attention. The WAAFs stood, set aside their knitting and their letters, and adjusted their headsets.

"Prime Minister," Park said, setting down a telephone. "It appears Kesselring is preparing to send us some trade."

FIVE

Q: *Dame Eleanor, did you have any sense that the fifteenth of September might be a climactic day?*

A: *My analysis for Keith Park was that it might be busy, but I didn't think it would be pivotal. Besides, in life, unlike calculus, one cannot predict pivots; one can only detect them in arrears.*

Q: *What—*

A: *When the second derivative of a function is zero, the function reverses concavity; it is inflecting.*

Q: *Oh . . .*

A: *Anyway, please remember that from early August until the end of September, we were just one day away from losing. One day! In that regard, Battle of Britain Day, as we now call it, Sunday the fifteenth of September, was just another day of fighting, just "another bloody Sunday," if I can be a little melodramatic.*

Q: *What—*

A: Park was stretched to the limit. Leigh-Mallory in 12 Group was providing too little, too late. My husband and all the pilots were just trying to stay alive. The ground crews were working eighteen hours a day to repair and patch up the aircraft and rearm and refuel them. The WAAFs were trying to decipher blips on cathode ray screens and scrambled voices amid the static in their headsets. The controllers were confronting the confusion of contradictory and incomplete information gushing in from Chain Home and Observer Corps stations. The only question that counted was: When dawn breaks, would Park still have enough aircraft to defend us for another day, or would we have been broken?

Q: Did your husband—

A: I think it has been forgotten that the pilots actually fighting the battle had almost no idea of what was going on. They sat around in their dispersal huts, waiting for the phone to ring. Then they were ordered to take off and then vectored to an interception point where there might or might not be enemy aircraft. All they knew of the battle was what they could see around them, and, depending on the weather, that might not be very much at all. Clouds could conceal the enemy or the sun. Pilots could see what was above them but had only a restricted view of what was below and behind them. In Uxbridge I could stand beside Park and see the battle laid out before me. My husband could see only a little patch of sky in the midst of the battle.

Q: Did he fly that day?

A: He did. Indeed he did . . .

Shaux finished a walk beside the hedgerow that separated the airfield from a wheat field. A farmer was harvesting, seated on an ancient reaping machine drawn by two plodding shire horses. A woman Shaux assumed was his wife followed behind, picking up the sheaves and stacking them to dry. She must have the body of an athlete, muscled and toned, he thought, to stoop, lift, and stack; walk a few paces; and stoop, lift and stack again, seemingly tirelessly. They had started at the edges of the field, Shaux saw, and were slowly working their way towards the center, leaving a diminishing island of uncut wheat in the center of the field. The machine clicked and clattered, and a rabbit sprang from the island of wheat and raced for the safety of the hedgerow. Nothing could offer a more vivid contrast to the peaceful rustic scene beyond the hedge than the Spitfires and their attendant crews. It had been a glorious summer, or so the newspapers said, and it was now a splendid autumn, but the seasons meant nothing on Shaux's side of the hedge.

In the summer of 1918, at the end of the last war just twenty-two years ago, Shaux thought, his father had been killed, shot down in a Sopwith Camel fighter by a German Albatross, and his mother had died shortly afterward from a bomb dropped on London from a Zeppelin airship. The politicians had all promised that that was the war to end all wars and nothing like it could ever happen again. Now Shaux was flying against German fighters, and bombs were falling on London by day and by night.

Another rabbit broke cover and raced for the hedgerow, but this time a hawk swooped down out of the sunshine and took it, ruthlessly, precisely, mercilessly. Perhaps the two sides of the hedge were not so different after all.

"No, no, Dobson. Don't use a pliers, slip-joint. Use a pliers, locking."

Shaux's ponderings were interrupted by the voice of a ground crew sergeant working on a nearby Spitfire. The quartermasters who maintained RAF inventories used descriptive phrases for supplies and stores so that a pair of pliers would be categorized by its type, size, and so on, as in "pliers, slip-joint" as opposed to "pliers, locking." These descriptions had become part of 339's general language, so that one might have an "eggs, scrambled" for breakfast or a "pints, brown ale" at the local pub.

Shaux checked with Digby and Potter; 339's status had been raised from "Available 30 Minutes" to "Available."

There was still nothing to do. Shaux reclaimed his seat—rank had its privileges—closed his eyes, and attempted to think of nothing. Harry Pound, Shaux's former station commander who was killed a week ago in a 110 sneak attack, had told him to "concentrate on nothingness" in order to relax and prepare for battle, to be completely aware but without specific focus. "Close your eyes to see more clearly," Pound had said. Pound had spent some time in India and studied yoga. Shaux didn't believe in anything he couldn't see or touch but was willing to give it a try; if it was good enough for Pound, it was surely good enough for him.

Pound had expressed it as a state in which two opposites could both be true, like the alert watchfulness necessary to survive in the air and the calm necessary to make rapid rational decisions. Pound had likened it to the state of Schrödinger's famous hypothetical cat in quantum physics, which had been both alive and dead at the same time. It had become a private joke between them. "How's Schrödinger's cat today?" Pound would ask him.

Shaux willed himself to remain calm. He hated the waiting, waiting, waiting, not knowing if they would fly or not and, if they did fly, whether they would find the enemy or not, and if they did find the enemy . . .

Perhaps he should get a book to read or do some of the paperwork that was piling up on his desk. Shaux was far from thinking about nothing; his thoughts were careening hither and yon.

Keith Park, Eleanor's boss, had flown in a few days ago—was it only yesterday? Shaux had not met him before, but he felt he already knew the AOC from Eleanor's glowing descriptions. In person, Park struck Shaux as a simple, straightforward man, direct and to the point. He had arrived flying his own Hurricane, and he was wearing old-fashioned white flying overalls. Other senior officers, conscious of their rank, arrived in grand staff cars dressed in splendid uniforms.

"Ah, Shaux," Park had said, "I'm glad to meet you at last. I had the pleasure of knowing your father. He was a fine man. I'm sure he would be very proud to know you're following in his footsteps."

"Yes, sir," Shaux replied, not knowing what else to say; his father's footsteps led to being shot down and killed in aerial combat, but Shaux knew that Park didn't mean that.

"Harry Pound knew him as well. Pound was a very good man too, a good friend, and it's a tragedy he was killed."

Pound had been in command of RAF Oldchurch when a formation of Messerschmitt 110s had erupted out of nowhere in a sneak attack. Pound had been killed on the ground, manning an antiaircraft gun position of his own design. Shaux had run to the only operational aircraft available, an obsolescent Boulton Paul Defiant. Eleanor, who had been visiting Pound, followed him. Since the Defiant's guns were in a separate turret, inaccessible to the pilot, Shaux had had no choice but to bring her as his gunner. They'd been able to shoot down one of the 110s.

"Yes, sir," Shaux said again.

"I don't know if a Defiant has managed to shoot down a 110 before or if you're the first," Park said. "Anyway, it was a damned good show, and a damned good show by Eleanor Rand, of course. Churchill told me to give her a medal, which I was delighted to do."

"It was very well deserved," Shaux said. "She was wonderful." He stopped abruptly, lest he reveal just how wonderful he really thought she was.

"Well, you certainly deserve one as well, Shaux. It was a remarkable piece of flying," Park said, offering his hand. "A second DFC! Congratulations!"

Shaux had mumbled something as Park shook his hand; Shaux loathed public accolades and wished he hadn't been singled out. Now everyone would stare at him on buses and trains and on the London Underground.

Pound had been a brilliant mathematician in civilian life, a Cambridge professor. He had also been an inspired amateur engineer, delighting in projects such as creating hydraulic gun platforms out of old Defiant turrets powered by Morris Oxford bullnose cars.

He'd been helping Eleanor develop her zero-sum model. Now she had his advice no more. Eleanor's team had also been killed in a different bombing raid on London, so she'd been scrambling to rebuild a team and keep her model up-to-date.

Shaux had therefore formulated the brilliant idea of volunteering to assist her. He was, after all, one of the few mathematicians in England who had actually studied minimax while he was at Oxford. It was obviously important; Churchill had told Eleanor he wanted her to expand her studies. And, coincidentally, it would allow him to spend a minimum of twelve hours every day in her company, preferably twenty-four.

It was interesting that Park had given him a medal for a "remarkable piece of flying," rather than a victory. Park was a pilot, a professional; he understood the skill involved in getting a tired old Defiant into a position where it could avoid the vastly superior firepower of three 110s and still find a way to bring one of them down.

"Excuse me, sir," a voice intruded. "Sector says readiness at 1100 hours."

"Thank you," Shaux said, without opening his eyes. Eleanor would see the lights on the 339 Tote Board move to "Ordered to Readiness." She would be thinking of him.

Shaux and Eleanor had met at Oxford and become close friends. Well, in truth, he had adored her, and she had permitted him to be an acolyte. Unable to find the courage to declare his feelings, Shaux had watched mutely and painfully as she had bumbled through a series of unsuccessful relationships with other men. She was always searching for someone, or so it seemed, but never for him.

Then Oxford ended and the war started. Shaux was swept up in the RAF's desperate fight for survival, while Eleanor joined the WAAFs and eventually moved to Park's staff in 11 Group, where she developed her model.

Their paths had crossed again when she came down to visit Pound at RAF Oldchurch, where 339 was stationed. Suddenly, miraculously, totally unexpectedly, inexplicably, she returned his love. He did not understand why, but he didn't care. It was as if the sun had suddenly come out on a spring day after a long and grueling winter.

Shaux had never been loved. He had no family and few friends. He had taught himself to be happy—or, at least, content—in his own company. He had never even kissed a girl. Now, suddenly, he felt as if he had been transported to the Garden of Eden in the time before God had mandated the use of fig leaves.

But there was a rub: he was flying against the Luftwaffe every day. He had already been shot down twice. The laws of probability dictated that he would meet his fate very soon—perhaps today, perhaps this morning. He carried within the innermost corners of his brain the poem by William Butler Yeats that began:

I know that I will meet my fate
Somewhere among the clouds above.

He knew it; he just knew it: paradise found, and lost, in the twinkling of an eye.

SIX

Q: What did the mathematical model tell you on a day-by-day basis? Did it tell Park what Kesselring was going to do?

A: It gave him probabilities. There were no certainties.

Q: Just how accurate was Red Tape? That was the model's code name, was it not?

A: It wasn't called Red Tape then. It was still just called a zero-sum model. Churchill coined that name months later, as a joke, because I always sent him files in red folders. During the Battle of Britain, each day we input the Luftwaffe's activities, the number and type of aircraft they flew, their targets, our interception rates, and so on, and used the model to estimate probabilities for the future. I know it's been hyped as some kind of crystal ball, but it wasn't . . .

"What does your model tell us, Eleanor?" Park asked.

"I'll see if we've calculated any new updates," Eleanor said, and picked up a telephone.

Eleanor's original zero-sum model team had been killed a week ago in the first blitz attack on London—Millie, Eleanor's effervescent assistant, as sharp as a tack, pert, blond, and a slayer of men's hearts with a single, flashing glance; and Kristoffer, who described himself as just a good old country hog farmer from North Carolina but who also just happened to be a Princeton-trained mathematician completing his second PhD.

Millie had bent the RAF's supine administrative bureaucracy to her will, or at least the male half of the bureaucracy, so that accurate data on each day's fighting flowed smoothly to the model team. Kristoffer had brought order and discipline to the model itself and had fine-tuned it just as a racing mechanic fine-tunes a sports car so that the model now outperformed Eleanor's wildest hopes.

Millie had been replaced by Jayne Jackson, a primly severe grammar school arithmetic teacher, and Kristoffer had been replaced by Algernon Bramble, a highly competent but also highly annoying Cambridge mathematician. While Millie had used charm to extract the data from the bureaucracy, Jayne used intimidation—it seemed to work just as well. While Kris had used the power of rigorous thought to refine the model, Bramble brought a sort of nervous intellectual energy, a cerebral dynamism, which also seemed to work in its own way.

"Statistical Research Office, Sergeant Jackson speaking," the voice on the telephone announced.

"Jayne, is that you?" Eleanor asked. "What on earth is the Statistical Research Office?"

"Mr. Bramble told me to use that name, ma'am. He said we didn't have a name, and we needed one."

Eleanor sighed. Very soon she would have to decide if Bramble's extensive eccentricities were worth his undoubted abilities.

"Is he there?"

"Just a moment, ma'am."

"Bramble speaking, 11 Group SRO."

"Mr. Bramble, stop using that ridiculous expression immediately."

"We need a name."

"Why?"

"If we don't have a name, we don't exist."

"Who said that?"

"René Descartes."

"No, he didn't—you're making that up!"

"Well, it might have been Schopenhauer—or Confucius. I can't remember exactly which."

"Rubbish!"

"Well, all right, true, but Confucius would have said it if he'd thought of it—in Mandarin, of course. He probably thought of it but didn't write it down. Or he did think of it and wrote it down, but it got lost over the centuries. It's why every culture has naming ceremonies, baptisms and so forth, launchings for ships, and it's why—"

"Stop!"

"The relationship between linguistics and human cognition suggests—"

"Mr. Bramble, stop! What are we predicting for today?"

She could almost hear the gears in his mind resetting into a different thought configuration.

"Given the weather pattern, we think he'll try for London again," Bramble said. "The best bet is that he'll try a moderate bomber force with heavy fighter protection this morning, say four or five fighters to every bomber, and then a second, larger raid this afternoon. The second raid will be dependent on the results of the first, of course, and whether he thinks he can catch us off guard."

"London? Not the airfields?"

"We have London at forty percent, Southampton at thirty percent, and nothing else above ten percent."

"Thank you, Mr. Bramble," Eleanor said. She heard him saying: "It's a very good name . . ." as she replaced the telephone.

She had been hesitant to take him on when she interviewed him. She had only done so because he had been taught at Cambridge by H. W. A. Pound, and she had been desperate for staff.

Q: Red Tape is a fascinating subject. We didn't really know a lot about it until Sir Algernon Bramble published his memoirs in the seventies. It was a long-held secret, like the breaking of the Enigma code at Bletchley Park. Quite extraordinary! Was he with you on Battle of Britain Day?

A: He was. He'd just started a few days before, in fact.

Q: What was he like?

A: Bramble? Well, I remember the first time I met him . . .

The Military Intelligence recruitment machine fed Eleanor a never-ending stream of mathematicians, almost all young men and women from Oxford and Cambridge and the Imperial College London, almost all exhibiting, in varying degrees, some combination of arrogance and insecurity. Their high intelligence made them think—made them *know*—they were superior to everyone else, and they couldn't understand why everyone else found them obnoxious.

Eleanor looked at her current candidate warily.

"Mr. . . . er, Mr. Bramble, I see you are in the second year of your research towards a doctorate," she began. "Let's see . . . you're studying fractals?"

"Yes," he answered, as if he was expecting her to ask what fractals were.

"Tell me a little about your research, please."

"Fractals are infinitely recursive, self-symmetrical," Bramble began in a haughty, singsong tone.

"Yes, Mr. Bramble, indeed they are, or, at least some of them are," she cut him off. "What is your specific field of study?"

"Well, it's complicated. I don't wish to be rude, but I'm not sure you'd understand."

"I'm not sure either, Mr. Bramble," she said. "Wait! I've just had a wonderful idea, Mr. Bramble! We can solve this conundrum together! If you tell me what you're studying, we'll both know for sure if I can understand fractals or not."

Bramble stared down his pimply nose at her, clearly irritated by her sarcasm. He glanced at his watch.

"Look, again, I don't wish to be rude, Miss . . . er . . . Miss . . . er, but I was told I would be interviewed by the director himself. When will I meet him?"

"You're talking to him, Mr. Bramble."

"*You're* the director?" he asked. "Really? Are you sure?" He looked around the room uncertainly. "This is MI6-3b, isn't it?"

"It is, or it will be shortly."

"I assumed you were the director's secretary, or a personnel person, or . . ."

"I assumed you did," Eleanor said.

"But to your credit, you must have some basic knowledge of mathematics, of course, to work in a place like this," Bramble added, as if he believed that would somehow reduce the insult.

"You're very kind to say so, Mr. Bramble."

She was not angry. This often happened; it was a product of male chauvinism and academic arrogance.

"Now, let me explain the situation to you, Mr. Bramble," she said. "I don't want you to make another false assumption. You are being interviewed to join a highly secret project that can only be explained in detail to those who have been selected to work on it. In other words, you are being interviewed for a job you cannot know in advance."

He raised his eyebrows, but she continued.

"If you decline to work here once the job is explained to you, or if you start here but your work is unsatisfactory, you will be reassigned to a new experimental weather station."

"That sounds a bit arbitrary, a bit authoritarian, I must say," Bramble said.

"Indeed so. That's a very apt description of the Emergency Powers Defence Act of 1939, Mr. Bramble." He opened his mouth to object, but she overrode him.

"In order to determine exactly how truly arbitrary and authoritarian the Emergency Powers Defence Act of 1939 really is, Mr. Bramble, I have a copy of it here, if you wish to borrow it."

He closed his mouth and she continued.

"Now, let me tell you what we're doing. We are pursuing von Neumann's minimax theory. As you know, von Neumann described games such as draughts—checkers, as he called them in America—as zero-sum, in which one side's advantage is equal to the other side's disadvantage, a concept we have extended to include asymmetric advantages and disadvantages. The formulae necessary to model and value these asymmetries require mathematical skills of the highest order."

Bramble continued to stare down his nose at her.

"We are using the model to predict events on an iterative stochastic basis. Are you familiar with von Neumann's work, Mr. Bramble?"

"Well, I'm aware of it, although I've never studied it," he said with a slight shrug. "I think I may have attended a lecture on it once . . . It doesn't seem very interesting, frankly. A bit pointless—superficial, if you will."

"Oh dear," Eleanor murmured. "Well, I was considering you for a position as a mathematician on the project, but if you'd be bored by game theory, there's always Scotland. The weather station is in the Shetland Islands. I'm told it holds the record for the fewest days with sunshine and most days of rain in the British Isles. The station is located on a small island of its own and disguises itself as a sheep farm; the staff members also tend to the animals under the direction of a local shepherd. A small ferry boat brings supplies every three months, weather permitting. I imagine it's very peaceful."

"Wait, wait!" said Bramble. "Perhaps I didn't really give minimax sufficient thought."

"Perhaps."

In the ensuing days Bramble had thrown himself into the model and shown himself to be a gifted mathematician. Eleanor decided to put up with his annoying foibles. She also added a Hungarian professor who had studied under von Neumann and left Budapest just before the first anti-Jewish laws were promulgated in 1938. He was classified, in the heartless bureaucratic terminology of the war, as a DP, a displaced person, one without a clearly defined nationality and an uncertain future.

Eleanor had hired Jayne Jackson in part for her competence in managing large volumes of data and in part because Eleanor hoped Jayne's experience in controlling unruly adolescents in school would help in managing Bramble.

Of course, she realized with a sinking heart, once MI6-3b was established, she would need many more Brambles and Jacksons.

Q: Can you just remind our viewers exactly what the Red Tape model was? It's been described as the first war game, the ancestor of modern war gaming.

A: Oh no, not at all! The first war game—if you exclude chess, which is at least two thousand years old, and similar imperial Chinese games—was the Prussian game Kriegsspeil, popularized by Field Marshall Helmuth von Moltke the Elder in the nineteenth century.

Q: Well . . .

A: Park was heavily outnumbered and always reacting. He was defending; Kesselring was attacking. So Park was always responding to Kesselring's initiatives. The model permitted Park to anticipate Kesselring a little better.

But Keith Park was also a brilliant tactician, a brilliant counter-puncher and feinter. Kesselring kept sending over waves of 110s on "free hunts," as they were called. The 110s couldn't bomb, and they were not a significant threat, so Park simply left them alone. That created the impression in Kesselring's mind that Park couldn't stop them because he was running out of aircraft. So Kesselring kept underestimating Park and sending over large formations of vulnerable bombers, which suffered heavy losses. Kesselring and Goring never seemed to understand.

Q: And Red Tape . . .

A: The mathematical analysis was not on strategies to win, but on strategies not to lose. Park never did anything to make it possible for Kesselring to win, even though Kesselring always outnumbered Park by two or three to one. Park's strategies were brilliant exercises in deception.

Many people think that the Luftwaffe lost because they didn't understand radar and Chain Home, which is true, to an extent, but it shortchanges Park; the Luftwaffe lost because Park deceived them. Of course, many people in Fighter Command didn't understand Park, either—that's why he lost his job. But that's a story for another time.

SEVEN

Q: Describe the first raid of that fateful day, if you would, Dame Eleanor. You said the early morning was quiet. When did the first raid reach England?

A: Let's see; it started building up over France around eleven in the morning and consisted of well over a hundred Messerschmitt 109 fighters and twenty-five or so Dornier 17 medium bombers. Of course, we didn't know the actual composition of the raid until much later; all we knew was that there was a big radar contact building up over northern France. In those days we thought radar was miraculous, which indeed it was, but it was a far cry from today's precision. Keith Park had to make the best of what little we knew.

Q: So how did Keith Park make his decisions? Was it guesswork?

A: You could say it was guesswork, if you like, except his guesses were correct over ninety percent of the time. I prefer to describe it as informed planning. He knew from experience what Kesselring might try, and he defended against those possibilities. He had to keep reserves for contingencies, and so on. He had to decide if there would be another raid after the one the radar could see.

Q: So many variables . . .

A: Yes. He also had to make assumptions about what types of aircraft were coming and at what height. If the raid consisted of only fighters, he'd let it through unopposed, but if it was bombers, he had to respond . . .

Q: But your new model helped?

A: Yes, but only to a limited extent. It gave him statistical probabilities, but he still had to make the actual decisions. For example, that morning there was a forty percent chance Kesselring would go for London, but that means there was a sixty percent chance he wouldn't. In the end, it all came down to Park's judgment.

"What's Kesselring up to this morning?" Park asked rhetorically. "Is this a feint or is it a real raid?" He picked up a phone. "This is the AOC. Give me the latest weather information, please." He was silent for a while. "Thank you," he said, and hung up.

"It's quite cloudy, from two thousand feet up to eleven thousand. Several layers but patchy. Not good bombing weather. But, on the other hand, it'll be hard for us to spot them, so they could slip through and hit us hard. Eleanor, any thoughts?"

Eleanor saw Churchill looking at her quizzically from behind his unlit cigar. She always felt a certain amount of pressure when Park asked for her advice in private, but with Churchill staring at her, she felt the whole British government, indeed the whole nation, was weighing her in the balance.

"Kesselring's been overweighting his 109s and 110s recently, sir," she said. "Two or three or four fighters for every one bomber."

"True," Park murmured.

Eleanor watched him looking down at the map. Every day he had to make these critical decisions. If he over-responded to the raid and the raiders were all fighters, he could be drawn into a costly dogfight that had no strategic value—a waste of scarce resources. Worse, it could expose Hurricanes to 109s unnecessarily. Hurricanes were excellent fighters, excellent gun platforms, but they weren't quite as agile as 109s. Park preferred to use them against bombers, relying on Spitfires to chase 109s away.

In addition, if it was an all-fighter raid, when Park's fighters had to come down to rearm and refuel, a second raid consisting of bombers could sweep across England unopposed. There was nothing on the radar to suggest a second raid, Eleanor saw, but that could change in an instant.

Park was pulling on his chin, lost in calculations. If he under responded and this first wave of raiders consisted mostly of bombers, then they could inflict a great deal of damage while Park's squadrons were still trying to climb and reach them.

Across the English Channel—in Lille, if the intelligence was correct—she imagined Kesselring, the commander of Luftflotte II, staring at a similar map, trying to anticipate Park's reactions. They had fought this duel for a month, Kesselring's thrusts against Park's parries, and both sides had suffered grievous losses.

Park picked up the phone again. "What are the latest reports on wind conditions over Kent? Very well. Thank you.

"The Luftwaffe will have strong headwinds against them," he said. "They'll be slow getting to their targets, wherever they are, and quick getting home."

He stared at the map for another minute, doubtless engrossed in a private debate. Eleanor wondered if he was conscious of Churchill gazing at him. Probably not, she thought. Park was concerned only with the balance of forces and Kesselring's likely actions.

"Very well," he said, straightening up. "We'll respond in strength."

"Why, pray, have you reached that conclusion, Air Vice-Marshal?" Churchill asked.

"He's done this before, sir," Park said. "We have no indication of another raid forming up behind this one. If he tries again, as he may, it won't be until the early afternoon. We'll have time to rearm and refuel."

He glanced at Eleanor and raised his eyebrows.

"I agree, sir," she said, feeling immensely grateful—honored—that Park had solicited her opinion in front of Churchill.

Park turned away to discuss his plans with the controllers, leaving Eleanor with Churchill.

"Perhaps we should await developments before we commit our forces," Churchill pondered, staring down at the thicket of markers the WAAFs were assembling over Calais. "They're still in France."

"We don't have time, sir," Eleanor said. "Those aircraft may be bombers at fifteen thousand feet and 109 fighters at twenty-five thousand feet. The Chain Home radio detection system cannot distinguish heights. It takes a Spitfire ten minutes to climb to twenty-five thousand feet, flat out, burning lots of fuel. A 109 can fly six miles in a minute, so they can be across the Channel and forty miles towards London by the time the Spitfires are at their height."

Churchill looked dubious, and Eleanor pressed on.

"The 109s can be only twenty miles from where we sit in a quarter of an hour from now, only three minutes away from Uxbridge."

Churchill glanced at the concrete ceiling. Eleanor was struck with sudden anxiety: Churchill was almost seventy, he'd fought wars on horseback, and he'd ridden in an actual cavalry charge, just like the medieval knights in armor, for God's sake! Now he was running the country, with the fate of Britain in his hands. Could an elderly man possibly comprehend the intricacies of modern warfare, which was as much a question of machine against machine as man against man? Her own father was about the same age, she thought. And he was starting to slow down, sometimes beginning conversations and then losing the thread.

Well, she thought, whether Churchill understood modern warfare or not, it was her job to try to explain it to him anyway.

"We discussed dimensions before, Prime Minister," she said. "We imagined the map as three-dimensional. Now imagine we are twenty-five thousand feet above the map, as we sit up here on the balcony. But the distance between the ground level on the table and us up here on the balcony is not only twenty-five thousand feet, sir; it's also ten minutes. This balcony is ten minutes away for the fastest fighter in the world."

"That's remarkable, young lady!" Churchill burst out. "Now I see what you mean—it's all coming to life! How on earth did you ever think of it?"

"I didn't, sir. Einstein did, when he saw that space and time are inextricably bound together by four dimensions: three spatial and one temporal. Time is distance and vice versa. Mine is a simple adaptation of that truth."

Eleanor told herself to calm down. The objective was to give Park support, not try to bedazzle the prime minister with science.

"Mr. Park has to position our defenses now or face disaster: a hundred bombers roaming over London unopposed."

Churchill seemed to calm down too.

"How does he know where to position our defenses?" he growled.

"Remember, sir, we're not trying to win—we're trying not to lose. Not losing can be defined by disrupting and frustrating Luftwaffe bomber attacks, preventing them from reaching their targets without significant losses on our side. So he'll probably set up a series of defenses all the way from the coast to London, a series of hurdles for the Luftwaffe to surmount."

Park returned.

"I'm going to put up eight squadrons, Prime Minister," he said. "I'm going to assume Kesselring's going for the East End of London, and I'll ask Leigh-Mallory to put up his Big Wing. If nothing else, it'll shock the Luftwaffe to see a pack of Hurricanes and Spitfires coming out of the north."

"Where will you deploy your forces, pray tell me?"

"Defense in depth." He gestured at the map below. "Two squadrons high over Canterbury, four more just south of London over Biggin, and two more in reserve over Chelmsford. The two over Canterbury will be high, at twenty-five thousand feet, to take out high 109 escorts."

He gestured at the map.

"I've requested the Big Wing to wait over Hornchurch, over here, to cover the docks and the east of London. The Luftwaffe crews have a tendency to fly north until they can see the Thames estuary as a landmark and then turn west towards London. Douglas Bader is putting up five squadrons from Duxford in his Big Wing. Just for once, with a bit of luck, Kesselring will be outnumbered."

It occurred to Eleanor that Churchill was evaluating Park. Park, in charge of 11 Group, and Dowding, in charge of Fighter Command, were subject to nonstop criticism, a barrage of complaints coming from Sholto Douglas and Trafford Leigh-Mallory. Douglas wanted Dowding's job, and Leigh-Mallory wanted Park's. Perhaps Churchill was deciding if Park was good enough for the job or whether his critics were right about him.

"If the bombers get through, I want them disorganized and frightened, Prime Minister," Park continued. "I want them harried. I want them dropping their loads at random and turning around and running home as fast as possible. Just when they're turning into a rabble, and just when the 109s are leaving them before they run out of fuel, then bang! Douglas Bader jumps out of the sun!"

Churchill nodded slowly, but Eleanor wasn't sure he was convinced.

"Mr. Park is wearing Luftflotte II down, sir, eroding it away," she told him. "It's a shadow of what it was. Kesselring keeps coming, thinking Mr. Park is running out of aircraft, and Kesselring is wrong. Mr. Park has more aircraft now than he ever has had. Kesselring has lost almost a thousand aircraft since 13 August. Many of his Kampfgeschwaders, his bomber wings, are becoming empty shells."

Out of the corner of her eye, she saw the Tote Board lights for 339 move to "Ordered to Stand By." Johnnie was being called upon once more.

"A thousand, did you say?" Churchill was asking. "I know their losses are high, but . . ."

"Almost a thousand, sir. Nine hundred and seventy-nine, to be exact, until midnight last night."

"There are those that say . . . ," Churchill began, but Eleanor risked interrupting him again.

"Kesselring is in the process of losing, Prime Minister, slowly but surely. We just have to be patient and wait while he finishes the job."

EIGHT

Q: When did the raid actually start?

A: At 1115 hours. We saw the markers building up over Calais, and we knew it would take our squadrons at least fifteen minutes to get into position. One of the first Park called up was 339 . . .

"We're under starter's orders, gentlemen," Digby called through the doorway of the dispersal hut. "Five minutes, if you please."

Shaux stood up and stretched. At long, long last, the waiting was over.

"The wind's from the north, chaps," Potter announced, and 339 lined up facing southward to piss downwind. It was a squadron ritual. On cue, Charlie, the squadron mascot, a big black Belgian Bouvier, trotted out to a wheel on Shaux's Spitfire and raised his leg.

Diggers and Froggie Potter, Shaux's two flight commanders, were both excellent leaders, and between them they had honed 339 into a highly effective force. Shaux felt that all he had to do was to point 339 in the right direction, and Diggers and Froggie would take care of everything else.

In many ways they were opposites. Diggers was calm and disciplined, with superb eyesight and excellent aeronautical skills, a man of exactitude and rocklike reliability. Froggie was instinctive, full of natural exuberance, an intuitive pilot with the looks of a film star.

Diggers was one of the oldest pilots in 11 Group at the ripe old age of twenty-three; Froggie had lied about his age to enter the RAF and was only eighteen. Diggers was contemplative; Shaux knew he was an ornithologist, happiest when sitting motionless in a bush for hours, waiting to get a glimpse of an unusual bird—a rara avis, as he liked to say. Froggie, in contrast, was a devotee of American jazz bands and played the saxophone. He was known to break into the jitterbug at unpredictable moments.

But despite their differences, they both exuded confidence so that even the newest, rawest pilots who joined 339 felt safe. Given that the operational life expectancy of a Spitfire pilot in a frontline squadron was five hours, it was essential for new pilots to trust their leaders. Fighter Command pilots were all young men in their late teens or early twenties, full of bravado and willing to take extraordinary risks. But they were not suicidal; if they did not believe that their leaders would bring them home again safely, they would find a reason not to fly.

Shaux began to pull on his equipment: leather jacket, life vest, helmet, parachute, two pairs of gloves, and all the rest. The newsreels tended to show pilots dashing out to their waiting Spitfires in dramatic fashion. In real life, fully equipped pilots waddled to their aircraft, with their parachutes flapping against their backsides in an ungainly fashion. They barely walked, let alone ran.

"I say," said someone. "Has anyone seen a gloves, leather?" It was that new chap, Henderson, the aerial golfer.

The pilots gathered around their leaders, pulling on their flying gear and taking last puffs at their cigarettes.

"We're being vectored to Canterbury at angels two-five," Digby said. "We'll be joined by 314, the Polish chaps."

"Twenty-five thousand feet," Shaux said, just in case one of the new chaps didn't know what "angels two-five" meant. "So Group's sending us up above the fray to chase away any stray 109s wandering around up there."

He kept his tone light and conversational, as if meeting 109s would be just a stroll in the park.

"They'll be flying into a strong headwind," Shaux said. "It'll slow down their bombers. Therefore, the 109s will have to slow down to keep pace with them. They'll be crawling; they might even be flaps-down. If they see us, it will take them quite a while to speed up."

The effective groundspeed of the Luftwaffe bombers, and therefore their 109 escorts, would be as little as 200 miles per hour and possibly even less. If 339 could attack downwind, they could be 100 miles per hour faster.

"Now, chaps, listen to me, particularly you new chaps," Potter said. "It's follow-my-leader. Just stay in formation and wait for orders from the skipper or Diggers or me. I will personally fry the balls of any pilot who breaks formation and serve them on toast for dinner this evening."

"Balls, fried, pilots, Froggie?" someone asked.

"*Testes frixi*, old chap," Digby murmured. "Stay together. Stay tight. Remember, 339's official motto is *Odiosis bonum est*, which as you all know is Latin for 'Boring is good.'"

Shaux chuckled, knowing that Digby had just invented the motto on the spot.

The pilots walked out to their waiting Spitfires.

"Is that really our motto?" Henderson asked.

"It is," Potter said.

"I always stank at Latin," Henderson said.

"You probably found it *odiosis*."

Shaux eased his way into the Spitfire's tiny cockpit, and the ground crew warrant officer strapped him in. They had been together ever since the Battle of France two months ago—a lifetime. The cockpit smelled of a pungent combination of exhaust fumes, rubber, oil, cordite, and oxygen—the smell of danger. He went through his pre-start checklist and pressed the starter. The Rolls-Royce Merlin grumbled briefly before roaring to life. It was unquestionably the finest liquid-cooled engine ever built, Shaux thought, all twenty-seven liters of it, all twelve cylinders of it, better even than the thirty-four-liter inverted V-12 Daimler-Benz 602 that powered the 109s. At these slow revs the Merlin sounded and felt lumpy and uneven, but given its head, it would become silky smooth, and its sound would rise to a howl of triumph.

He settled back to wait, tapping the instruments to make sure that the needles weren't stuck, and waggling the control surfaces. Readiness could last a long time or be cancelled. It was the Fighter Command way: hurry up and wait.

But on this occasion the squadron flight sergeant appeared within a couple of minutes and fired a flare from a Very pistol, commanding them into the air. Shaux gave the Merlin a little more juice and took his feet off the brakes. His Spitfire grumbled forward. He moved each of the control surfaces to make sure they were all working freely. He reached the end of the field, stepped on his right brake, and swung into the wind. Looking back he could see 339 following in good order.

In the distance he could see Charlie, the squadron Bouvier. His pink tongue was lolling as he sat beside Flight Sergeant Jenkins. Charlie, whose full name was Le Grand Charles, had belonged to a Belgian pilot who had escaped the German blitzkrieg that had over-run his country in the spring. He flew out in a tiny Renard R.31 with the seventy-five-pound dog sitting on his crotch. The pilot—his name was Jacques something, if Shaux remembered correctly—had been killed a few days after his arrival. Charlie had been bereft, searching and searching for his master, but had now formed a new bond with Froggie Potter, who had taught him to howl while Froggie played the saxophone. Froggie claimed that Charlie had already mastered Glenn Miller's "String of Pearls" and was now working on the brand-new "Tuxedo Junction." Charlie was not howling, Froggie insisted, but giv-ing his version of a trombone.

Charlie, along with every living creature on the airfield, would wait patiently for 339's return. Even the farmer and his wife, beyond the hedgerow, had paused from their labors.

Shaux took a deep breath and opened the throttle. The Merlin roared. The Spitfire accelerated swiftly, and the rear wheel lifted within seconds. Now the aircraft was rocking as it bounced across the uneven surface of the field, and the whole airframe vibrated as the revs spun up. The thunder of the Merlin and the deep reverberation of the aircraft combined to produce an exhilarating tremor of power—not humming, Shaux thought, but thrumming, like the complex harmonics of the strings of a double bass. Then came the magical moment when Shaux knew the Spitfire was ready to fly, its wheels scarcely on the grass, and it was quivering as the air swept over the wings. It reminded Shaux of how a fishing rod tingles as a fish nuzzles the bait—almost, almost, but not quite, not yet.

Shaux didn't pull back on the control column or make any overt conscious action. He just released the Spitfire and gave it its head, and it leapt into the air, as if delighted to be back in its natural element. Off to his right he saw Digby's Spitfire rising, with the rest of A Flight behind him. Potter and B Flight would be a hundred yards behind and to the left.

The ground fell away, and the trees shrunk beneath him. Glancing down, he saw the farmer had climbed down from his harvester and stood at attention beside it, his arm raised in salute. His wife fluttered a white handkerchief.

Shaux raised the undercarriage and closed the canopy, and the noise and turbulence abated. He adjusted the revs for the long climb towards the sun; towards the thin, cold air far above them; towards the hunting grounds where 109s preyed. The Spitfire Mk II had the fastest sustained rate of climb of any aircraft in the world, two thousand five hundred feet per minute, but twenty-five thousand feet was a long way up and ten minutes away from the ground. There was cloud from two thousand feet to ten thousand feet, Shaux knew, which would protect 339 from any marauding 109s or 110s, but it might play havoc with their formation. Above the clouds they would be at a huge tactical disadvantage against anyone above them, but Shaux trusted that Park and the controllers had given them at least ten minutes before the first ethereal radar blips over France turned into real enemy aircraft over England.

Last week, RAF Oldchurch, 339's old base, had been badly damaged in the raid in which Pound had died, and 339 had moved twenty miles along the coast to RAF Hawkinge, just outside Folkestone. Hawkinge was so close to France, the local joke ran, that the pilots stationed there had to speak French. Hawkinge was only twenty-five miles from Calais, perhaps thirty miles from Dunkirk, and forty miles from Arras. The closest 109s were based at Calais-Marck, only five minutes away from Hawkinge in level flight.

The nearest Dornier 17 bombers were in Arras. Shaux had been shot down over Dunkirk. The launch that had evacuated him from the Dunkirk beaches had been sunk by a Stuka dive-bomber in the English

Channel off Folkestone. Then he had been stationed in Arras during the Battle of France, before the French had collapsed in June—less than three months ago. Earlier in September, a week or so ago, he had been shot down again, a few miles north of Canterbury. Shaux had been fighting over these few square miles of Channel and coastline forever, or so it seemed, and was fighting still.

Shaux led 339 north overhead Canterbury and out into the Thames estuary near Whitstable, battling the headwinds. They broke through the clouds at ten thousand feet, and 339 was still well together, in surprisingly good formation. Shaux took no credit; this was entirely due to Digby and Potter.

"Red Leader to Shadow: tighten up," Digby's voice sounded through Shaux's headset, evidently not satisfied. Shadow was 339's call sign. Shaux could see 339 tightening but apparently not enough.

A minute passed.

"Green Leader to Shadow: *testes frixi*," said Potter's voice.

"Lumba calling Green Leader. Repeat, not understood," came the plaintive voice of the Hornchurch Sector controller.

Shaux grinned. He was as relaxed as he could be under the circumstances. He knew that every pilot in 339 would be searching above them for 109s, and the higher they rose, the safer they would be. They rose through fifteen thousand feet and turned back south, and now the wind was behind them, blowing them back towards any Luftwaffe formations coming from France. In another four minutes, they were at twenty-five thousand feet. Shaux could not see the great, gray mass of Canterbury Cathedral below them, but he knew it was there.

He had trained 339 to search the skies for enemy aircraft. Whoever saw the other side first had a huge, often decisive, advantage. If you saw your enemy before he saw you, you could move first, either defensively or offensively, to change the odds in your favor—to make it less likely that you would lose, as Eleanor would say. It was the same advantage as going first in a game of noughts and crosses.

The enemy, if you were fortunate enough to see him first, would appear as a line of little black dots in the sky, seemingly harmless. But the dots would rapidly grow larger and sprout wings and fuselages and tails. If they developed two engines, you knew they might be bombers, carrying death and destruction, to be stopped at all costs. But they might also be fast, cannon-armed 110 fighters. Recognizing the difference—not being confused—was vital.

Otherwise they were single-engine fighters, 109s, to be feared and evaded if possible and to be confronted if necessary.

The role of the 109s was to keep RAF fighters—usually Hurricanes—away from the bombers. The role of the Spitfires was to get the 109s away from the bombers so that Hurricanes could attack the bombers. The lumbering bombers were essentially defenseless. The 109s could defeat Hurricanes, but Spitfires could defeat the 109s—with luck. It was an intricate balance of forces, an intricate hierarchy of dominance like the hierarchy of predators in the jungle or the hawk above the farmer's wheat field.

Perhaps that was why he loved Spitfires, Shaux thought—because of all the aircraft in the war, they were the top predators.

Now there really were aircraft in sight, little black dots at the same altitude swimming slowly towards 339.

"Uniform Yacht," said Digby's voice, and Shaux knew he could read 314's squadron markings painted on the sides of their fuselages, UY. The 314's code name was Hawkeye.

"Shadow calling Lumba," he said quietly. "We are in position. Hawkeye in sight." He wondered if Eleanor, back at 11 Group, was listening.

NINE

Q: How many Spitfires did Park use that morning?

A: Spitfires and Hurricanes—Hurricanes tend to be overlooked because they were always considered to be less glamorous. But there were far more Hurricanes than Spitfires in Fighter Command, and they accounted for the large majority of 11 Group victories. But, to your question, we had almost two hundred and fifty aircraft in the air by noon. It was one of the rare occasions we outnumbered the Luftwaffe.

A WAAF pushed a marker labeled 339 onto Canterbury. Another marker labeled 314 joined it. The Tote Board lights for 339 moved to from "Left Ground" to "In Position." Once again Johnnie was in harm's way.

Eleanor knew that 314 was one of the squadrons manned by Polish pilots who had escaped after the collapse of Poland under Hitler's onslaught a year ago. The Polish squadrons had outstanding reputations; the pilots were very well trained—in many cases better trained than British pilots—and were utterly committed to destroying the enemy. Johnnie was in good company.

She wondered how many 109s Johnnie would encounter and prayed there would be none. In spite of the ferocious fighting, in spite of there being hundreds of aircraft converging into the tight airspace above southeastern England, Eleanor knew that most patrols ended without the pilots even sighting the enemy, let alone engaging it. Indeed, she had built the probability of encountering hostile aircraft into her model of the battle. You calculated the number of cubic miles of air above southern England and estimated the number of aircraft to give you aircraft density per cubic mile. Each square mile of English countryside had five cubic miles of airspace above it . . . you realized how empty the skies were, even during the largest raids.

The 339 had accumulated more operational flying hours than almost any other squadron, and its roll of victories was steadily increasing. Yet, despite almost constant operations, 339 had one of the lowest casualty rates in 11 Group. Johnnie claimed no credit for any of this; she knew that in his mind, it was all due to his flight leaders, Digby and Potter—Diggers and Froggie, as he affectionately called them. Eleanor—who had no brothers, only sisters—thought that Diggers was the kind of man she'd like as a big brother, calm and reliable but with an impish sense of humor. He had the bluest eyes that Eleanor had ever seen. Froggie was simply an exuberant schoolboy, seemingly without a care in the world and handsome to the point of being beautiful but, according to Johnnie, also a naturally gifted fighter pilot. He would be the fun-loving younger brother, always mildly in trouble over something or other.

Dowding had recently introduced a new policy that she considered to be blatantly unfair. He had divided Fighter Command squadrons into three categories. Squadrons in Category A, like 339, were the best and would fly as often as possible. Category B squadrons would be used as reserves, only flying during major raids, and would provide replacement pilots to replenish Category A pilot losses. Category C squadrons were essentially training units to be used only in emergencies; their primary role was feeding replacement pilots up to Category B squadrons.

Dowding's policy meant that 339 and other elite squadrons were placed continuously in circumstances of extreme danger, where injury or death was very likely, and kept there until the very likely occurred.

Park, she knew, accepted Dowding's plan with great reluctance. To Park, the greatest problem facing 11 Group was the lack of qualified flight and squadron commanders—the Johnnies and the Diggerses and the Froggies—men who had engaged with the enemy and survived, men with steel nerves, men who could hold their squadrons together. The best leaders were invaluable, and they needed to be conserved whenever possible. Park hated the idea that, under Dowding's plan, they would simply be flown until they could fly no more.

Johnnie had become one of the squadron leaders that people talked about. She had heard Johnnie mentioned in the same league as Sailor Milan of 74 Squadron and Stanford Tuck of 257. There was a tale that he was so relaxed, so calm in the air, that he had to be woken when the enemy appeared. Some joked he had nine lives, like a cat. It was said that he had some sort of magical power of survival—he had been shot down twice without a scratch. He had escaped from the beaches of Dunkirk, escaped from France when it collapsed—when he was said to have been the last pilot out—and escaped drowning when a Stuka dive-bombed the launch that rescued him from Dunkirk. He was a Fighter Command escape artist, an 11 Group Houdini.

Now, once again, he was waiting to encounter the enemy. The 339 marker was only eighteen inches from the nearest enemy marker. An armada of Luftflotte II markers advanced from northern France and Belgium into Kent; 339 and 314 would be the first squadrons to meet the onslaught.

Eleanor felt a sudden rising wave of panic. She turned away from the map and said something incoherent to one of the controllers, who stared at her in surprise.

Get a grip on yourself, she told herself harshly. Behaving like a panicky little girl, particularly in front of Park and Churchill, was not going to help. Take a deep breath and deal with the situation calmly.

The problem had started a week ago, when she had launched herself into a sudden and completely unexpected affair with Johnnie, an affair of such intensity that she had not thought it possible. She had known Johnnie as a friend at Oxford where they both studied mathematics; a close friend certainly, but nothing more. She had been busy with other relationships, and he had been clothed in seemingly impenetrable diffidence, emotional chain mail. She had taken him for granted.

Earlier this month they had reconnected by chance, when she had visited Oldchurch to see Harry Pound. She had known the appalling odds the fighter pilots faced, but as statistics, as mathematical abstractions. These statistics, it now struck her like a blow, were the odds against Johnnie. When she said goodbye to him, she was vividly conscious of the fact that he would probably die—almost certainly die—before she saw him again.

She marveled at Johnnie's almost preternatural calmness in the face of danger. He was a stoic, but that was not really an adequate explanation. He had a remarkable ability to absorb stress—but not, she thought, in a healthy way. She was no psychiatrist, far from it, but Johnnie, it seemed to her, had simply shut down his emotions and became an automaton, a zombie. He had willed himself to be utterly indifferent to his fate. He had put his humanity on hold.

He had hollowed out his soul and become a man of straw.

He had told her that his favorite poet was William Butler Yeats, and she had found, in a collection of Yeats' poetry, the key—the Rosetta stone—to Johnnie. She realized that he lived—tried to live—within the confines of a poem that described the emotions of a young man, a fighter pilot in the Great War, who was certain he would die. The poem began, "I know that I shall meet my fate . . ." The young man in the poem concludes, persuades himself, that his life is a waste of breath; he simply waits for the enemy to end it. Johnnie, she realized, was also simply waiting.

She discovered Johnnie was an orphan, brought up without love in an orphanage and sentenced from birth to loneliness. He had never felt love and never would. He would die unloved. He and the world would both be indifferent to his fate.

Suddenly she had found herself compulsively committed to filling that void, to giving him the love he had never experienced. Her love would replace his fatalism—or stoicism, or nihilism, or whatever -ism it was—and give his life meaning. She would rescue him from the shadow world of the poem by Yeats, reclaim his soul, and fill it with passion.

In so doing she would also rescue herself from her previously unsuccessful relationships with men. She realized she had been feckless, self-indulgent, and shallow. She would redeem herself and find true love by giving it to him.

But her love, however strong, was not armor plating. He was at twenty-five thousand feet over Canterbury with more than a hundred 109s approaching. In the first encounters, when 339 and 314 were the tip of Park's defensive spear, he would be outnumbered perhaps by five or six to one. He was engaged in a battle on a knife edge, in which the merest unlucky chance or miscalculation could send him spinning earthward. Statistically 11 Group would lose at least ten percent of its forces today, twenty or more Hurricanes or Spitfires. Would he be one of those?

How many times had he seen a 109 bursting out of the sun, cannons firing as it grew huge and malevolent? How many times had he experienced the shock of—

"Are you all right, Eleanor?" Park asked, jerking her back into reality. He was staring at her closely.

"Yes, of course, sir," she said, knowing he knew she was lying.

He took her by the elbow and steered her away from the hearing of Churchill and his retinue and the controllers.

"Look, Eleanor, it's none of my business, and I have no right to intrude on your privacy, but . . . well, to get to the point, I noticed you seemed upset when you saw 339 was in position waiting for the 109s, and, well, to be frank, not to beat about the bush, I'm told Johnnie Shaux is a friend of yours."

"Yes," she said, in surprise. This was not like the reserved, austere Park. She paused for a moment. If she couldn't trust Park, she could trust no one. She plunged on. "In fact, sir, he's more than a friend. I hope we'll get married."

"Well, I'm very happy for you, Eleanor," Park said, and she saw that it was true. "I had the pleasure of meeting him just yesterday, I don't know if he mentioned it. A good chap—but you know that far better than I do!"

He smiled. "Anyway, the reason I'm intruding is that I've decided to pull him out of the line in a few days to give him a break and a chance to rest."

"Really, sir?" she asked, and she was suddenly on the edge of tears. "But what about Dowding's A Squadrons policy? Can 339 do without him?"

"They'll have to, Eleanor. Shaux deserves—no, he needs—a break. He's been in the thick of things since the start of August. Yes, I know Stuffy Dowding's A Squadrons policy, but there are limits to what we can ask people to do. Besides, he's trained up a couple of excellent flight commanders, so 339 will still be very much a force to be reckoned with."

"Thank—"

"I'm going to transfer him to the A&AEE," Park said, cutting her off. "They're the chaps who test new aircraft and engines and updated versions. They're very short of expert pilots too. It's not risk-free, far from it, but at least he won't have 109s on his tail."

"Thank you, sir, I really appreciate it. I . . ." She couldn't go on.

Every day she expected Johnnie to die. He'd flown over two hundred hours in the face of the enemy. Only a tiny, tiny handful of pilots on either side could survive those odds. He'd been shot down twice, miraculously without a scratch. It was statistically inevitable he'd be shot down again, and statistically highly, *highly* unlikely he'd survive. It was a reality he lived every day, a cold black dread in whose shadow she walked. Now Park would lift the shadow. But, oh God, he might not survive today . . . Her eyes filled with tears.

Park wordlessly handed her a handkerchief and turned away. She knew he understood.

TEN

Q: The first contacts were when, Dame Eleanor?

A: At 1130, over Canterbury . . .

"Bandits three o'clock low!" Digby's voice erupted in Shaux's headset, and he almost jumped through the cockpit canopy.

"Steady, 339," Shaux said immediately, to himself as much as anybody. The new pilots would almost certainly have turned blindly in that direction.

Shaux gazed out to his right and almost immediately saw little black dots crawling across the white clouds below them. They were 109s, perhaps five thousand feet below, moving northeast, and, Shaux guessed, they really were crawling, chained to lumbering Dornier 17s or Junkers 88s hidden somewhere in the clouds beneath them. He could see five *schwarms* of four aircraft each, scattered loosely in a line, perhaps two miles to the south of Canterbury.

Each schwarm was flying in finger-four formation, with two pairs of aircraft positioned roughly like the tips of one's fingers. It was a far more flexible and effective formation than the rigid v-shaped arrowhead pattern, the "vic," that Fighter Command demanded. Shaux and many of the other experienced pilots flew finger-four and simply ignored Fighter Command.

There were probably more 109s close by, but there was no telling where they were or how many. Perhaps the Germans had been stupid enough, once again, to have the rest of the escorts down below with the bombers. They'd been doing it for two weeks or more, robbing the lower 109s of all their tactical advantages.

At this point in their holding pattern, 339 was flying east, away from the 109s; Shaux calculated that a shallow diving turn to the right would position 339 for a flank attack, hopefully before the 109s saw them. Let's see: A circle with a diameter of two miles has a circumference of $2\pi r$, or six miles, Shaux calculated, and therefore 339 would travel three miles to complete a half turn. The current speed of 339 equated to a mile every fifteen seconds, so the diving turn would take forty-five seconds. In the meantime, the 109s would have flown about two miles northeast, meaning that 339 would arrive at the point of intersection slightly behind the 109s, at their four o'clock, over their right shoulders.

Shaux could count on the Polish squadron to watch his back should there be more 109s up at this altitude. The important thing was to chase the 109s away from the invisible bombers so that Hurricanes from other squadrons could find the bombers unprotected.

"Follow me," he said, letting his starboard wing dip, beginning his turn.

Spitfires always did everything perfectly, he thought, as 339 described a graceful arc through the sky. Spitfires swam through the air just as sharks swam through water, in a perfect balance of forces. Lift created by the wings raised the planes up, gravity pulled them down; the thrust of the prop drove them forward, and the drag of friction across the airframe pulled them back. Like sharks, Spitfires had to keep moving or sink and die. Well, Shaux thought, abruptly pulling his thoughts together, the combined result was this graceful, silky, smooth turn towards the enemy.

"*Testes frixi,*" growled Potter's voice once more. Evidently the arc was not as graceful as it should be.

Back at Uxbridge, someone would be saying, "Now 339 is engaging the enemy, sir," and Park would be nodding in acknowledgment. Eleanor would have her fingers crossed. Eleanor is wishing me luck, Shaux thought. I can feel it, and therefore I am invincible.

Shaux did not need to look at the enemy—he had calculated where they would be and when they would be there. Instead he searched the skies above and behind them. The easiest and most foolish way to get jumped was to assume that the enemy you could see was the only enemy close by and in range. Seasoned pilots learned the hard way to assume the worst, and Digby in particular seemed to have a sixth sense for danger, a sort of natural radar. Shaux had read somewhere that bats had something of the same sort. If there was ever a single reason for 339's record of relative safety, it was Digby's vigilance, his batlike sixth sense. Froggie had a new American comic book about a character called Batman—perhaps 339 could give Diggers that as a nickname, although he'd probably prefer *Homo Vespertilio*.

Shaux's plan of attack would bring 339 to the right flank of the 109s, and they would fly laterally across the strung-out line of schwarms. Each 109 would be in his field of fire for only a fleeting moment, but the effect of being jumped from the flank, totally unexpectedly, would be devastating. Shaux didn't need to shoot the 109s down; he just needed to scatter them hither and yon so that it would take them a long time to reorient themselves and regroup and even longer to relocate the bombers they were supposed to be escorting. Given the fierce headwinds they were facing, they might never catch up. It would almost as if they'd never flown across the Channel in the first place.

Shaux had seen a 109 that had been forced down in a field near Chichester a couple of weeks ago. He had sat in the cockpit to get a sense of what a 109 pilot could see—and what he could not. Unlike the Spitfire, with its clear curving canopy, the 109 had heavy struts that impeded the pilot's vision, particularly towards the rear. By planning an attack that approached the 109s from the right flank and slightly behind, Shaux hoped the enemy would not see them until it was too late.

Halfway through 339's turn, Shaux saw the 109s lift their noses and begin to climb. Looking up to his right, Shaux saw the silhouettes of the Polish 314 Squadron above them in the glare. Now was the critical moment. Would the 109 leader focus on the menace of 314, or would he keep searching and see 339 on his flank? In another twenty seconds, the 109s would be all but defenseless, slowing as they started to climb, unable to turn fast enough to evade 339's attack.

Luftflotte II had lost so many aircraft over the course of the last month, Shaux thought, and so many pilots, that they were probably short of experienced leaders, just like 11 Group, but even worse. The survivors got better and better, more and more deadly, like that chap Galland, but the chaps now getting promoted into leadership positions were probably still wet behind the ears.

Shaux's Spitfire approached the end of its turn. The nearest 109s grew larger. How can they not see us? Shaux wondered. Well, I have Diggers, and they do not.

Now the 109s were growing to full size in the sky. Their closing speed with 339 was over 100 miles per hour. He saw the profile of the nearest pilot looking up towards 314, unaware of 339.

"Tallyho, gentlemen," Shaux said and opened fire.

His Spitfire was armed with eight .303-caliber machine guns, four in each wing, with a firing rate of approximately nineteen rounds per second per gun or 150 rounds per second in total. Each round consisted of a lead core encased in a hardened cupro-nickel jacket with a muzzle velocity of approximately 2,500 feet per second or roughly 1,500 miles per hour. Thus Shaux delivered 150 rounds into and around the nearest 109's cockpit before he flashed over it and moved on to the next. The schwarms were only about three hundred yards apart, Shaux estimated, so that the entire formation was stretched less than a mile from one side to the other. It took 339 approximately twenty seconds to fly across the entire formation. It was only as they crossed the fifth and final schwarm that the last 109s seemed to realize 339 was there, presumably from the shouts of their colleagues in their headsets, "*Achtung, Achtung,* Spitfire, Spitfire!"

"Follow me right," Shaux said, and led 339 into a hard right turn.

It was a maneuver he insisted they practice over and over. Many squadrons on both sides would make a coordinated first attack, and then break left and right and up and down into individual dogfights. But a squadron that stayed in formation retained the full force of its combined firepower. "Those who stay together, prey together," Digby liked to say. Shaux could not recall the Latin.

It was not the actual effect of having eighty or ninety machine guns trained as one, because they never were. It was the massive shock wave created by one tightly organized and disciplined formation flashing through another. Shaux knew they didn't really have to fire at all—the chances of hitting the enemy were pretty low, but tracer rounds with visible trails of brightly burning phosphorus so that the pilots could see where they were firing would have a dramatic and unnerving effect. The sudden appearance of the Spitfires and the cascade of tracer would be enough to make the 109 pilots flinch and break formation. Even a Galland would not be immune.

Looking back as they turned, Shaux saw that the orderly ranks of the schwarms had been turned into chaos. It would take long minutes—too long, from the enemy's perspective—to reorganize. Some of them might use up so much fuel that they'd give up and turn for home.

"This is Red Two. I'm damaged, the wheels are down."

"This is Red Leader," Digby's voice said. "Return home, Red Two."

A lucky shot from one of the 109s must have broken a hydraulic line, Shaux thought. He couldn't fight like that, his Spitfire's aerodynamics would be hopelessly impaired, and he'd be fortunate to land in one piece.

As well as being disruptive, 339's attack must also have been deeply demoralizing to the enemy. The 109s had been overhead England less than five minutes before they were jumped. Now they'd be searching frantically, flitting through the scattered clouds, wondering when the next Spitfire squadron would burst out of nowhere. Perhaps 314 would descend upon them. Shaux saw that at least one 109 was falling; that, too, would hurt the enemy's morale.

They completed their right turn, and Shaux saw Red Two breaking away with one wheel up and one wheel down. That would make for a tricky landing. There were no more schwarms in sight, no other targets. Shaux would take 339 back up to twenty-five thousand feet and await further developments. He opened his mouth to give the order.

"Bandits seven o'clock level," snapped Digby's voice.

"Shadow, left," Shaux said, with an immediate gut-wrenching turn towards the enemy—split seconds meant the difference between life and death. Over his left shoulder he saw at least eight, possibly more, 109s coming at 339 head-on, just seconds away.

It was now 339's turn to get attacked, but Digby had given them just enough warning to be able to turn so that these new 109s could only deliver a glancing blow. The two formations raced through each other. Shaux saw lots of 109s but none he could fire at. One 109 crossed so closely above him that he cringed. He saw tracer flashing all around, but he did not hear or feel anything hit him. It was over in a second.

"Oh dear, I've been hit!" said a voice in his headset. It had to be one of the new chaps. Shaux didn't recognize his voice.

"Shadow, regroup," Shaux said. It was essential that 339 regroup as fast as possible to remain a fighting unit rather than a bunch of individuals so that they could continue to "prey together." That took priority over everything else. The "regroup" command meant they would all turn north and climb to twenty-five thousand feet—that was their standard procedure—where, hopefully, 339 would find each other and regain formation. Sector would give them a rendezvous point if necessary.

Shaux believed in a short list of default actions and reactions that he and Digby and Potter had drilled into the squadron until they were instinctive. Far too many squadrons, in Shaux's opinion, fell apart after being attacked or attacking and sacrificed all the advantages of a cohesive formation. Thus, after being jumped and thrown into disarray, 339 would automatically know how to regroup.

He turned north and applied more power to climb, searching for more 109s. He could see no other aircraft, including no other 339 Spitfires. He was alone for the moment, without the benefit of Digby's eyesight and 339's protection.

"Green Three, this is Green Leader," Potter's voice said. "Return to base. Bearing three-one-oh."

Green Three was the new chap, Henderson, who had broken the dispersal hut window a half an hour ago. Potter was exactly right, Shaux thought. If Green Three had been hit, he needed to get out of the way and back to safety as soon as possible. Henderson probably couldn't tell the difference between superficial damage and something more severe. Trying to stay up here would just invite more damage.

"It hurts," said Green Three.

Shaux suddenly felt cold. Henderson had been hit, not just his Spitfire.

"It really, really hurts."

ELEVEN

Q: How quickly did you know what was happening during the battle?

A: We knew very quickly. The pilots talked to the Sector controllers on the R/T—

Q: R/T?

A: Sorry, on the radio telephone. The Sector controllers talked to the Group controllers in Uxbridge. The observers and Chain Home radar stations reported to Fighter Command first for filtering, and then to us as soon as they had verified the information.

Q: So Park's information was up-to-date?

A: I think it's safe to say we were seldom more than a minute or two out-of-date, unless it was very cloudy. Therefore, from Park's perspective about his ability to direct 11 Group during the battle, on a clear day the map table was only seven or eight miles out of position. The WAAFs at Uxbridge and Bentley Priory—Fighter Command—were really excellent. It's actually very difficult to interpret the data and maneuver the markers accurately.

The map table below them was now a confused jumble of markers scattered across southeastern England that were being pushed back and forth by the WAAFs. The lights on the Tote Board on the far wall were constantly changing to reflect each squadron's status. Telephones shrilled incessantly on the controllers' and supervisors' desks.

It struck Eleanor that the Operations Room was like an ants' nest filled with furious but organized activity, with each worker fulfilling his or her special role as quickly and as efficiently as possible. The WAAFs were listening to Fighter Command voices in their ears, relaying reports and moving the markers as bidden. Teleprinters were burping tape. Other information was pouring in from Pip-Squeak IFF transmitters via Huff Duff RDF receivers, Chain Home RDF, ROC observation posts, and a litany of other acronyms—the whole Dowding Fighter Command system. It was like a person perceiving a situation through each of his or her disparate senses and combining everything to understand what was going on.

The information she could see was being filtered and synthesized by more WAAFs at Fighter Command HQ at Bentley Priory, sent to Uxbridge, and displayed on the table. Park and his controllers looked down from the balconies with telephones glued to their ears, made their decisions, and relayed them to the Sectors.

Out in the Sectors, at Biggin and Hornchurch and Tangmere and the rest, the decisions made in this room would be relayed to the pilots by R/T. And there was a whole flow of information in the reverse direction, back from the pilots over R/T to their Sector controllers and by telephone back to Fighter Command and 11 Group.

All those messages, all those communications, all that electrical instrumentation and paraphernalia . . . and, standing above it all, Park was like the conductor of a vast orchestra. Eleanor grinned to herself secretly and told herself to steady up; she'd had a tutor at Oxford who described an analogy as a dull mind's substitute for reasoning.

Churchill was staring down at the table, seemingly befuddled. Every few seconds, Eleanor noticed, he put his unlit cigar in his mouth, inhaled pointlessly, and reluctantly removed it.

"What is happening?" he demanded, almost like an impatient infant—here, Eleanor conceded, the analogy was apt. "Are we winning, are we holding our own, are we losing—pray tell me? What is going on?" He shook his massive head. "The fate of the nation is in the balance, I am the prime minister, I should know, and I have no idea what is happening!"

Eleanor had spent the past few weeks understanding the Dowding system and reinterpreting it into a mathematical model, her minimax zero-sum simulation. Now she could read the positional implications of the markers at a glance. She had also spent those weeks at Park's side, observing his strategies, watching his decisions, and admiring his tactical skills. Now she could see how Kesselring, in the Luftflotte II headquarters in Brussels, was aiming to outfox Park and how Park had positioned his forces to outmaneuver Kesselring. Now she could read the map like a narrative.

She must help Churchill see what she could see. He was said to have a vivid imagination. All she could do was to try.

She pointed downwards, towards the south of London.

"Sir, look at that crescent of markers with Luftwaffe labels on them, over there towards the far side of the table under the Tote Board. They represent what the enemy calls a *Kampfgeschwader*, KG for short, a bomber wing at fifteen thousand feet. Imagine they're not markers on the table—imagine they're miniature bombers four feet above the table, flying north by northwest."

Churchill gazed down at the table, rapt, and Eleanor knew he could see them as she described them. Down below the WAAFs adjusted the line of markers, inching them towards central London.

"Those are Dorniers, it's been reported and confirmed, twin-engine bombers. They are approaching London, each with two thousand pounds of bombs. There are an estimated twenty-five Dorniers, so they're carrying fifty thousand pounds of high explosive. Or the bombs might contain jellified petroleum incendiaries capable of starting enormous, violent fires."

Churchill grunted, absorbed, and she continued.

"The Dorniers are just crossing the outer suburbs now, perhaps as near as Croydon and Bromley, perhaps back as far as Sevenoaks. The people in the streets can look up and see them and hear them and wonder if the bombs will start falling, if it's their turn to be blown to pieces or burned to a crisp."

"Yes, yes, I see the bombers," said Churchill.

"The closest bombers are seven to ten miles south of the Thames, south of central London. At a ground speed of 200 miles per hour, it'll take them no more than two or three minutes to reach the river."

"Yes, yes."

"They're flying in intermittent cloud, hard to spot from the air."

"Yes, I see it."

"On the scale of the map, they're coming towards London at a rate of six inches a minute, an inch every ten seconds."

"Great Scott! So fast? Can they not be stopped?" Churchill demanded. "Where are the Spitfires? Where are the Hurricanes?"

"Look further back into Kent, Prime Minister," she said, ignoring his question. "You'll see all those other enemy markers scattered back across Kent all the way to the Channel and all the 11 Group markers. Imagine those markers are at twenty thousand feet or higher, let's say almost as high as this balcony, much higher than the bombers, above the clouds. Those are the Luftwaffe escort fighters, Messerschmitt 109s, dozens and dozens of them, perhaps some Messerschmitt 110s as well, and our own Spitfires and Hurricanes."

"Yes, yes, I can see it, but . . ."

Again the WAAFs moved Luftwaffe markers towards London, and again she ignored his question.

"The higher enemy markers, the fighters over Kent, are locked in dogfights. They're not advancing, as you can see. Mr. Park has managed to slow them down, to stop them, to peel them away from the bombers, leaving the bombers exposed as they fly on towards London. The escorts have had to stop and fight all the way down through Kent from Biggin Hill and all the way back to Dungeness."

"Now I see it."

"Mr. Park said he would set up hurdles, sir. Well, the enemy has stumbled over them."

"Yes, yes, he did."

"There are perhaps a hundred fifty fighters on each side, sir, three hundred in all, all engaged," she said. "Our fighters are directly above their stations. They can stay until the last moment before they have to break off for refueling. But the 109s, on the other hand, have to go all the way back to France."

Johnnie's 339 was one of those markers, she thought; it was reported as waiting over Whitstable for fresh vectoring instructions. She'd heard at least one 339 Spitfire had been hit. She willed herself not to think about it. The Polish squadron, 314, was moving north, perhaps to catch the bombers as they returned to France after bombing their targets. That left 339 alone, a few inches from a line of enemy markers approaching Canterbury on their journey home.

"Yes, but . . . ," Churchill began.

"Now look over there, sir," she said, pointing. "Look at those RAF markers flying southeast over central London, over there, all by themselves."

"Yes, yes, I see them. But who on earth are they? Where did they spring from? I don't understand!"

It was a moment of high drama, and she permitted herself to be dramatic.

"That's the Duxford Wing, Prime Minister!" she told him. "That's five squadrons from 12 Group, fifty aircraft, mostly Hurricanes, led by Douglas Bader. The Dornier 17s are unescorted: no 109s. There may be twenty-five Dorniers still in formation. That's all that are left. Twenty-five slow bombers against fifty Hurricanes and Spitfires."

"Great Scott!"

"All the Dorniers' escorts are still going round in circles over Kent, dodging Spitfires, and soon they'll be running low on fuel."

Churchill had risen to his feet in excitement.

"The bombers are all alone and more or less defenseless," she said. "Mr. Park has set a trap for the Germans, sir, and they're flying straight into it!"

"By God, they are!" Churchill roared. "By God, they are! The Duxford Wing! I wish I was up there to see it!"

She supposed a mass attack by a wing of fighters was probably the modern equivalent of a calvary charge.

"Where are the bombers heading, do you think?" Churchill asked, sobering. "What are their targets?"

"Well, sir, I don't know . . . They're currently flying towards west central London, as you can see. Unless they turn again, they'll reach Battersea, or Chelsea, or Fulham, very shortly, but there aren't any real military targets in those areas. They could be making for Victoria Station, I suppose, or Battersea Power Station . . ."

"May God have mercy on whoever it may be," said Churchill.

Eleanor permitted herself a wicked thought.

"Actually, sir, on further reflection, if they keep going, they're aiming straight at us!"

"The devil you say!" Churchill said, glancing up at the concrete ceiling in shock. "Do you think so? Where's the Duxford Wing?"

"They are in contact, sir," Park said, turning from the senior controller's desk. "Now we'll finally see what the Big Wing can do."

TWELVE

Q: To give our viewers some perspective, how many of the pilots were fresh to the battle and had not fought before?

A: Well, that depended on which group they were in. The pilots in 10 Group in the west of England and 12 Group in the Midlands had seen very little fighting. So, on 15 September, the day we now call Battle of Britain Day, many of the pilots in the Duxford Wing were in contact with the enemy for the first time.

Q: And 11 Group?

A: They did almost all the fighting. I don't mean that in a disparaging manner; it's just because the Luftwaffe was launching its attacks into 11 Group territory. Anyway, at the rate that 11 Group was replacing pilots at that stage of the battle, I would guess that perhaps twenty-five percent—fifty pilots, say—had never encountered the enemy. In terms of how many pilots were experienced—who had, for example, flown in operations against the enemy for more than a week—I'd say no more than thirty or forty.

Q: They were the survivors?

A: Exactly. The problem was that the new pilots lacked survival instincts or hadn't had a chance to develop them. Experienced pilots, like my husband, reacted without thinking. New pilots were much more easily confused and therefore much more vulnerable. They became disoriented and had to stop to think and often made poor decisions. But, of course, there was nothing that could be done to prevent that. As long as the Luftwaffe kept sending bombers, we had to put Spitfires and Hurricanes in their way, even if their pilots weren't always able to meet the challenge . . .

"There are holes in the side of the cockpit," said Green Three, Henderson. "And bits of metal sticking in. I can actually see the ground."

"Fly southeast, Green Three," said Potter. "One-three-five degrees on your compass."

"I'm so sorry," said Henderson. "I didn't want to let you down."

"You're not," said Potter. "Fly southeast and reduce height gradually as you go. You'll find Hawkinge ahead of you."

"I'm not sure where southeast is."

"Just turn to your right until your compass reads one-three-five, Green Three. See you for tea this afternoon."

Shaux sent a silent message of thanks to Potter for handling the situation gently but firmly. Shaux himself was almost back up to twenty-five thousand feet, just about over the coast. He could see aircraft out to his right, but they were too far away to identify. They could be part of 339, but they could also be 109s.

"I can't move my legs," Henderson said. "I can't feel the rudder pedals."

An icy hand had gripped Shaux's stomach ever since Henderson had reported he'd been hit. Now the icy hand tightened its grip. A skilled pilot might be able to fly without rudder control, but not a novice.

"I can't turn," Henderson said, and there was an edge of desperation in his voice. "I can't get to three-five-one degrees."

There were ways of turning without the rudder, and three-five-one was the wrong bearing, but Shaux said nothing. Nor did Potter. It was understood with agonizing clarity that Henderson's fate was now beyond instruction or help. He was on his own.

"There are also holes in the side of my leg," said Henderson, in a tone of surprised discovery. "And bits of metal sticking in. Good Lord! So that's why it hurts so much!"

Shaux groaned silently. To be a fighter pilot required a suspension of belief. Nobody in 11 Group was suicidal; nor, Shaux was certain, were their Luftwaffe enemies. If you were to climb into your cockpit and fly, it was therefore essential—fundamental—to believe that you would come back safely and unharmed, even when you knew there were significant odds against coming back at all. You had to be able to ignore the obvious.

Now Henderson's plight was stripping away the mask, forcing everyone in hearing range to face reality: an inexperienced pilot in a damaged aircraft with shrapnel in his leg would almost certainly die.

Shaux had fought this battle with himself over and over again, for days, weeks, months. Every pilot had his own unique way of dealing with danger, and with the odds of survival. In Shaux's case, he had developed a sort of stoic indifference to survival. He had fallen under the spell of a siren song, the bewitching words of a poem by the Irish poet William Butler Yeats, who had written about a fighter pilot in the last war. The poem began:

> *I know that I shall meet my fate,*
> *Somewhere among the clouds above;*

Yeats's airman expected to die—knew he would die—just as Shaux expected to die. But it didn't matter, Shaux had convinced himself, because his life was not really worth living. Yeats' poem ended:

> *I balanced all, brought all to mind*
> *The years to come seemed waste of breath,*
> *A waste of breath the years behind*
> *In balance with this life, this death.*

And thus, hey presto! Shaux didn't care. On careful consideration, as the poem explained, losing a life that would be a waste of breath was no loss at all and nothing to regret. Therefore death had no further dominion over him.

That fatalist philosophy had carried him through innumerable encounters with the Luftwaffe over Holland, Belgium, France, and the Channel against 109s and 110s and Dorniers and Heinkels and Junkers 88s and Stukas. It had sustained him from May until now in September.

Forget Henderson, who was beyond help, and look for 109s, Shaux told himself; focus on the rest of 339.

He had seen a nature film about herds of antelope, or wildebeest, or some such animals, being chased by lions, or, perhaps, cheetahs, somewhere in Africa. As the antelopes fled, they abandoned the older and sicker animals that could not keep up with the herd as well as the newborn that simply couldn't run fast enough. So it was up here: 339 must stay together as a fighting unit to survive; Henderson, like a wounded young antelope, was unfortunately but necessarily on his own.

"It really, really hurts," said Henderson's voice, in a sort of gasp.

There was absolutely nothing that Shaux—or anyone else—could do for Henderson. You could put a racehorse with a broken leg out of its misery but not a Spitfire pilot.

It was up to God, and Shaux did not believe in God.

Shaux's job was to keep 339 safe and together. There were bound to be more 109s. The aircraft on his right were approaching. Instinct told him it was part of 339, but he turned towards them just to be on the safe side. Looking down, he could see the north coast of Kent. There was a small harbor town. It could be Whitstable or Herne Bay. Let's see . . . the harbor opened to the northwest. It was Whitstable.

"Shadow, regroup overhead Whitstable, angels two-five," he said.

"Shadow leader, I am on your three o'clock," Digby's voice said. Shaux's instincts had been right.

Digby appeared on his starboard wing almost immediately, with A Flight miraculously in position behind him.

"I'm so sorry, but I don't know where Whitstable is," Henderson said, and began to sob. "I don't know where I am. I'm in the clouds. I don't know what to do."

Shaux wanted to tell Green Three to stop talking, but he did not have the heart. There were thirty or forty Spitfire and Hurricane pilots listening to Henderson, all four squadrons on the Hornchurch Sector D R/T frequency, knowing he would almost certainly die absolutely alone, absolutely beyond help and in extreme pain, just as they would also die if the same fate were to befall them.

Shaux wanted to tell 339 to disperse in a general hunt for Henderson, to somehow find him and guide him back to safety, but he could not.

"Oh God, I've let everybody down."

Shaux could tell that Henderson was trying to suppress his sobs.

"I'm so ashamed. I'm a complete joke."

Everyone on the Hornchurch Sector operational R/T system could hear Henderson, not only the pilots and the controllers and the operations staff back at the station, but also all the WAAFs at the plotting tables and in the Huff Duff stations all over Kent and Surrey. Nothing could be worse for morale than to hear this hideously public end. It was like looking through the window of one of those American prison gas chambers, watching the condemned man die.

Shaux opened his mouth to tell Henderson that far from being a joke or a failure, he was a brave man doing his duty as best he could, and Shaux was privileged to have him in his squadron.

But: "Shadow, eyes wide open," Shaux said instead. There had to be more 109s than just the few they'd seen so far.

"A complete joke . . . I stank at Latin and now I stink at flying . . ."

Potter and B Flight arrived. Shaux knew that Potter would be in anguish. Henderson was one of his chaps, and Potter would feel he was somehow to blame for not protecting him.

"I can't see the ground. I think I'm diving."

"Follow me, Shadow," Shaux said unnecessarily, but he had to keep 339 focused and alert and not lost in the agony of Henderson's lonely fate.

"Now I can't even blow my nose. My handkerchief's soaked in blood," Henderson sobbed. "What a complete joke I am, a bloody joke."

Less than an hour ago, Henderson had been celebrating a birdie at aerial golf. Now he was lost, in pain, and stripped of all dignity, of all self-respect.

"I see you!" Henderson suddenly yelled. "Thank God! Thank God! Coming up behind me! Thank God! I see you, Green . . ."

His transmission ended as abruptly as it had begun.

"Stay alert, Shadow," Shaux said into the sudden silence. His voice sounded harsh and ruthless in his ears. Uncaring.

"What is your status, Shadow?" the Sector controller asked, a little unsteadily.

One aircraft down, Shaux thought, and another retired damaged. Two out of eleven, nine left. Tanks still half full, probably better than that for the ammunition belts; par for the course.

"Shadow is open for trade, Lumba. Bent but not broken," he replied.

It sounded a bit bombastic, a bit jingoistic, and certainly uncaring, he thought, but this was no time to mourn. The listening WAAFs would think he was a heartless bastard. They would be right, he thought.

THIRTEEN

Q: Were you aware of victories and losses as they occurred?

A: Not immediately. The pilots talked to the Sector controllers, so they could hear what was happening. Some of the WAAFs at Fighter Command and 11 Group and the liaison functions could hear the conversations on their headsets, but Park and the Group controllers did not. It would have been overwhelming to try to listen to hundreds of communications.

Q: So you couldn't listen in to your husband or his squadron, for example?

A: Sometimes, I admit . . . It drove me crazy, it was stupid, but sometimes I just couldn't help it . . .

Park replaced a telephone.

"Sector D reports that 339 Squadron describes its condition as bent but not broken, Prime Minister," he said solemnly. "I believe that can also be said of 11 Group in general."

"Bent but not broken," Churchill repeated slowly, his face wreathed with smiles, as if chewing the words with delight. "Bent but not broken. I shall so report it to Parliament."

Eleanor had heard that Churchill collected phrases he could use in future speeches.

"No new formations are crossing the coast, Prime Minister, at least not yet," Park said. "We may have seen the worst of it for the time being."

"Has there been much damage?" Churchill asked.

"The Dorniers were successful in bombing the railway lines leading to Victoria Station, sir," Park said. "They damaged the lines and a viaduct in Battersea. That will cause problems with both Victoria and Waterloo. I don't know if that was their real target or just a lucky hit."

"Is that all?"

"Well, sir, there are reports that a Dornier crashed into Victoria Station," Park said. "And apparently a couple of bombs hit Buckingham Palace, but I don't have confirmation."

A telephone rang and he excused himself.

"Well, I'm sure the royal family isn't there today," Churchill said. "It's Sunday. But they'll be pleased, nonetheless."

"Why on earth would the king and queen be pleased, sir?" Eleanor asked.

"The queen told me recently that she wished they'd be bombed so she could look the poor people of East London in the eye."

Eleanor wasn't sure that was a sign of genuine royal empathy or a cynical appeal for popularity. Park was distracted, and Churchill was staring at her, waiting for her response. Perhaps it would be best to steer the conversation in a different direction.

"There are still more than a hundred Luftwaffe aircraft over England, sir," Eleanor said. "The Dorniers are turning for home, and there are still a lot of 109s and 110s farther south."

"How many of them have we shot down so far?"

"We can't tell yet, sir, until all the reports are in," Eleanor said. "And I beg you to remember that the estimated number of victories is almost always greatly exaggerated."

"Well, I'm sure the Big Wing gave a good account of itself," Churchill said. To Eleanor's annoyance he seemed to imply that most of the victories would have been won by Douglas Bader's Big Wing, part of Leigh-Mallory's 12 Group, rather than by 11 Group's squadrons.

The map table was still a jumble of markers stretching all the way from London to the coast. The Tote Board reported that 339 was still on patrol. Johnnie was still in danger.

"The Luftwaffe still has to fly back across Kent, sir. Mr. Park still has several squadrons in the air."

"Yes, exactly," Park said, returning. "I'm ordering some of the Spitfires down lower."

"I thought you preferred not to send Spitfires against bombers, Air Vice-Marshal?" Churchill asked. Eleanor wondered again if he was testing Park.

"There are a great many 109s mixed in with the bomber stream, sir," Park said. "We have several reports of Hurricanes getting jumped at low altitudes."

He turned away and picked up a telephone. Eleanor needed to get away from Churchill's barrage of questions, at least for a few minutes. She mumbled something and slipped downstairs to the main floor. She scrounged a cup of tea and wished she hadn't promised to give up smoking.

The WAAFs moved efficiently all around, talking quietly into their headsets, adjusting the markers on the table, and updating the squadron displays. They seemed oblivious to Churchill's looming presence in the gallery above. Eleanor had never seen the WAAFs become flustered, even in the heat of the greatest raids with dozens of markers scattered across the table. In everyday life they would be shopgirls, or factory workers, or perhaps young wives, the kind of young women who, in normal society, would not be expected to manage major responsibilities. They would be scrubbing floors and cooking simple meals to put in front of their husbands and certainly not expected to manage major responsibilities in a military organization.

What nonsense! These women were performing their duties flawlessly, just as competently as the male controllers and intelligence officers sitting up in the balcony. The Dowding system—the Fighter Command control system—relied on WAAFs in a dozen different roles. In fact, Eleanor thought, there were women in the Supermarine factories building Spitfires and in the Hawker factories building Hurricanes. There were women assembling the Merlin engines that powered them.

Eleanor shook her head slowly. There were women down here doing the work, and men up there on the balconies, seated in comfortable chairs and watching them. One day the world would change. One day, perhaps, the prime minister would be a woman. Yes, she said to herself, and one day pigs will fly!

The WAAF in charge this morning was Section Officer Susan Smith, Eleanor saw. Susan had the cubicle next to Eleanor's in the WAAF officers' sleeping quarters. They weren't close friends, but they had gravitated towards each other, planning trips to the mess and dining hall together in order to escape the unwanted attentions of the male officers, who vastly outnumbered them. Susan wasn't looking well, Eleanor thought. In truth, the demanding pressures of the job, the remorseless daily raids, and their squalid living conditions must be taking their toll on everyone.

Susan was wearing a headset marked "Sector D R/T," allowing her to listen directly to the pilots and controllers as the battle unfolded. A set of spare headphones lay on the table. Without making a conscious decision, Eleanor saw her own hand reach out and pick them up. The same hand adjusted the headset and settled it on her head.

"Lumba calling Shadow," she heard the Hornchurch controller say through the static. "Shadow vector two-zero-zero direction Ashford, descend to angels one-five."

"Vector two-zero-zero," she heard Johnnie say. "Angels one-five. Follow me, Shadow."

Almost immediately Eleanor saw that the 339 marker was moving southwest. Johnnie was rejoining the hunt. She never did this, never listened in to pilots, but the need to hear his voice was overpowering. Park had promised to take him out of 339 and to give him a well-deserved break from his daily encounters with the enemy, but in the meantime, now, he was in the middle of a sky full of 109s.

Two minutes of silence followed. Meanwhile a nearby WAAF inched the 339 marker southwestward across the table in response to information relayed from the Observer Corps and Huff Duff stations. Other WAAFs moved a ragged line of Luftwaffe markers southward from London towards Maidstone and Dover. Down here at table level, the fight seemed closer somehow, and more immediate, and the waiting more unbearable. "Lumba calling Shadow. Bandits at angels one-eight overhead Ashford heading southeast."

Yes, there was the enemy marker, the remnants of a Dornier *staffel*, a bomber formation on a path that would intersect with the 339 marker.

"Shadow," Johnnie's voice responded.

Johnnie was known for the monosyllabic brevity of his R/T messages. Other squadron leaders encouraged communication, believing it reinforced teamwork and esprit de corps and made their pilots feel less alone. Some squadron leaders even told jokes. The Polish squadrons in particular were known for their constant chatter, sometimes in accented English and sometimes in Polish—much to their English-speaking leaders and controllers' frustration. Johnnie, the minimalist, believed that important information and orders could get lost in unnecessary chitchat.

Susan had told her the WAAFs had favorites among the pilots just from listening to their voices. Eleanor wondered if Johnnie was one of them.

More silence: Johnnie's last order, "Follow me," was still in effect.

"Red Leader. Bandits one o'clock at angels one-six." This had to be Digby, Johnnie's trusted right-hand man who was blessed with superb eyesight. Johnnie said that flying with Diggers was like flying with airborne radar. Digby sounded no more excited about spotting the enemy than about noticing a stray piece of fluff on his sleeve.

"Red Leader. Bandits are Dorniers."

Perhaps this was the formation that had bombed the railway lines in Battersea.

"Red Leader. There are twelve Dorniers."

Finally Johnnie broke his silence.

"Green Flight, engage the bandits. Red Flight, cover Green Flight."

Johnnie was splitting his force. Green Flight was led by Froggie Potter. The other half of 339, Digby's Red Flight, would climb higher, searching for 109s.

"Follow me, Green Flight," Potter's voice said. "Stay tight and hold your fire."

Several voices spoke through the static at once. Then Potter's voice came through, saying, "*Testes frixi*, Green Flight."

Testes frixi? Obviously he hadn't really said "fried testicles" in Latin, Eleanor thought—that would be absurd. Had he said, "Test sixty," perhaps, using some private 339 code? "This is tricky" might make sense, or even "Fiddlesticks." It was hard to tell through the crackling static. She'd ask Johnnie tonight.

Eleanor tried to envision what was happening. Potter, with four or five aircraft closing in on a dozen Dorniers and coming up behind them over the Dornier pilots' left shoulders. Digby was climbing above Potter and the Dorniers, searching for 109s. Where was Johnnie? The map table was no help: all the markers were bunched together over Ashford.

"Tallyho!" came Potter's laconic voice. Green Flight was engaging.

"Bandits right!" Digby's voice broke in, no longer laconic. "Right, right, right!"

"Shadow, buster! Buster!" Johnnie said. "Shadow, climb."

"Jesus Christ!" yelled an unknown voice.

"Green Flight, climb!" That must be Potter.

Susan Smith was staring at Eleanor with her eyes wide. What was happening? "Buster," Eleanor knew, meant to open the throttle wide for maximum speed and was used only in dire emergencies. Enemy aircraft must have jumped 339 again on their right, possibly a formation of 109s that was not showing on the map table.

The level of static doubled, making it much harder to hear. This sometimes happened, Eleanor knew, when a damaged R/T in one of the Spitfires was jammed in the transmit position.

"Shadow, re-form, re-form, buster, buster," Johnnie instructed through the static. Whatever was going on, Johnnie wanted 339 to break off contact and climb as fast as possible. His voice revealed no fear, no uncertainty.

Johnnie had split 339 into two formations, one—Green Flight led by Potter—to attack the Dorniers trying to escape back to France and the other—Red Flight led by Digby—to fly above Green Flight to protect them. Eleanor couldn't tell which flight had been jumped or whether both had been. How many 109s were there? Why weren't the bandits on the map? Where was Johnnie?

"Lumba calling Shadow. What is your status?" Evidently the Sector D controller in Hornchurch was just as uncertain as Eleanor.

"Look out, Red Leader!" someone yelled. "Behind you. Behind you."

"Thank you," Digby's precise voice came dimly through the static.

"Bandits at six o'clock!" someone else said.

The static grew worse.

"Bandits twelve o'clock high!" someone yelled. That had to mean yet more 109s making a direct frontal attack, diving down onto 339. Could there be two or even three formations attacking 339? Why weren't these schwarms on the map table? How had they managed to escape observation? How had 339 been dispatched into the eye of a storm?

Where was Johnnie?

The static stopped abruptly, replaced by a shocking silence. Susan and Eleanor were still staring at each other.

"Lumba calling Shadow. What is your status?" the controller asked again.

Silence.

"Lumba calling all Shadow aircraft. Acknowledge."

Silence.

"Lumba calling all Shadow aircraft. Acknowledge."

Silence.

There was a look of horror on Susan Smith's face. Eleanor felt as if she were staring into a mirror.

FOURTEEN

Q: All you could hear was silence? That must have been very frightening.

A: Yes, it was. There's really nothing else to say . . .

"Red Leader," Digby said. "Bandits one o'clock at angels one-six."

Shaux stared forward down past the right side of his engine cowling and saw aircraft below him flickering in and out through the wispy clouds, gray, almost black, hard to see against the ground far below them. He glanced at the compass between his knees. The bandits were flying southeast towards Folkestone and the coast.

"Red Leader. Bandits are Dorniers.

"Red Leader. There are twelve Dorniers."

So the Hornchurch controller had been exactly right. This should be an excellent opportunity. The Luftwaffe bombers were only about ten miles from the Channel and less than thirty from their bases in France. They now had a tailwind, and they'd probably already dropped their bombs, so they would be much lighter and faster than on their journey in. That meant they'd only be over England for another two or three minutes, but two or three minutes would be ample time to mount an attack against them. Even though they'd probably already dropped their bombs, it should be possible to damage or down at least one or two of them so that they would never return to bomb again.

There was also, however, an excellent chance that these Dorniers had covering 109s. With so many aircraft up here throughout the morning, there were bound to be at least some stray 109s if not an organized schwarm or two. He'd let Froggie Potter and Green Flight go for the Dorniers while Digby and Red Flight stayed up here to provide cover. He glanced over his left shoulder to look at Green Flight. Froggie was a hundred feet behind him and perhaps twenty feet below. Over his right shoulder, he could see Digby and Red Flight.

"Green Flight, engage the bandits. Red Flight, cover Green Flight."

It was a tactic they had practiced on many occasions and had used with considerable success against the enemy. They even had a name for it: Red Eyes, Green Guns. Potter's Flight could concentrate on attacking the bombers without worrying about being jumped while Digby's searched the skies above them for other aircraft.

"Follow me, Green Flight," Potter's voice said. "Stay tight and hold your fire." His voice was calm, almost laconic, but Shaux knew his pulse would be racing in excitement and anticipation.

Potter's Spitfire lifted its right wing, and Green Flight began an arcing, descending turn, five Spitfires moving as one, displaying their elegant silhouettes. Shaux felt he had a ringside seat at an airshow featuring an unusually fine display of graceful aircraft and precision formation flying. He had no doubt that Potter had instinctively selected the exact rate of bank and turn that would bring them to the perfect position to attack the Dorniers, arriving over the Dornier pilots' left shoulders at a point-blank range of two hundred yards—two hundred yards exactly, where the eight guns in a Spitfire's wings were calibrated to merge.

How sad, Shaux thought, that all that elegance and skill were brought together by the demands of a brutal, savage war, that the only purpose of Potter's banking turn was to shoot other aircraft out of the sky, and that some young airmen, boys still in their teens, perhaps Luftwaffe, perhaps 339, would probably die in the next two or three minutes.

Shaux shook his head and told himself to shut up—this was definitely *not* the time for daydreaming or pretentious moralizing—and began a systematic search for covering 109s.

"*Testes frixi*, Green Flight," Potter said.

Evidently Potter had detected an imperfection in the turn as Green Flight curved away. Shaux smiled. The concept of "balls, fried" would pass into 339 lore. It would be another thread in the intangible skein of esprit de corps that bound the pilots together and kept them sane and confident and willing to fly again.

At some point he would lose Potter—and Digby as well. They were just too good to be flight leaders; they'd get their own squadrons to command. And 11 Group would be the better for it, but he, Shaux, would suddenly be on his own.

No 109s in sight. Perhaps it was time to ask for a break. Some chaps with his seniority were getting spells of extended leave or being posted to ground-based jobs in Sector Ops and things like that. He probably had as many operational hours as just about anyone by now. His first sorties against the enemy had been back in June, more than three months ago, flying Boulton Paul Defiants over Holland and Belgium, and then, as the Allies collapsed and the Germans advanced, he'd fought over Dunkirk and France. Now he'd been with 339 for a month, flying against the enemy almost every day, sometimes several times a day. In that month the Luftwaffe had been bombed 339 out of two of its airfields—Hawkinge was the third—and yet 339 was still intact, still fighting.

Surely the powers that be, the pencil-pushers, would grant him a sabbatical? And it really was true that he was uniquely qualified to help Eleanor with her mathematical model, although it was also true that he was desperately anxious to spend all day and all night with her, mathematical model or no.

His world had been turned upside down ever since she had summoned him to a London hotel room just a week ago. It was not just the physical passion she had unleashed in him; it was the matching passion he had seen unleashed in her. He had always thought of girls as prim and proper—ladylike—and assumed they were beyond the carnal desires felt by men; he was shocked to discover that they—Eleanor at least—were not. He had thought that girls were supposed to put up with all that stuff reluctantly—not to demand it.

He dragged himself back to reality, as he did a hundred times a day. Tonight she had summoned him to London once again, but he could not permit himself to think about it, not now.

No 109s; perhaps they had already returned to France, given their notoriously limited range and endurance.

Another minute passed. No visible 109s . . . Potter and Green Flight were out of sight below him, but they should be just about to attack any moment now.

Let's see, how much time had 339 been flying? Shaux was going to have to bring 339 down for rearming and refueling fairly soon, perhaps in another five minutes, after Potter had completed his attack. Perhaps 339 would be released this afternoon, and he could leave for London early.

"Tallyho!" Potter said. Green Flight, somewhere below him, had reached the Dorniers. Still no sign of . . .

"Bandits right!" Digby snapped, and Shaux almost jumped out of his skin. "Right, right, right!"

Even as Shaux turned his head to look, the air around him was filled with tracer. There were four or five 109s, shockingly close, almost on top of them, cannons blazing.

"Shadow, buster! Buster!" Shaux said, as calmly as he could, pushing the throttle wide open for emergency power and easing the control column back. The note from the Merlin changed from a roar to a howl as the revs surged up. He was jumping into a torrent of tracer.

Whack! Whack! Whack! Cannon shells tore into the engine housing ahead of him. Something flew off and smashed into the armored glass ahead of the gunsight. For a second Shaux thought the entire canopy might fly off.

"Shadow, climb!"

The 109s swept over them, no more than twenty feet above their cockpits, *huge* in the sky, buffeting Shaux's Spitfire with their prop wash. They were kings of the killing grounds, top predators, at least this time.

"Jesus Christ!" yelled an unknown voice.

There was a gigantic flash of an explosion just out of Shaux's vision off to his left, so close that the blast canted his aircraft. Something massive struck his engine housing with a sound like a sledgehammer and spiraled away. Could that really have been an actual propeller blade? Something else, something oblong, detached itself and smashed into the port wing before flashing past him and out of sight. The Spitfire jerked violently, and for a second Shaux feared the entire Merlin engine had been knocked off its mountings. The aircraft careened to the right, no longer flying in an aeronautical sense, just thrown aside by whatever had struck the engine.

It took Shaux long seconds to persuade the Spitfire to return to something approaching normal flight, and when it did, he saw that he had lost the entire left engine cowling. The Merlin was open to the wind for fully eight feet, just as if the ground crew was inspecting it. There was no exhaust manifold on that side, causing the Merlin to shudder as the timing of the two banks of the V-12 engine became unsynchronized. The stubs of the exhaust pipes, leading directly from the cylinders, were glowing yellow-red hot and burping fire.

The drag of the open engine pulled the Spitfire to the left, and Shaux had to apply constant right rudder to keep the aircraft flying straight. He had never heard of a Spitfire flying without an engine cowling; now he would find out if it could.

A few minutes ago, 339 had jumped a 109 schwarm; now it was 339's turn to be jumped.

Shaux's headset was filled with loud static. Someone's R/T had been hit and jammed in constant transmit, making communication impossible, at least for the moment.

Shaux twisted back and forth in his seat, trying to find the rest of 339 and the 109s, but, as often happened in a sudden encounter, the sky had emptied itself.

The attack had come from the right. The attackers had to have reached him through Digby's Red Flight. Where was Digby? The explosion had been on his left, where Potter's Green Flight had been—but Potter was several thousand feet below him, attacking the Dorniers. Where was Potter now?

Shaux checked his compass and saw that he was flying—more accurately, he was limping crabwise—west. There was nothing he could do for 339 in this condition and without R/T.

He began to execute a painfully erratic turn back eastward for a course towards Hawkinge. He didn't need to make the Spitfire descend; it was doing so all by itself. The needle in the oil pressure gauge was sinking; beside it, to its right, the oil temperature gauge was climbing. Looking back, he saw that his Merlin was emitting a long gray trail, like a giant advertisement in the sky beckoning any stray 109s in sight, and saying, "Look here. Follow this trail to find a wounded Spitfire."

It was very simple. Ten minutes from now he'd either be safely on the ground at Hawkinge, wondering what was for lunch, or he'd be dead. Yeats had explained it all, very efficiently:

> *I know that I will meet my fate*
> *Somewhere among the clouds above.*

The only uncertainty had always been the exact nature of his fate. That thought had sustained him through three months of constant fighting, two occasions on which he had been shot down, and innumerable times—like now—when he had been shot up and damaged.

His rate of descent seemed constant, so he should make it to Hawkinge. If he couldn't get that far, he'd try to put down in Lympne.

Where had those 109s come from? What had happened to Red Flight? Would the Spitfire keep flying? The oil and coolant temperature gauges were as high as he had ever seen them. Soon the Merlin would run out of oil and seize up.

He completed his turn towards Hawkinge. Out to his left he could see his own trail of gray gossamer, stretching back to where he had begun his turn. Interesting: there was an aircraft following his trail.

Perhaps it was another 339 Spitfire. He wished he had Digby's phenomenal eyesight. He strained against the glare. Now he could see a second aircraft—two aircraft were following him. The first aircraft banked to follow his turn: two engines. It was inconceivable that a pair of German bombers would follow a Spitfire. So the only other possible twin-engine aircraft they could be were 110s.

The Luftwaffe often dispatched Messerschmitt 110s on small independent raids, looking for targets of opportunity. Well, Shaux thought, doubtless they were looking at him and seeing opportunity.

Shaux ran through a catalog of possible evasive maneuvers and came up with nothing. His Spitfire was dying. He might conceivably be able to outmaneuver one 110 but certainly not two. Perhaps he should bail out before they caught up with him.

He took his hand off the control stick, and the Spitfire immediately yawed wildly. He would have to let the controls go to open the canopy—assuming the canopy would open after whatever-that-was had crashed into it. Then he would have to undo his straps and climb up on the seat in order to jump—but clearly the Spitfire wouldn't fly by itself, even for fifteen or twenty seconds. He considered undoing the straps and opening the canopy, somehow using one hand only, and then inverting the Spitfire and letting himself fall out. He put the probability of success at one in a million.

> *I know that I will meet my fate*
> *Somewhere among the clouds above . . .*

He'd had his share of luck, more than his share, and now it had run out. Someone had played the ace of trumps against him. It was a huge, huge pity about Eleanor, but he'd be dead and wouldn't know what he was missing, so it wouldn't matter, and she'd move on. She was irrepressible. She'd become famous one day—well, she was almost becoming famous already; actually, secretly famous, to be more accurate.

The two aircraft behind him had disappeared into the clouds and the hazy trail of oil the Merlin was shedding. When he saw them again, they'd be right behind him.

In the meantime, Eleanor had fulfilled his wildest dreams. She had loved him, however briefly, and made love to him. She had wanted him and wanted him to make love to her. He had stared deep into her eyes, unmasked, primordial, when the moment came. Every dream he had ever had, every future he had ever imagined, had been surpassed. If his life was a race, then Eleanor was both the finishing line and first prize, the gold medal. He had won—game, set, and match. Anything else was trivial.

He recalled another verse, from John Dryden, about a man who was truly happy:

> *Tomorrow, do thy worst, for I have lived today.*

It was a suitable summation to his life: he had had his today. The 110s would finish off a contented man.

FIFTEEN

Q: I appreciate that there were several different battles going on at the same time, engagements and skirmishes, Dame Eleanor.

A: There was fighting all across southeastern England, a long line of encounters, if you will; some were triggered by the Luftwaffe flying into Park's defensive lines, and some were chance meetings.

Q: Let's take it a step at a time so that the audience can appreciate what was happening at noon that day. To start with, what happened to the Big Wing over London? That was the decisive victory, was it not?

A: Well, it was heralded as a brilliant success. The bombing raid was very dramatic because a Dornier fell on Victoria Station in the middle of the day, and some of its bombs hit Buckingham Palace. The Duxford Wing attacked the Dorniers, as Park had planned. They claimed twenty-six victories.

Q: Amazing! How many Dorniers were there?

A: We weren't quite certain at the time, of course, but after the war it was established there were twenty-seven, of which twenty-one returned to France and landed safely.

Q: Er, that doesn't add up.

A: Very true . . .

"There appears to be a lull in enemy operations, Prime Minister," Park said.

"Do we know the score at the end of this inning?" Churchill asked. "Did we win?"

"It's very early to tell, Prime Minister. We have to wait for the pilots to land and make their reports, and then everything has to be tabulated and cross-checked and confirmed over the next few days."

"Stuff and nonsense!" Eleanor thought that Churchill looked like an impatient schoolboy. "What do the controllers say now?"

"What do we know, Eleanor?"

"Well, sir, we don't have results for 11 Group," she said. "But so far 12 Group are already claiming twenty-six victories for the Duxford Wing, but of course . . ."

"Twenty-six? Twenty-six?" Churchill roared. "Splendid! Splendid!"

"Well, sir, that has to be verified. The pilots are still in the air."

Eleanor saw that Park was attempting not to roll his eyes at such an absurdly high claim.

"We'll know in good time," he said. "In the meantime, Prime Minister, may I suggest lunch in the officers' mess?"

"Thank you, Air Vice-Marshal. That's really very good of you. But no," Churchill replied with ponderous formality. "You may recall that I have been here before and have experienced your mess, and, as they say, forewarned is forearmed."

"Very wise, sir." Park smiled.

"I came prepared," Churchill said.

With that, his secretary opened a wicker picnic basket from which she drew a red-and-white checkered tablecloth, cutlery, several packages wrapped in greaseproof paper, a champagne flute, and an impressive-looking bottle.

Eleanor stared—she just couldn't help it.

"With age comes wisdom, Squadron Officer," Churchill rumbled with an impish smile. "With great age comes great wisdom. With great wisdom comes smoked salmon and Pol Roger. Enjoy your lunch in the mess. Bon appétit!"

Eleanor grinned in spite of her inner horror—what had happened to Johnnie?—and left the balcony. As she climbed down the stairs to the main floor, she heard the pop of a champagne cork.

She hurried up the long flights of stairs that led to the surface and fresh air. She lit a cigarette and inhaled deeply, even though she had promised not to smoke. She walked alone across the grass for a few minutes, facing the memory of the shattering silence when they lost R/T contact with 339.

Where was he? Safe? Injured but safe? Injured but not . . . She stopped herself.

She swore she would never, ever listen to the R/T again. She swore she would stick to her self-imposed discipline: always assume that Johnnie was all right. Anything else would drive her crazy. Although he had wrapped himself in Yeats's bleak and hopeless poem, he was a survivor. What had he said? That 339 was bent but not broken. He might bend in the wind, like a tree in a storm, but he would not break.

She had always assumed that being in love would make one gloriously happy, but it was far from it—it was making her a nervous wreck. Of course, she thought, if one fell in love with a fighter pilot in the midst of the greatest aerial battle in history, one could not reasonably expect to experience a frothy romantic comedy, like a Hollywood film with Fred Astaire and Ginger Rogers. Her thoughts careened sideways as it occurred to her that she had never danced with Johnnie; indeed, she didn't even know if he could dance. She had slept with him before dancing with him; her aunt Matilda, who had taught etiquette to Eleanor and her sisters, would be shocked. "Really, my dear," Aunt Matilda would have said. "That seems a trifle impetuous to me; one might even say it was precipitate!"

Her thoughts careened again. Her model was predicting that the battle could only last a few more days—the Luftwaffe simply could not absorb the rate at which it was losing aircraft. Park had promised to pull Shaux out of the line soon, but would "soon" be soon enough? Even just a few more days could spell catastrophe for Johnnie, assuming, God forbid, catastrophe had not already struck.

She willed herself to stop this train of thought—these trains of thought. She must focus her attention elsewhere. She was at the very center of England's resistance to Hitler. She was the senior strategic advisor to Keith Park, AOC 11 Group. She was explaining and interpreting the battle to Churchill, one of the three or four most powerful men in the world, who had just placed her in charge of a top secret intelligence department.

Surely all that must be more important than whether or not she would be in Johnnie's arms tonight. She was a professional mathematician, a creature of reason, of cold logic—not some daydreaming girl fretting over her lover. Except that she was.

Very well, she told herself severely. As a mathematician I will define Johnnie's status and prospects as indeterminate and in a state of unresolved quantum superimposition, both simultaneously alive *and* dead, exactly like Schrödinger's cat. Since I cannot know more until I get more information, I cannot worry about it.

Faint hope, she thought, but it was all she had. In the meantime she had work to do.

She blew her nose, ground out her cigarette, and returned to her office in Hillesden House. An armed RAF Regiment policeman had stood outside her door ever since Churchill had decided to set up a special department for her work. It was all becoming a little ridiculous. The system, Whitehall's all-powerful administrative bureaucracy, was consuming her model. In the past few days, she had received several thick manuals prescribing the proper operation of government departments. She was receiving numerous résumés for potential additions to her staff—and not just mathematicians but clerks, bookkeepers, and an adjutant and support staff. Someone from the Treasury had written to her to complain that she was behind on her expense reporting.

Another official had written to her to point out that she had not yet been approved to receive intelligence as defined in Section 1(1) of the Official Secrets Act of 1911. Therefore, if she communicated to herself any information she created using her own model, "any secret official code word; or password; or any sketch, plan, model, article, or note; or other document or information that is calculated to be or might be or is intended to be directly or indirectly useful to an enemy," then she would be guilty of a felony. In sum, it was treasonous for her to think, until told she could do so.

To add insult to injury, as she reached her door, she saw that Bramble had placed a new sign on the door: 11 Group SRO.

She groaned. She'd had an idea based on von Neumann's work on game theory and written some equations. The original equations each contained statistical variables, such as the number of aircraft Park had available; the average observed size of a 109 Jagdgeschwader; the length of time to build, test, and deliver a Hurricane; or how long it took to take off from Biggin Hill and climb to twenty thousand feet over Hastings. Each morning, data flowing into 11 Group from the Sectors and the fighter stations provided new values for the variables.

Managing this data had been Millie's job, and since her death it was now Jayne's. Kristoffer—and now Bramble—recalculated the results of the equations based on the new values. The results might, or might not, be useful in predicting Kesselring's next moves.

That's all there was: data series laid out in tabular fashion on page after page of loose-leaf paper and two dozen or so equations: a growing pile of notebooks that would be unintelligible to all but a handful of advanced mathematicians. The original formulae had evolved and adapted, like Darwin's creatures in the Galápagos Islands; those that could predict events had survived and spawned other formulae, while those that could not withered away.

And yet the pile of notebooks now had an armed guard and a name and a growing staff and the prime minister's imprimatur and an attendant bureaucracy and its own government department and an overdue expense budget. Soon, she feared, it would also have its own isolated country house.

She often wondered whether her model really was important or whether people just wanted it to be important. Perhaps that was why she was no longer allowed to discuss her equations with anybody besides a chosen few: if people didn't know what her model was, they could assume it was important.

She entered her office, a small room jammed with two desks and four people. Jayne and an assistant, Vera, were tabulating data as it was called in by the Sectors and airfields. Bramble was hard at work calculating the latest results, assisted by the new Hungarian mathematician.

He had a lean and hungry look, and a name she couldn't pronounce, so Eleanor had nicknamed him Cassius in her mind.

One of Jayne's folders held the squadron reports. She flipped through the pages until she came to 339.

1135 Engaged 20+ Bf 109
1139 Spitfire damaged RTB
1141 Spitfire shot down pilot KIA

1209 Engaged 5+ Bf 109, 12+ Do17
1209 Spitfire shot down pilot KIA
1211 Spitfire damaged RTB

RTB meant "returned to base." KIA meant "killed in action." The time when 339 had been jumped was 1209. Was Johnnie an RTB or a KIA, or had he simply returned to base unscathed, not needing a report? She could take the phone from Jayne and call the airfield and find out. On the other hand, that would delay the statistical production process and make the recalculation of the model late, and consequently she might not be able to give Park any new insights. She stared at the report helplessly, undecided. She had never been in love before, and she'd had no idea how complicated—how difficult—love made everything.

"Excuse me, ma'am," Jayne said very firmly, and took the 339 report from Eleanor's hands. Jayne's look suggested that she thought things would go much more smoothly if Eleanor left the room again. She had her hair pulled back into a severe bun, with a pencil sticking through it. Jayne handed the page to Vera, who inserted it into her typewriter with a professionally skillful twirl of the carriage. Eleanor was struck by a momentary pang of sorrow for Millie. Millie had never twirled.

Jayne, meanwhile, was listening on the telephone, repeating information in staccato bursts to Vera, who was typing fast.

"Next, Sector D, 339," Jayne announced. Vera's fingers poised in anticipation above the keyboard, like talons ready to strike. Eleanor stopped breathing.

"Sector D, 339: P/O Henderson, K, KIA; F/O Roberts, J, KIA; S/L Shaux, spelt Sugar-Harry-Ace-Uncle-X-ray, RTB uninjured, A/C unsalvageable; ten pilots available, twelve aircraft available," Jayne dictated, as Vera struck the keys in a high-speed cacophony. "Next is Sector D, 601 . . ."

Vera extracted the 339 report from her typewriter with another professional whirring of gears and passed it to Cassius, who observed it for a moment just as a cat observes a mouse before pouncing. He began to scribble calculations rapidly. Eleanor gripped the table to stop her hands from shaking. Johnnie's state of quantum superimposition had been resolved: he had survived.

She willed herself to transform from anxious lover to cool military professional.

"Well, Mr. Bramble, what do we have so far?" she asked. She was still uncertain how to address him. She was far his senior in rank but junior in age, not to mention the complexities of women working in male professions. "Mr. Bramble" sounded too formal, and "Bramble" sounded too curt, too schoolboyish, too dominating. His first name was Algernon, she knew, and her rank allowed her to address him by that name, while he had to address her respectfully as "ma'am." But somehow she felt she could not call him by that name, and certainly not by Algie, for that matter—no one, however difficult, deserved to be addressed as pond slime.

"There's a sixty-two-point-five percent chance they'll send a much larger raid this afternoon," Bramble said. His manner suggested he was instructing a kindergarten student. "The mean aggregate sizes from comparable previous raids would suggest at least two hundred bombers and twice as many fighters. These numbers, coincidentally, approximate the available aircraft Luftflotte II did not employ this morning. That adds some additional credibility to the estimate."

"Are you sure, Bramble?" Cassius asked. He was one of those people who could arch a single eyebrow in a look of incredulity, a skill that Eleanor greatly envied and secretly practiced in her mirror but, alas, without success.

"I'm sure."

"It seems a bit . . . exact," Cassius demurred.

"I understand—I also thought this was all a bit silly when I first joined," Bramble said, gesturing at the room at large with a dismissive hand. "Asymmetric zero-sums are intuitively unlikely, almost self-contradictory—dichotomous, if you will—and far less intriguing than fractals. But, nonetheless, the predictions tend to be surprisingly correct, indeed robust, and I'm coming to the conclusion that asymmetric minimax may not be as completely foolish an idea as it seems to be at first blush. You'll see!"

"Thank you, Mr. Bramble," Eleanor said, curtsying slightly. "High praise, indeed!"

SIXTEEN

Q: The morning raids were over by 1:00 p.m., Dame Eleanor?

A: Yes. The last 11 Group squadrons were touching down and starting to refuel and rearm. And we could tell from the Chain Home stations that the Luftwaffe aircraft were also landing.

Q: So there was a short lull?

A: In the fighting, yes, but the ground crews on both sides of the Channel were working at top speed, all the WAAFs and the operations and intelligence staff and observers were going through a shift change, and so on. We were getting battle damage reports and bombing assessments. I had to prepare to give my best estimate of the enemy's intentions for the afternoon so that Park could make his decisions. When I went back down to the Operations Room, Churchill was still ecstatic at the initial reports and was dictating congratulations to 12 Group and the Duxford Wing . . .

"Twenty-six victories to the Big Wing!" Churchill exalted. "What a triumph for 12 Group! I must write a memorandum of commendation to Leigh-Mallory."

Park and Eleanor exchanged glances.

"With respect, Prime Minister, the initial claims by pilots are often overestimated," Park said. He gave no sign of anger at 12 Group's preposterous claims or at Churchill's credulity. "It's easy to be mistaken."

"I know that very well," Churchill responded. "Perhaps it was only twenty. Young officers are wont to exaggerate their own prowess, particularly in the presence of young ladies. And how did 11 Group do, pray tell me?"

"Eleanor, do we have the numbers yet?" Park asked.

"So far there's about fifty claimed, sir," she said. "Based on past analyses, we probably shot down somewhere between fifteen and twenty, almost all 109s."

"Then 12 Group outdid you, Park!" Churchill grinned.

"The Royal Observer Corps is very reliable at identifying crash sites, sir," Park said. "We'll know exactly in a few days."

Eleanor could tell Park was seething with fury. The Duxford Wing was claiming to have shot down every Dornier—their numbers were preposterous. If all the Dorniers had been shot down, what phantoms had 339 engaged over Ashford? And 11 Group had done ninety percent of the fighting, and now 12 Group was claiming ninety percent of the victory! What was a polite way of telling Churchill that Leigh-Mallory was almost certainly lying?

"I'm afraid the Duxford claims are statistically unlikely, sir," she told Churchill. "We've never had results like that before."

"We've never had the Duxford Wing engaged before," Churchill snapped, and Eleanor saw Park swallow an angry retort.

Looking past Churchill's shoulder, she saw that 339's status on the Tote Board had jumped to "Landed and Refueling."

"I trust our own losses are not too severe," Churchill said. "Do we have an estimate?"

"Not yet, sir," she said. "We don't know who's back safely and who isn't."

"I'm sure the Duxford Wing will have fared well," Churchill said. "They have safety in numbers."

"No doubt of it, sir," she said. There was no point in arguing.

Q: Was this the basis of the so-called Big Wing controversy?

A: Well, the Big Wing controversy is a whole subject in its own right that had been building for some time, but certainly the claims made on that day added fuel to the fire.

Q: Tell us what was involved, Dame Eleanor.

A: Oh dear; it's a very difficult subject. Besides, it was not really germane to the events of the day, only to subsequent perceptions.

Q: But, surely, it's important to our understanding of what happened?

A: Well, there was a popular theory that the best way to employ fighters was en masse, in groups of thirty or forty or more. It was promoted by an Italian named Italo Balbo, who was in Mussolini's air force, the Regia Aeronautica. In fact, big wings were even called Balbos for a while.

Q: So 12 Group, with Leigh-Mallory and Bader, favored large formations, and Park favored small formations. Since 11 Group actually won the Battle of Britain using small formations, why was there a dispute?

A: It's really hard to imagine, looking back. We think of the Battle of Britain as a great victory, against overwhelming odds, fought with brilliance. Now we see Dowding and Park as great heroes who saved the country.

But at the time the view was completely opposite. Dowding and Park were considered to be losing or barely hanging on at best. It was only in retrospect that people understood what had happened, the magnitude of the odds that Dowding and Park overcame, the brilliance of Dowding's foresight, and the genius of Park's tactics.

People saw hundreds of bombers damaging London and other cities, and they blamed Dowding and Park for letting them get through. They also blamed Dowding and Park for having no defense against bombing by night. That was grossly unfair—at that stage of the war, before airborne radar, it was technically impossible to stop bombers at night.

They saw that Park was letting the nuisance raids through unopposed, to conserve our strength while the Luftwaffe wasted theirs . . .

Q: But when Park won . . .

A: The battle was not won in a visible manner—the enemy ramparts were not overrun, as it were. The trenches were not stormed. There was no cry of triumph, no ceremonial surrender, no parade, no flyby. The Germans simply stopped coming by day. It was a submission, a silent defeat, but an absolute one. One morning we got up and the skies were clear of aircraft. The aircrews snoozed in their disposal huts. The map remained empty all day. The WAAFs knitted. That's how we knew.

Later we had confirmation: we deciphered the Enigma message postponing the Sea Lion invasion, although that was much too secret to be broadcast.

Meanwhile Beaverbrook and Sholto Douglas and all the rest gathered and convinced Churchill to clean house and dismiss the winning team. Dowding and his boss, Newall, and Park all went, and the snipers—Douglas and Leigh-Mallory and Charles Porter—took over.

I remember . . .

Q: What?

A: It's nothing.

Q: Please?

A: Very well: I remember in 1945, after the war, when Hitler was dead and Nazi Germany was in ruins and in unconditional surrender, and Churchill was triumphantly victorious, he called a general election, expecting to be reelected by a landslide. He expected to be treated as a conquering hero. He wasn't. He was defeated by the voters quite decisively—thrown out, cast aside, dismissed.

He was stunned at what he perceived to be the gross ingratitude of the people he had saved. Shocked to be utterly excluded from the conferences in which the postwar world order was decided— conferences he itched to attend but couldn't. He went from being one of the three most powerful men in the world to being a nobody . . . excluded . . . unwanted . . .

I remember thinking to myself, well, sir, now you know how it feels.

Q: Ah, I see . . . Were you involved personally in the Big Wing dispute?

A: No, not at the time. It was all done secretly, behind Dowding's and Park's backs. In any case, I was off setting up MI6-3b, and I didn't find out until I went to see Park a couple of weeks later . . .

"Ah, Eleanor, how pleasant to see you," Park greeted her, and she saw he meant it. "I see you've been promoted again; now Shaux has to address you as ma'am and stand to attention when you enter a room! Can I offer you a cup of tea? How is your new job shaping up?"

He made a fuss of calling for tea and offering her a cigarette.

"Well, sir, I'm doing my best, but they've locked me away in a dreary mansion house in Suffolk, miles from anywhere, and surrounded me with tedious bureaucrats and loutish academics."

"It sounds delightful." Park laughed.

"I'd much rather be back here with you, sir."

"I feel the same way."

"Anyway, sir, what's done is done. I came to say goodbye and to thank you for everything."

"On the contrary, Eleanor," Park said. "It's I who should be thanking you for all your contributions."

"Sir, it's not easy for a woman to get men to take her seriously— intellectually or professionally, I mean. You gave me a chance. Otherwise the model would never have been built. That's what I came to tell you."

"I take no credit for that," Park said, shaking his head. "I've always thought it was very stupid to waste half of all human brainpower just because it happens to be in female heads. In fact, there are more women than men, so it's more than half the human brainpower. Anyway, the last war moved women along and got them the vote; perhaps this war will advance women some more. After all, we'll lose the war without the contributions of your gender."

"I just wish I could keep on working for you, sir, rather than someone in Military Intelligence I haven't even met."

Park's face darkened.

"Look, Eleanor, there are a couple of things you need to know. You're better off where you are."

"Why, sir?"

An orderly entered with tea, and Park waited until she served them and left.

"I'm afraid the knives are out for me, and Stuffy Dowding, too," Park said. "We'll be gone, banished, within a week or two."

"That's preposterous!" Eleanor objected. "You've just won the greatest battle in the history of aviation and possibly one of the greatest battles in all history!"

"Leigh-Mallory is a smooth operator," Park said, shaking his head. "He wants Fighter Command, and he sees me as standing in his way. So, first he'll get me thrown out and he'll take over 11 Group, and then he'll take Fighter Command. Sholto Douglas and he are as thick as thieves. They're running round Whitehall, telling everyone who'll listen that I totally mishandled the battle."

"That's totally unfair!"

"Fair or not, he's succeeding."

He looked completely exhausted, she thought. Drained. More—it was the first time she had ever seen him look defeated. Göring and Kesselring and the entire might of the Luftwaffe had not been able to overcome him, but Leigh-Mallory and his cronies had. He could handle a thousand Luftwaffe raiders, but not a handful of air vice-marshals.

"You're off to continue with your model, Eleanor," he said. "I won't be able to help you, I'm afraid, but I've mentioned you to Edward Bridges, the cabinet secretary. He's a friend of mine and a first-class chap. He isn't widely known, but he's one of the most powerful men in England."

"I'm afraid I've never heard of him, sir."

"He runs the civil service, and that's more powerful than running the army, the navy, and the RAF combined. Anyway, if you ever need help, go to him."

"Thank you, sir. I will."

"There's another matter I want to mention," he continued. "I've tried to take care of things before the ax falls on me and Stuffy Dowding. As you know, I've already given your Johnnie Shaux a long leave, and now I'm transferring him to the experimental chaps at Martlesham Heath, the A&AEE, as they call it, to be a test pilot. The paperwork's all done.

It's not a completely safe job, but at least the Luftwaffe won't be shooting at him every day."

It was typical of Park to be so generous and thorough—punctilious—in recognizing the contributions of others, but she was still overwhelmed by the injustice of his dismissal.

"I can't believe they're going to move you out."

"Look, Eleanor, it's easy," he said. "Because of the Battle of Britain, 11 Group is the most glamorous Group in the RAF, and Fighter Command is the most prestigious. Ambitious men want the most glamorous and prestigious commands, I'm afraid, and I'm not going to go, cap in hand, around Whitehall, ingratiating myself. I only care we were able to stop the invasion."

"But it's not fair. Leigh-Mallory did nothing but undermine you, and Sholto Douglas wasn't even in the fight!"

"Eleanor, whoever told you life is fair?" he asked. It was the closest he came to expressing the bitterness that must have been bubbling up inside him. "*I* know I stopped Kesselring, and so do you, and so does Dowding and a few others whose opinions I value. I don't care what the rest of the world thinks."

He stared out of the window for a second, as if to regain control of his emotions.

"Look, one more thing before I forget. I've spoken to Edward Bridges about you, and I'll speak to Wilfrid Freeman about Shaux. He's the Air Council member of research and development, and he's absolutely top-notch. So you'll each have a friend in high places if you need one."

He made a gesture of frustration.

"That's all I can do, Eleanor, I'm afraid. Now, off you go and help Johnnie Shaux enjoy the rest of his leave."

He stood to say goodbye and held out his hand.

"Goodbye, sir," she whispered, fighting down sudden tears.

She pushed past his arm and hugged him. She knew he understood.

Q: So your model predicted another raid in the afternoon, Dame Eleanor?

A: The model said it was more likely than not. That's all. People don't really understand probabilities.

Q: Do you gamble, Dame Eleanor?

A: Certainly not! There's a good reason why casino owners are very rich and almost all gamblers are poor.

Q: Did you feel Fighter Command had won a victory that morning?

A: Absolutely yes, but not in the manner I think you mean. We had won because, once again, the Luftwaffe had come in force and, once again, had failed to inflict significant damage, either on the ground or in the air. Therefore we had not lost. Therefore we had won.

That was Keith Park's entire plan for the battle: to survive, to live to fight another day, to deny Kesselring control of England's southern skies.

Q: And, from a personal point of view, your husband had survived in spite of being jumped?

A: Yes. Johnnie's Spitfire was quite seriously damaged, but he flew it back to Hawkinge and landed safely. The entire cowling and half the tail skin were missing. The Supermarine engineers came to look at it—they couldn't believe it was airworthy.

Q: "Bent but not broken," I believe he said at some point, a phrase Churchill repeated to the House of Commons.

A: Exactly so.

Q: On that note—with 11 Group bent but not broken, in the middle of that fateful day in 1940—let us bring this segment of our interview with Dame Eleanor Shaux to a close. Our special series on the Battle of Britain, with Dame Eleanor, will continue tomorrow evening at the same time. Good night.

PART TWO

15 September 1940

1300 to 1700 Hours

SEVENTEEN

Q: (To camera:) *Good evening, and welcome to the second installment of our series about the Battle of Britain, the aerial campaign between the British RAF and the Nazi German Luftwaffe in 1940, early in the Second World War.*

Once again we are fortunate to have Dame Eleanor Shaux with us, someone who scarcely needs an introduction. She was in 11 Group headquarters, the famous Battle of Britain Bunker in Uxbridge, throughout the battle. That's where she developed her well-known Red Tape model, the first modern war game simulator, based on the pioneering mathematical theories of John von Neumann of Princeton University.

(To guest:) Good evening, Dame Eleanor.

A: *Good evening.*

Q: (To camera:) *Last time we traced, with Dame Eleanor's help, the events of the morning of 15 September 1940, a day now known as Battle of Britain Day. That morning involved an attack by approximately thirty Luftwaffe bombers supported and protected by one hundred and twenty-five Messerschmitt 109 fighters. Southern England was defended by more than two hundred Spitfires and Hurricanes. The Luftwaffe managed to inflict minor damage on London's railway system but suffered over thirty aircraft shot down. The RAF lost thirteen aircraft.*

(To guest:) *Dame Eleanor, remind us why the Luftwaffe was attacking England in 1940.*

A: Hitler planned to invade England. He had stripped northern Europe of barges to create an invasion fleet that could bring the German army across the Straits of Dover. All he needed to be successful was air superiority. He needed to drive the RAF away. To do so he launched intense attacks on RAF airfields, radar stations, and similar military targets.

Q: Without success?

A: Without success. Early in September he switched tactics and began direct bombing attacks on London and other British cities in a campaign we now call the blitz. Actually, let me correct myself, if I may. He attacked without apparent success. Several times he came close to breaking 11 Group, but not quite.

One of the Luftwaffe's strategies was to try to overwhelm the RAF with sheer numbers, and that was the case on the afternoon of September 15, when he launched the last big daylight raid of the Battle of Britain.

Q: Just to remind our viewers, you had spent the morning explaining the situation to Winston Churchill, who was visiting 11 Group headquarters and watching the famous map table, while your future husband, Johnnie Shaux, was heavily engaged in the skies over Kent. His Spitfire suffered serious damage in one encounter with the enemy, but he was able to land safely.

A: Yes, we were both quite busy—Johnnie more so than I, of course.

Q: I'm exhausted just hearing about it. And when the morning raids were over, Churchill had a private picnic of smoked salmon sandwiches washed down with champagne! What a story! Now, to resume when we left off, if we may: you were expecting another attack in the afternoon.

A: Yes. My model predicted that Luftflotte II would attack in force, with two or three times as many aircraft as the morning. Keith Park, the 11

Group AOC, my boss, had to anticipate what Albert Kesselring, the Luftflotte II commander, would do . . .

"Eleanor, you estimate a heavier attack this afternoon?" Park asked.

"The model puts that as the highest probability, sir," she said. "The most likely targets are the London docks. We think Kesselring could put up more than a hundred bombers and as many as three hundred fighters. He may be betting that you'll release some of the squadrons that flew this morning."

She realized with surprise that she was quoting Bramble with complete confidence. Was she being foolish? No—Bramble might wear his insecurities on his sleeve, but she trusted his mathematics fully.

"Surely, Squadron Officer, the appearance of the Duxford Wing would have deterred him?" Churchill boomed.

She answered in her mind: "Surely, Prime Minister, the ineffectiveness of the Duxford Wing would have encouraged him." But "Perhaps, sir" was all she allowed herself to say aloud.

Why did everyone continue to believe that forty or fifty Spitfires all together were more effective than small flights of four or five, when Park was proving it false every day?

"Then we will plan a defense in depth," Park said. "We'll set a line of hurdles the length of Kent, from the coast to Biggin, and we'll ask 12 Group to cover London once more."

"A steeplechase, Air Vice-Marshal?"

"Exactly so, Prime Minister. A race over the hurdles." Park nodded.

He stared down at the map, setting his defenses in his mind.

"All our squadrons are operational?" he asked Eleanor.

"Yes, sir," she said. "We lost thirteen aircraft this morning, based on reports so far, about one in twenty, and we have reserves for those aircraft and aircrew in place. We'll have twenty-one squadrons available as soon as they've finished refueling and rearming."

"Very well."

Q: So the 11 Group squadrons were ready? They could fly again so quickly?

A: Yes. There had been some losses, but nothing we couldn't absorb. The worst hit was 339, with two losses and two more badly damaged aircraft, but they were still an A squadron, still a fighting unit . . .

"I should have done something," Potter said, not trying to hide his tearstained cheeks. "He was my chap, a Greenie, on his first op, and . . . and . . ."

"There was nothing to be done, old chap," Digby said. "You can't punish yourself for things beyond your control. You know that."

"Yes, I do know, but it was just so horrible to listen to him on the R/T," Potter choked. "I felt so *helpless.*" He blew his nose several times. "He was in pain, with some sort of shrapnel in his legs. And then he thought I was coming up behind him to save him, when it was really a 109 coming to finish him off. What must he have thought when he believed I was opening fire on him? Oh, God!"

His face disappeared into his handkerchief. Charlie was gently pushing his massive head against Potter's knees, sensing his distress and trying to comfort Potter with his presence.

Shaux patted Potter on the shoulder, feeling a hundred years old. Potter might be a highly successful fighter pilot, with a growing number of victories to his name, a top predator in this most ruthless of all arenas, but he also remained a sensitive eighteen-year-old appalled by the carnage he witnessed every day.

"Are you all right to fly this afternoon, Froggie?" Shaux asked. "Should I stand you down?"

"Of course not, skipper. I'm fine, really. I am. I'm so sorry I'm behaving like this."

"Don't be sorry, Froggie," Shaux said. "We all have to remind ourselves not to get callous or cynical, in spite of seeing chaps shot down day in, day out."

"Please don't leave me behind, skipper. I wouldn't know what to do with myself."

That was undoubtedly true, Shaux thought. Besides, if you fell off a bicycle when you were learning to ride, you were supposed to get back on and try again immediately. He would let Potter fly.

Shaux wondered how any of them could keep their humanity in the midst of the slaughter. They might well be up there again within the hour. Eleanor was very confident that the relative strengths of 11 Group and Luftflotte II were shifting, slowly but surely, in Fighter Command's favor. It was only a question of time before Kesselring would have to give up attacking in daylight.

Well, Eleanor was paid to look at the big picture, and she did it very well. Shaux, on the other hand, was paid to look at a very small picture—what he could see out of his cockpit. She dealt in dozens, hundreds, of aircraft; he dealt in one aircraft at a time.

"I have to thank you, Diggers, old chap," Shaux said, moving the conversation on, giving Potter a moment to recover. "Thanks for chasing that 110 away."

"Not at all, skipper," Digby said.

As Shaux had been heading for home, approaching Hawkinge, he was spewing oil and dropping random bits and pieces of his engine right, left, and center. A 110—two, he had thought originally—had followed him, closing in for the kill. It had fired a burst at him, but the tracer missed him completely—not even close. Perhaps the intelligence reports about the declining quality of Luftwaffe crews were really true.

Shaux had thought initially that there were two 110s on his tail, but the second aircraft had turned out to be Digby, thank God. Digby had proceeded to chase the 110 out into the Channel. It had engine problems of its own.

"I must say, skipper, that's an interesting new modification for a Spitfire," Potter said, looking across to Shaux's aircraft. He had blown his nose once more, put his handkerchief away, and squared his shoulders. "I've always thought that cowlings, engines, were totally unnecessary."

The left cowling of Shaux's Spitfire was missing, exposing fully eight feet of the Merlin, and the skin on the left wing root and the left tailplane and elevator was missing. Once again Shaux was left to marvel at his own survival and the ability of a Spitfire to absorb punishment.

Digby had shepherded him back to Hawkinge, lest any more 110s appear, and Shaux had more or less flown his aircraft into the ground rather than landing it, fighting the yawing drag of the exposed engine and stripped spars.

Well, only this morning Shaux had thought his Spitfire was looking a little worse for wear—now it definitely was. KN-J, King Nuts Johnnie, would probably be broken up for spare parts. In the meantime the ground crews had warmed up KN-H, King Nuts Harry, for him, and Charlie had duly baptized it.

"Readiness in fifteen minutes, gentlemen," said Flight Sergeant Jenkins, approaching them from the dispersal hut. "It seems they're coming back for a second try."

"The cloud won't help them find their targets," Digby said, looking up. "One wonders why they bother."

"True, and the wind's still strong against 'em, and all," Jenkins added.

Shaux also wondered what Kesselring, or Göring, or Hitler, or whoever was making the decision, was hoping to achieve. Perhaps they were hoping that Park would make some hideous mistake and all their bombers would get through unharmed and inflict a major blow. Perhaps they thought that 11 Group was running out of aircraft.

None of that mattered, of course, when the skies were full of 109s. He still didn't understand how 339 had been jumped this morning. It must have been one of those fluke encounters when an attacking formation is presented with a perfect targeting situation: 109s emerging by chance from clouds and finding Spitfires directly in the center of their gunsights. He had learned over the past few weeks that there really were such things as good and bad luck, and no pilot, however expert, is exempt from them.

He wondered if the enemy had been visible from the ground and how hundreds of observers could have missed them.

Well, he'd leave the strategic implications of this afternoon's raids in Park's and Eleanor's capable hands, and worry about getting 339 through one more encounter. He hoped he'd be back on the ground by four o'clock, in time to have a quick bath before hopping that lorry to London, where Eleanor would be waiting for him.

"Are we fully rearmed and refueled, Flight?" Shaux asked Jenkins.

"All present and correct, sir. Ten aircraft, including H-for-Harry," Jenkins replied. "One new pilot arrived who could replace Pilot Officer Henderson, if you wish, sir?"

"Does he have any experience?"

"No, sir, not really, not that I know of," Jenkins said slowly. "Bit of a risk, if you ask me, sir."

"Then let him sit," Shaux said.

He'd far rather fly shorthanded than take the chance of another debacle like poor Henderson this morning. Perhaps I'm getting soft in my old age, Shaux thought to himself. Potter and Digby both looked at him without speaking, and he knew they knew what he was thinking.

"Sector now says readiness in five minutes," an airman called through the dispersal hut door.

"Once more unto the breach, dear friends," Digby said.

Potter had offered the end of his scarf to Charlie for a tug-of-war, and Charlie was winning. The scarf soon ripped in two, and Charlie gamboled round them in a victory lap, his stumpy tail wagging, tongue lolling. He was shaking his mighty head, half the scarf dangling from his jaws.

"Listen, Charlie, thou wretched hound, I've still got just about enough left," Potter said, wrapping the remainder round his neck.

Shaux knew that the prospect of immediate action had dispelled Potter's lingering feelings of guilt at Henderson's death. It wasn't callousness; it was a basic survival technique. Shaux had told himself a thousand times that the only battle that matters is not the last one but the next. That was a battle that would be fought by pilots present, not pilots past.

"I think you mean *canis miserabilis*, old chap," Digby offered.

"Sector says we're the first ones up," the airman called again.

"It's déjà vu," Potter said.

"*Odiosis est*," Digby agreed, pretending to yawn.

Q: How many aircraft were involved in the afternoon?

A: At the height of the battle, there were nineteen squadrons. But initially Park sent up four groups of two squadrons, his hurdles, if you will, from the coast to London, all designed to separate the bombers from their defending fighters. He was trying to peel the 109s away from the bombers, just as he had successfully done in the morning.

Q: And your husband was one of the first?

A: Yes, it seemed as if every time Luftflotte II came across the Channel, Johnnie and 339 would be waiting somewhere over southern Kent— loitering, as Johnnie used to say.

Q: Loitering?

A: That's how he described those patrols: loitering with intent.

"You are repeating this morning's plan, pray tell me?" Churchill asked Park.

"Yes, Prime Minister. We will run Luftflotte II through another steeplechase and concentrate additional squadrons over London for a counterblow."

"The Duxford Wing, I trust?"

"Of course, Prime Minister," Park said. "But with due respect to Leigh-Mallory's Wing, the key lies in our ability to wear down the enemy by attrition on the way up to London and on the way back."

"Doubtless," Churchill grunted, evidently unconvinced.

"We will have two squadrons, 339 and 314, waiting to greet Luftflotte II over Sheerness. Spitfires are with the 339, and 314, one of the excellent Polish squadrons, has Hurricanes. Then 339 will meet the 109s, and 314 the bombers. And then, twenty miles on, we will have another pair of squadrons, and so on, all the way up to London, Prime Minister."

"Let us wish them good hunting."

Let us wish them safety and long lives, Eleanor thought to herself. Let Johnnie eke out one more sortie and come safely to London tonight. Let him survive unscathed.

EIGHTEEN

Q: Did this seem like a climactic battle?

A: Not really. It seemed like a larger raid than usual, certainly, as it was building up, but it did not seem to be a climax. It didn't even last very long—most of the fighting took place between two o'clock and three o'clock in the afternoon. It just seemed like the twenty-seventh round of a ten-round boxing match.

We received radar warnings from Chain Home a little before two, and Park ordered the first squadrons up to be ready to meet the 109s in any high-fighter cover. It took eight minutes for a Spitfire to reach twenty thousand feet and about as long for the enemy bomber staffels to cross the Channel into that headwind, so Park didn't want to be caught napping . . .

Telephones began to ring around the room, and WAAFs at the map table were beginning to push markers towards Calais: thirty aircraft in one group, fifty in another, and sixty in a third. Kesselring liked to send his attacking aircraft in waves, Eleanor thought, hoping to catch Park with a significant number of squadrons on the ground, refueling and rearming. If that was just the first wave, and there could be one or two more, it looked as if Bramble's calculations might prove true.

Jayne Jackson climbed the stairs to the balcony and beckoned to Eleanor. This was unusual. Perhaps Bramble and Cassius had recalculated and had new predictions.

"Excuse me, ma'am, but I thought you ought to know, in case you hear it unexpected," Jayne said, sotto voce. "I will not beat about the bush; Section Officer Smith did away with herself over lunchtime."

"What?"

"Stabbed herself with her knitting needles in her cubicle. She bled to death on the floor."

"What?"

"It seems she was listening on the R/T last week and heard her fiancé get shot down," Sergeant Jackson continued. "He was a Hurricane pilot; screaming he was, all in flames, as he was going down, so it seems. A lot of the girls on duty were all upset listening to him. Anyway, Miss Smith heard the whole thing on her headphones."

Eleanor remembered the look of horror on Susan Smith's face this morning when 339 was jumped. She must have been reliving the appalling experience of hearing her fiancé die.

"Well, also, ma'am, it seems Miss Smith is, or was, I should say, in the family way, and of course she couldn't get married if he was dead."

"What?" It appeared to be the only thing Eleanor was capable of saying.

"She went to see the WAAF Queen Bee this morning to ask for a leave of absence. The Queen Bee said under WAAF rules, Miss Smith could have compassionate leave for a fiancé, but couldn't stay in the service in her condition. And it seems Miss Smith's mother is devout and wouldn't take her back in, on account of the shame. Miss Smith hadn't got any money. So the Queen Bee gave her the name of a Church of England home for fallen women and five quid and told her to pack up her belongings."

"How awful!"

"She shouldn't have given him what he wanted, not if they weren't married," Sergeant Jackson sniffed. "Should've told him to keep it in his trousers, in my opinion. She brought it all on herself."

Eleanor thought she saw a glimmer of satisfaction on Jayne Jackson's face, the sort of glimmer that might have been seen on Madam Defarge's face at the foot of the guillotine.

"How . . . how do you know all this, Jayne?"

"I'm friendly with the Queen Bee's orderly clerk."

Eleanor told herself to never, under any circumstances whatsoever, communicate personal information to the Queen Bee, as the senior WAAF officer was known. And she hadn't liked that look on Jayne's face; she'd have to think about whether to keep her, although she was highly competent . . .

Poor Susan! She had gone from being a cheerful, competent young woman making a valuable contribution to the war effort, with a fiancé and her whole future ahead of her, to nothing: an outcast, a "fallen woman."

Oh God. Eleanor thought about herself. Suppose Johnnie made her pregnant . . . She had no intention of asking him to keep it in his trousers, as Jayne had put it, nor did she wish him to. Perhaps she and Johnnie should . . .

"Eleanor?" Park's voice intruded. "Do we have an update?"

"No, sir. Not yet, but shortly," she replied, drowning in guilt for ignoring her responsibilities. "Jayne, ask Bramble if he's changed his forecast, will you?"

The war's the only thing that matters, Eleanor told herself sternly. She was here in the 11 Group Operations Room, with Park and even Winston Churchill, as a major enemy attack built up over Calais. She glanced guiltily at the map and the Tote Board beyond it and at the controllers in the galleries around her. Young men had already died this morning, and more were about to die, attackers and defenders alike. Tens of thousands of people were preparing to defend the country—radar operators, radio communicators, WAAFs, information filterers, Home Guard volunteers on patrol, Royal Observer Corps watchers with their binoculars turned to the skies over the white cliffs of Dover, ambulance drivers and firemen preparing themselves for a savage onslaught for which they had never been equipped or trained, ack-ack antiaircraft gunners gazing up in frustration at the low clouds, barrage balloon operators, doctors, nurses, policemen, and special constables . . . the list was endless. Fires still burned from this morning's raid, and searchers still combed through the wreckage for survivors. Soon more civilians would die as bombs rained down upon them.

Park relied upon her logic and analysis. Therefore all of 11 Group, of Fighter Command, was depending on her. Matters of everyday existence, people's private lives, their hopes and fears, their loves, were insignificant in comparison.

Park was on the telephone. Eleanor saw 339's status move from "Ordered to Stand By" to "At Standby." Johnnie would be sitting in his Spitfire. This was not the time to be analyzing the pros and cons of keeping it in his trousers, or not.

Q: Your husband's squadron was involved in the afternoon attacks?

A: It was. The first squadron Park put on standby was 339.

Johnnie sat in his replacement Spitfire, waggling the control surfaces to get a feel for them. Every aircraft was unique, even when they were built to be identical. H-for-Harry seemed tighter than J-for-Johnnie, probably because it had flown far fewer hours. Wires and elbow joints and couplings stretch over time. He guessed H-for-Harry would be more responsive, even twitchy, but probably a little slower, not yet really run in.

Once again they were in position, hurrying up and waiting. He wondered idly how high they'd be ordered to fly—up to angels one-five meant they be facing the bomber stream, 17s and 111s, doubtless with protective 109s and 110s mixed in; if they were ordered higher, it would be the bombers' high 109 escorts once more. Park seemed to like 339 up high and forward on the coast. Perhaps someone had told him about Digby's phenomenal eyesight.

Should he have let Froggie fly? It was so hard to know how much any one pilot could stand. He was normally so exuberant, like an overgrown schoolboy—well, he'd been a schoolboy only a few months ago—that it was hard to imagine he was ready to crack. He was always at the center of the crowd, often with his saxophone at the ready and girls emerging from the woodwork to make eyes at him.

Things seemed to come easily to Froggie, like attracting the prettiest girls. He was a natural marksman, a crack shot, who could effortlessly solve the very tricky problem of getting eight machine guns synchronized to merge at a range of two hundred yards onto a skittering target at more than 300 miles per hour. How many confirmed victories did Potter have? Had he earned another Distinguished Flying Cross? Shaux made a mental note to check the records.

The schoolboy had changed into a skilled Spitfire pilot, but his inner self remained. Froggie had told Shaux that his proudest achievement, prior to joining 11 Group, had been being appointed captain of his school's second eleven cricket team. He had exulted in their victories and wept at their defeats, he confessed.

"I always thought it was my fault, skipper, if we lost. I was the captain; I was supposed to make sure we won."

He had carried that principle into the infinitely more brutal world of aerial combat. He was a flight commander, and, in his mind, responsible for every failure. One could shake off the shame of losing a cricket match to some neighboring school, Shaux supposed, but how did one live through the violent death of one of one's flight members?

Diggers, on the other hand, had a rocklike calm and perseverance. He always seemed to be in the right place at the right time and was unflappable. He absorbed tragedy privately, Shaux supposed, without visible commotion. He would disappear for hours, walking in the woods and looking for rare birds, doubtless finding solace in the immutable ways of nature.

H-for-Harry's Merlin was not overheating, but Shaux always hated standing by, the highest level of readiness without actually taking off. Once they took off, they'd have at least eight minutes to climb to angels two-zero. Shaux would much rather be loitering at angels two-five, above the oncoming 109s, versus facing the prospect of having to climb through them.

As if Park somehow magically heard him and agreed, Flight Sergeant Jenkins appeared through the distant dispersal hut door and fired a green flare into the air. Charlie stood beside him, his red tongue lolling. It was too far to see if he was still holding the scarf, although Diggers could have seen easily. Shaux released the brakes, tweaked the throttle, and let H-for-Harry rumble forward. He turned into the wind, paused to give 339 half a minute to get organized, and then opened the throttle.

Shaux glanced back as 339 accelerated. Digby and Potter were, as ever, one hundred feet behind him on either side, with their wing men another one hundred behind them, and the rest of their flights ech-eloned back farther still. With Diggers and Froggie at my back and Eleanor awaiting me, I am invincible, he thought in a sudden moment of unexpected elation. H-for Harry's tail came up at 40 miles per hour; in a few more seconds his Spitfire would be ready for that magical moment of first flight. Elation! He took one more glance back.

Potter's aircraft stumbled, as a galloping horse might stumble in a steeplechase as it gathers itself to jump a hurdle. The right under-carriage strut collapsed, or perhaps the wheel fell into an invisible rut and the strut snapped off. Potter's propeller struck the grass, throwing up dirt and mud like a manic lawn mower, slewing his Spitfire sharply round to the right and directly into the path of Green Four; Klaus, the Czech pilot, coming up behind him at 50 miles per hour. Klaus's Spitfire rammed into Potter's Spitfire just behind its right wing root. Klaus's propeller scythed through Potter's cockpit, and the force of the impact began to rip Potter's Spitfire into two separate pieces before both Spitfires exploded as one.

Some tremor, some primeval sixth sense, caused Shaux to realize he was airborne and to catch his Spitfire before it fell back to earth, downed by his own inattention.

"Follow me," he said, to grab 339's attention and to make sure that they were focusing on flying and not on the black smoke billowing up behind them.

He adjusted the controls and raised the wheels. Potter's funeral pyre receded from view as 339 climbed. He flashed over the farmer and his wife. He could tell, even in that split second, that they were transfixed, staring in silent horror at the rising column of smoke on the airfield.

"Lumba, this is Shadow," he said, forcing his voice to be utterly devoid of emotion. "Two aircraft down on takeoff. Eight remaining."

"Shadow, repeat?" the Sector controller's voice replied. Shaux didn't recognize it—it must be someone new, and he didn't feel much like re-announcing Potter's death.

"Green Two, you are now Green Leader," he said. "And 339 will re-form, re-form."

"Green Leader," said Jacko Welsh. The Australian must have ice water in his veins, Shaux thought—he had been behind Potter and Klaus and had taken off through the explosion.

Now only eight strong, 339 commenced their droning climb towards angels two-zero, re-forming their formation as they did so, with Green Flight, now led by Welsh, down to three aircraft and Digby's Red Flight having four. Unfortunately, Shaux thought, 339 was really good at re-forming to compensate for casualties, because they had to do it so often.

They climbed in stony silence. The shock of Potter's death had robbed 339, famous for its laconic brevity, of their voices. Shaux refused to permit himself to dwell on it; there would be plenty of time for mourning later. He checked back to make sure 339 had re-formed itself to fill the missing slots—not too bad, in the circumstances, although looser than Froggie would have liked.

"*Testes frixi,*" Digby's voice growled, and Shaux swallowed a sob.

NINETEEN

Q: Casualties were suffered by 339 even before it was airborne?

A: Yes. I think people forget that a significant portion of losses in the Battle of Britain occurred on the ground—on both sides. A lot of damaged Luftflotte II bombers managed to make it back across the Channel to their bases in France or Belgium, only to crash on landing. And it was the same for damaged 11 Group fighters.

Squadron takeoffs were also dangerous, with up to a dozen aircraft all taking off at once, or in close succession, I should say, from a grass field. It saved time, and time was of the essence, but it was quite costly.

Q: But Park kept 339 in the fight?

A: He did.

Park hung up the telephone.

"The 339 has suffered losses on the ground," he announced to the room in general. "Their skipper is not among the casualties," he added, looking at Eleanor. She felt her heart stop for what seemed to be an eternity before restarting. She sent Park a secret "thank you" for telling her Johnnie was safe.

"Can they still fight?" Churchill asked. "Should they be employed?"

"Believe me, sir, if anyone can fight, it's 339." He paused for thought. "I'm going to leave them up because I've a sense we'll need everything we've got. Our most forward squadron is 339, up over the coast. If nothing else, they'll be worth their weight in gold reporting incoming bandits."

Johnnie should be very proud of Park's comments, Eleanor thought, taking a deep breath to calm herself, although Johnnie would probably say something dismissive and self-deprecating.

Jayne Jackson returned, this time with Bramble in tow, and Eleanor crossed the balcony to speak to them.

"We ran the model again," Bramble said. "The same result: a heavy raid with the East End of London as the most likely target. I don't know why they're doing it, given the weather, which is more or less continuous cloud cover."

"Anything new, Eleanor?" Park called over, his eyes on the map. He must be very nervous, Eleanor thought, despite his outward calm.

"No, sir. We still think London is the best bet, but there's cloud from two to twelve thousand feet, so they won't be very accurate."

"Then why are they coming at all?" Churchill rumbled.

Bramble's eyes opened wide as he realized who had spoken. He opened his mouth to speak and then closed it again. Eleanor formed the distinct impression that Jayne had kicked him in the ankle.

"There is no real strategic purpose, sir, in a military sense," Eleanor said. "They're probably hoping that the AOC will make a mistake, perhaps allowing them to catch 11 Group on the ground, and they're probably hoping to convince you they can't be stopped."

"Well, 11 Group couldn't stop them this morning," Churchill said.

Oh God, Eleanor thought, I'm about to argue with the prime minister. So be it.

"True, sir, they reached London, but we won. We won because they lost a lot of aircraft and did very little damage in return. We won because Mr. Park still has nineteen squadrons flying or ready to fly. We won because you have no intention of giving up—none whatsoever. We won because we didn't lose. They lost because they didn't win."

"Does Reichsmarschall Hermann Göring understand that, do you suppose, Squadron Officer?" Churchill shot back.

"No, Prime Minister. I'm certain he does not. And that is precisely why he's losing."

"Ha!" Churchill barked. "Excellent! I think I'll put you in the cabinet, Squadron Officer, if Mr. Park can spare you?"

"Absolutely out of the question, Prime Minister." Park smiled.

Bramble continued to stare open-mouthed at Churchill, as if seeing a vision.

"Thank you, Mr. Bramble," Eleanor said firmly, edging him towards the stairs.

"Oh, yes, of course," he said, and retreated.

"You actually spoke to him!" she heard him say over his shoulder. "To Mr. Churchill!"

Eleanor had a sudden image of Bramble sitting in bed in his pajamas, with his knees drawn up and a guttering candle for light, making an entry in his journal that began: "Dear Diary, Today I actually saw Winston Churchill in person . . ."

Eleanor followed him down to the main floor and borrowed one of the WAAF supervisor's phones to telephone D Sector. She shouldn't be doing this, she thought; she was again using official channels for personal reasons. She sat idly in an empty seat until she abruptly realized that this was Susan Smith's station and jumped up as if scalded. She wondered what the other WAAFs around her would think. She didn't know who knew and who didn't.

When Sector D finally connected, they informed her that Potter and Klaus had collided on takeoff and had died instantly. She thanked them and hung up the telephone. Poor Johnnie! Froggie had been one of his two favorites. His death would be another cross for Johnnie to bear, another grief to suppress so deep that even nightmares could not plumb the stygian depths. Oh, Johnnie, she thought in silent despair, how many griefs have you buried in the last month? How can I ever rescue you? I'll just have to dig them up and assuage them, one by one.

Q: I don't think people have any idea of what those men went through.

A: I'm sure you're right . . .

As 339 climbed steadily through overcast skies towards twenty thousand feet, Shaux tried unsuccessfully to think of anything but Froggie Potter. It was almost a relief, in a strange and horrible way. They flirted with death and the uncertainty of whether they would be alive tomorrow every day; there was a certain sense of grotesque resolution when the uncertainty was laid to rest—well, now we know Potter's fate. At least he had died instantly and not in long, drawn-out anguish like the wretched Henderson this morning.

They were now climbing in intermittent cloud, the kind of conditions—indeed, the very same cloud conditions—as those in which they had been jumped this morning. Shaux wondered if he should remind 339 to stay alert, but somehow he couldn't break the silence.

Potter had been struck directly, at 50 miles per hour, by a ten-foot-diameter propeller spinning at 1,500 rpm and driven by a roaring twenty-seven-liter, 1,000-horsepower Merlin. The propeller had three blades, each some five feet long. The propeller would have carved through the cockpit in less than half a second, rotating perhaps a dozen times; thus the individual blades would have sliced their way through Potter's seated body about forty times as the propeller traversed it; from there the propellers would have cut open the fuel tanks directly ahead of the cockpit instrument panel, thereby spraying high-octane fuel onto the superheated burning gases and white-hot surfaces of Potter's Merlin's exhaust manifolds and causing an instant explosion that had engulfed and incinerated both aircraft.

Potter probably hadn't had time to see death coming as his undercarriage leg collapsed. It was an interesting philosophical point, Shaux felt, as to whether or not Potter actually knew that he was dead. And since Potter was in a least a dozen pieces, did each piece know or only some?

They emerged into clear air at angels one-five and continued to climb. The strong winds had blown them out over the North Sea, and now Shaux led them back with the wind, flying southwest towards the Channel and France. He had done so this morning with twelve aircraft; now he had eight.

Shaux saw a long, dirty smear across the clear blue skies ahead.

"Lumba, this is Red Leader," Digby's voice sounded in Shaux's headphones. "Bandits ahead."

It sounded like a sigh.

Q: Let's see. The raids started after two o'clock?

A: Yes, a little later. Park was building up his defensive lines above Kent and preparing a large force to meet the Luftwaffe in London.

The status lights for 339 showed "In Position," Eleanor saw. Looking across the Tote Board, she saw 603 and 222 were also "In Position"; 17 and 257 were "Left Ground"; 501 and 605 were also "In Position"; 249 and 504 were "Left Ground." Park had nine squadrons of Spitfires and Hurricanes waiting for Luftflotte II.

The WAAFs around the map table readjusted the cluster of markers over northern France and the Channel. When they were done, Eleanor saw that the oncoming enemy had split into three columns.

Park was on the telephone.

"Yes, there are 109s on free hunts as well as 109s in with the bombers . . . Yes, I want 41 and 92 from Biggin . . . Yes, now."

He hung up the telephone and picked up another.

"This is the AOC . . . Oh, sorry, Fred, good afternoon to you, too . . . Northolt should put up 1 and 229 as soon as possible . . . Oh, it's a big one, all right. Perhaps five hundred E/As—or even six."

Park was estimating five or six hundred enemy aircraft, Eleanor thought, and Park had only two hundred at best.

The WAAFs were moving quickly but efficiently, preparing markers for more and more 11 Group squadrons. The enemy markers inched their way across the map towards London. The lights on the Tote Board obeyed Park's instructions as the WAAFs raised the status lights of more and more squadrons to "Left Ground" and "In Position."

Park was taking no chances. She had thought he was nervous, but now she thought he was worried. She saw him pick up the dedicated telephone to 12 Group and knew that Douglas Bader's Big Wing would also be engaged. She saw him speak to his friend Quinton Brand of 10 Group and knew that one or two squadrons from Middle Wallop—she guessed 238 and 609—would also be added to the cause.

Churchill sat like a sphinx in a Zen-like trance, his unlit cigar between his lips, his eyes on the map and the Tote Board, his thoughts inscrutable. If England loses, Eleanor thought, Churchill will go down in history as one of the great losers of all time, like Napoleon at Waterloo or Robert E. Lee at Gettysburg . . .

Q: How many planes were involved altogether?

A: Aircraft, I think you mean. Planes are boundless, two-dimensional surfaces generated by a straight line moving at a constant velocity with respect to a fixed point . . . Sorry. Accuracy is a virtue, but pedantry is a vice. But to answer your question, the total number varied, of course, at various stages of the afternoon, but it was somewhere in the region of two hundred fifty Fighter Command aircraft and between four hundred fifty and five hundred from Luftflotte II.

"Lumba calling Shadow; eyes in the skies."

"Shadow," Shaux replied. So, Sector wanted them to stay on station and report on the incoming enemy formations, staying above the fray. It would be frustrating to let bomber staffels go by unchallenged on their way to maim and kill innocent men, women, and children, but Shaux understood Park's paramount need for accurate information.

It was a duty for which Digby had been born. The rest of 339 would form a protective barrier around him, and he would report on the armada passing below them.

They would be only partially successful, however. The cloud cover was likely obstructing the Observer Corps watchers who were look-ing up from the coastline far below, and it was obscuring 339's vision as they looked down. Large numbers of bandits might be sneaking in undetected. Shaux doubted they'd be able to attack 11 Group airfields successfully—they'd have to be below two thousand feet, where the bombers would be highly vulnerable to antiaircraft fire—so they were probably heading for London, which, with this headwind, was per-haps twenty minutes away. That, in turn, meant the bombers would be returning home beneath him in less than an hour, at which time Sector might order them to attack.

Eleanor said that Luftflotte II would soon be running out of aircraft, but Shaux saw no evidence of it. Staffel after staffel passed beneath him, as annotated and reported by Digby. Perhaps the Luftflotte II chaps thought the same thing about 11 Group.

"Red Leader looks down; everyone else looks up," he said, to remind himself as much as the rest of 339. They were witnessing the greatest air fleet ever assembled, a far greater force than the RAF's own Bomber Command. The job for 339 was to witness, not to get jumped by 109s.

"Hitler knows that he must break us in this island or lose the war," Shaux recalled Churchill saying in one of his speeches. Well, he's certainly trying to break us this afternoon, he thought.

TWENTY

Q: When did the bombers reach London?

A: At about 1430—half past two. The first formations reached the Thames at Gravesend and turned west towards the East End of London.

Q: Is it true that Churchill asked about reserves?

A: Yes. At that point Park had every squadron from 11 Group in the air, plus the Duxford Wing from 12 Group and two squadrons from 10 Group. Later he decided to order three squadrons to land, just in case they were needed as a reserve against a late-afternoon raid.

Reports from the Observer Corps on the south coast, and from 339 high above them, put the total number of enemy aircraft in the five hundred range. If you consider that they were in a formation about five miles wide and twenty miles long, Kesselring had about one aircraft for every cubic mile they occupied—a very high density.

One can only imagine how terrifying it must have been for the people of northern Kent and East London to look up through breaks in the clouds and catch glimpses of formation after formation of Dorniers and Heinkels bearing random death and destruction.

Q: What exactly did Churchill say when he asked about reserves?

Park put down a telephone.

"Everyone is now airborne," he said. "Nineteen 11 Group squadrons, the Duxford Wing from 12 Group, and two squadrons from 10 Group."

A WAAF pushed the leading enemy marker into the Thames estuary and edged it towards London. A long line of Luftflotte II markers followed in its train. A group of RAF markers awaited them over Hornchurch.

"We are still, however, outnumbered two to one," Park added.

"What other reserves have we?" Churchill asked him, staring down at the map table.

"There are none."

"None? Did you say none, pray tell me?" Churchill asked, as if unwilling to believe it.

"None, Prime Minister."

Q: *In his account in his books covering the history of the Second World War, Churchill wrote that Park looked grave.*

A: *I don't think that's fair. Park looked calm, as he almost always did. He made up his mind, positioned his resources, and then awaited the outcome. One must remember that we'd been doing this day after day after day. His stomach might have been in knots, but you'd never know it.*

Churchill, on the other hand, was not used to seeing the fate of England—the fate, if you will, of the British Empire, from his perspective—laid out on a map table in real time, about to be decided in the next twenty minutes. I think he saw, for the first time, the scale of the threat and how thin our margins truly were. I think he saw all those markers scattered across the map and realized there really were far more of them than there were of us. It shocked him, I think. "The Few" was not just a finely turned phrase; it was a mathematical fact.

I think he had been judging Park, sitting back and observing him, weighing him in the balance, as it were. Now, all of a sudden, I think Churchill realized that the only thing saving him from being Adolf Hitler's special guest in Spandau Prison in Berlin was Keith Park's judgment.

Q: It was really that dramatic? I thought you said earlier that this did not feel like the decisive day in the battle.

A: I did. That was because we'd had a month of decisive days, and this, as I believe I said on a previous occasion, was just another bloody Sunday. But Churchill was not used to the knife edge. He wrote afterwards that "the odds were great; our margins small; the stakes infinite." He was seeing it for the first time.

Q: The stakes were infinite?

A: Just everything that's happened since 1940, just the entire modern world as we know it—that's all.

Churchill glowered.

"The bombers will reach London, sir," Eleanor said to him, feeling a need to protect Park, although she wasn't really sure why. "They will hurt the East End, I'm afraid, once again, but they won't do decisive damage. In the meantime Mr. Park has made sure they'll pay a very high price."

"Let us hope, Squadron Officer."

Eleanor felt something snap inside her mind.

"Hope has nothing to do with it, sir," she said.

Park had invented, out of thin air, a brilliant defense against overwhelming odds. Johnnie was grimly clinging to his sanity amid the mayhem somewhere among the clouds above, outnumbered two to one. Froggie Potter had died a few minutes ago, the promise of his life squandered and unfulfilled. Churchill must understand what all that sacrifice had achieved.

"They outnumber us two to one, as Mr. Park has said, but we are shooting down more than two of their aircraft for every one of ours." She was surprised by the harshness in her voice. "That's a simple, bounded, negative arithmetic series, sir, tending to zero, and it leads to inevitable Luftwaffe defeat."

She waited for a sharp retort, but none came. Churchill simply stared at her. Park stared at her, too, for a long second. Then a telephone rang, commanding his attention.

Q: "The odds were great; our margins small; the stakes infinite." That was Churchill's description?

A: Yes. That's what he wrote after the war, seven or eight years later, I suppose.

At 1430 that afternoon, when he asked Park about reserves, approximately two hundred bombers were approaching London. They had almost four hundred 109s to protect them, some in tight formation with them, some flying in free hunts. The cloud cover made it difficult to find the enemy aircraft, so the Dorniers and Heinkels were advancing successfully even though they were flying into a heavy headwind and flying into scores of Spitfires and Hurricanes.

All we could do in Uxbridge was to wait for the reports. It was like watching the ball bouncing round a roulette wheel, waiting for it to settle. On the way in, the battle was very ragged because of the weather conditions. There were lots of indecisive encounters. But as the bombers turned for home, the balance seemed to shift in our favor . . .

"Shadow, Lumba calling. Vector three-zero-zero at angels one-five."

"Shadow."

At long last, Sector was releasing 339 from sentry duty high above the fray and directing them inland. Presumably, Shaux thought, the bombers and their escorts were now beginning to make their way home to France and Belgium, and 339 was being directed to intercept them as they sought safety. And presumably the radar screens were clear, so there were no more incoming bandits for Digby to spot.

As usual, Shaux knew virtually nothing about what was going on. He had seen large numbers of enemy aircraft flying northeast below him. The timing suggested they had hit London and were now returning. Without bomb loads, and now with a tailwind, they'd be much faster. The cloud would make it difficult to spot them from afar and plan a coordinated attack.

These were the right conditions for the sort of sudden random melee they had suffered this morning, and chance could overcome discipline and training.

Perhaps Luftflotte II had finally broken through and scored a major victory. Perhaps Park had snookered them once more. Eleanor would know. In the meantime it didn't matter who was winning or losing, only that 339 was on an intersection vector with the enemy.

In these conditions, with eight aircraft, it would be best to fly as two finger-four formations, one behind the other. Shaux decided he had better lead Green Flight himself. Potter was gone; Jacko Welsh had great promise but lacked the experience to lead them in this unpredictable situation.

"Shadow, Green Flight leads," Shaux said. "Follow me. Re-form."

"Shadow, Lumba calling," said the Sector controller's voice. "Advise?"

Shaux ignored him; he was not about to debate tactical formations with a new and inexperienced controller—and clearly whoever the voice belonged to was new and inexperienced because he didn't have the good sense to leave the flying up to the pilots and restrict himself to telling them where to go. Shaux debated sending a stinging response, wondering why he was so irked, until he realized he must be reacting to Potter's death.

Shaux always accepted that shooting down enemy aircraft was a necessary part of the job, even though he felt no personal animosity towards the Luftwaffe pilots, who he considered to be young men like himself just doing their duty as best they could. He did not see them as evil mass murderers, as Nazis, the way some of the newspapers portrayed them, or as barbarian hordes of Huns, as some of his fellow pilots thought. But on this occasion Shaux found he was hoping to find the enemy, hoping to inflict some retribution. He felt ashamed of himself but could not shake it.

Still almost exactly overhead Hawkinge, the 339 was between Folkestone and Dover. A vector of three hundred, approximately west-northwest, would bring them back to Ashford, where they had been jumped this morning. This was beginning to feel like déjà vu, just as Potter had said this morning. Damn! How many days or weeks or months would it take until Froggie Potter stopped erupting into his train of thought?

"Stay awake," he said, to himself as much as anyone else. This was a perfect opportunity for a 109 or a 110 to come sneaking up behind them from the direction of France, just when they least expected it.

"Aircraft three o'clock low," said Digby, his miraculous eyesight as all-seeing as ever. The aircraft were single-engined, Shaux saw, flying south towards France at angels one-three. They must be 109s making a run for it, and 339 could probably catch them if he made an immediate decision. He opened his mouth to speak.

"Aircraft are Hurricanes," Digby said.

Shaux closed his mouth again. That was another mistake by the controller, he thought, who was supposed to tell them the whereabouts of all 11 Group aircraft in order to avoid a friendly fire accident. Shaux decided to make a stink about it when they got back to Hawkinge. It was ridiculous that . . .

"Bandits twelve o'clock low," Digby said. Shaux's attention had been wandering yet again. "Bandits are 17s and 109s."

Here they came, two thousand feet below 339, three unmistakable Dorniers in tight formation with three unmistakable 109s behind them. Shaux estimated a closing speed of a mile every twenty seconds and a distance of four miles. Two thousand feet to descend to the bombers' altitude.

Shaux considered his options. He needed a firing solution that maximized the chances of damaging the Dorniers while forcing the 109s out of the picture. He had ten seconds to decide.

The bandits were crossing in front of him from left to right. He needed to fly a quarter of the way around a circle with a two-minute duration circumference in order to intersect thirty seconds from now. Shaux often found it convenient to measure distances in time rather than yards or miles, a practice that baffled his fellow pilots who lacked his mathematical abilities.

"Follow me," he said, banking right and choosing what he hoped was the correct rate of turn. "Green Flight take the 109s; Red Flight take the Dorniers."

If he was correct, the bandits would present themselves in the center of his gunsight in thirty seconds. Mr. Finlay, his high school mathematics teacher, leapt into his head. "The proof of the pudding is in the eating," he would always say, a phrase Shaux had never really understood.

Shaux searched above and behind for other bandits, knowing Digby would be searching too; there was no need to look at the enemy as they approached, if his calculations were correct. There were no other aircraft beyond 339 that he could see. Finally he looked forward, and there, in the center of his sights, were the 109s. Mr. Finlay would have nodded his approval—a proven pudding.

Shaux opened fire at the leading 109 and saw his tracer striking the right wing and engine cowling. He fired for two, perhaps three, seconds, as the guns barked and the Spitfire shuddered from the recoil, and eight lines of white-hot ordnance converged on the 109 before he flashed over it and began a sharp right turn. In three seconds Shaux's eight machine guns had delivered four hundred rounds, and he was confident that many of them had struck home.

Yes, the 109 was descending, streaming oil, as Shaux completed his turn behind it. The 109 was flying in an awkward, crablike attitude, and Shaux knew the pilot must be fighting serious structural damage, perhaps to the ailerons.

Shaux checked the horizons and the skies above and saw that Jacko had stayed with him, as all good wingmen should, a hundred feet or so behind him.

The 109 was forty or so miles from safety, and even so he might still have difficulty landing if his control surfaces were damaged, and had slowed to a crawl, probably hobbled by whatever was losing that oil. Shaux calculated he could chase him down in two minutes or less, and the 109 had very little chance of escape. This would be for Froggie Potter, Shaux thought, a 109 for a Spitfire, an eye for an eye, a tooth for a tooth, a pilot for a pilot.

No, Shaux thought, it is more fitting to turn away and hope that the pilot survives the war and lives a long and fruitful life worthy of Froggie. Who knew—perhaps he played the saxophone.

"Shadow, re-form, re-form," he said. He turned north and climbed, and Jacko followed in his wake.

TWENTY-ONE

Q: It must have been extremely confusing, hard to tell much with so many battles going on.

A: It was. Clausewitz's old phrase "the fog of war" is very apposite...

"Would someone have the common decency, the mercy, to tell me what the *devil* is going on?" Churchill demanded, gesticulating vaguely at the map, the Tote Board, the WAAFs and controllers, and the hodge-podge of markers stretched across the table. He had risen to his feet. Now he dropped his curled fists to his sides, like an impotent, frustrated infant.

"Am I to conclude by the silence that no one knows?" he barked.

Park was operating at full speed, a separate telephone to each ear as he leaned over the senior controller's desk to read a note the controller was holding up for him.

Eleanor saw Churchill was about to throw a tantrum—there was no other way to describe it—triggered by the tension and uncertainty of the moment.

"Let me report, sir," she said, stepping between Churchill and Park's back.

She looked down at the map and across at the Tote Board.

"There are three groups of bandits, sir," she said, in a voice she hoped was both authoritative and calming. "In total there are an estimated two hundred bombers, mostly Dornier 17s and Heinkel 110s, although we also have unsubstantiated reports of Junkers 88s and Dornier 205s as well. Flying with each group are 109s and 110s, and there are also staffels of 109s in free hunt formations ahead of each bomber group. I hope that is clear, sir?"

She was afraid that she sounded like an announcer on the loud-speakers at a railway station, reading off endless lists of destinations.

"Clear."

"The bombers crossed the coast of Kent at 1415, 1430, and 1440 respectively."

Churchill stared down at the map and across at the clock. Her voice seemed to calm him.

"Each bomber group has an inner core of sixty to eighty bombers flying in close formation surrounded by a similar number of 109s and 110s in close support, with an outer shell of an additional sixty or eighty 109s to ward off our fighters."

She paused for breath.

"Each bomber group took about twenty minutes to reach London, pursued and attacked by several squadrons of Hurricanes and Spitfires."

"Ah," said Churchill. "I see now. You make it sound like those Western wagon trains of settlers on the American frontier under attack by marauders."

It was not an analogy Eleanor would have chosen, but if it satisfied Churchill, so be it.

"Exactly so, sir."

Churchill sat down.

"Go on," he said.

"You will recall, sir, that Mr. Park arranged the 11 Group squadrons as a series of hurdles so that as each enemy bomber group made its way past one set of squadrons, perhaps losing one or two bombers in the process, the bomber group was immediately attacked by fresh 11 Group squadrons."

"Go on," Churchill said again.

"Well, sir, the situation is very fluid, but it appears that seven squadrons are attacking the western and central groups—let's see, 419, 92, 222, 605, 105, I think. I'm not sure who the others are; and the remainder are attacking the eastern bomber group, which is the biggest. The tactical situation is being made very difficult by the cloud cover, which makes it hard for the controllers to tell our pilots exactly where the enemy is and for our pilots to find the enemy in the clouds; further, even though Mr. Park has every squadron available in the air, he is still outnumbered two to one."

Churchill grunted, but he seemed placated.

"The last of the enemy is over East London—East Ham, it seems. Approximately a hundred bombers—no more than half—managed to drop their loads."

"The rest were shot down?"

"No sir; some were, but most were damaged and forced to turn back."

Churchill brightened.

"What of the Big Wing?" he asked. "Have they engaged yet?"

"It appears they were jumped, sir, over Maidenhead."

"Jumped? How could they be jumped?" he demanded. He glowered down at the table, as if his favorite football team had been unexpectedly defeated, and chewed his cigar.

Q: The Luftwaffe's target was London, both for the morning and afternoon raids. But London was a very difficult target to reach and damage, if I understand you correctly, and, obviously, the history of the Battle of Britain proves it. The raids were a disaster for the Luftwaffe. So why did the Luftwaffe High Command order these expensive, unsuccessful attacks?

A: It's a very good question. There are books about enormous mistakes in history, like the charge of the Light Brigade or the Trojan horse. One wonders how the people involved could have been so monumentally stupid. The London blitz was one such mistake; from Hitler's perspective, it dragged defeat from the jaws of victory. Churchill was very fortunate that Hitler made such a blunder. I recall telling him that if—

Q: Were you Churchill's favorite advisor, do you think, looking back?

A: God, no! Far from it! I think I intrigued him; I think in his view I was this sort of quirky child prodigy, this sort of intellectual enfant terrible.

He enjoyed seeing me take on the heavy hitters in Whitehall, but I was never his favorite, even in the early days. That was his good friend Frederick Lindemann, who was his official scientific advisor throughout the war. I remember, sometime after the Battle of Britain was over, Lindemann and I disagreed over bombing London . . .

Churchill poured himself a glass of brandy and puffed on his mighty cigar.

"Mrs. Shaux disagrees with you on bombing, Fred," he said mischievously.

"Then she is wrong, Winston," Frederick Lindemann replied. He did not bother to look at Eleanor.

"She thinks that bombing London is a mistake."

"Nonsense!"

Eleanor sat between them as dinner ended. She had not been dismissed from the table when brandy and port were offered, for which she was grateful, but she had not been invited to have a drink. She might be the head of her own intelligence department, MI6-3b, but she was still a young girl in a man's world. Churchill glanced at her impishly—she knew he was goading her. So be it.

"Why is bombing London a good idea, Mr. Lindemann?" she asked.

"Why? Don't you know?" he replied, staring down his nose at her. "There are several reasons: firstly, the terror-inducing psychological effects of modern bombing on common working-class civilians have been well established, and—"

"Then why are the citizens of East London not terrorized?" she interrupted him. "On the contrary, they are grimly enduring nightly air raids—one might say proudly enduring nightly air raids."

She decided that if Churchill wanted a performing monkey, she might as well act like one.

"May I join you, gentlemen?" she asked, and took the brandy decanter in front of Lindemann. She glanced at Churchill and received a twinkle in his eye and the slightest nod.

"Strategic bombing, as I term it, is—"

"I read your theory of de-housing, sir, in which you recommend that we deliberately bomb poor civilian areas of Germany cities to make the common working people suffer and go homeless and hungry and unable to work, and I find it—how can I put it?—er, unfortunate."

"That's—"

"The whole point of the Battle of Britain was to defeat Fighter Command, not to kill innocent civilians. We know that from the intelligence intercepts. If Göring had stuck to bombing the 11 Group airfields, he'd have gained air superiority over the Channel and southern England, thus permitting an invasion."

Lindemann started to interrupt again, but again she overrode him.

"That was the point, the only point. Bombing London has no strategic purpose, and daylight bombing has proved to be hideously expensive. Hitler threw away a thousand aircraft, most of his experienced aircrew, and his aura of invincibility and gained nothing in return. Nothing!"

"The psychological—"

"On the day after Mr. Churchill's visit to us in 11 Group, on 16 September, the *New York Times* banner headline ran, if memory serves: 'BRITISH DOWN 185 GERMAN PLANES IN DAY OF AIR FURY.' That's the result that matters."

"That number was grossly inflated."

"Who cares, Mr. Lindemann? It was a psychological victory. I thought you believed in psychological effects?"

Q: So, as I understand it, the bombing did no serious damage, in spite of two hundred bombers being employed, and the Luftwaffe's losses were very high, in spite of a two-to-one advantage, even if they were not as high as Fighter Command claimed?

A: Correct. The Luftwaffe aircrews faced another grim journey back to France, harried by the Spitfires and Hurricanes their commanders had promised them no longer existed.

Shaux found the rest of 339 at angels two-zero, overhead Hawkinge, just as they had been twenty minutes before. He reported to Sector and waited for a new vector. Jacko Welsh had been in 339 for about two weeks, which made him a seasoned pilot by 11 Group standards. Shaux would give him Green Flight, at least for a few days, to see if he had the unusual but essential mix of caution and clarity of thought on the one hand and aggression on the other required in leading a fighter flight.

Jacko was one of the growing contingent of Australians joining 11 Group. Shaux recalled the evening he had arrived, when 339 was still in Oldchurch. They had gathered, as they always did, at the village inn for one or two pints, bitter.

"I understand you are from a sheep station in New South Wales, Jacko, if I may be so bold?" Harry Pound, the Oldchurch station commander, had asked.

"I can't say I'm not, sir," Welsh had replied.

"How old were you when you first flew?"

"Well, I've no idea . . . the first time I soloed, I was ten."

"Ten? So young?" Froggie had asked.

"So old! Dad said I had to be able to reach the pedals *and* see out of the windscreen at the same time before I could fly solo. I didn't grow tall enough until I was ten."

This had prompted a general order of another pints, bitter, all round, and toasts to dads on stations, sheep, and down under.

Shaux had often pondered the almost random way in which pilots came together in transitory groupings as a result of 11 Group's very high casualty rates, the way that schoolboys and young men, thrown together by forces beyond their control, were required to go out and face existential threats together as a mutually supportive team. Often the only thing they had in common was a pints, bitter in the pub the night before. Shaux himself was an orphan, Froggie the son of a member of Parliament, Digby a highland Scot, and now Jacko from Mustamistit, New South Wales, somewhere beyond Gundagai.

"We call it Mustamistit because strangers keep coming into town and turning around and leaving again, saying, 'This can't be it, mustamistit!'"

Shaux considered telling 339 to stay alert, but he knew it was unnecessary. They were flying in a loose box pattern above Canterbury. There were aircraft below: fleeing bombers and pursuing fighters. No need to intervene.

They were down to eight aircraft, but 339 was an A squadron, and Shaux expected pilots and replacement aircraft would arrive later tonight or in the morning. He wondered if life was the same in a Luftwaffe Jagdgeschwader, a fighter group, and guessed it was. They, too, would have inner groups of seasoned pilots, survivors, and an endlessly revolving door of raw recruits. He wondered if the Jagdgeschwader pilots thought they were winning or losing. He wondered what they talked about as they drank their biers, lager—exactly the same things as 11 Group pilots, he was sure: aircraft and girls, cars and girls, sports and girls, and heroic conquests accomplished with each, but never, ever, ever the pilots who had gone before them and been lost.

"Shadow, this is Lumba," a voice in his headset said. "I have some trade for you."

TWENTY-TWO

Q: I think your model had correctly forecasted the size of the raid and the target. You must have been feeling very pleased with its accuracy.

A: Actually the reverse: I was terrified that we would start to depend on it and then it would collapse and then there'd be a disaster, and I would have caused it.

Q: How could that have happened?

A: Well, it didn't, but we were stretched so thin that we only had enough aircraft if things went reasonably well. If things went badly, we could have been overwhelmed by sheer numbers. I admit that it kept me awake at night.

Q: But you were right . . .

Eleanor glanced at the clock: it was 1600. It would all be over in less than an hour. The map was full of scattered markers, as if swept in by a wave and now being swept out again. No—that wasn't right. The tide had swept in superbly disciplined Jagdgeschwaders and Kampfgeschwaders that were holding their positions even though they would be mauled and mauled again, and now the tide was sweeping out shattered formations pockmarked with the empty spaces left by missing aircraft.

Why was she here? How had it all come to this? Only a month ago, when she had been attached to the Air Ministry with the task of tabulating statistics somewhere deep in the dusty catacombs of Whitehall, it had occurred to her that some aspects of the battle could be expressed in discrete mathematical terms, perhaps using von Neumann's zero-sum theory of games as a starting point.

She had started with a few simple functions to compare 11 Group with Luftflotte II to tabulate the results of each day's battle. That had led, in a moment of insight, to measurements not of how the two sides were similar but how they were dissimilar. In chess, for example, both sides started out with exactly the same numbers of the same pieces and competed to control the board, taking each other's pieces in a series of encounters. But in the aerial battle, the two sides had completely different pieces and different numbers of them. Then, in a torrent of thought, she had jumped from simple zero-sum advantages and disadvantages where one side's gain was exactly proportional to the other side's loss, to asymmetric zero-sums in which the two sides competed head-on but for different gains and losses.

From there she had leapt from the measurement of the big Operations Room map in terms of distance to measuring it in terms of time. Dover was not sixty miles from London, for example, but fifteen minutes, assuming constant height and wind conditions. Time permitted her to view the two-dimensional map as if it were three-dimensional, because the vertical movements of aircraft added or subtracted flight time. A Spitfire, for example, was not five thousand feet directly below a Dornier bomber, but two minutes below it. The speed of each aircraft would tell how far away they were, not in distance but in time.

With less than three hundred fighters, 11 Group could not possibly compete with Luftflotte II, which had fifteen hundred fighters and a thousand bombers. But in the dimension of time, 11 Group could cover the battlefield far more rapidly, thus multiplying its force from hopelessly outnumbered to equal, nullifying Luftflotte II numerical advantages.

The simple mathematical functions she wrote had grown more complex, more subtle; within days they seemed to take on a life of their own, fitting together into combinations and derivatives she had not anticipated and was delighted to discover. The cascade of functions came to describe more and more aspects of the battle, with more and more reliability, and began to predict its outcome. They became a replication of the battle, a mathematical representation of it: a model.

Then—she remembered the exact moment—it had all fallen into place, and she knew she was right. She had been standing next to Park, staring down from the Operations Room balcony at the jumble of markers on the map below, idly wondering who would win or lose in these particular encounters. Then it had struck her: 11 Group did not need to win; it simply needed not to lose. Luftflotte II, as the aggressor, had to win, but 11 Group, as the defender, didn't have to win, it just had to not lose and to keep on not losing until Luftflotte II gave up and went home.

She was reminded of the time when she was thirteen or fourteen, when her eyesight had become so blurry that she could not see the blackboard at school. Her mother resisted the idea of glasses, because glasses made girls less attractive, and it was not necessary for girls to learn a lot in school but very necessary, indeed essential, that they look attractive—within the bounds of gentility and decorum, of course—so that they could find appropriate husbands in due season.

But Eleanor, in an act of rebellion, went in secret to an oculist who fitted her for eyeglasses. When they came, she paid for them out of her post office savings and put them on and—abracadabra—the world was suddenly, miraculously in focus. She remembered staring at her hands as if seeing them for the first time.

In the same manner, the battle laid out on the Operations Room map table leapt into sharp focus, as if she were seeing it for the first time.

"Well, Eleanor, how are we doing this afternoon?" Park had interrupted her thoughts with a smile. "Are we winning?"

"No, sir, not yet, but we're not losing—that's all that matters. Of that I'm certain."

Now here she was, less than a month later, explaining a massive bombing raid to the prime minister himself, with her own staff working the model and her own intelligence department being prepared for her. She was far out on a limb, she was far out of her depth, but her sense of certainty had not left her.

Bramble brought a wonderful combination of arrogance and insecurity to the project—arrogance that he could carry it forward and
improve it in ways she could never have fathomed, and insecurity that
he might not be able to and therefore had to work twice as hard to
prove his superiority.

Cassius brought a different emotion: hatred. Eleanor had never
imagined that hatred could inspire an intellectual exercise, but his
hatred of Hitler, and what Hitler had done to his family, his country,
and his entire way of life, drove him like a goad. And yet, she glimpsed,
he was not naturally a creature of hatred; he had an impish sense of fun.
When she was first interviewing him, she had asked how his research
had been going before he had to flee.

"Well, ma'am, I would have to admit my research was gressing
before I escaped."

"You mean it was *pro*-gressing, advancing."

"No. They were neither progressing nor regressing. They were
stuck, going nowhere. They were simply gressing."

"There is no such word as *gressing*."

"Then there should be."

But Luftflotte II kept coming, and their raids were not diminishing
in scale or frequency. More of southern England was becoming pockmarked with bomb craters, and the list of 11 Group pilots lost in action
kept growing longer. Perhaps I'm wrong, she thought in sudden panic.
After all, she had been completely wrong about Johnnie, and he was
the only other thing that mattered in her life.

And to make matters worse, most people thought the notion of
"not losing" as a strategy was ridiculous. Her polite detractors said she
had made a mountain out of a tautology. It didn't help that the same
thought had occurred to Thomas Inskip, who had said that the role of
the RAF was not to achieve an early knockout blow but to prevent the
Germans from knocking the RAF out.

Eleanor knew that Inskip was considered to be one of the least successful and most foolish men in government—ever! In 1937, Stanley
Baldwin, then prime minister, a noted appeaser of Hitler and passive
enabler of German rearmament, had been forced by popular demand to
appoint a minister for coordination of defense to reinvigorate Britain's
military planning and capabilities. It was widely held that Baldwin had

appointed Inskip, a professional lawyer who was solicitor general, to head the ministry in order to make sure the ministry failed, because an energetic and capable minister might have upset the Germans he was busy appeasing.

There was even a book titled *Guilty Men* that had been published just a few months ago, blaming Inskip and others for failing to prepare for the war.

Eleanor was secretly amused by the fact that Inskip had been promoted to the peerage in spite of his failure and was now a viscount. Well, she thought, if "not losing" proves to be the wrong strategy, I'll be made a countess.

But she knew that it was *not* the wrong strategy. Dowding and Park believed it, as had Harry Pound, England's premier mathematician. As she had said to Churchill, we just have to be patient and wait while the Luftwaffe defeats itself.

She glanced over at him. He was leafing through his paperwork, dictating to his secretary sotto voce, and dealing with the rest of the world, perhaps satisfied that Park really did know what he was doing.

She glanced down at the map, her eyes automatically seeking out 339's marker. They were holding overhead Hawkinge at angels two-five. Johnnie probably had fuel for another hour or so of waiting and enough ammunition for one more interception, if necessary. He was probably wondering how long it would be before Sector recalled them. Targets were dwindling as Luftflotte II retreated. It would take him a good two hours to get to London this evening, and bomb damage to the roads and bridges could make it much longer. Knowing Johnnie, he was probably forcing himself *not* to think about the evening.

She glanced at the Tote Board and then at Park, sending him a secret wish to recall 339, but he seemed oblivious. She glanced down at the WAAFs at the table, hoping one of them would move 339's marker to safety, but no one did. Perhaps she should go down and listen on the Sector D R/T headset, just to hear his voice. She could see the headset lying on Susan Smith's desk, tempting her.

Poor Susan Smith—how horrible to die like that, to be so wretched, so hopeless, that you could do that to yourself. Eleanor would never be able to look at a pair of knitting needles again without thinking of that ghastly act.

Eleanor would have to make an instant decision. She would have to drop Johnnie like a hot potato, now, or marry him, because if she didn't marry him, it was very possible that she'd find herself in Susan's position: unmarried and pregnant.

Eleanor would be thrown out of the WAAFs. Her mother would have a field day heaping ignominy upon her, and her sisters would enjoy the spectacle. Fortunately, poor George's money meant that she wouldn't be without resources, as Susan had been, but it would not be pleasant to be an unwed mother.

She'd known Johnnie for three years, but she'd only been in love with him for a week. That was the issue: was she in love or was she just overwhelmed, intoxicated, by the strain of her own job and the extreme danger of his? Perhaps she should let some time go by. Park had promised to transfer him out of 11 Group, so they'd have more time to take things step by step. But she didn't want to take things step by step; she wanted him, all of him, now.

Perhaps she was bad for Johnnie. He was surviving by suppressing his feelings. He had made himself into a cold automaton on the outside, calmly flying his Spitfire, while all the dangers, all the tragedies, all the fears, all the emotions were battened down below the hatches where he didn't have to deal with them. He had convinced himself his life was a waste of breath. He had adopted Yeats's poem as his coat of armor. She could quote it verbatim:

The years to come seemed waste of breath,
A waste of breath the years behind
In balance with this life, this death.

The cold automaton who expected the rest of his life, the years to come, to be a waste of breath was a survivor because he was indifferent to his fate. But what if, because of her, the emotions burst out? What if she was unlocking Pandora's Box, and disasters would flood out and overwhelm him in a mighty cataract of calamity, as Churchill might say?

Her relationship with Johnnie, once so calm and reassuring, once so relaxingly even-keeled, had become a bit frantic—a lot frantic. She had, ridiculously, flown in a Defiant with him and helped him shoot down a 110. In the circumstances it was just about comprehensible—kill or be killed; he needed a gunner, and she was literally the only person there. But it had been absurdly, wildly dangerous. So, as a catharsis, she supposed, she had immediately summoned him to her bed—one wild, outrageous act to expunge another. In that one extreme circumstance, it was, possibly, understandable as a compulsive affirmation of life, but she'd better think very carefully before the next time—before tonight.

Tonight there would be no such excuse or explanation. Tonight she would not be acting from any motive other than desire aforethought.

TWENTY-THREE

Q: You mentioned Churchill's frustration with not being able to tell how the battle was going—the fog of war. Was it always like this—I mean, as the engagements continued?

A: Yes. We'd have dozens of reports of enemy losses, our losses, bombs falling, and so on, but it would take several days to really get an accurate picture.

Q: So he wasn't being unreasonable?

A: Well, that's not the point. The point is that each person has a set of skills and experiences that allow them to operate successfully in different situations. I had a detailed understanding of 11 Group, how these engagements evolved, and the quality of the information we were receiving, and so I understood what we knew and what we didn't.

Churchill didn't have that understanding. On the other hand, he had a level of understanding far deeper than mine, indeed, far deeper than everyone.

Q: Meaning?

A: He understood the British people—the British people at that time, I mean—and what they could and could not bear, far better than anyone else, or anyone since, for that matter. He understood the stakes, which he described as "infinite." He also understood, I think, what the pilots, the "Few," as he had named them, were going through . . .

"Shadow, this is Lumba. Vector one-six-zero direction Dover at angels one-five."

This controller's voice sounded familiar; the irritating controller must have gone off shift, or got stuck in the lavatory, or something, thank goodness.

"Shadow," Shaux said. "Follow me."

Shaux turned south. They were still in two finger-four formations, with Green Flight in the lead and Red Flight, led by Digby, a little behind and a little above. They had fuel for another thirty minutes or so and plenty of ammunition. Sector was sending other squadrons back to base; Shaux assumed the supply of targets must be dwindling as the remaining bandits escaped across the Channel. The major battles of the day had been won or lost; only the mopping up remained.

"Aircraft below at two o'clock," Digby said. "Aircraft are Dornier bandits and Hurricanes."

Sector acknowledged but did not tell 339 to get involved. They would be overhead Dover in five minutes.

"Aircraft below at two o'clock," Digby said again, some two minutes later. "Aircraft are Dornier bandits."

"Shadow, engage," said the controller.

"Bandits are six 17s flying southeast at angels one-two," said Digby.

"Red eyes, green guns," Shaux said. "Watch for escorts."

"Correction," Digby said. "Bandits are three 17s and three 110s. Mea culpa."

Digby had made a rare error, but there was no one else, as far as Shaux knew, who could even begin to identify aircraft four miles away and five thousand feet below through scattered clouds. A twin-engine Bf 110 Destroyer heavy fighter looked a lot like a 17 at this distance.

"Ego te absolvo a peccatis tuis," the controller said.

"Gratias tibi, Lumba."

"Omni tempore, Red Leader. *Bonum dies habeas."*

Everyone was going a little crazy, Shaux thought, as he listened to Digby and the controller chatting in Latin over the Sector R/T. The endless tension punctuated by sudden, violent clashes was probably eroding everybody's common sense.

"Follow me," he said, for what seemed like the hundredth time today. He briefly considered saying *"Sequi me,"* but thought better of it.

The best angle to attack these aircraft was from the side. Both the 17s and the 110s could fire forward and back but were vulnerable on their flanks, particularly to nimble Spitfires. The bandits were tightly bunched for mutual safety, but from Shaux's planned angle of attack, that simply made them into a single, larger target. He wondered if this group had already been attacked before. Almost certainly they had, in which case they might be running low on ammunition and therefore also vulnerable to an attack from the rear, which would give 339 a much longer time on target. He adjusted 339's curving flight path to bring them round almost behind the bandits and a little below, and matched speeds.

Only two of the rear gunners fired as they closed. The bandit aircrews must be terrified. On top of whatever horrors they had already suffered at the hands of 11 Group, on top of however many encounters they had survived or evaded, on top of however many of their comrades' deaths they had witnessed, they were now looking back at eight Spitfires and sixty-four machine guns three hundred yards behind them; 339 must have looked like a firing squad.

Digby and the rest of Green Flight would be looking above and all around for danger but had reported none. Well, thought Shaux, there's no point in delaying the inevitable.

"Tallyho," he said, in accordance with 11 Group ritual.

He opened the throttle to close the gap with the bandits and opened fire on the closest 17 at a range of two hundred yards. Jacko, just behind him and to his right, fired at the same time. Sixteen machine guns, firing at a combined rate of 270 rounds per second, sawed at the Dornier. With this attack solution they could fire an abnormally long burst lasting about four seconds so that the Dornier absorbed as many as a thousand rounds. It staggered and its right wing and right engine sheared off as a complete single piece, severed from the fuselage. The wing struck the 17 next to it, flipping it over on its back. Both aircraft began to spin earthward.

The remaining bandits began to break formation in all directions.

Shaux heard sharp rapping noises from shards of metal and debris as his Spitfire flew through the space where the 17s had been. He reflected that he had seen many aircraft damaged and shot down, on both sides and in many ways, but never had he seen a complete wing sawn off in midflight.

There was no point in pursuing the remaining bandits. It would take a while to track them down, and he did not want to take 339 out over the Channel unnecessarily. Besides, he had to admit, there was a limit to how much carnage he could endure.

He suddenly felt exhausted, drained, chilled to the bone, and a hundred years old. Poor Charlie, he thought, *canis miserablis*. He'd never get the chance to win the rest of Froggie's scarf.

"Follow me," he said, and turned northward.

Q: Those were the last Luftwaffe losses of the day?

A: Not quite. There was a subsequent raid, later on, on Southampton. But those were the last losses of the big raid.

"D Sector reports two Dorniers shot down by 339 over the coast," Park reported. "No losses to 339," he added, looking at Eleanor.

The map table was clearing rapidly as the Luftwaffe retreated to France and Belgium. The Tote Board for 399's status moved down one, from "Enemy Sighted" to "Ordered to Land." The WAAFs around the table seemed to relax a trifle. Eleanor looked at Park and sensed an easing of the tension within him. People were clattering up and down the stairs on their way—at long last—to and from the lavatories. Eleanor thought of joining them but knew there was always a long line as soon as a raid was over.

There would be no easing of tension in the East End of London, she thought—not in the ambulance stations and the hospitals; nor in the overworked fire stations and police stations; nor in the overflowing mortuaries; nor among the Home Guard and Air Raid Warden rescue parties digging their way through bomb-damaged buildings, hunting for trapped survivors; nor among the injured struggling to absorb relentless waves of pain; nor among the bereaved, grappling to grasp the loss of a son, or a daughter, or a mother, someone infinitely familiar and now infinitely far away; nor among the populace numbly assessing the violence and destruction wrought upon their neighborhoods; nor among the toddlers and schoolchildren searching, with growing panic, for their parents.

Nor would tensions be easing across Kent—not among the volunteers searching aircraft crash sites, Luftwaffe and Fighter Command alike; nor among the bomb disposal squads beginning the excruciating process of defusing unexploded bombs; nor among the radar operators in their Chain Home stations and the observers on the clifftops still watching, with aching eyes, for signs of yet another raid, yet more Kampfgeschwaders in remorseless phalanxes of droning black aircraft bearing death and destruction; nor among the 11 Group ground crews hastily refueling and rearming their serviceable Spitfires and Hurricanes against the possibility of a late-afternoon strike; nor among the RAF station intelligence officers and chaplains compiling lists of the missing and the dead.

If this is it, Eleanor thought—if Park has warded off yet another savage onslaught, and Johnnie has survived another encounter with the enemy—then we have lived to fight another day.

Churchill's secretary was busy packing up his refreshment boxes and tidying up his file folders. She, at least, had decided the day was over. Churchill himself was lost in silent contemplation, staring down at the table. Perhaps he was committing the scene to his memory, she thought, so that he could write about it in his memoirs in years to come.

Eleanor anticipated his next question and spoke quietly into a telephone.

"Jayne, do we have preliminary estimates of each side's losses?"

"Mr. Bramble's just adding them up, those we've got so far, that is. Just a minute . . . We have eighty victories claimed by 11 Group and another eighty by 12 Group, so far, all unverified, of course."

"And our losses?"

"Mr. Bramble says forty so far."

Eleanor hung up the telephone.

"Well, Air Vice-Marshal, is it over?" Churchill asked Park.

"It appears so, Prime Minister, for the time being."

"And what are the results? Do we know our margin of victory?"

"Not yet, sir," Eleanor interceded. "We have lost at least forty aircraft, but we haven't tabulated enemy losses yet." She simply was not going to repeat Leigh-Mallory's exaggerated claims. "Bromley-by-Bow gasworks is badly damaged and on fire, the East Upton tube station was hit, and there are numerous reports of scattered bomb damage across East London. I suspect many, perhaps most, of the bombers simply dropped their loads at random."

"That is all the damage, Squadron Officer? A gasworks and an Underground station?"

"All that's been reported so far, sir, and the damage to the railway lines this morning."

"And for that they sent six hundred aircraft this afternoon, after sending two hundred this morning?" Churchill asked, shaking his head.

She did not reply.

"Eight hundred sorties for a gasworks and an Underground station and some damaged railway lines in Vauxhall?"

"So it appears, sir."

"So many for so little," he mused. Again she thought he might have his memoirs in mind—"so many for so little" would be a fine contrapuntal note to his famous "so much to so few."

"Will they return tomorrow? What do your formulae predict?"

"They will return, without question, sir, but they will almost certainly return at night. We can hunt them down in daylight, when we can see them, but not at night, when we cannot."

"Well, then, Squadron Officer, Reichsmarschall Göring may yet win, if he cannot be stopped."

"Oh no, sir. He has already lost," she said.

He raised his eyebrows.

"He lost a week ago, sir, when he gave up bombing 11 Group airfields and started bombing London. That means he cannot control the air over England and the Channel, and therefore he cannot invade us. There will be no Nazi armada."

Churchill stared at her for a moment, and she feared an explosion. He turned to Park.

"Are you sure you cannot spare this young lady to serve in the cabinet?" he asked.

"Quite sure, sir." Park grinned.

"Then I shall take my leave of you, Air Vice-Marshal. This has been a very interesting day, and I shall long remember it."

"You are always welcome, sir, of course," Park said, as they shook hands.

"As for you, Squadron Officer, I await our next encounter with great interest," Churchill said. "Are you quite sure Göring has lost?"

"Quite sure, Prime Minister. Unfortunately he doesn't know it yet."

"And now, on to more important matters," Churchill said, placing his hat on his head. "I shall now ascend fifty feet, into the open air, and there I shall rejoice in the flavor of a fine cigar. I leave you to these stygian depths."

He waved to the room in general.

"Good afternoon to you all."

Then he was gone, leaving a strange vacuum in the room, a sort of loss of energy.

"Well, we survived another day, sir," she said to Park.

"Yes, indeed, and thank you for looking after Churchill," Park said. "I couldn't have survived without you."

"Sir, you may recall that I have a forty-eight-hour leave starting tonight. Is there anything else I can do before I go? I promise you Bramble is very competent, although I admit he is also weird!"

"Off you go, Eleanor, and thank you." He paused, and she saw the faintest twinkle in his eye. "If, by complete and unlikely coincidence, you happen to run into Johnnie Shaux, thank him for another excellent effort by 339."

Eleanor grinned and hurried away.

Now, for important matters, she thought. Should I wear my uniform or a dress? Or wear my uniform now but pack a dress? Could she sweet-talk her way into the WAAF warrant officers' bathrooms, which had real hot water?

She glanced down at the map table one last time, out of habit. The table was almost empty. A WAAF pulled the 339 marker—so often and so long the center of Eleanor's attention—from the table and casually tossed it into a jumbled tray of discarded markers, where it lay upside down and half hidden, no longer of significance or value.

Q: And 339 landed safely?

A: It did.

Shaux led the remnants of 339 back home. Hawkinge was easy to find: a long column of black smoke, stretching out all the way to Folkestone, marked Froggie's funeral pyre.

Shaux landed, taxied, and climbed slowly from H-for-Harry. Charlie came to greet him, still carrying the scarf. Digby and then the others joined him, a small gaggle of men in a large field staring helplessly at the smoldering remnants of two Spitfires.

Charlie ran back and forth uncertainly, looking for Potter. He sat down; his eyes turned skyward, the scarf clenched between his teeth, to wait.

One of the younger pilots, one of Froggie's Greenies, shuddered as if about to weep.

"Right, chaps," Shaux said, commanding their attention. "I've just got time for a quick pints, bitter, before I have to get up to London. Chop, chop!"

"But—" the Greenie began.

"Excellent idea, Skipper," Digby overrode him. "If we hurry, there'll be time for two."

Q: I can't believe it just ended like that . . . the greatest aerial assault in history just petered out? So little for so many, Churchill said?

A: So many for so little, he said, but I don't recall him using those words in a speech.

Q: So many for so little . . .

A: Wars and battles have a way of doing that, if you look back through history. They tend to end, as T. S. Eliot wrote, "not with a bang but a whimper."

TWENTY-FOUR

Q: So that was the end?

A: It was the end of daylight bombing raids.

Q: How did you know you'd won?

A: Well, I hate to be pedantic, but we didn't know we'd won. We just knew we hadn't lost.

We knew from the end of the daylight raids that Luftflotte II could not sustain any more losses of that magnitude, and we knew two days later, on the seventeenth, when Bletchley Park intercepted the order to suspend Operation Sea Lion, the invasion, indefinitely. The Luftwaffe had lost thirteen hundred aircraft in less than five weeks, with nothing to show for it.

Q: So you did know you'd won!

A: No. The raids simply shifted from daylight bombing to nighttime bombing.

From Hitler's perspective, he hadn't been able to invade us, but he could try to bomb us into submission. "Strategic bombing," as it is now called, was a very popular theory in those days. The theory was widely supported before the start of the war—Mitchell and Doolittle on the American side, Trenchard on ours, the Italian Douhet, and so on. Göring was a great believer.

There was no invasion, but we continued to suffer from another series of disasters as the Germans switched to intense night bombing— the blitz. In the eight months following that day, forty-three thousand people were killed and another one hundred and forty thousand were wounded.

It cost Dowding and Park their jobs, because they couldn't stop the bombers at night. The technology simply did not exist. As a consequence, London was bombed on seventy-six consecutive nights. Coventry, of course . . .

Q: Did you say seventy-six consecutive nights?

A: I did.

Q: That's . . . that's . . . barbaric!

A: That's as good a word as any. And, in due course, the same fate was visited on countless German and Japanese cities by the RAF and the USAAF. But that's another story in its own right. I always remember . . .

Q: What?

A: I remember the long lines of children in railway stations who were waiting patiently to be evacuated. They were being sent to safe places in the country, rather like children being placed in foster homes today, to be saved from the bombing. They had labels hanging round their necks with their names on them . . . they were so sad, so frightened, and yet so still.

Q: But when all is said and done, 15 September, Battle of Britain Day, didn't resolve anything?

A: As I believe I said earlier, it was just another bloody Sunday.

Q: That was your last day in 11 Group?

A: Yes, I was off to MI6-3b. It was my husband's last day in 339, too, because Park pulled him out of operational flying that evening and transferred him to A&AEE shortly thereafter, just as he had promised. He never said so, but I think it was a farewell present to me.

Eleanor entered the saloon bar of the Bunch of Grapes public house on the corner of Brompton Road and Yeoman's Row. The room was already crowded, but she managed to find a stool at the bar. The publican approached her with slightly raised eyebrows.

"I'm waiting for someone, thank you," she said. He appraised her for a moment and then turned to serve another customer; evidently he had decided she was not a streetwalker. Perhaps the day would come when a girl could go into a pub unescorted and not be assumed to be a tramp, she thought, but it probably wouldn't come for a long time.

Everyone in 11 Group now accepted that the WAAFs were every bit as competent as their male colleagues. The Air Transport Auxiliary, the ATA, the newly formed aircraft-ferrying organization, was accepting female pilots—"Attagirls," they were called. But the WAAFs only received half the pay that men did, and the Attagirls were only allowed to fly obsolescent aircraft. Men could pinch women's bottoms with impunity, but women had to justify their moral propriety to publicans.

Johnnie was a little late, she thought, glancing towards the door. It still seemed strange that she would now be waiting for him with bated breath, having seen him so casually every day at Oxford. He had been like a pair of old slippers, she thought, comfortable and comforting. Now, through an abrupt metamorphosis she really did not understand, he was an object of consuming desire.

She remembered the day, the minute, the exact moment when everything had changed. She had been visiting Harry Pound, her advisor on her minimax model, at the airfield at Oldchurch where Johnnie was stationed. And 339 was ordered to readiness and then into the sky. She had stood beside Pound, watching the Spitfires depart. Pound had wished Johnnie "good hunting," and she had wanted to wish him good luck, but she hadn't, feeling it was too trite; she'd even considered "be careful," but that would have been absurd.

And so he had taken off and flown against the Luftwaffe without the protective cloaking of her luck, naked against the 109s. She felt as if she had condemned him to death. She feared he would face a 109 pilot who had been wished good luck by a girl, and that would be the margin between them: the pilot with luck wished upon him and the pilot without. She had suffered for seventy-five minutes, sure she had killed him, until he had landed again, unscathed. He had survived, but she had been unable to forgive herself.

Her emotions had shocked her. They were totally unexpected and unprecedented. Why was she feeling this? Then it had dawned on her: this unexpected and unprecedented turmoil was love, an emotion made as much of pain as it was of pleasure.

No Johnnie yet. He must have been delayed coming up from Hawkinge. The talk in the pub around her was all about the bombing attacks, the bombs hitting the palace, and the bomber crashing into Victoria Station. Evidently a mob had caught a German pilot when he landed by parachute in Kennington and had beaten him severely until he was rescued by the police.

The BBC announced that over 150 German aircraft had been downed, a number Eleanor knew was pure nonsense. It had been a good day, a very good day, but the Luftwaffe had lost no more than sixty or so aircraft. The exaggeration was mostly due to the absurd claims made by the Duxford Wing. When Eleanor had seen Jayne's latest tabulations, she had noted that six different pilots had claimed the Dornier that crashed into Victoria Station.

There would almost certainly be more bombs tonight, but the Londoners in the pub were angry rather than scared. If Hitler was trying to terrorize Londoners, he was being singularly unsuccessful.

Cassius, who had grasped the minimax model as a weapon to wield against the Nazis and was working eighteen hours a day, was projecting that the Luftwaffe would bomb every night that the weather was clear over France and would continue indefinitely.

"You mean over England?" she had asked him.

"No. The Luftwaffe cares about taking off and landing safely. They don't care about finding legitimate targets. They are happy to blow things up at random. Besides, London is a big target. It's hard to miss, even in darkness. Someone starts a fire, and then everyone else bombs the fire. If you miss, you just start another fire. Who cares? It's easy."

Eleanor thought there was some truth in that, although in her new role as head of MI6-3b, she had been told of the Lorenz radio guidance beams the Luftwaffe was using to find targets at night.

After today's losses Göring and Kesselring might be forced to scale back daylight bombing, she thought, in which case Hitler might have to postpone the invasion and Park and Dowding would have accomplished their miracle. She had said as much to Churchill when he left Uxbridge. She had followed him up the stairs and found him smoking by his car.

"They lost at least ten percent of their forces today, sir, and accomplished nothing. If the frequency and intensity of daylight raids fall, as I predict they will, you will know that Hitler has postponed, or even cancelled, the invasion."

"Then, you think we have won?" Churchill asked.

"No, sir, I think we haven't lost."

"Ha!" Churchill barked, and climbed into his car. Eleanor had been left to wonder if he was pleased or annoyed with her.

Now, finally, just when she was beginning to worry about him, Johnnie pushed through the door.

There was a momentary hush in the bar, a sort of rippling tide of silence, as people noticed his uniform, his Squadron leader's stripes, his pilot's wings, and his DFC and bar medal ribbon.

"Look here, here's one of the Few," someone said loudly. "Good for you, mate!"

"Hear, hear," said several others, and there was a smattering of applause.

Johnnie turned bright pink with embarrassment and flapped his hands in a gesture of self-deprecation. He ducked his head as if willing himself to disappear. George had once described Johnnie as "conspicuously unnoticeable." Now she could not stop gazing at him. As he came through the crowd, several people shook his hand. Poor Johnnie, she thought. All that attention for a man who asked for nothing.

"I'm so sorry I'm late. The lorry broke down," Johnnie said as he reached her.

They stared at each other, too reticent to kiss in public. She touched his arm instead and knew he understood.

He ordered a shandy for her and a bitter for himself.

"It's on the house, Squadron Leader," the publican said, when Johnnie reached into his pocket to pay. "Proud to serve you."

"Cheers," they said, and drank.

She took off her raincoat.

"You're wearing that dress!" he exclaimed, staring.

It was a dress she had worn in their last summer in Oxford—only a year ago, but it seemed like fifty years—when they went punting on the river. It was china blue with little white flowers, like cherry blossoms against a spring sky.

"For the time being," she said, and he almost choked on his beer.

"The weather forecast is for ten-tenths cloud tomorrow," he said, recovering. "We've been stood down."

"I know," she said. "Park's given me the day off too."

"I don't have to be back until 0500 on Tuesday," he said.

"Neither do I," she said.

They tried to talk casually, but they were far too nervous and far too conscious of the friendly scrutiny of the crowded bar.

"Excuse me for asking, sir, but did you fly today?" someone asked Shaux.

She could see him wriggling, trying to escape the spotlight.

"Yes, he did," she answered for him. "Twice."

Johnnie seemed to be hoping the ground would open up beneath his feet so he could escape into oblivion.

"Did you get one?" a woman asked.

"Yes, he did," Eleanor said, standing and pulling on her raincoat. "We have to leave," she added, to save them both from further public scrutiny.

"Make sure he gets what he deserves this evening, young lady," someone called out as they left, and there was a roar of approval. Now it was her turn to turn scarlet.

As the doors closed behind them someone called out "Twice!" and the crowd roared again.

They walked a block along Knightsbridge towards Harrods before turning into Ovington Gardens and then into Ovington Mews, a tiny cobbled street once filled with carriage houses and servants' quarters. She fumbled for the key. Her friend's flat occupied the upper floor above a garage and consisted of a kitchen, a bathroom, and one room that served as a living room and bedroom combined.

They stood looking at each other helplessly, almost too tense to proceed.

"I think you should start by undressing me," she said.

TWENTY-FIVE

First Epilogue

Q: *Suppose, for a moment, Dame Eleanor, that Germany had won the Battle of Britain. Suppose the losses on 15 September and on the preceding days had been reversed. What would have happened, do you suppose?*

A: *Well, the whole point of the aerial campaign, from the Luftwaffe's perspective, was to push the RAF out of southern England in order to permit Operation Sea Lion to occur. If the Luftwaffe had gained and held air superiority by defeating 11 Group, the next question is whether the Germans would have been able to accomplish a successful cross-Channel invasion.*

Q: *So, what do you think would have happened?*

A: *Well, it's counterfactual, of course, but it's interesting to measure the probabilities using a zero-sum approach.*

With regard to an actual invasion, a cross-Channel attack, the Luftwaffe had proved to be very effective against naval assets. With no Spitfires or Hurricanes to distract them, the Luftwaffe could have systematically bombed every Royal Navy ship that tried to come close to the invasion force. Stuka dive-bombers were very effective against large naval assets, and 110s were successful at suppressing smaller vessels, and the Luftwaffe had many Stukas and 110s.

In addition, without 11 Group to oppose them, Luftflotte II could have carried out low-level bombing attacks on the Channel ports using 17s and 111s, to devastating effect. From Dover to Poole, Hitler would have had five or six deep-water harbors to choose from.

So I think a Channel crossing would have been successful. The German invasion fleet—consisting of hundreds of big Rhine barges suitable for carrying troops, tanks, and artillery pieces——would have been substantially unopposed. In addition, we must remember that the English coast in 1940 was far less well defended than the coast of Normandy on D-Day in 1944. There were a few fortifications, but nothing remotely like Hitler's Atlantic Wall.

Q: Then what?

A: The English army had lost its armor and its artillery at Dunkirk and hadn't had time to replace them. The regular army was still disorganized, and the territorial forces—volunteers and the Home Guard—were ill-trained and ill-equipped. There was a chronic shortage of transportation; General Montgomery, who in later years became England's most victorious general, was relying on local buses to transport his defensive forces . . . Can you imagine?

And there was also a lot of turmoil among the senior command. General Ironside—what a wonderful name for a soldier—the most obvious choice to command the army, kept failing . . . in other words, a bit of a mess.

Once the Wehrmacht—the German army—was in England, I think their equipment and tactics would have proved superior. Panzers on the ground and Stukas from the air would have outmaneuvered and destroyed the British army. Southern England has few natural defenses—no deep forests or high hills or wide rivers. There would have been nowhere to hide and nothing to stop the Panzer advances.

The Wehrmacht would probably have reached London in a week or ten days.

Q: So Britain would have lost the war?

A: Yes. I think the Wehrmacht would have taken the rest of England in a month or less. Scotland and Wales might have taken another month or two more—they're much more difficult territory for armored vehicles. The combined forces of the British Commonwealth could not have retaken Britain. By the end of—

Q: Why couldn't they have recaptured Britain?

A: Well, for the very practical reason that there was nowhere to launch a counterinvasion from. Germany would have occupied Northern Ireland, of course, and would probably have grabbed Ireland and Iceland as well. The British couldn't have launched an invasion from Canada; it's too far away.

Without Britain as a base, the United States could never have staged a counterinvasion like D-Day. America—which was still neutral in 1940 and 1941—would have found itself facing an expansionist Japan in the Pacific and an expansionist Germany in the Atlantic.

Q: What would have happened then, if the Battle of Britain was lost and Germany was triumphant?

A: If Hitler had been wise, which he was not, he would have concentrated on the Desert War in North Africa, seizing the Suez Canal and then going on into the Arabian Peninsula. That's a war the Afrika Korps almost won in 1941, led by Erwin Rommel, the Desert Fox. He'd certainly have won if Britain had already been defeated, in which case Malta would have fallen and the Australians—who were fighting in the desert—would probably have given up and gone home to defend their own country.

Once he controlled the whole Mediterranean and the Middle East, Hitler might have stopped. He'd have had no need to invade Russia. He'd have had plenty of room for Lebensraum, open doors into Africa and India, plenty of oil, and control of the Suez Canal and the trade routes between Europe and Asia. SS storm troopers would have occupied what is now Israel. In fact, Hitler could have made Jerusalem his eastern capital! A swastika flying over Temple Mount!

He would have been greater than Napoleon, greater than Frederick the Great, greater even than the Emperor Augustus or Charlemagne, the most powerful men in European history.

Q: What would the United States have done?

A: War is the most consuming, the most exhausting of all human activities. The United States would have entered the war only if it was forced to—as the Japanese forced the United States into war in the Pacific by attacking Pearl Harbor. The United States would only have needed to fight Hitler if it was similarly provoked, as it was in World War I.

In the end it would have come down to the atomic bomb. When Hitler had developed that . . .

Q: Are you serious? Hitler was a long way behind in atomic research; he tried and gave up. The United States had the Manhattan Project. They would have developed the bomb first.

A: Well, yes, but we are theorizing a British defeat in 1940. At the beginning of the war, the British were well ahead in atomic research. It was the highly secret British MAUD report, as it was called, that demonstrated that an atomic bomb was practical. Churchill gave everything we had on nuclear fission to the Americans as part of Lend-Lease, and that was the intellectual and scientific basis of the Manhattan Project. Enrico Fermi took the MAUD report and started building an experimental reactor at Columbia University in New York.

If, however, Hitler had won the Battle of Britain, he'd have had all that MAUD research material in 1940 and all the British and refugee atomic physicists, including Rudolf Peierls and Otto Frisch, instead of the Americans having it, so he'd have had a jump start on developing atomic weapons.

Q: Are you saying . . .

A: *I'm saying that a logical and credible result of Britain losing the Battle of Britain would have been a Nazi nuclear bomb on top of a V1 cruise missile or a V2 ballistic missile.*

Thus one can imagine, sometime in 1944 or 1945, the Nazi battleship Bismarck patrolling the eastern coast of the United States, armed with V1 cruise missiles and V2 ballistic missiles tipped with atomic warheads. The United States would not have possessed those technologies and would not have been able to defend against them.

Q: *Are you serious?*

A: *Certainly. The Germans would have had a two-year lead over everyone else in atomic research. They certainly had the intellectual and technical skills necessary, and an even greater incentive to develop the V1 and V2 missiles as delivery vehicles.*

Q: *What would the United States have done?*

A: *Well, President Roosevelt, or President Truman, would have had some very, very tough decisions to make . . .*

Q: *You mean, faced by a Nazi bomb?*

A: *Well, of course, the Luftwaffe didn't win the Battle of Britain, thank goodness, so the point is moot. But it might give pause to your American viewers to reflect that Churchill's famous expression, "Never have so many owed so much to so few," doesn't just apply to the English.*

Q: *The Battle of Britain pilots saved the world, including America, from a Nazi bomb? Are you serious?*

A: *Well, counterfactual hypotheses are always fun, I think, particularly with a good glass of port.*

(Deleted:

Q: Wow! That's a whole show in its own right! Jesus Christ! Would you consider doing a "what if" type of show? That's amazing!

A: Scarcely amazing, I would hope: merely logical.

Q: But would you do it?

A: Certainly, if you offer a vintage port and a good, sharp cheddar.

End of deletion.)

Q: Wow! That's a whole interview in its own right! But we're running out of time for this segment, I'm afraid.

So, coming back to what actually happened, Dame Eleanor, what was the mood like, after the Battle of Britain? You must have been very hopeful, back in September 1940, that the tide of war was finally shifting in your favor.

A: Oh no, not at all! There was no light at the end of the tunnel, only darkness. The year 1940 had been brutal, but 1941 would turn out to be even worse.

Q: Worse?

A: By far.

Q: That's a question we'll have to explore in our next episode.

PART THREE

15 March 1941

to

6 December 1941

TWENTY-SIX

Q: (To camera:) *Good evening and welcome to our third program in a series of interviews with our distinguished guest, Dame Eleanor Shaux, examining the Battle of Britain.*

Dame Eleanor was a senior intelligence officer in the 11 Group Operations Room on 15 September 1940, what we now celebrate as Battle of Britain Day, and her future husband, Johnnie Shaux, was in command of 339 Squadron, one of the 11 Group Spitfire squadrons stationed at Hawkinge in Kent.

(To guest:) *Good evening again, Dame Eleanor.*

A: *Good evening.*

Q: (To camera:) *In our last episode Dame Eleanor helped us understand what the pilots went through and how the Fighter Command command-and-control system worked. We talked about the raids that took place on Battle of Britain Day, raids that cost the Luftwaffe almost eighty aircraft without any significant damage to Fighter Command or London.*

We also asked her to speculate on what might have happened if the Luftwaffe had won—a fascinating subject in its own right, one to which I hope we'll be able to return.

In this episode we will explore what really happened after the RAF's success in the Battle of Britain. We'll ask Dame Eleanor to guide us through the next year of the war, through the dark days of 1941. At the end of our last show, Dame Eleanor told us that 1940 had been—and, let me look at my notes, yes, I can quote her—"1940 had been brutal, but 1941 would turn out to be even worse. There was no light at the end of the tunnel, only darkness."

A: Alas, yes, these were very difficult times. We were alone. I think people forget that we fought for more than two years before America entered the war, from September 1939 until December 1941. The Battle of Britain, which ended in September 1940, was fought fifteen months before Pearl Harbor.

Q: Perhaps we could use that thought to frame this session, Dame Eleanor? "From the Battle of Britain to Pearl Harbor," as it were? From no light at the end of the tunnel until light?

A: Oh no! There was still no light at the end of 1941; in fact, to strain the analogy further, at the end of 1941 we were still searching in the dark to find the beginning of the tunnel, much less the end of it!

Q: But surely Churchill said, in one of his famous speeches, "Now this is not the end. It is not even the beginning of the end. But it is, perhaps, the end of the beginning."

A: Alas not; he did say that, indeed he did, but not until the end of 1942, a year after Pearl Harbor, two years after the Battle of Britain, three years after the start of the war.

Q: I'm beginning to realize this was a very, very long war!

A: Well, it certainly seemed so at the time.

(Deleted:

Q: (Laughs) Sorry, I shouldn't have laughed.

A: Why not? It was supposed to be funny.

End of deletion.)

Q: Well, let's start on that journey, beginning with the Battle of Britain and moving towards Pearl Harbor. I think one of the most extraordinary aspects of the Battle of Britain is that the losers, Hermann Göring and Albert Kesselring, kept their jobs and remained in Hitler's favor for years to come, whereas the victors, Air Chief Marshal Hugh Dowding and Air Vice-Marshal Keith Park, were sacked within a few weeks, as if they had been the losers.

A: True; Park was transferred to a lesser job supervising pilot training, and Dowding was sent on a meaningless mission to Washington D.C. And, coincidentally, I was sent into exile, or so it seemed, in Malvern House.

Eleanor awoke reluctantly. In her dreams she was still entwined with Johnnie, but in the cold reality of predawn Malvern House, he was already up and away to RAF Martlesham Heath. She tried to linger within the boundaries of her dreams—dreams that were now receding into an indistinct erotic blur beyond her reach—but her alarm clock would not permit her. She groaned and acknowledged the inevitability of getting up.

Her cavernous bedroom was chilly and damp; her vast bathroom even more so. The antique plumbing system had probably never, ever worked, even when it was first installed, as the height of modernity and efficiency, sometime in Queen Victoria's reign. Her wartime toothpaste seemed to be made from chalk. She glanced at herself briefly in an ornate gilt mirror as she tugged on her sacklike, unbecoming uniform. She grimaced at her reflection and shrugged.

Eleanor felt she was a prisoner within this decaying mansion instead of its mistress. Yet mistress she was: commanding officer of Section 3b of Military Intelligence Department 6, MI6-3b, as it was called, stationed here in the requisitioned Malvern House in Suffolk on the east coast of England.

It was all Winston Churchill's fault.

It had been six months since Winston Churchill, the prime minister, had given her his enigmatic instructions. She had been summoned to Downing Street on September 7, 1940, the day after the Luftwaffe had unleashed its bombers against London at the start of the blitz, a fearsome turn of events that she alone had predicted using the zero-sum mathematical model she had created.

Churchill had glowered at her.

"The fate of this island is teetering in the balance, Mrs. Rand."

"I know, sir." There wasn't anything else to say.

He pondered for a moment.

"I know you're not a gypsy fortune-teller with a crystal ball, Mrs. Rand, nor yet a savant with a pack of tarot cards. Nevertheless, I want you to paint with a broader brush, to look beyond the immediate. I shall give you whatever resources you may require, and you will extend your analysis as widely as you can."

What did he mean? Surely not . . . he actually wanted her to predict Hitler's actions? He might just as well have told her to design a rocket ship to the moon—but this was not a moment for equivocation. She had no choice.

"I . . . I'll do my best, sir."

"As shall we all, Mrs. Rand, as shall we all, with gathering skill and might, until, in the fullness of time, Herr Hitler and his monstrous ménage lie choking in their own vile excrement."

A week later, Churchill had visited 11 Group headquarters in Uxbridge and watched from the balcony as the climactic aerial battles unfolded on the map table beneath him. He had not changed his mind and let her off the hook, as she had fervently wished, and within a few days she had been dispatched to this gloomy mansion deep in the soggy English countryside, hidden far from curious eyes.

That had been in September; now it was March. It should be close to spring, but, Eleanor feared, perhaps it was always winter in Malvern House. The mansion's sole saving grace was that Aldeburgh was only twenty miles from Martlesham Heath, where Johnnie was based.

Eleanor's mathematical model was now a state secret—even its existence was denied. Therefore, in order to give Malvern House an apparent purpose, and after much discussion, Bramble and Cassius had designed a large contraption that was twenty feet wide and six feet high and made out of several sets of bedsprings wired together. This contraption was attached to masts above the roof, creating the impression of radio receivers or antennae.

Local rumors sprang up about experimental radar projects and were not vigorously denied. Initially the structure was positioned along the ridge of the main roofline for engineering simplicity, until the local vicar was heard to wonder why England feared invasion from Scotland, upon which a detachment of Royal Engineers was brought in very quickly to reorient the bedsprings to face southeast, towards Belgium and France.

Q: (Chuckles) *The bedsprings worked?*

A: *They did. After the war, we discovered that the Abwehr believed we really were doing radar work because the bedsprings were so obviously a cheap fake they had to be a very clever disguise for a real antenna. They even tried to reverse-engineer it as their so-called Bettfeder Freya radar system, their bedspring radar.*

Q: *The Abwehr?*

A: *German military intelligence.*

Q: *Did you know you were being spied on?*

A: *In the beginning we assumed so. Later on we knew so.*

Meanwhile the zero-sum model, which Eleanor had designed and built based on the factors determining advantages and disadvantages in aerial warfare, was being reinvented to record and forecast the war in Europe. It required a vast expansion both in terms of complexity and scale. Cassius had dubbed the original model "Luftflotte II versus 11 Group," measuring the balance of forces involved in aerial conflict. In his spare time Bramble was toying with creating a map game, like the American game Monopoly, with a greatly simplified version of zero-sum rules. Spitfires battled 109s and 17s, and individual dogfights were determined by the throw of dice. The biggest problem, he said, was finding the right name for the game.

The new model had to have a "broader brush"—Eleanor was very conscious of Churchill's expression—capable of encompassing the far more complex parameters involved in "Third Reich versus British Empire."

Eleanor had started using folders with red covers for her reports to Churchill, and the model had now been given the unofficial code name of Red Tape.

Churchill had asked Eleanor to address two initial questions, partly because he needed answers and partly as a test of the model's potential. The first was a fairly narrow question about what Fighter Command should be doing now that it had beaten back the Luftwaffe in the Battle of Britain, and the nighttime blitz was finally beginning to slow. This was almost an extension of last year's work, and Bramble had redefined Red Tape to encompass alternative campaigns, both offensive and defensive, over Europe.

Churchill's second question asked what Hitler would do next, with particular regard to the future relationship between Germany and Russia. Would the Molotov-Ribbentrop Pact survive? That required not just military capabilities, but also economic and political considerations.

Cassius, in particular, had torn into that question with all the energy that his volcanic hatred for Hitler generated. He was working twelve hours a day or more, pausing only to eat or sleep or to pace the grounds, muttering to himself and smoking a tobacco pipe large enough to act as an auxiliary heating system for Malvern House's woeful plumbing.

For Eleanor, second-guessing Hitler's intentions was like a trip into Dante's *Inferno*, a study in evil and its consequences.

Bramble, meanwhile, seemed calmer as he developed options for the aerial war. Evidently Eleanor's idea of using Jayne Jackson to control him was having some effect, and he seemed to be at Jayne's constant back and call. Occasionally Eleanor had seen him open his mouth, almost certainly to say something outrageous, and Jayne had jumped in with some diversion or other before he could do so.

Jayne herself was blossoming. With the exception of the higher mathematics involved in designing and redesigning the Red Tape model, most of what Malvern House did on a day-to-day basis was the routine, repetitive compilation of statistical tables. Here Jayne excelled, transforming these humdrum processes into a series of rigidly applied protocols with fearsome consequences for anyone who strayed outside her boundaries. She called it "coloring inside the lines."

M-I6, Eleanor's nominal supervisor, was a distant irritant. M-I6 had sent a representative named Crenshaw to Malvern House. He handled the unending flow of paperwork that washed over them from the upper reaches of His Majesty's Civil Service, and Eleanor was delighted to let him deal with all that nonsense. She was amused to see a growing rivalry between Crenshaw and Jayne as to who could be the most rigidly bureaucratic. Eleanor arranged for Jayne to be commissioned as a WAAF flight officer, partly as a reward for all her hard work and partly to strengthen her hand against Crenshaw.

Periodically dispatch riders would appear with sealed letters from Whitehall. Edward Bridges, the cabinet secretary, would advise Eleanor that "the prime minister wishes to be informed of MI6-3b's opinion on" this or that aspect of the war, causing a sudden spurt of activity to retune Red Tape to provide such an opinion.

Malvern House was less than a mile from Aldeburgh, a delightful fishing town with beautiful sandy beaches on the North Sea that was sadly acquiring the same sort of run-down, weary look as the rest of wartime England. Still, it was home to several friendly pubs where the "radar research blokes" were welcome and any as yet unattached WAAFs were greeted with enthusiasm.

Every evening Johnnie would arrive on his thunderous motorcycle, and the rest of the world would recede into the darkness, and nothing else would matter beyond the four corners of their bed.

Johnnie was testing new versions of aircraft. His work was not completely safe, but at least he was not being shot at on a daily basis. He was currently testing experimental airborne radars in Bristol Beaufighters as part of the frantic effort to find ways to combat the nightly bombing blitz. He was also testing a twin-engine fighter, the Whirlwind, which held promise, he said, but suffered from unreliable engines.

They had married soon after Battle of Britain Day, in a shopworn ritual performed in the Kensington and Chelsea Register Office by officials already bored by the third such rushed formality that morning. It was over in less than ten minutes. Eleanor's solicitor's office had arranged the whole thing, smoothing over whatever legalities might be applicable, and all she and Johnnie had had to do was show up.

Johnnie, usually so reticent, had been unable to stop grinning.

TWENTY-SEVEN

Q: Your department was part of MI6, now the SIS, the Secret Intelligence Service, was it not?

A: It was.

Q: I don't think it's a museum, like Bletchley Park is now?

A: No, I believe Malvern House is owned by a German company, ironically enough, that makes avionics and radar equipment. Besides, Red Tape was a far lesser contributor to the war effort than Ultra.

Q: Well, I don't know about that . . .

A: It's true. Ultra—our ability to read German Enigma codes—was vital to our success in many campaigns and theaters of operation. The work that Turing and the others did was as great an intellectual accomplishment as the Manhattan Project, I think. I wish someone would make a film out of it—it's a great story.

Q: It's always struck me as amazing that your work remained completely secret for so many years, just as the Ultra Project and Bletchley Park remained secret. We didn't know about Ultra until F. W. Winterbotham published his memoirs in 1974, and we didn't know about Red Tape

until the late seventies, I think it was, when Sir Algernon Bramble pub-
lished his autobiography. And, if I recall, Malvern House was described
by General Ernest Pondsford in his memoirs. He was your first MI6 boss,
I believe.

A: I believe so too.

(Deleted:

Q: (Laughs) *Stop making me laugh!*

A: Why?

End of deletion.)

Q: (Chuckles) *While you were in the secret intelligence world, did you*
meet Bond, James Bond?

A: I wish I had. (Laughs) *He would have been in prime physical condi-*
tion, in his early twenties. Alas, the members of the intelligence services
I did meet were somewhat less dashing, shall we say . . .

Eleanor's new boss, Brigadier Ernest Pondsford, a deputy director of
Military Intelligence, MI-1, found her existence profoundly annoying,
for he was not permitted to know the nature of her work even though
he was nominally in charge of her. He was told to provide her with
whatever she required immediately, without asking why, and to keep
his mouth shut.

The stars of the Military Intelligence world were Departments MI5
and MI6, for domestic and foreign intelligence respectively, with their
mysterious and dramatic espionage and counterespionage roles and
their secret agents and spies skulking in the shadows, all cloak-and-
dagger and derring-do, all with a delicious whiff of danger. MI5 and
MI6 inspired novels and cinema films by that chap Alfred Hitchcock.
At a less glamorous level, there were prosaic but necessary functions
such as MI-8, which did signals interception and communications
security, and MI1b, which did cryptography—code breaking.

But who had even *heard* of MI6-3b? *What* was MI6-3b? Pondsford feared that if Eleanor failed at whatever she was doing, he might get the blame; if she succeeded, he would get no credit. He was reaching retirement age; one more promotion to major general would mean a useful addition to his pension and perhaps even an appropriate and imposing medal to impress the chaps at the golf club—he might even be asked to join the board.

In his youth in the previous war, the rank of brigadier had been a general officer's rank—brigadier general. But when Pondsford had finally crawled up the ranks to reach that level, the rank of brigadier general was reduced to merely brigadier, and the accoutrements and privileges of general rank were all stripped away so that he was little better than a jumped-up colonel. That one additional promotion was therefore critical to both his sense of status and his financial well-being.

Of course, as his wife had pointed out to him on numerous occasions, he could volunteer for something more visible, something more likely to ensure promotion and reward. He could request a transfer back to his old battalion, which was now fighting in the desert in North Africa, or out to the Far East, where it was only a question of time before the Japanese descended upon some hapless British possession.

But any such move would involve grave discomfort at the least and acute danger at the most. He thought it very possible—perhaps likely— that she might prefer to be a general's widow, with a general's widow's pension, rather than a live brigadier's wife.

Pondsford sent a babysitter to Malvern House, a retired naval officer named Crenshaw. It was Commander Crenshaw's official responsibility as the MI6-3b adjutant to take care of the administrative detritus that grows like mushrooms in the dank gloom of all government departments. His real mission, however, was to report regularly to Pondsford on what Eleanor was actually doing, or at least seeming to do. Pondsford was confident that, sooner or later, the endless stream of administrative paperwork flowing through Crenshaw's hands would reveal MI6-3b's true purpose. Just as dustbins and wastepaper baskets reveal evidence of last night's peccadilloes, MI6-3b's manifests and requisitions would reveal its hidden secrets.

But what was she doing? Who was she? Eleanor was a wing officer in the WAAF. She seemed very young to hold so high a rank (although the women's services did not really count for anything, of course, in a man's world—just a sop for their vanity to make them think they were important, to make the women keep quiet and work harder and accept far lower rates of pay, if truth were known). She wore the ribbon of the Military Medal on her tunic, which was very unusual. Crenshaw made discreet inquiries at WAAF headquarters but was told her personnel file had been mislaid. She was married—supposedly, although who knew or even cared these lax days?—to a fighter pilot, a squadron leader who arrived on a motorcycle each evening at dusk and accompanied by an extremely large black dog wearing a white scarf. He left each morning before dawn. Crenshaw was not surprised that his file was also inexplicably unavailable.

Eleanor had a team of intensely nonmilitary assistants with pimpled faces and thick eyeglasses who slouched around Malvern House and talked in unfathomable scientific gobbledygook. They were eggheads hoovered up from Cambridge and the Imperial College London. They occupied their off-duty hours playing bridge and chess and building model railways. They raced each other doing large jigsaw puzzles without looking at the picture. They complained that the *Times* crossword puzzle was far too simple.

They were listed in the personnel manifests as technical research officers, with commissions as acting temporary lieutenants (hostilities only) in the Royal Artillery, seconded to MI6. Crenshaw arranged for certain ladies to engage them in conversation at the local pub, but he learned only that the TROs had boorish manners and groping hands.

Malvern House hosted four disparate tribes: the TROs and their assistant WAAFs; a detachment of dispirited, excruciatingly bored soldiers from the 4th/5th Battalion, Suffolk Regiment, Territorial Army, who guarded the house and grounds; a growing tribe of even more dispirited administrative assistants who labored over Crenshaw's ever-expanding administrative files; and last and very least, a small cadre of emigres, refugees from Hitler's Third Reich, ragtag escapees from half of Europe who were officially classified as displaced persons—DPs for short—and were billeted in the former stables and eked out their existence as gardeners, handymen, cleaners, and cooks.

Early each morning, a dispatch rider on a Matchless G3 motor bicycle brought mysterious files to Malvern House. Eleanor and her team of TROs would disappear behind locked doors and absorb the contents of the files. But to what end? At 11 o'clock or so, the documents would be placed in a locked vault, and the team would retreat to a room with small desks and large blackboards that Crenshaw called the schoolroom. There, they would write incomprehensible mathematical formulae on the boards.

Eventually Eleanor or her principal assistant, Bramble, would emerge from the schoolroom and type a report, which would be carried away by a dispatch rider. After lunch the TROs might write more formulae or build model railway locomotives powered by small handmade electrical transformers that had a tendency to overheat and catch fire.

The TROs were, presumably, in charge of whatever it was that Malvern House existed to do, but they seemed to be subordinate to a WAAF flight officer named Jackson who was prim, proper, and completely ruthless. Although Crenshaw was a master at managing bureaucracies, he found himself losing ground against her. All the files, all the paperwork, all the reports created by the TROs were within her steely purview and locked securely beyond his reach. Even the DPs seemed to be at her command.

Crenshaw broke into Eleanor's office. There were no copies of her reports that he could find. Instead he could simply steal her typewriter ribbon and so re-create what she had typed, but, alas, she had removed it.

Crenshaw discreetly photographed the big blackboards filled with scribbled formulae and sent the film off to Brigadier Pondsford at MI-1. Pondsford made inquiries, but evidently the scribbles matched no known branch of science or mathematics.

Perhaps a key to the conundrum was that the dispatch riders were members of the Women's Royal Navy Service, the Wrens. Crenshaw had a minion follow one of the Matchless dispatch riders when she left Malvern House and was shocked to hear that Eleanor's report had been carried to the Cabinet Office beside 10 Downing Street, Churchill's official residence. The minion had to admit, to his deep chagrin, that the Wren was a far better rider, and he could only just keep up.

Crenshaw knew it was strongly rumored in intelligence circles that there was a secret cypher operation at Bletchley Park, somewhere near

Bedford and Luton, north of London, devoted to breaking Enigma and other German codes. Crenshaw concluded that Malvern House was a similar establishment, perhaps an offshoot of Bletchley Park. He told Pondsford that in the morning the dispatch riders brought copies of intercepted German naval Kriegsmarine radio signals and returned to Whitehall later in the day with the decoded results.

Pondsford did not question this conclusion. It was simply another example, in his opinion, of the sloppy civilian amateurism and moral decadence that was infecting the armed forces at every turn. At Bletchley Park, everyone genuflected over that disgusting chap Alan Turing, who should be sent to prison, in Pondsford's opinion, not given an important post entrusted with official government secrets. He'd heard that Turing had been to Princeton, in America, which probably explained a lot. He'd heard vaguely that Eleanor also had something to do with Princeton, but he lacked the energy to make inquiries. At Malvern House, it was bad enough that men had to defer to women, as if women were fit to fill positions of command.

How could you expect to win a war like that? The whole country was going to the dogs—or to the bitches, he chuckled to himself.

Q: You didn't like the intelligence world?

A: I did not. There were too many secrets, too many ugly things hiding under rocks.

Q: For example?

Eleanor stared at her visitor in horror.

"You did *what*?" she finally managed.

Her visitor, Henry Tizard, shifted uncomfortably in his chair.

"Everything was explicitly authorized by Mr. Churchill himself!"

Eleanor took a deep breath. As part of her ever-expanding access to secret information, Churchill had given instructions that she be briefed on secret military research and development programs. Her early days at Malvern House had been so busy with these reports and briefings that she had all but abandoned the model and its derivatives and delivered them into Bramble's and Cassius' hands.

"I want you to know what's going on," Churchill had said. "I want you to see inside the secret confines of the boffins' innermost research establishments and deepest laboratories, where what will be the modern world is being invented. I cannot ask you to predict the future if you don't know what might drive it."

She had been astounded by what she had learned and humbled by the intellectual powerhouses that had produced these ideas. There was the concept of an air-breathing, gasoline-fueled, rocket engine designed by an RAF officer named Whittle—a jet, he called it for short—far faster and many times more powerful than reciprocating propeller engines like the mighty Merlin. There was a magnetron capable of increasing the power of radar by a thousand times. There were secret explosives made of putty-like substances, gunsights that aimed where a moving enemy *would be* when you fired, and more designs and devices than she could imagine.

And there was a short, dense memorandum from a couple of DP scientists in Birmingham, of all people and all places, positing that uranium could be used to create a bomb one thousand times as powerful as TNT. The paper began by saying that the only defense against such a weapon would be to get one before one's enemy.

Let's see, she thought to herself. A Dornier 17 can carry about two thousand pounds of TNT explosive, for example, or—God help us— the equivalent of two million pounds, using the Frisch–Peierls uranium calculation.

She lit a cigarette. In spite of her best efforts, she needed the calming influence of tobacco to counter the stresses of this horrible MI6-3b job. Hitler would only need to send two or three Dorniers to destroy London and wipe it off the map, forcing Churchill to surrender; or, of course, for Churchill to bomb Berlin before Hitler could bomb London.

Whoever possessed such a weapon would become, instantly, the most powerful person in the world, in the entire history of the human race. Mythology was full of stories of super-powerful gods and heroes, of unstoppable weapons like Thor's mighty hammer or King Arthur's magical, unbreakable Excalibur or Zeus's all-powerful thunderbolt.

Such a weapon would level a city and destroy its inhabitants, just as Joshua's trumpets had knocked down the walls of Jericho and "utterly destroyed all that was in it," as the bible succinctly put it.

But now, here was her visitor, Henry Tizard, of the Aeronautical Research Committee, calmly telling her that he had, on the instructions of Winston Churchill, gone to America with a delegation of British scientists and given everything—*everything*—to the Americans, with nothing promised or committed in return. She couldn't believe it.

"Randall and Boot's cavity magnetron, Mr. Tizard?"

"Yes."

"Frank Whittle's turbojet?"

"Yes."

So now the Americans had the secret to accurate day and night navigation and the next generation of aircraft: in short, the future of the skies.

"Gyroscopic gunsights? Chain Home? Explosive 808? Curran's proximity fuse designs?"

"Yes."

She hesitated.

"The Frisch–Peierls memorandum?"

"Yes."

Q: But surely the Lend-Lease agreement included an exchange of British assets for American support?

A: The Lend-Lease Act didn't occur until the following year, and full cooperation on weapons development didn't occur until after Pearl Harbor. The truth is, I think, that Churchill didn't understand what he was giving away. In 1940, I think, he was just trying to woo Roosevelt with shiny objects.

Q: Did you discuss this with him?

A: Yes, but much later, when the Frisch–Peierls memorandum had evolved into the MAUD report and Tube Alloys.

Q: Once again, that's an area I want to explore, but first I want to finish the early days of MI6-3b, if we may.

A: Of course. Sorry . . .

TWENTY-EIGHT

Q: You've mentioned that your husband had been transferred out of 339 after the Battle of Britain and was working in aircraft development as a test pilot. Tell us a little about that.

A: Actually, there's a lot to tell. You see, one of the things I don't think people think about is that armed conflict is the ultimate clash of technologies. If both sides have the same technology, then there's a horrible stalemate, like the Western Front in the first war. The Cold War remained cold because the two sides had equal, self-cancelling ICBM technology, which made MAD work. But . . .

Q: I'm sorry. ICBM? MAD?

A: Oh, that's intercontinental ballistic missiles and mutually assured destruction, a doctrine of frozen stalemate.

Q: Thank you.

A: Anyway, if one side gains a technological advantage, say, for example, the introduction of the English yew longbow against French armored cavalry in the fifteenth century, the results can be dramatic. Or, in American terms, the repeating rifle of the US Cavalry, such as the Winchester 73, against the arrows and spears of the indigenous American Indians.

The war in the air over Europe seesawed back and forth as one side gained a technical advantage and then the other caught up or surpassed it. The Dowding system's technology combined with the air superiority of the Spitfire brought us victory in the Battle of Britain. But then Hitler switched to night bombing—the blitz—and we had no defensive technology to resist it. The pendulum swung in the Luftwaffe's favor. Then we developed airborne radar for the cannon-armed Beaufighter and GCI, and we were able to knock down the bombers, leading, in large part, to the end of the blitz.

Q: GCI?

A: Sorry. Ground-controlled interception. We developed better radars on the ground to see German bombers at night, and then we directed Beaufighters to the bombers until they were close enough to find them with their own airborne radars, even though they were still quite crude. Hitler lost only twenty aircraft at night in January 1941, but he lost almost two hundred in May. That's a tenfold improvement in the effectiveness of our technology in four months.

It was the same with fighters. The machine-gun-armed Spitfire Is and IIs had outperformed the 109Es in the Battle of Britain, but within a few months the Luftwaffe introduced the cannon-armed Focke-Wulf 190, and it completely overpowered the Spitfires. It took us over a year to catch up, with the widespread deployment of the Spitfire Mark IX.

Q: That's what you argued with Trafford Leigh-Mallory?

A: Exactly so. And on and on, all through the war, it was the same: one technology leapfrogging another and then being leapfrogged itself. It's a whole, dramatic story in its own right—why the Germans developed V1 and V2 rockets and the Allies didn't; why the poorly armored, poorly gunned American Sherman tanks were able to defeat the vastly superior Panzer Tigers; why the—but I digress.

Q: But that's another subject to which I'd like to return, if we may.

A: As you wish. Anyway, the specific technological competition early in 1941 was the ability of the German bombers to find their targets at night versus the ability of RAF fighters to find the bombers without being able to see them. Johnnie, my husband, worked on Beaufighter radar development, among other things.

Johnnie Shaux awoke with a start. He had been dozing in the unexpected luxury of a first-class railway carriage as an elderly tank engine pulled a decrepit passenger train from Birmingham up towards Derby. They were arriving in Litchfield, he saw; still a few miles to go. He sank back in his seat and let his mind wander.

What a difference a few short months had made! His new job as a test pilot and Eleanor had changed everything.

Park had transferred him out of Fighter Command and into the A&AEE, the Aeroplane and Armament Experimental Establishment. He was out of the crucible of daily battles against the 109s of Luftflotte II and into the relatively safe job of testing experimental aircraft and equipment, and out of the drama of forward 11 Group fighter stations on the Channel to the relative calm of a flight testing station in Suffolk. It was a chance to rediscover the joy of flying.

He had loved flying before the war. He had counted the minutes until he could climb into the cockpit of a Tiger Moth or a mighty Gladiator or even a tiny Avro 621—in fact, any aircraft at all—and escape into the sky. In particular he had savored the magical moment when an aircraft is not yet airborne but is ready to fly, waiting for the slightest twitch on the controls to release it, to cast off the shackles of mere gravity and soar into the aircraft's natural element.

The war had changed all that. Last year, in 1940, the Battle of France and the Battle of Britain had been exercises in brutality, turning the skies of England, France, and Belgium into slaughterhouses. Flying was to be feared, to be survived, and certainly not enjoyed. Fighter Command and the Luftwaffe had been like two punch-drunk prizefighters, Johnnie thought, battering each other to pieces, too strong to surrender but too weak to win—until the middle of September, when Luftflotte II had failed to answer the bell. As Eleanor would say, 11 Group had not won the Battle of Britain; Luftflotte II had lost it.

In the dark days of the Battle of Britain, he had awakened every morning expecting that day would be his last, and that expectation had almost been proved right so often that he'd lost count. He had survived, but many, many others had not; he had watched as they had been blown up in midair, or crashed into the unyielding earth, or been burned to death like fiery tapers in the sky, or drowned in the chill waters of the Channel. And some of them had been members of the Luftwaffe, young men just like him, sent to their deaths by his thumb on the trigger button.

In those days the moment of preflight had not been a moment of exultation but the opening act, the prologue, of a violent tragedy.

Out of the front edge of his window, Shaux watched the tank engine slowly dragging the train out of Litchfield, burping smoke and steam. Acrid fumes drifted back through his window. He lit a cigarette and settled back into the cushions and wished he could get a cup of tea.

Froggie Potter had almost made it to the end. It still ached, like an old wound on a cold day, to remember that Froggie had been killed in a freak accident on the ground. He should have been a squadron skipper by now, rising through the ranks despite his youth—he was simply too good not to rise. He should have been playing cricket and playing his saxophone and walking out with the prettiest girls in the neighborhood and drinking more than his share of pints, bitter.

Instead he was buried—what little the ground crews had found of him was buried—beneath an old yew tree somewhere towards the back of a village churchyard in Kent, a little off the beaten path where the lawn mowers didn't reach and the thistles and dandelions grew unchallenged. Digby had purchased a little marble statue of a frog playing a saxophone, and it sat at the foot of Froggie's grave. Shaux had not attended the funeral—he just couldn't—but he had visited the churchyard a couple of months ago and swore he'd heard, somewhere in the treetops, the sound of a saxophone playing a mournful blues song. He hadn't taken Charlie with him for fear of upsetting him.

But all of that was long ago, locked away, banished forever. Since his transfer he was now employed to explore the endlessly fascinating questions of why some aircraft fly better than others, why some slip easily through the sky and others struggle, and why some engines purr sweetly on, come what may, and why others hesitate, knock, overheat, or simply die.

His primary task was supposed to be test-flying developmental upgrades of the Westland Whirlwind, a small experimental heavy fighter powered by two Rolls-Royce Peregrine engines. But the need to develop effective radar to combat bombers at night had taken priority, and he had spent endless hours flying Beaufighters, testing version after version of Airborne Interception radar, until finally they installed the AI Mk IV version and—voilà!—they could actually find another aircraft in the sky. Suddenly, dramatically, the Luftwaffe could no longer fly with impunity at night, skulking in the darkness, and the long agony of the London blitz—seventy nights without respite or mercy—could soon be broken.

Where were they now? Walton-on-Trent. They chugged through without stopping.

The Whirlwind was a potentially great idea, Shaux mused.

In a single-engined Hurricane or Spitfire, everything had to be jammed into the fuselage in a line—the engine, the fuel tank, the pilot, and all the other bits and pieces. The wings were full of machine guns and ammunition belts, outboard to keep clear of the propeller blades. But in the Whirlwind, the engines and the fuel tanks were in the wings, leaving room for a ferocious armament of four 20-millimeter cannons in the nose, with plenty of room for the cockpit and everything else behind. Four cannons located closely together directly in line with the pilot's gunsight, with plenty of space for ammunition belts, meant that the Whirlwind could blow any Luftwaffe aircraft out of the sky.

Johnnie loved the idea—the principle—of the Whirlwind, a petite, saucy-looking aircraft with a high tail and a vicious sting in its nose. The wings and chubby little engine housings were low-slung and far forward. The pilot sat high on the fuselage in a bubble canopy offering a superb field of vision. The Whirlwind was just forty-five feet wide and thirty-two feet long, only slightly bigger than a Hurricane but with much more punch and power. With its upright tail and deadly armament, Johnnie would have called it a Scorpion, but there was doubtless a naming committee somewhere in Whitehall that decided such things. Hurricane, Tempest, Tornado, Whirlwind, Typhoon . . . he'd hate to have to pilot an aircraft named "Squall" or "Gale."

He had always thought of some aircraft as masculine—the 109, for example—and some as feminine; the Whirlwind was definitely feminine.

But, unfortunately, the Peregrine-powered Whirlwind was not a successful aircraft. The Rolls-Royce Peregrines lacked power and over-heated far too often, so they could only be flown at lower revs and lower altitudes. The engines were based on old-fashioned design principles from the mid-1920s, and they had been starved of development resources by the engineers at Rolls-Royce, who—correctly, in Shaux's opinion—were giving top priority to the mighty Merlin.

And while the Whirlwind was an aerodynamically superior airframe, it was made of complicated and costly materials—the Whirlwind used three times as much alloyed materials as a Spitfire, making it very expensive and time-consuming to build.

In sum, Shaux considered the Peregrine-powered Whirlwind to be a good idea but not good enough. It reminded him of the underpowered Boulton Paul Defiant, an aircraft similar to a Hurricane but with a separate rotating gun turret behind the cockpit—also a good idea, but not good enough. Shaux had flown Defiants against the Luftwaffe for several months early in the war and considered himself lucky to have survived.

Worse yet, Rolls-Royce was in the process of taking two V-12 Peregrines and converting them into a single X-24 engine called a Vulture by taking a second Peregrine, inverting it, and adding it to a common crankshaft. Some poor bastards, Shaux thought, would actually have to fly aircraft that relied on such a crazy idea. The "Vulture," he thought. What a name!

He hoped that the Whirlwind, the Peregrine, and the Vulture would all be abandoned. In complete contrast, he had flown a new experimental aircraft he judged to be vastly superior—the Merlin-powered wooden-bodied De Havilland Mosquito. On his first flight, the hair on the back of his neck had stood up when it catapulted itself into the air. In fact, the Mosquito was so good, so balanced, and so naturally *right* that it had shocked him—had tempted him into a great blasphemy: it could be even better than a Spitfire!

But he feared that the bureaucratic inertia of the various bodies involved—the Air Ministry, the Ministry of Aircraft Production, the

A&AEE, the RAF, Rolls-Royce, Westland, and the inscrutable and omniscient Treasury—would not make obvious decisions easily. He had learned that facts and figures counted for little in the world of aircraft development, while committees of men who seldom or never flew counted for a great deal. He was on his way to a committee meeting now; it would be interesting to see what transpired.

He roused himself and lit another cigarette. They had reached Burton upon Trent—still a way to go. The rain seemed to be getting heavier the farther north he traveled.

Despite the rain, this was a welcome and exciting break from the routine of testing aircraft. Every day he flew five or six test flights— usually to assess slight modifications to existing production versions of this equipment or that—and almost all his flights were without incident. He would work his way through a list of drills and then return to the ground to fill out long reports. The only occasional excitement was being shot at by an inexperienced antiaircraft flak battery that mistook him for an enemy aircraft—he sometimes wondered if Grimsby had been captured and had become National Socialist Grimsby or if the Grimsby Home Guard had joined the Axis powers.

TWENTY-NINE

Shaux stood and stretched. He had the window open a crack, but now the rain was managing to find its way in, and he closed it reluctantly.

It would be at least fifteen minutes before they reached Derby. The engine chugged around the next bend, burping and wheezing; it wasn't the engine's fault they were late, Shaux thought, it should have been put out to pasture ages ago. Like so many other things—and people—the demands of the war were stretching the railways to their limits.

He would be late for his meeting at Rolls-Royce; he wondered if they would wait for him and bet they would not. Government committees, he had come to learn, had only a limited tolerance for facts and those that bear them. He rehearsed his report in his mind: the continuing weaknesses plaguing the Peregrine engine and therefore the continuing unreliability of the Whirlwind as an operation fighter, in sharp contrast to the vastly superior Merlin-powered Mosquito, and therefore his recommendation that the Whirlwinds and Peregrines be discontinued.

But all of that—the powers that be, the committees, the aircraft, the engines, and indeed the war itself—seemed irrelevant in comparison to Eleanor.

He had known her for almost three years at Oxford, seeing her almost every day. She had been a close friend and companion but never more. She seemed to be one of those girls who just magically seem to attract men without trying, and Shaux had been routinely shouldered aside by the onrushing stampede of all the men she had attracted. His role in her life, he supposed, was to provide quiet interludes, moments of relaxation. He had been like a comfortable pair of old slippers—no, better yet, he had been a faithful dog, a trusted companion requiring no effort, always happy just to be there, grateful to be taken for granted. She had never actually patted his head or given him a dog biscuit, he thought, but she had a tiny lopsided almost-smile that achieved the same effect.

They parted ways. He had returned to the RAF after Oxford, and she had gone off to Paris. When war was declared a few months later, he had been sent to Holland, and she had volunteered for the WAAF.

Joining Park in 11 Group in Uxbridge, she had made her great intellectual leap—that the war in the air could be modeled in mathematical formulae and that the model could be used on a heuristic and stochastic basis to project possible future results—seemingly out of the blue. The idea had occurred to no one before, but once she had proposed it, it suddenly seemed blindingly obvious. Of course you could model a battle as it happened, in its midst! Of course one could construct a branch of calculus to do so! Of course you could measure comparative strengths and weaknesses and advantages and disadvantages and project them into the future!

The mythical Greek goddess Athena was said not to have been born but to have leapt fully armed from the forehead of her father Zeus, ready for battle, Shaux remembered. Eleanor's model, in similar fashion, seemed to have leapt, fully expressed and proven, from Eleanor's forehead. Her formulae were like a symphony by Beethoven, or a Spitfire, or a poem by Yeats—things that were self-evidently right, beyond question. Of course!

Suddenly Eleanor was a major contributor to war planning at the highest levels, with a complete secret government department being formed around her. She was no longer just a protégé of Park but of Winston Churchill himself.

But all that was nothing in comparison to her next volte-face; she had changed from being his good friend to being his ardent lover. He had no idea why, and he did not want or dare to ask her. Just like her mathematical model, it was a self-contained miracle, sui generis and complete unto itself.

During the desperate fighting of the Battle of France and the Battle of Britain, before her conversion, he had tried to inoculate himself against the probability of death by building—as best he could—a stoic indifference to his own survival. After all, he had thought, he'd never have Eleanor, and no other woman could ever compare, and he was therefore destined to a long and arid bachelorhood, so what was the point of living? Some other man would share her moments of elation and despair, the quiet intimacy of their humdrum domestic existence, her tiny lopsided almost-smile, and the secrets of her bed. In which case, for Shaux the years to come, as Yeats had said in his poem, would be a waste of breath.

Now, even though he had magically become that man, even as he luxuriated in the heat of her passion, he tried to inoculate himself, to convince himself that it couldn't last, that one day she would move on to someone else, perhaps leaving him with an apologetic smile but leaving him nonetheless.

Perhaps her intellectual brilliance and her abrupt emotional changes stemmed from some sort of deep-rooted imbalance. Aristotle had said that the greatest artists of his time alternated between creative mania and the coils of melancholia. In modern times Vincent van Gogh, for example, went from artistic brilliance one day to despair the next, and back again.

Van Gogh had chopped off his ear. Eleanor had taken Johnnie to her bed. Perhaps they were simply two examples of the same kind of self-destructive psychotic catharsis.

Or there was another possible explanation. She had studied the battle in the skies in theory, and she had analyzed the dangers the pilots faced—as abstract statistics. Then she, like everyone else, had been immersed in the wartime propaganda that turned mediocre pilots such as himself into mythical heroes, like the Spartans of Greek mythology—that Churchill had ennobled as "the Few." Then she had come face to face with the only 11 Group pilot she actually knew, himself, and, voilà: she had convinced herself she loved him passionately and it was her patriotic duty to take him to her bed. Churchill had said that "never have so many owed so much to so few." Well, perhaps she felt she should start to make a repayment of the debt on behalf of all Englishwomen.

He didn't care: he had suspended all disbelief and reveled in her attention. RAF Martlesham Heath, in Suffolk, where A&AEE was based, was only twenty miles from Aldeburgh, where Eleanor presided over her secret MI6-3b group in Malvern House. He had purchased a 1937 Sunbeam Model 9 motorcycle with a mighty 600-cc motor that could convey him that distance in less than half an hour. The motorcycle had a sidecar that was the perfect size for Charlie. The ground crews maintained the Sunbeam in perfect order and, miraculously, the fuel tank was always full.

He found he could finish the day's test-flying, write up his reports and logs, bathe, eat dinner, and be at Malvern House by seven o'clock or so. By ten he and Eleanor would fall into an exhausted sleep. Charlie slept outside their door, ready to repel any invader who threatened their sanctuary. Shaux could get up before dawn, and he and Charlie could be back at Martlesham in time for breakfast.

Charlie still had a somewhat worried air, and Shaux knew he feared that one day—perhaps today—Shaux would fly away and never come back, just like Jacques and Froggie. But there was no question that Charlie was far more relaxed and cheerful since Shaux had started talking to him in French, the language he had learned as a puppy.

"Allons nous, mon brave," he said to Charlie each morning, and Charlie would bound down the stairs, pause briefly to baptize the new day, and then vault into the sidecar like an Olympic champion. The whole contraption would shake under the impact.

Thus, he thought, after the grim days of 1940, 1941 was turning out to be a wonderful year. He flew every day without anyone trying to shoot him out of the sky, and Eleanor awaited him each evening. He could imagine no more perfect an existence.

John Dryden's poem fitted his mood perfectly: *"Tomorrow, do thy worst, for I have lived today."* Perhaps he had found a poem that could trump even Yeats.

They were only twenty-two, still less than two years out of Oxford. Their lives were ahead of them—the war permitting. In the meantime, unless and until she moved on, she had taken their separate lives and made them one.

The orphanage in which he had grown up had single beds, of course, and only boys. He was aware of girls only in the vaguest manner and certainly had no knowledge of the differences between the sexes and the various purposes to which those differences could be employed.

In the rough-and-tumble of an RAF barracks, when he was fifteen, he was finally told the great secret of the sexes and was persecuted endlessly for being unaware of it, but there were still no actual females in the vicinity, and it was not until he was eighteen and at Oxford that he had his first real contacts with girls.

Eleanor was also studying mathematics, and she had asked him to lend her a textbook. She had looked at him and he had jumped, as if he had been shocked by an electric current. He had never before stared into a girl's eyes or vice versa. She had thanked him with a little half-smile, just in the left corner of her mouth, needing no words to convey her meaning, and he had been captivated on the spot. They had gradually become friends—after all, she needed a pair of slippers—and he had been enslaved ever since; she, in the meantime, was too knee-deep in suppliant men to notice him as a possible suitor.

She had quickly become a meteor, blazing across the Oxford skies, while he, a dim dwarf star, had plodded in her wake.

And so it had remained until just a few months ago, when she had suddenly and inexplicably turned to him.

But all was not well.

He had always thought of her as the center of the crowd—her extensive family, her friends, the cohorts of admirers, and, more recently, her growing staff and her obligations and commitments in Whitehall. But to her telling, her family was a nightmare to be avoided, her friends were no more than acquaintances, the admirers were wasp-like pests, and MI6-3b was like a vast quicksand into which she was sinking without hope.

He knew she was increasingly uncomfortable in her new role, partly because her Red Tape model was becoming overstretched and expectations were becoming too high and partly because what she considered to be the objective results of mathematics were becoming policy footballs to be kicked back and forth by contending teams of Whitehall cognoscenti.

So, for example, to Eleanor it was a simple fact that the new Luftwaffe Focke-Wulf 190 fighter could outperform Spitfire Mark Vs. Therefore, she reasoned, sending Spitfires against 190s was foolish and dangerous. But that ran into RAF official dogma, which stated that it was necessary to send Spitfires over France, where the 190s waited for them, although the reasons for this necessity were never quite explained or justified.

Sometimes—his most wicked thought—he hoped he wouldn't survive the war. In these straitened circumstances, they could overlook all the normal, humdrum decisions in life and their consequences—where to live, what jobs to take, whether to take on the burden of a mortgage, when to start a family, and so forth—because normal decisions were suspended for the duration of the war. They weren't in charge of their own lives. But, once the war was over, and they could retake command of their destiny, would she again see him simply as a pair of slippers, and if so, of the safe and welcome kind, or the boring, threadbare kind?

And what would postwar England be like, particularly if under German occupation?

Eleanor believed that England would lose, unless Hitler made a truly colossal misjudgment or unless America entered the war. The cold logic of her model dictated that their survival depended on both those events coming true—both the mistake to weaken Germany and the American intervention to rescue England.

She thought that Hitler was capable of such an error—she expected him to invade Russia—but that the Americans were far too sensible to find themselves at war. After all, Europeans had been slaughtering each other for hundreds—thousands—of years and would probably continue to do so; there wasn't much America could do to stop them, and there was little benefit for America in trying to stop them.

American forces had arrived late in the previous war, dragged in during the last few months, but had suffered brutally at Belleau Wood, Château-Thierry, and other slaughterhouses. Americans were generous and magnanimous, but would they really want to rescue the Europeans from themselves a second time in twenty years, at such great cost?

Shaux did not doubt her analysis. It made his own efforts with Whirlwinds and Beaufighters and Mosquitos seem inconsequential in comparison. It made the 11 Group deaths he had witnessed, and the Luftflotte II deaths he had caused, utterly trivial and irrelevant. It made her model pointless—an intellectual artifact created by the losing side.

THIRTY

Shaux stared out of the window as the train pulled slowly into Derby station. The cloud base was less than a thousand feet, and the only colors he could see were variations of gray. He was very conscious of the fact that he always checked the skies for 109s whenever he went outside, even just getting off a train. He wondered how long the reflex would continue—perhaps for months or even years?

There were no taxis or buses outside the station. He turned up his raincoat collar against the remorseless drizzle and set off to walk a mile or so to the buildings housing the Rolls-Royce engineering department. By the time he reached them, he was soaked.

The meeting was an official interdepartmental committee formed to evaluate the future direction of the Whirlwind. There would be engineers from Rolls-Royce, designers from Westland, and a coterie of civil servants representing the various branches of government involved. His role was to offer an assessment of the latest, most advanced versions of the fighter from a pilot's perspective.

He was torn between his interest in and admiration for Rolls-Royce, the finest engineers and motorcar manufacturers in the world, on the one hand and his pessimistic view of committees on the other. It was as if he were visiting Michelangelo's studio to attend a meeting of art critics.

The meeting room was too big for the gathering and had a dusty, Dickensian feel, with exposed brick walls and ancient oil-stained floorboards of random widths and lengths. Shaux guessed this had once been part of an eighteenth-century cotton mill. He had been right: he had predicted he would be the last to arrive and that the meeting would already be in progress—the air was thick with tobacco smoke, and the table was littered with teacups.

He took off his cap and raincoat and added them to several others on an elderly coat rack behind the door; a puddle was forming beneath it.

"My name is Blackwell," said one of the civil servants, coming forward. He had a tobacco pipe clenched between his teeth, mournful eyes, and a droopy mustache. "I'm from the Ministry of Aircraft Production."

As he shook Blackwell's hand, Shaux saw the man's eyes drop to his pilot's wings and medal ribbon, and Shaux cringed inwardly. Eleanor always said that men look at a woman's chest before looking at her face; Shaux felt the same thing with men inspecting his ribbon.

"Yes, sir, you're right," he groaned silently. "That really is a DFC and bar. My, my! One of the Few! A Battle of Britain ace! A hero of the skies!"

Shaux only wore his ribbon out of respect for Harry Pound, who had recommended it shortly before he died. The bar or second award, given to him by Keith Park, reminded him of Eleanor's astonishing bravery in climbing into a Defiant fighter to fly against Messerschmitt 110s.

The other attendees greeted him in turn, each covertly repeating the scrutiny of his medal ribbon. One of them was from Westland, the Whirlwind designer and manufacturer, and two were from Rolls-Royce. There was an elderly air marshal from the Air Council, a civil servant from the Air Ministry, another from the Treasury, and two from the Ministry of Supply. Everyone seemed very deferential to the Treasury man; he, after all, held the purse strings. More tea was served—of course, Shaux thought, no meeting could proceed until tea had been served—and Blackwell called them to order.

The engineers and civil servants occupied one side of a long table. The Rolls-Royce engineers wore white coverall jackets, like doctors, as badges of honor, an array of fountain pens and slide rules projecting from the pockets. There was a single chair for Shaux facing them. He was reminded of his viva voce exams in college.

"Gentlemen, let us continue to our next agenda item," Blackwell said, confirming Shaux's guess that the meeting had started well before his arrival. "As you know, Squadron Leader Shaux has been testing the Whirlwind. He's been testing modifications advised by Westland and Rolls-Royce as well as suggestions from 263 Squadron, where the Whirlwind is already in operational service. Squadron Leader Shaux's reports are before us."

Blackwell picked up a manila folder, and there was a general shuffling of papers around the table. The engineers seemed to have a defensive air about them, as if they had read his reports and found them too critical.

"Would you be so kind as to present your opinions, Squadron Leader?"

Shaux felt as if he were about to be cross-examined by the Spanish Inquisition, as if Blackwell had asked, "Would you begin by confessing your most grievous heresies?"

"Thank you, sir," Shaux said. "Gentlemen, I've grouped my thoughts into four areas of concern, if that's helpful."

"Please proceed."

Shaux squared his shoulders and launched into his report. He realized he didn't have to read it: he knew it verbatim.

"Thank you, sir. The first is the practical matter that you make two versions of the Peregrine that spin in opposite directions in a twin-engined aircraft, eliminating the effects of torque. Several Luftwaffe aircraft do the same with Daimler-Benz and BMW engines. It may be a good idea in theory, but it turns out to be a maintenance and inventory nightmare. Rather than making the entire engine contra-rotating, I suggest you could—"

"That's an RAF ground crew training problem, surely," interrupted a balding engineer towards the end of the table. "It's just a matter of your chaps knowing the difference between left and right. There's nothing wrong with the Peregrines. Your chaps will just have to get cracking and turn it up a notch or two."

"We've had Peregrines delivered from Rolls-Royce with back-to-front parts, sir," Shaux said.

"Rubbish!" the balding engineer snorted. "All our engines are fully inspected before they leave Rolls-Royce."

Shaux had no wish for acrimony, but he could not let the dedicated, hardworking RAF ground crews be maligned.

"It's been documented, sir," he said. "Perhaps your inspection chaps could turn it up a notch or two as well."

"That's an outrageous thing to—" the balding engineer began, but Blackwell intervened.

"Let's move on," he said, with a frosty glare at Shaux, as if he were to blame.

"The Peregrine has a tendency to overheat, as I've detailed in my reports," Shaux said. "I know you've been working on this for quite some time. Unfortunately, the pressurized cooling system simply isn't efficient enough, and . . ."

"Be specific," snapped another white-coated engineer. Evidently Rolls-Royce engineers did not take kindly to criticism. "What overheats?"

"Well, the gudgeon pins, for example, sir, will overheat and can warp out of true at—"

"We are reengineering the gudgeon pins, as well as other components you've mentioned in your reports. We are modifying the alloys. You'll just have to be patient. Rome wasn't built in a day and neither is an aero engine or, indeed, an aircraft for it to power."

There was a ripple of nods down the table and even a sotto voce "Hear, hear."

"Sir, with respect, I just don't think—"

"Squadron Leader," Bald Head interrupted him. "The Peregrine-powered Whirlwind is already in production and in squadron service. It has been accepted by the RAF, if not, apparently, by you. I'm sure all these, um, teething troubles, will get sorted out; in any case, all these problems will be solved in the new Vulture."

Shaux said nothing, and Bald Head stared at him.

"Come, come, come, Squadron Leader, you don't like the Vulture, either?"

Shaux groaned inwardly. It seemed that aeronautical engineers were no different from the rest of humanity. Perhaps he didn't want to work at Rolls-Royce after all.

"Are there any of our products that rise to your exacting standards?" Bald Head raised his eyebrows in an evident attempt at sarcastic humor, and a titter ran down the table just as the nods of approval had done a moment ago. Shaux decided he definitely did not want to work at Rolls-Royce.

"Sir, I'm a mathematician, not an engineer," Shaux said, as deferentially as he could muster. "In mathematics, there are limits beyond which functions—trend lines, if you will—cannot go. Perhaps the same is true in engineering. Perhaps the Peregrine is pushing the Kestrel beyond its limits. If the Peregrine is reaching its limits, the Vulture is also unlikely to succeed."

"But . . . ," said Bald Head and Westland together, but Shaux was determined to make his point.

"I've flown Merlins for hundreds of hours. They've never let me down. Every few months you come up with a new version that's even better. And they're all totally reliable. Clearly the Merlin hasn't reached its limits. So, I'm just suggesting, with due respect, that the Merlin still has enormous potential, while the Peregrine apparently does not."

"There's absolutely nothing wrong with the P—" Bald Head interrupted.

"The Merlin is, in my opinion, the finest fluid-cooled engine ever built."

"Well, then . . . ," Blackwell began, but Shaux continued.

"Unfortunately the Peregrine, on the other hand, is prone to failure."

"We need the Peregrine to power the Whirlwind," the engineer for Westland said.

"The Peregrine is based on the Kestrel, a wonderful and highly successful engine but by 1920s standards. The Peregrine can't disguise its pedigree."

"All that's irrelevant; we need the Peregrine to power the Whirlwind," the Westland engineer repeated, as if Shaux had failed to grasp his point.

"I'm not sure we need the Whirlwind, sir."

The Westland man was almost struck dumb by this blasphemy, but not quite.

"We need a light two-engine fighter bomber. Everyone knows that."

"Yes, sir," Shaux said. "Preferably one that uses Merlins, like the Beaufighter."

"Or the Vulture," Blackwell interceded.

"With due respect, sir," Shaux said, afraid he was exacerbating an argument, "I think if Rolls-Royce can't make a single V-12 Peregrine work, it certainly won't be able to make an X-24 version work."

Bald Head looked as if Shaux had just reached across and punched him on the nose, but Shaux was determined to get his point across.

"The Beau is a wonderful aircraft, but it's not really fast enough—it's too heavy. A lighter aircraft with two Merlins instead of two Peregrines would be excellent."

"There is no suitable airframe," Blackwell retorted.

"Yes, sir, there is: the Mosquito."

"Surely you jest?" Blackwell did not disguise his sneer. "The wooden wonder?"

Shaux sighed inwardly. The meeting was descending into a shouting match, and he feared it was all his fault.

The door swung open abruptly, and a burly man entered. The engineers scrambled to their feet, and Shaux guessed he was someone important.

"My name's Hives," he said, shaking Shaux's hand. "I work for Rolls-Royce."

Shaux judged him to be in his midfifties. He was wearing a brown coverall work coat with several pens and small tools jammed in his pockets and even a stethoscope around his neck, like a doctor. He had an open, no-nonsense air, and Shaux took to him immediately.

Hives wasted no time in getting to the point.

"I've read your reports, Squadron Leader. How many times has the Peregrine malfunctioned to the point of failure while you've been flying it?"

"I have a list, sir," Shaux said, reaching into his briefcase.

"How many times altogether, Squadron Leader?"

"Twelve, sir, including a double failure."

"Double failure?" Bald Head asked. "What is a so-called double failure?"

"At five thousand feet, the starboard engine overheated, sir, and began emitting heavy black smoke. I shut it down. We subsequently identified a supercharger failure."

Bald Head grunted.

"Then, as I was returning to Martlesham, the port engine began to overheat."

"Began? How did you know?" Bald Head demanded. "What did the temperature gauge indicate?"

"I don't know—I didn't look at it, sir."

"Then how could you possibly know the engine was overheating without looking at the gauge?"

"I relied on the flames coming out of the engine, sir."

"That's enough!" Hives said, and Shaux suspected he was trying to swallow a chuckle. "Gentlemen, I think I have the information necessary to make a recommendation."

Hives stood, and the room rose with him. Blackwell began to speak, but Hives cut him off.

"Thank you, gentlemen," he said. "Mr. Shaux, I'd appreciate a moment of your time."

Suddenly the gathering was over, and Shaux found Hives leading him away. Shaux wondered who he was, exactly, but for some strange reason didn't feel he could ask.

"Sorry about that, Mr. Shaux," he said, pulling out a tobacco pipe and standing under an eave to avoid the drizzle. "And I'm sorry that chaps like you have to fly aircraft powered by problems just because the engineers don't want to admit failure."

"The Whirlwind is an almost, sir, just like the Defiant was. It's hard to acknowledge it's not quite good enough."

"Well said," Hives grunted. "I'll mention your comment to Wilfrid Freeman. What do you think of the Vulture?"

"I haven't flown it, sir. But reliability is closely related to simplicity, so each new wrinkle creates another opportunity for failure. Taking two problematic V-12 Peregrines and combining them into an X-24 single engine seems very problematic indeed."

Hives pondered for a moment.

"I've had the pleasure—I think the privilege—of working on our aero engines for twenty-five years or so. I've managed seventeen types, and each type has had dozens of versions. Of all those, just three have been truly successful, and therefore fourteen have not. A truly successful engine, like the Merlin, is the exception; the good-but-not-good-enough, like the Peregrine, is the rule. Unfortunately, some engineers become so wedded to a good-but-not-good-enough design that they just can't let it go."

He knocked out his pipe on a window ledge as they strolled past it.

"Let me ask you something else, Squadron Leader: The day both Peregrines failed, one after the other, and caught on fire, why didn't you bail out? Why keep flying?"

"Well, sir, it's always better to get the engines back on the ground in one piece, if possible, so they could be examined. Besides . . ."

Shaux stopped.

"Besides what, Mr. Shaux?"

"I'm paid to fly, not bail out, that's all."

Hives seemed about to reply, but simply smiled, shook his hand, and turned away.

THIRTY-ONE

Q: In the aftermath of the Battle of Britain, Trafford Leigh-Mallory, Park's bitterest opponent, replaced Park and was subsequently promoted time and again. Were you still in 11 Group when he took over?

A: No, I was already gone. I had transferred to MI6-3b.

Q: But you did encounter Leigh-Mallory again?

A: I did. But let me make something clear. It's now fashionable among military historians to classify Leigh-Mallory as the bad guy. But we have to remember that he was killed in 1944 in a flying accident, and he never wrote his memoir. His critics were free to criticize him in their memoirs without rebuttal, as it were.

In my view he was just trapped into conventional thinking that dictated using very large formations, whereas Park understood intuitively that small formations were much more effective.

Churchill once said that he thought history would be kind to Churchill, because he intended to write it himself. It's one of my favorite Churchillisms. Leigh-Mallory never had a chance to write his own history.

Q: But you didn't like Leigh-Mallory, did you?

A: No, I didn't, but I was concerned with results, not feelings. His policies were unsuccessful.

Q: The failure of the Big Wing?

A: Yes, and the failure of the rhubarbs.

Q: Did you say "rhubarbs," Dame Eleanor?

A: I did. Rhubarbs were fighter sweeps over France, conducted by 11 Group after Leigh-Mallory took over late in 1940. I crossed swords with Leigh-Mallory the following spring, the spring of 1941. Churchill had asked me to analyze Leigh-Mallory's strategy of fighter raids— rhubarbs—over France.

Q: This was part of your job at the MI6-3b group?

A: Indeed it was. There was a concern that Leigh-Mallory's sweeps were too expensive . . .

The underground bomb shelters holding the Cabinet War Rooms were buried deep and ran, like the catacombs of ancient Rome, beneath the stately government buildings above them. They were crudely fashioned from concrete and steel beams and zigzagged through the foundations in a haphazard manner, wherever there was room for a corridor or an office. Telephone and electrical cables hung in festoons from the ceilings. Naked light bulbs blazed harshly at inadequate intervals. The air, thick with stale tobacco smoke, was laced with the pervasive evidence of inadequate bathroom facilities multiplied by inadequate ventilation.

Even the largest room was hopelessly overcrowded. Churchill sat with some of his inner council and senior officers of the armed forces, gazing at Eleanor across a pile of report folders—her reports, she realized, seeing their red covers.

"Now, Wing Officer," he rumbled, "I have read your reports with considerable interest. You are not afraid to take . . . shall we say, unconventional positions."

Eleanor did not know what to say and therefore said nothing.

"We are gathered to consider one of your recent findings," he continued. "I refer to your recent analysis of RAF fighter sweeps into France, Holland, and Belgium—sweeps, I might add, under the direction of Air Marshal Leigh-Mallory."

"Yes, sir," Eleanor said.

Churchill was wreathed in cigar smoke, as if he were smoldering. Anthony Eden, handsome and erudite, the foreign secretary and, she'd heard it said, Churchill's political enforcer, appeared to be appraising her, but for what purpose she chose not to imagine—her mother had warned her long ago never to trust men in their forties with impeccably groomed hair. The senior service officers, Trafford Leigh-Mallory among them, glared at her with ill-disguised hostility. These officers, she realized, had built their careers and reputations on being experts in their various forms of warfare, and they clearly considered it absurd, as well as threatening, that Churchill would waste his time—and theirs— on the opinions of a mere slip of a girl.

There had been no introductions; she had no idea who some of these men were. If they were friends of Leigh-Mallory, she was in for a difficult morning. Their stares made her feel as if she were a specimen of an inferior species under a microscope. She took a deep breath.

"Sir, let me preface my remarks by reminding you of the mathematical principle upon which our research is based."

"Namely?" Churchill asked.

"Our objective, at both a tactical and at a strategic level, is not to lose. The side that does not lose can survive to win."

"Claptrap!" Leigh-Mallory snorted in derision. "Academic hogwash!" He spoke sotto voce but with the clear intention of being heard. One of his neighbors chuckled.

"Well, sir, with respect . . . ," she began.

"Prime Minister, this is sophistry!" Leigh-Mallory interrupted. "Flimflam and flapdoodle! The purpose of fighting is to win. We must carry the fight to the enemy. The best defense is a good offense, as someone-or-other said, or words to that effect. Why are we wasting our time on wordplay and nonsense? Why are we listening to some little . . . ?"

He stopped himself but no doubt everyone knew he meant "some little girl"—or worse. The same neighbor—or perhaps it was another one, who knew?—murmured, "Hear, hear."

Churchill did not respond. Eleanor knew she would have to fight for herself.

"George Washington," Eleanor said.

"What?" Leigh-Mallory asked, nonplussed.

"You didn't know who coined that phrase, sir. It was George Washington."

She saw that Leigh-Mallory was inflating himself in fury; she saw the other senior officers were shocked by her insolence; she saw Anthony Eden smirk. She knew this meeting was already a disaster; Leigh-Mallory would never permit a reasoned discussion of his tactics. All she could hope for was that Churchill would see through Leigh-Mallory's bluster. She plowed on.

"With respect, sir, not losing is the essential antecedent premise for winning."

"What—," Leigh-Mallory began, but Eleanor overrode him.

"As an example, we didn't lose the Battle of Britain; the Luftwaffe did. They made a series of strategic and tactical blunders that allowed us to shoot down large numbers of their aircraft, even though they heavily outnumbered us, even though they were better trained and equally well equipped, and even though they were within a few days—sometimes a few hours—of victory."

"What—"

"Their errors and blunders led to their defeat. They lost through their own stupidity. We, in the meantime, made no fatal errors, did not lose, and therefore survived until they lost. Therefore we won."

Leigh-Mallory was a large man and seemed to be becoming increasingly belligerent.

"What makes you an expert on the Battle of Britain, may I ask?"

"I was 11 Group AOC staff, sir."

He peered at her closely.

"You worked for Keith Park?"

"I did."

"Oh, I see," Leigh-Mallory said. His tone was one iota short of an open sneer. "Are you that mathematician girl he kept hanging around?

Well, Miss, Miss, Whomever, Park was relieved of command, and I run 11 Group now. Therefore—"

This time Churchill intervened.

"Mrs. Shaux developed the mathematical model that led to her predictions. She correctly predicted the start of the blitz, and she correctly predicted the outcome of the battle."

"Guesswork," Leigh-Mallory muttered.

"Now she leads the team that sends in the estimates of enemy intentions and actions."

"The red intelligence report files?"

"MI6-3b reports—Red Tape, as I call them," Churchill said. "May we now continue with the briefing? What is your view of fighter sorties over France, pray tell me, and how are you analyzing them?"

"At a strategic level, we ask: What is the purpose of an action, and what is the result? Did the action achieve the purpose, or not, and why? In the case of Air . . ."

Leigh-Mallory took out a large tobacco pipe and rapped it loudly on the table to empty it, and then began searching his tunic pockets for tobacco and matches.

Eleanor spoke through the interruption, determined not to be diverted or intimidated.

"In the case of Air Marshal Leigh-Mallory's fighter sweeps over France, we can ask: What are they designed to achieve, and are they succeeding? Their nominal purpose is to disrupt German military transportation within northern France. Are they succeeding? Is *Wehrmacht* transportation being disrupted? So far these sweeps, known as 'rhubarbs,' do not appear to be inflicting any appreciable harm on the enemy but are resulting in very high 11 Group aircraft losses; nor—"

"Do you have a lighter I can borrow, old chap?" Leigh-Mallory asked his neighbor. "I seem to have mislaid mine."

"Nor is there any likelihood they will be successful in the future," Eleanor continued, ignoring him. "Therefore, Prime—"

"Thanks, old chap."

"Therefore, Prime Minister, I recommend they be abandoned."

Churchill raised his eyebrows in inquiry towards Leigh-Mallory.

"We are showing the flag, Prime Minister," he said, between puffs on his pipe. He positioned his burly shoulders in such a manner that the conversation seemed to be between himself and Churchill, excluding Eleanor. "We are giving the occupied countries some hope. We are giving our own newspapers something to write about."

"We are letting the occupied countries see our fighters shot down," Eleanor countered.

"We are attacking from the air," Leigh-Mallory said, leaning sideways so that Eleanor had to look over his shoulder to see Churchill. "We are carrying the fight to the enemy."

"We are shooting up French trains and killing Frenchmen. The French are our allies. The French are not pleased."

"How on earth do you know what the French think?" Leigh-Mallory barked, swinging around to face her.

"I asked MI6 to ask them, and that's what they reported."

For a moment Leigh-Mallory was stumped but then returned to the attack.

"We are damaging the enemy's supply lines."

"Yes, sir, by bombing French towns and villages."

"Prime Minister, this is ridiculous," Leigh-Mallory snapped. "We must carry the fight to the enemy. The enemy is in France. Therefore we must attack in France. QED, as I believe a mathematician might say."

"Here, here," his neighbor offered in sotto voce support.

Leigh-Mallory shrugged his shoulders.

"Besides, Prime Minister, does it really matter what the French think?" he asked, and gained a supporting smirk from Eden.

Eleanor looked around the room of hostile masculine faces. None of them seemed inclined to come to her aid. Were their egos so large that they could not acknowledge a mistake, even if it was costing lives? Churchill seemed content to sit back and see who won the debate.

"Sir, we are losing four Spitfires for every Focke-Wulf 190 we shoot down," Eleanor tried again. "Every time we cross the Channel, we help the enemy to take a step towards victory in the air."

"Rubbish!" Leigh-Mallory said. "That's an outrageous thing to say!"

"So far we've lost more than two hundred Spitfires over Europe since this strategy began—two hundred in four months, with nothing to show for it. If we hadn't conducted these raids, that's two hundred more aircraft we'd have at the ready and two hundred more trained pilots."

"What should we do?" Leigh-Mallory asked the room at large, as if not expecting an answer. "What do academic theories suggest?"

"We should wait until we won't lose. We are using the wrong weapons against the wrong targets at the wrong time."

"Claptrap!"

"Spitfires and Focke-Wulf 190s are air superiority fighters, and currently the 190 Mark A-1 is superior to the Spitfire V. We should wait for an upgraded model Spitfire. I'm told the Mark IX with the Merlin 60 Series engine will beat the 190. We should wait until we can take down the 190s. Given the current state of Spitfire development, that will be mid-1942. The Hawker Typhoon might be ready earlier, but it's not doing well in-flight testing. Its Napier Sabre engine . . ."

Leigh-Mallory rose to his feet and leaned towards Eleanor, as if he might be contemplating slapping her.

"How the devil do you know all this?"

"I'm paid to know it, sir. It's my job. I am employed to advise Mr. Churchill whether we are winning or losing and, if we are losing, as 11 Group is currently doing over France, how we can stop losing."

Leigh-Mallory paused, shrugged, and turned to Churchill.

"Prime Minister," he said. "I have absolutely no intention of suspending these raids. Indeed, I have every intention of increasing them."

Eleanor did not rise.

"The purpose of these raids is to disrupt German military transportation," she said. "It is not being disrupted. We are failing, at great cost. In order to avoid additional losses, we should wait until we have Spitfire Mark IXs available."

"That's enough, Wing Officer!" Leigh-Mallory thundered. "I'll not have some chit of a girl demeaning my pilots."

"I'm not demeaning them, sir. On the contrary, I admire them deeply. I'm simply trying to save their lives."

"Prime Minister, you have a choice!" Leigh-Mallory thundered.

Q: And I believe Churchill sided with Leigh-Mallory?

A: Churchill did. I became persona non grata in Whitehall. He didn't fire me, but he hid me away for a while.

Q: Banished back to Malvern House?

A: No, to America.

THIRTY-TWO

Q: When did you go to America?

A: In the summer of 1941. I had two more meetings with Churchill, and he sent me off.

"You have upset Trafford Leigh-Mallory," Churchill said, glowering at Eleanor from beneath his eyebrows.

He was wreathed in cigar smoke, indistinct but utterly recognizable. Just as Monet's hazy painting *Impression, soleil levant* had redefined the essence of sunrise, she thought, and launched the entire Impressionist school of art, indeed, the whole glorious explosion of Modern Art, this sight of him, glimpsed though the smoky haze—*Impression, Churchill*—could have defined the prime minister and Britain's resistance to the Nazi onslaught.

He was seated in the center chair at the table in the cabinet room at 10 Downing Street. Anthony Eden sat beside him on his left, and Lord Beaverbrook sat on his right. Scattered farther down the table were several other men, lesser lights she did not recognize.

Eleanor said nothing. She had assumed Leigh-Mallory would complain about her, but there was nothing she could do about it. It was just a question of what, if anything, Churchill would do about it.

Churchill shook his massive head.

"Do not consider it a significant achievement, Wing Officer, for he is very easily upset," he said.

Eleanor grinned and relaxed. She wasn't in trouble, at least, not yet.

"Now, let us now move on to more consequential matters," Churchill said, reaching for his smoldering cigar. "I asked you to apply your mathematical analysis to Eastern Europe, to Germany and Russia. Tell me what Hitler will do."

He held up his hand to stop her from responding, as if he were an actor delivering a soliloquy.

"Will the pact between Molotov and Ribbentrop hold?" he asked. "Fascist Germany and Soviet Russia have carved up Eastern Europe between them, like a juicy plum pudding, and many famous races and territories have been consumed. But Stalin and Hitler are not natural allies, nor are the Huns and Slavs of common blood, and they are both brutal and ruthless men. Will they continue to work together, in a monstrous and criminal conspiracy, or will they fall out?"

Eleanor began to reply, but Churchill was still not finished.

"Of all the cruel fates that might befall one, to be born to the east of Berlin and to the west of St. Petersburg must surely rank as one of the cruelest. Prussians on one side, Russians on the other . . . It is not to be contemplated . . ."

His voice trailed away.

Oh dear! she thought. Churchill seemed to be playing with phraseology for some future book he would write, *History of the World, Part Seven*, or some such title, and she was supposed to use a half-baked mathematical model to predict the next stages in the war. At least Churchill had not picked up a skull and declaimed: "Alas, poor Yorick."

Well, half-baked or not, she and Bramble had fed the model what they believed were pertinent parameters in anticipation of Churchill's question.

"Hitler will invade Russia," Eleanor said flatly. The model ascribed a probability of over ninety percent.

"That's absurd!" said Anthony Eden, the foreign secretary. "On what grounds? Hitler knows what happened to Napoleon. He knows he can't possibly win. He definitely will not invade Russia, Prime Minister, of that I'm certain. Absurd!"

"Why do you think he will, pray tell me?" Churchill asked Eleanor, ignoring Eden.

"He believes that Germans need Lebensraum, sir, space to expand, space to live. He probably imagines he can reduce the Slavs to serfdom, serving future generations of Aryans. He might simply plan to starve the Russians and Ukrainians to death."

"That's absurd," Eden repeated.

"You are suggesting genocide," Beaverbrook said, shaking his head. "This is the twentieth century, not the tenth. These things simply don't happen anymore."

"That'll cheer up the Armenians," she almost said but managed to hold her tongue. Over a million Armenians had been slaughtered during the Great War less than twenty-five years ago. Besides, intelligence reports suggested similar treatment of Jewish people, not just by the Nazis but throughout Eastern Europe.

"Russia is unconquerable," Eden said. "That's an acknowledged fact."

"Russia is vast and empty and poorly defended, sir," Eleanor responded. "In any case, Hitler has no choice."

"Why does Hitler have no choice, pray tell me?" Churchill asked.

"Hitler needs oil, so he needs the Caucasus, sir, if he can't get to Arabia. He may think Russia an easier target than Arabia, with much easier supply lines, given that supply lines are his Achilles' heel. He needs the minerals and the food produced in the Ukraine. The Ukrainians have no love for Stalin; they might even side with Hitler."

"That's absurd rubbish," Eden said again. "We must be prepared for Russia and Germany to work together against us in North Africa, pushing towards Suez and Arabia."

"We must consider how we can help Russia resist Germany."

"When does your crystal ball tell you that this invasion will take place?" Eden asked, his tone dripping with contempt.

"I don't know, sir, but we'll know a month or so before it happens."

"You're counting on Ultra intercepts? Or Operation Magic, perhaps?"

"No, sir. We'll know on our own. We'll know that when the blitz ends, the invasion of Russia is drawing very close."

"Your crystal ball tells you the blitz will end?"

"Sir, I have no crystal ball, as you know," Eleanor responded, determined not to let Eden needle her. "All I have is a mathematical probability tending to one."

Eden sighed a loud theatrical sigh and rolled his eyes. Churchill glanced around the table to see if anyone else wished to comment.

"If I may, Prime Minister?" asked a mild-looking man in old-fashioned, rounded spectacles. Churchill nodded through his smoke screen.

"Wing Officer, good morning. My name is Edward Bridges. I've been reading your reports with great interest."

So this was Park's friend, the cabinet secretary, one of the most powerful men in England.

"Please tell us why a possible end to the blitz and a start to a possible invasion of Russia are causally interrelated?"

"Sir, the Luftwaffe cannot operate on two fronts. They don't have enough aircraft. Even now there are very few 109s and 110s in France or Belgium or Holland. They're in Poland, ready to attack. But 109s and 110s are not sufficient to defeat the Russian air force. They'll need every Dornier 17 and Heinkel 111 they can lay their hands on to destroy the Russian airfields and the aircraft on the ground."

She glanced across the table and saw that she had everyone's attention, even Eden's.

"They'll be successful, not only because the Soviet Union lacks Spitfires and Hurricanes, but also because it lacks the Dowding system and it lacks Keith Park."

She saw a couple of frowns—clearly they did not want any suggestion that they might have been wrong to sack Dowding and Park. She turned to Bridges.

"Therefore, sir, when Hitler stops bombing us, it will be so that he can transfer his bombers to bomb Russia."

"Just idle conjecture," Eden murmured.

"It might be conjecture, Foreign Secretary," Bridges said, turning to Eden. "But it is, in my opinion, far from idle; it is cogent and compelling conjecture."

Oh dear, she thought, not daring to look at Eden but confident he was scowling. Oh dear, now everyone in Whitehall will be out to get me . . .

Q: When was that meeting?

A: Early in May, if I recall correctly.

Q: When did the blitz end?

A: Well, it didn't really end. It just petered out by the end of May, by which time Kesselring and Luftflotte II had been transferred to Germany and Poland. The order to commence the move of Luftflotte II came on 11 May, I believe.

Q: When did Hitler invade Russia?

A: He launched Operation Barbarossa on 22 June.

Q: So you were right. Did Eden apologize?

A: He did not. It proved to be the last straw, and I was dispatched to Washington.

"I'm being sent to a conference overseas, Mr. Bramble," Eleanor said. "I'm going to leave you in charge." Even after all these months, she had not been able to decide how to address him.

"Are you sure?"

"Of course I'm sure. Why would I not know if I'm being sent somewhere?"

"No, I meant are you sure I'm going to be in charge?"

"Of course. They're setting up a committee to set our priorities. But I'll put you in touch with the cabinet secretary, Edward Bridges. He'll be someone you can go to for help, a friend in high places, and he's your pipeline to Churchill as well. He will listen to you, even if others will not."

"What about Commander Crenshaw and Brigadier Pondsford?"

"You mustn't tell them anything you're doing. Just use them to do the administrative work."

"Can I use Jayne Jackson?"

"Yes, of course. Why ever not?"

"Just asking."

She was beginning to have second thoughts about putting Bramble in charge. She had never doubted his mathematical abilities—she was leaving the model in good hands—but perhaps his insecurities would make it too hard for him to run Malvern House. Unfortunately the only other possibility was Cassius, but he wouldn't survive in Whitehall for more than five minutes.

No, Cassius was not the only other choice! Johnnie would be perfect! But, alas, there was no time.

In the meantime, there was a lot to do before she left.

Jayne came to see her within minutes.

"I believe you're going away, ma'am, and leaving Bramble in charge?"

"Yes, I am. The news is out already? I haven't made an announcement yet."

"Bramble told me. He's concerned . . ."

"Bramble told you he is concerned? What—"

"We're engaged to be married, ma'am," she burst out.

"Engaged?"

"You might as well know it all, ma'am, since you'll be gone." The words were tumbling out of her mouth. "He's a bit all over the place, I know, because his brain works too quickly for everything else to keep up, like good, old-fashioned plain common sense, but he does do what he's told to do. I had a dog like that once: wild if he was off the leash but docile on it. Bramble's happiest when he's under firm discipline."

Eleanor could not decide if she was hearing this or dreaming.

"After the war he'll be a college professor in Cambridge, a good provider, a PhD, and I could be a private tutor. It'll be a nice step up for a high school teacher, to be completely honest. He'll be respectable. And he does need someone to tell him what to do."

Eleanor struggled to visualize a union between the prim, highly organized Jayne Jackson and the brilliant, obsessive Bramble. Actually, come to think of it, it made a lot of sense!

"Well, congratulations, Jayne!" she managed. "I hope you'll be very happy."

"Since I'm telling you all this, you might as well know the rest. I'm having a baby. We're getting married later this month."

Now Eleanor was speechless.

"Well, I knew what he wanted—of course I did—so I thought I might as well, because he needs someone like me to look after him, tell him what to do, keep him in line, firmly, so it's in his own best interests."

Oh . . . my . . . God, Eleanor thought, frantically suppressing the giggles that were bubbling up within her: Jayne hadn't made Bramble keep it in his trousers in his own best interests, because he needed firm discipline for his own good. A sudden image of Jayne applying smart corporal punishment to Bramble's bare buttocks in chastisement for some disciplinary misdemeanor was almost too much to bear.

"I see," she managed.

Q: When did you leave for Washington?

A: Soon after Operation Barbarossa; I got there in time for the Fourth of July.

Churchill summoned Eleanor. On this occasion only Bridges was in attendance.

"You have two very unusual talents, Wing Officer," Churchill said. "One is your remarkable mathematical insight. The other is your outstanding ability to annoy senior members of the government and the armed forces."

Eleanor grinned but said nothing.

"I shall send you to Washington to annoy their officials and senior officers instead."

"I'll do my best, sir."

"Ha!" Churchill responded, and sucked on his cigar.

"But this is no laughing matter," he continued, and Eleanor saw he was in deadly earnest. "It is of the gravest importance. It will be your purpose to convince them that Hitler must be opposed regardless of the cost and regardless of the strong preference of the American people to remain neutral in the present conflict. You must seek out Mr. Harry Hopkins. I'll write to tell him you are coming."

"I'm not sure they'll listen to me any more than our people do, sir. If I can't convince members of your own government to—"

"You must convince them, Wing Officer, you must, as must I!" he said. "It is essential that America commits to the fight; otherwise we will surely lose this war, lose our empire, and lose our island. We shall become just another minor principality with a glorious past and, I fear, an inglorious future."

He shook his head.

"Our island will become a museum filled with gawking foreigners on guided omnibus tours with Zeiss Ikon cameras who fill our pubs and inns with a babel of alien tongues. We shall be of no more consequence in the world than Egypt or Greece or even, God forbid, France. The king will be but an impoverished émigré, eking out a shabby existence in some frigid province of northern Canada."

He rose to bid her goodbye.

"We cannot last much longer. We barely survived Dunkirk. We barely survived the Battle of Britain. We have barely survived the blitz. We are struggling against Rommel in the desert in North Africa. We are struggling to survive the U-boats in the Atlantic. I doubt we can defend Hong Kong or Singapore, if it should come to that. Our prospects are very grim. Our only hope is to survive until Roosevelt can persuade his countrymen to join us."

He held out his hand.

"Good luck, Wing Officer."

"Thank you, sir."

THIRTY-THREE

Q: *You've mentioned your opposition to Leigh-Mallory's strategies, Dame Eleanor, his so-called rhubarb sweeps. But your husband was transferred back into Fighter Command and fought in those sweeps. He flew the Whirlwinds, the very fighter he had opposed as a test pilot. Didn't you both find that ironic—doubly ironic?*

A: *I'll leave it to you to find irony where you wish.*

Q: *Well . . .*

A: *The war in the air was a tragedy. Hundreds of young men on both sides were being killed, not to mention the thousands of civilians. The war shouldn't be trivialized, and it shouldn't be aggrandized. Irony was a luxury we couldn't afford.*

Q: *Well . . .*

A: *I'm sorry; I'm getting a bit preachy in my old age. One of the ironies of old age is that one recognizes finally one's weaknesses but cannot correct them. Forgive me?*

Q: *Of course!*

A: You were asking about Johnnie's new squadron. Fighter Command formed one final Whirlwind squadron, 188 XD, in the middle of 1941, and Johnnie was transferred out of A&AEE to command it. The last of the four American Eagle Squadrons was 188.

Q: Those were American volunteers?

A: Yes. Obviously America was neutral before Pearl Harbor, but many individual Americans were sympathetic to Britain and what was then the British Empire. Most of the volunteer American pilots went to Canada and joined the RCAF and then came to England to fight, although there was also a remarkable American businessman called Charles Sweeney, who organized—and paid for—a complete recruiting drive, first for the French and then for the RAF.

Q: They didn't have an American to command the new squadron?

A: They did subsequently, but in those days there were no Americans who had experience in commanding squadrons in battle. It was all a bit slapdash, a bit hurried, in a way.

Q: What do you mean?

A: Well . . .

"I've been posted, El," Shaux said as soon as they had hugged hello, a self-conscious, public, railway station sort of semi-hug.

"What?"

"They're forming a new squadron, 188. It's going to have American volunteers, and we'll be flying Whirlwinds."

"What? Are you serious?"

"It seems they have enough extra Whirlwinds sitting idle that they don't want to waste them."

"But you've always said they're no good."

"I know," Johnnie said. Words tumbled from his mouth. "Let me tell you what happened. When I got back to Martlesham from Rolls-Royce in Derby, there was a telegram waiting for me saying—"

"Wait! Stop! Should we be talking about this in the middle of Liverpool Street station?"

"Oh, sorry, El. Yes, I'm being very stupid," Shaux said, staring around them at the crowds of scurrying passengers. "Let's find somewhere to go."

He looked around vaguely.

"Oh, I know a place," Eleanor said. "Let's walk to Finsbury Circus and sit. It's only five minutes."

Shaux had never been there. It was a gracious oval lined with elegant, whitewashed buildings. The center formed a small park.

"So, a telegram?" Eleanor asked as they sat down on a bench.

"Yes, telling me I was being transferred. First I had to see Wilfrid Freeman, who's in charge of aircraft development for the Air Staff. I really liked him. Anyway, he told me he'd received a letter from Hives at Rolls-Royce mentioning my meeting there and urging Freeman to cancel the Kestrel engine. But Freeman said he can only cancel the Kestrel if Fighter Command cancels the Whirlwind, and Leigh-Mallory won't do it."

"I know Park thinks Freeman's a good man," Eleanor said.

"Oh, and Hives, the engineer I met, is general manager of the entire Rolls-Royce factory! I thought he was a bigwig, but I had no idea how big! Anyway, he told me that—"

"Hives?"

"No, sorry. Freeman. They were going to form one more Whirlwind squadron, and they needed someone with experience to command it, and I commanded 339, and I've probably flown the Whirlwind as much as anyone else, so I was the obvious choice."

"But you think the Whirlwind is a bad idea, Johnnie."

"I think it's a potentially good idea, but it's too expensive to make, and Rolls-Royce can't solve the engine problems. Anyway, Freeman said he wanted me to stay in A&AEE, but Fighter Command has priority and they're terribly short of squadron commanders. He was, well, he was quite complimentary."

She stared at him.

"Johnnie, what are you not telling me?"

"Well, it turned out that he'd heard about the double engine failure episode. He, er, well, he gave me the AFC."

"The Air Force Cross? That's wonderful!"

"No, it's not! It's another bloody medal ribbon I'll have to wear, dammit! Pretty soon I'll look like a Pearly King!"

"Don't be silly."

"He said if I'd stayed, I could have worked on the Mosquito, although that's in Boscombe Down so it's a long way from you."

"Well, on that note, Johnnie, I have news too. I have to go to Washington."

"Washington? You mean in America?"

"Yes, of course in America. Churchill's sending me there to participate in a conference."

Shaux was aghast at the thought of her being so far away, but he couldn't say so.

"El, that's amazing," he managed to say. "That's wonderful. I'm—"

"Johnnie! Stop it! You know I know when you're lying!"

"Well—"

She interrupted him again.

"I think he's sending me away because I cause too much trouble in Whitehall. He said it's only a short trip, but I'm not so sure. I think I'm being exiled."

"Rubbish!"

"I think it's true."

"Who will run your group? That chap Bramble?"

"A committee of babysitters, so it seems, appointed by the service chiefs and the Foreign Office. That means they will only work on the things the generals think are important, which is to say only the things that reinforce the generals' prejudices."

"That's ridiculous!"

"The powers that be, the generals and the mandarins, just don't like it when the model says they're wrong."

The thought of Eleanor leaving overwhelmed him.

"When are you leaving?"

"I'm not sure, Johnnie. In a couple of weeks, I think."

They were already holding hands tightly, but now his grip grew tighter.

"God, El, I don't want you to go! I don't want to go back to a squadron! Everything's been perfect these last few months, and now it's all ruined."

"Do you know when your new squadron will be formed?"

"Oh, I didn't finish telling you about my meetings. After I saw Freeman I had to go to see Leigh-Mallory at Bentley Priory."

He paused to light a cigarette, looked at Eleanor, grimaced, and ground it out again beneath his heel.

"He said he had very little confidence in the Whirlwind, which he described as an unreliable toy, and very little confidence in the American pilots, whom he described as playboys."

"That wasn't very nice."

Shaux remembered Leigh-Mallory's words very clearly.

"Nonetheless, we will put you in the forefront of the battle," Leigh-Mallory had said. "We need to take the fight to the enemy, whether they have the advantage or not. We need to put some stick about."

"Yes, sir," Shaux had said.

"Make sure 188 does a good job, even if you have to take some losses. Keep those Yanks in line. Put on a good show for the Frogs. I'm holding you personally responsible."

"Yes, sir."

At that, the telephone had rung, and Leigh-Mallory answered it.

"Good afternoon, Sholto," he had said and waved at Shaux in a vague gesture of dismissal.

"So that was that," Shaux said, and scowled.

"Don't pout," Eleanor said.

"I'll pout if I want to. I have a lot to pout about."

"And don't end sentences with prepositions."

"I have much about which to pout."

"I don't go to bed with pouty men."

"I've never pouted in my life. It's one of the seven mortal sins. 'Pout ye not,' as it says in the bible, 'lest ye shall also be pouted.'"

"Exactly so."

Q: So everything changed?

A: Everything changed. But that's the way it was during the war; you'd be doing one thing, and suddenly you'd be told to do something else.

Q: What did Churchill say?

Churchill adopted what she had come to call his soliloquy pose.

"There are four battlefields upon which this war is being decided and upon which our survival depends. One is in Russia, about which we can do little or nothing. One is in the Atlantic, as Karl Dönitz's U-boats devour our convoys. One is in the Mediterranean, where we struggle to keep Erwin Rommel, the Desert Fox, from winning the Suez Canal. The last is in Washington."

She began to ask him what he meant, but he continued.

"Our battle in Washington is as vital as any. It is the battle to win the Americans fully to our cause. This is the battlefield to which you are being dispatched. Nothing, I suppose, is more important. This is your mission."

Q: Please tell us about the American squadrons. What happened to the American Eagles?

A: They fought with distinction until they were transferred, intact, to the American Eighth Air Force in 1942. The other squadrons, 71, 121, and 133, were equipped with Hurricanes and Spitfires, and the Whirlwind was finally phased out. The Eagle Squadrons had almost a hundred pilots killed, missing, or taken as prisoners of war. It's important to remember that 1941 and 1942 were very difficult years for the RAF. These were brave men, and good pilots, but they had little or no battle experience . . .

"Good morning, chaps," Shaux said. "My name's Shaux. I'll have the privilege of being your CO for a while. And let me introduce Le Grand Charles, better known as Charlie, who has also been posted to 188. He's a volunteer transferred from the Belgian air force, just as you gentlemen have also volunteered."

He was facing fifteen or so pilots, all wearing the ES shoulder patch that distinguished Eagle Squadron volunteers. They seemed a little older than the English pilots, a little more mature than the schoolboys upon whom Fighter Command was increasingly reliant.

"We're going to be doing some training over the next few days, and then we'll become operational. I know you can all fly, and I know you've all been trained on the Whirlwind, and so the purpose of our training will be to get to know each other and to practice some basic tactics for when we meet the Luftwaffe."

"Pardon me for saying so, sir, but I'm a professional pilot, an air-mail pilot," said a tall man sitting in the back row. "Most guys here are professionals. I've been here in England for six months, and all I've done is training. I didn't come here to train, with due respect. I came here to fight."

There was a low murmur of support.

"Please don't call me 'sir,'" Shaux said. "'Skipper' is normal for squadron commanders. Fighter Command wants us in the line as soon as possible, so we'll move up as soon as I say we're ready. If I see that we're ready tomorrow, I'll tell them tomorrow."

The pilot did not seem convinced.

"What's your name?"

"Grady; Pete Grady."

"Well, Pete, let's see how we go," Shaux said. "Our primary mission will be hit-and-run sorties against enemy targets in France—small targets like E-boats, railway engines, convoys of lorries, that sort of thing. In Fighter Command vernacular, we call these raids 'rhubarbs.'"

Shaux paused and lit a cigarette. Now he had their attention.

"We will practice three things in order to prepare. Number one is ground attack against small targets of opportunity. It's why we have Whirlwinds. Our ability to contribute to the war effort is dependent on how accurate we can be. Ground attack requires low-level formation flying at forty to fifty feet, preferably lower, at up to 300 miles per hour."

"Forty or fifty feet?" asked another pilot.

"The lower the better." Shaux nodded. "If you shoot up a building, you need to just clear the chimneys. Or you need to be just clear of the radio mast of an E-boat. And so on. It's quite difficult to aim accurately in a diving attitude unless you're in a specifically designed aircraft like a Stuka. Subconsciously you're always worried about pulling up in time."

"You've done this?" Grady asked.

"Not in a Stuka, of course." Shaux laughed. "But yes; shipping in the docks in Antwerp and E-boats in the Channel, the occasional squirt at a railway engine, things like that. I found it best to be as level with the target as possible."

The pilots glanced at each other.

"That's what we'll practice. Twelve aircraft in three boxes of four, flying finger-four formation. Each aircraft will be fifty feet from the others, flying at treetop level at 300 miles per hour. Our separation will be approximately our wingspan. There are a couple of ruined abbeys in the countryside we can practice on. We'll start at fifty feet and work our way down. I'm not sure just how stable a gun platform a Whirlwind is at low levels—four cannons make a lot of recoil. You can fire safely in a Spit with the recoil of eight machine guns at ten feet, for example, but I don't know if a Whirlwind is that stable."

The pilots glanced at each other again.

"And we'll want to be as close to the target as possible for maximum effect. So we'll practice opening fire when we're three hundred yards away or less."

"Are you serious?" Grady asked.

"That'll be, say, two seconds to fire before we fly over the target. We have four 20-millimeter Hispano-Suizas, so that's about fifty rounds a second, one hundred rounds into the target. A hundred rounds per aircraft delivered from twenty feet above the ground will definitely wake them up."

"Are you serious?" Grady asked again.

"Piece of cake."

THIRTY-FOUR

Q: *You arrived in Washington early in July?*

A: *Yes. I remember being astonished at how hot and humid it was. I was in a heavy woolen WAAF uniform while all the American girls were wearing summer frocks. I was invited to a Fourth of July party, an open-air party, at the State Department, and I bought a dress to attend it. The rest of the British delegation was aghast at my temerity.*

Q: *What did—*

A: *Lord Halifax, who was the British ambassador, told me off in no uncertain terms. I distinctly remember seeing little beads of sweat rolling down his cheeks as he chastised me.*

Q: *(Laughing) Dame Eleanor, can you explain to our audience what was happening in the United States—with regard to the war, I mean, not the weather, in the middle of 1941?*

A: *Yes, of course. In 1941, the United States was facing one potential enemy across the Pacific and another across the Atlantic: the Nazis and the Japanese. But neither potential enemy was directly threatening, and both were heavily engaged in their own local theaters. There was no* causus belli—*no reason for the United States to go to war. If I had been an American, I wouldn't have wanted war either.*

All through 1941 it was as if Churchill was courting Roosevelt, trying to get him to commit. Churchill desperately needed American support and commitment. That's why I was sent to Washington. Churchill believed, as I did, that we would eventually lose the war unless the United States joined us. I was just one of many envoys sent to try to get the Americans to commit themselves. There was a whole series of conferences and delegations, like an elaborate mating ritual, all year.

Eleanor sipped a mint julep and tried to be polite to a United States Navy pilot who was attempting to flirt with her. He was one of several young officers who seemed prepared to do so.

"Have you ever met a military aviator before, Miss Shaux?" her escort asked. "It's kind of a specialized role. We fly escort from here all the way to Iceland, in a CVE, searching for U-boats. It's kind of dangerous, I admit, but someone has to do it."

"I suppose someone must."

He struck a pose, managing—quite skillfully, she acknowledged—to create the impression of scanning endless horizons for enemy ships while attempting to see down the front of her dress.

"Well, the call of duty . . . but, as I was asking, have you ever met a combat pilot before?"

"Well, as a matter of fact I have, Lieutenant. My husband is a Spitfire pilot who fought through the Battle of Britain. He's currently commanding an American Eagle Squadron, flying sweeps over occupied France."

"You're married? You have a husband?"

He seemed to find this news more disconcerting than the fact that her husband was a Battle of Britain fighter pilot.

"It's kind of dangerous, I admit, but someone has to do it."

The aviator mumbled something incoherent and withdrew, leaving Eleanor feeling a little guilty. Perhaps she'd been too rough?

An older, frailer man approached her—beating the young officers to the punch—as she was wondering what exactly might be in a mint julep and whether she dared have another.

"Good afternoon," he said. "I asked someone from the British embassy to point you out, Mrs. Shaux. My name is Harry Hopkins. Welcome to Washington."

Q: Can you remind our audience who Harry Hopkins was?

A: He was probably Roosevelt's closest advisor from the start of the New Deal in the 1930s all the way to the end of the war. He attended all the big wartime conferences; he was the leading man on Lend-Lease; he was Roosevelt's personal ambassador to Churchill. He was so close to Roosevelt that he actually lived in the White House.

Hopkins was a big man, but he gave the impression that he was smaller than he once had been, as if he were collapsing in on himself. Eleanor had been briefed that he had some terrible form of cancer eating away at him, as well as the day-to-day strain and punishing work schedule demanded of his role as President Roosevelt's closest confidant and emissary. It struck her that, given Roosevelt's crippling polio, the two most powerful men in America were both dying, slowly but inevitably, and might not survive to the end of hostilities.

"Your Mr. Churchill says you have a penchant for being right, Mrs. Shaux, and for upsetting the powers that be!"

"Well, sir, I'm afraid the latter part is true."

He had a straightforward manner, and she took to him immediately. He took her elbow with old-fashioned courtesy and drew her away from the crowd.

"I know Winston has held back on giving us details of your Red Tape system, but he has privately assured the president and me that you have an approach to strategic analytics that is both unique and accurate."

"He gives me far more credit than I deserve, Mr. Hopkins."

"Let me be the judge of that," he said. "Look, I'd like to get your views on a number of things, and time is of the essence. Are you free this evening?"

"Certainly, sir." Clearly Hopkins wasted no time.

"Have you met the secretary of state?" he asked, and led her back into the crowd. "Let me introduce you, and then we can slip away. It's far too hot, in my opinion. I see you were sensible enough to wear a dress, unlike the rest of your British colleagues, who look like they're dressed for a garden party at Buckingham Palace on a chilly day rather than a July fourth cookout in Washington."

Within minutes they were in a government limousine with an elaborate swan ornament on its hood. Not only was the motor car far larger than a Rolls-Royce, Eleanor thought in awe, but the swan was at least twice the size of the Rolls's Spirit of Ecstasy ornament. Hopkins was sitting quietly with his eyes closed. She supposed he alternated between moments of action and moments of rest in which to recharge his batteries. She found herself hoping that he would survive his illness.

She sat back and watched Washington roll by. She was struck by the city's peacetime vitality: its bright lights; its opulent, overflowing shops and stores and sumptuous restaurants; its vast, exuberant automobiles and its buzzing traffic; its petrol garages—gas stations— without queues or ration books; its feeling of complete safety and its lack of air raid sirens. All this was in sharp contrast to the grays and shadows of worn-down and weary wartime London, with bulbous antiaircraft barrage balloons above and grimy air raid shelters below its shabby streets.

They turned off a broad avenue and approached a tall wrought iron gate with a guardhouse beside it. Eleanor realized, with a shock of recognition, that they were entering the grounds of the White House.

Johnnie would love to see this, she thought. He took so much pride in her work, but he was, quite literally, an ocean away. It must be evening for him. Was he finishing his dinner before a trip to the local pub for a pints, bitter with his squadron?

Shaux turned for home. It was late in the evening and almost dark. He didn't want to have a stupid accident landing at the unlit field at Middle Wallop.

He stared at his gauges and wrote down a last set of readings. Flight Sergeant Jenkins—the best fitter in the RAF, in Shaux's opinion, and, like Charlie, another transferee from 339—and the ground crews had built a makeshift array of temperature and pressure gauges to try to find the most likely source of the Peregrine's perennial overheating. The mixture of petroleum and air that powered the Peregrine followed a tortuous route from the carburetor through the supercharger and the intercooler and finally into the cylinders. At every stage there was a fine line between raising the pressure of the fuel on the one hand, in order to increase the power of the engine, and keeping it below premature ignition on the other.

He and Jenkins had a feeling that overheating was occurring before the fuel ever reached the cylinders; somewhere—maybe, just maybe, in the intercooler. They had rigged two test harnesses. One, on the ground, kept running a Peregrine through an endless series of tiny adjustments, hoping to find the magical balance point. The second rig, attached to one of this Whirlwind's engines, found out whether the best results on the ground could be replicated in the air at different altitudes. There was only about a third as much oxygen in a cubic foot at twenty thousand feet in comparison to a cubic foot at sea level, and petroleum cannot ignite without oxygen.

He pondered if he could create a single graph of the temperatures as the fuel passed through the duel system and whether the graph would be a smooth curve or a ragged line of peaks and troughs. If he could, he could establish safety limits for using supercharger boost at various altitudes. It was just the kind of thing that Eleanor was really good at; she'd suggest the best way of doing it, but she was far away in Washington.

"I hope you enjoyed the meal, Mrs. Shaux?" Hopkins asked.

"It was delicious, sir, thank you. The crab was wonderful."

"Yes, indeed. We're very fortunate to live by the Chesapeake," he said, although Eleanor could not help noticing he had eaten very little and had disguised his lack of appetite by pushing his food round his plate.

"Now, Mrs. Shaux, let me repeat myself. Winston speaks very highly of you."

"Well, I don't . . ."

"He says you are courageous. He says you flew in a fighter aircraft in the Battle of Britain to fire the guns when no one else was available. But, he says, of even greater courage is the courage of your convictions. You make your point and stick to it."

He had pushed back from the table and crossed his knees, at ease. He was perhaps fifty, she guessed, old enough to be her father. He came from a village—a small town, she corrected herself—somewhere in the vast American West—and had risen from obscurity to great power.

"Sir, I'm not courageous at all. My mother would tell you I'm pig-headed, obstinate, and highly opinionated."

"Very well." He laughed. "Then tell me your opinion of where we stand. I believe you predicted that Hitler would invade Russia when almost everyone else said he would not. Will he win, in your opinion?"

If I am to persuade him, she decided, I must be completely honest.

"He will not."

"The State Department and the Department of the Army—all the military people, in fact—think he will win," Hopkins said. "Russia is weak, impoverished, and lacks anything approaching a modern military capability. Germany, on the other hand, has the best-equipped, best-trained, best-led armed forces in the world and a long list of victories to prove it."

"All of that is true, sir, and that's also the opinion of almost everyone in London. I'm in a minority of one. Nonetheless, I believe Hitler will find Russia just beyond his grasp."

"Why, Mrs. Shaux?"

"Well, sir, I'm a mathematician, not a strategist or military person."

"Then give me a mathematician's answer."

"All I have to work with are numbers, like how many men or how many aircraft does each side have, the distance from Berlin to Moscow, how far a Panzer tank can advance in a day, and so on—even how much hay a horse eats. I put these numbers into my formulae that Mr. Churchill calls the Red Tape model, and I plot the probability of Hitler getting to Moscow and defeating Stalin. I can draw the result as a graph, and I find that the line is asymptotic."

"Asymptotic?"

"The line approaches victory for Hitler but never reaches it. We can project the line of probability to infinity, and it never gets there. He won't get there."

Hopkins sat for a while. Eleanor feared he was concluding that her analysis was academic hogwash.

"I'm in charge of Lend-Lease, as you may know, Mrs. Shaux. Soon we have to decide if we're going to support Stalin or give him up as a lost cause."

"I know, sir."

"General Marshall thinks Hitler will win in Russia," Hopkins said, with a slight shake of his head. "Cordell Hull thinks Hitler will win."

This is ridiculous, she thought. Churchill had sent her to convince the Americans to do something that she thought was a bad idea. She had half a dozen formulae maintained by Bramble and Cassius in a dank country house disguised by bedsprings aligned in the wrong direction, while Hopkins commanded the resources of the most powerful nation in the world.

"Sir, it's not a question of whether Hitler will win. It's a question of whether he'll lose. Hitler should not have invaded Russia, but he did. It was a mistake."

"An asymptotic mistake, Mrs. Shaux?" he asked, smiling.

"Infinitely so, sir," she said, smiling back.

THIRTY-FIVE

Q: *It's an interesting coincidence, Dame Eleanor, that you went to America at exactly the time your husband took command of an American Eagle Squadron in England. How many of the pilots in the Battle of Britain were Americans? Can you tell us a little more about the Eagles?*

A: *They were manned by American volunteers, of course, just as we had Polish and Czech squadrons manned by volunteers from those countries. We also had Norwegians, Canadians—goodness, quite a few! Initially these squadrons had English squadron commanders because when the squadrons were initially formed, most of the volunteers were experienced pilots but had no operational experience.*

There were only ten or eleven American pilots in the Battle of Britain itself, but a total of about two hundred fifty served in the Eagle Squadrons before America joined the war at the end of 1941. About a hundred of those were lost—killed or taken prisoner.

Q: *That's almost half!*

A: *Aerial combat was not like having afternoon tea . . .*

"I've borrowed a Spitfire, chaps, and I'm going to simulate an attack," Shaux said. "You chaps will fly in three flights, finger-four, and I'll come looking for you."

"That'll be twelve of us against one of you," said a pilot named Paddock.

"Just remember what we've talked about," Shaux said, smiling. "Stay in formation and search the sky, especially the sun and your six o'clock. If you see me, turn towards me. Try to turn behind me, so you can attack me in my weak spot. If you're attacked, climb. Don't dive."

He led them out and waited until all three flights were airborne. He liked Paddock—he might make him a flight leader.

Shaux took off and climbed for five minutes until he found the rest of 188 wallowing along in loose formation. He positioned himself below them and to the left, opened the throttle, and made a climbing attack. When he was one hundred yards behind Red Flight, he decided they weren't going to see him.

"Bang, bang, bang," Shaux said. "Red Three, you're dead!"

"Dammit! Where the hell are you?"

"I'm at your six o'clock low, Red Three. Red Two, can you hear me?"

"Yes."

"Bang, bang, bang, Red Two. You're dead as well."

"That's not fair!"

"Who said war was fair, Red Two? The rest of you, stay alert. Search the sky."

He broke away in a gut-wrenching curve that brought him up behind Green Flight, with similar results.

He kept it up for another fifteen minutes, pretending to shoot down three more Whirlwinds. He didn't want to humiliate 188; he just wanted them to realize what they would be facing. And he wanted to see how the Whirlwinds would appear to the enemy and whether he could discern any tactical advantages or disadvantages.

Finally, when 188 was spread all across Dorset in disarray, he sent them home.

"OK, chaps, what did you learn?" Shaux asked when they were back on the ground and drinking tea in the dispersal hut.

"That we screwed up," said Paddock.

"That we didn't just screw up, we screwed up big time," said a pilot named Shultz.

"Not exactly." Shaux laughed again. "You should have learned, for example, that nine out of ten attacks come from the rear. It is simply too difficult for the attacker to fly an intercepting course from any other location."

"Why, skipper?" Shultz asked. "Why not from the side?"

"For two aircraft to intersect in three-dimensional space at the same time, the attacking pilot must not only be able predict the flight path of the aircraft he is pursuing, he must also be able to calculate a flight path for himself. That involves being able to do calculus in your head and converting distance into time, which few people can do."

"What about from the front?" Paddock asked.

"Head-on attacks are just stupid, as many dead pilots would tell you if they weren't dead."

Shaux accepted another mug of sweet tea.

"Can you do calculus in your head, skipper?" Grady asked.

"Only after two or three pints, bitter." Shaux smiled.

"No, seriously, skipper. Can you do calculus? Is that what it takes to survive?"

"You don't have to know calculus," Shaux said, evading the question. "You just have to remember what you've been taught."

He stood up.

"OK, smokes out, gentlemen. Flying gear on; let's do it again. This time Grady will lead you, with Paddock and Shultz leading Red and Green Flights."

An hour later, when Shaux had singlehandedly destroyed 188 for the second time, they were back in the dispersal hut.

"One advantage I notice is that the Whirlwind has wonderful rear vision," Shaux said. "You're sitting behind the wings, and the tail is very high. I could see the backs of your heads clearly."

"How does that help, skipper?"

"Because there are certain things your aircraft can do that the enemy can't do, and vice versa," Shaux said. "I remember sitting in a crashed 109 last year, in the Battle of Britain, realizing all the blind spots in the pilot's vision, all the places I could attack from."

He remembered being startled by how limited a 109 pilot's field of vision was, almost as if he was sitting behind a barred prison window.

"Anyway, in our case, Fw 190 pilots will underestimate your ability to see rearwards and you'll be able to start evasive action much more quickly than they expect."

He lit a cigarette.

"Let's assume that. Let's assume they're coming up behind, not realizing we can see them. When we take sharp evasive action, there's a good chance they'll overshoot. If they do—and we'll have to practice this over and over—if they get ahead of us, we can blow them out of the sky. So, gentlemen, we have two advantages so far: superior vision and superior firepower."

"Is that enough?" Shultz asked.

"I don't know, but it's a start. Anyway, managing these minor but vital differences—exploiting our advantages and minimizing theirs—are the keys to success. Once we work this out, I think we'll be very successful, even against 190s."

"Are you serious, skipper?" Paddock asked. "Even Spitfires can't beat 190s."

"I'm absolutely serious. They won't be used to dealing with Whirlwinds. They'll underestimate our agility and our firepower. Now, we're going up again, right now, and you will not, repeat not, get jumped from behind."

Shaux wanted them to fly five or six times every day, in part to simulate the stress of actual combat and in part to allow them to practice their operational skills. They were all proficient pilots—better than himself, in several cases—but normal flying and flying in the face of the enemy were two profoundly different things.

Each day's exercises ended in the local pub in Nether Wallop for consumption of pints, bitter and reflections on the lessons of the day.

"They say that a test pilot landed a Whirlwind with both engines on fire," Grady said to Shaux one evening. "It seems like he didn't bail out because he wanted to bring the engines back in one piece to show to Rolls-Royce so they could figure out what was wrong."

"Yes," Shaux said. "I've heard that story too."

"Well, skipper, you tested Whirlwinds. Is it true?"

"It sounds very unlikely. The chap would've been an idiot, if you ask me."

Every day their training included simulated low-level attacks. Each time Shaux would remind them of the basics.

"Remember, chaps, the key to low-level flying is to look at the horizon, not the ground or the water below you. Never look at your altimeter. It's not measuring your height; it's guessing your height from the air pressure. Besides, altimeters are useless at these levels."

Shaux would lead them to the Severn Estuary, in the west of England, the waterway leading to Cardiff in Wales and Bristol in England, where they practiced at progressively lower and lower levels. Shaux arranged for a decrepit trawler to be anchored near Cardiff, and they used that as a target. The ruins of Tintern Abbey lay close by and also made an excellent practice target.

Shaux assembled them early one morning.

"OK, chaps, another low-level live-fire attack this morning."

"Where to this time, skipper? Back to Cardiff?"

"No, that's getting boring, I think you'll agree. This morning we'll try Dieppe."

Several voices spoke at once.

"Dieppe is in France, skipper." Pete Grady's voice carried above the rest.

"Yes, at least it was the last time I looked, and I assume it hasn't moved."

"You mean this time it's for real?"

"Absolutely. I spoke to 11 Group yesterday and told them you were ready. Congratulations! You're operational!"

The 11 Group adjutant had been concerned that Shaux was rushing 188 into service too early—"Are you sure they can handle it, Johnnie?"—while Leigh-Mallory had taken the opposite view: "About bloody time too, Shaux; now get 188's ass in gear immediately and put some stick about."

Q: There's an interesting memoir by an American named Charles Shultz, who was one of the American Eagle volunteers. He flew in 188 when your husband commanded it. I'm sure you must have read it, Dame Eleanor?

A: He came to see me, oh, it must be thirty or forty years ago by now, when I was still teaching at Princeton, and presented me an autographed copy, which was very gracious of him. He wanted to know about Johnnie, so I told him, "There's not much to tell." "How can you say that?" he asked me. "Well," I told him, "that's a verbatim quote: that's exactly what Johnnie used to say about himself."

Q: Did you like the book?

A: I found it fascinating. I'd like, if I may, to read you a brief excerpt.

> So the very next day, the skipper, who is a mild, retiring kind of guy, the kind of guy you'd expect to be a minister, or an accountant, or behind the counter in a bank, or something like that, immediately leads us out over the Solent and the Isle of Wight and across the Channel, so low our balls are bouncing off the wave tops, and then there's the town of Dieppe coming up on the horizon, with the top of the castle actually above us. I couldn't believe how fast it was all happening. So I think, holy crap, that's actually the enemy coast!
>
> "OK, chaps, tallyho!" is all the skipper says, as if he was making a comment about the weather, and then we're across the beach and flying across the harbor at rooftop level. There are E-boats ahead of us, looking bigger than I expected. I was so surprised that I almost forgot to fire. Now we're out into the French countryside. "One-eighty-degree right turn, chaps," says the skipper, and he leads us into this screaming tight turn at zero feet, which is extremely dangerous unless you're really good, but the Whirlwinds are rock solid, and everyone stays in formation. Now I understand why the skipper made us practice day in, day out. Not a shot fired at us, not a 190 in sight. Now we're scraping our starboard wings on the treetops. We finish the turn, and there's the town and the harbor once more,

coming up fast. I take another squirt at the E-boats, and this time I think I might have hit one of them.

We turn sharp right and fly up the coast as far as Boulogne, super-low above the beaches. Now our balls are digging furrows in the sand, and we hit the harbor at Boulogne. More E-boats, same deal, and then we head west across the Channel, back to safety, and it's over in no time flat, and I think, Jesus Christ, I'm operational. The skipper's dog welcomes us home when we land, as he always does. That evening we're all in the local pub celebrating, and after a couple of pints, bitter, I ask the skipper what he thought.

"Piece of cake," he says. "We'll do it again tomorrow."

"I didn't expect it to be that easy," I admit.

"It wasn't," he says. "You're that good."

THIRTY-SIX

Q: How long did you stay in Washington?

A: Just a few weeks. I loved everything about America. I loved the Americans. I even imagined that Johnnie and I could live there after the war. But I made no progress in convincing anyone.

Eleanor left another indecisive meeting in which her American counterparts were polite but unmoved and strolled out towards the Washington Monument. She felt like crying. Johnnie was in Europe beneath the black thunderclouds of war, flying rhubarbs that were simply a series of futile gestures invented by men with limited imaginations in order to create the impression of activity. Not only was Johnnie expendable in those men's eyes, he was being expended.

What a contrast between the glorious summer skies of peaceful Washington and the wretched gloom of Europe suffering through yet another war . . . Hitler was advancing rapidly in Russia, making her predictions look ridiculous. Perhaps the Red Tape model was wrong . . . although she couldn't think how. Perhaps Bramble or Cassius had made an error. Johnnie would be exactly the right person to review their assumptions; he had such clarity of thought . . .

She returned slowly to the embassy, where she had been assigned the smallest and least convenient of all the offices available. She wrote a dispatch to Bridges, reporting her lack of progress and suggesting she return to England. She confessed a particularly disappointing failure in gaining Harry Hopkins's confidence.

What a contrast to a year ago! Park had recruited her, plucked her from the tedium and obscurity of the Air Ministry, and placed her at his side in 11 Group, in the epicenter of the storm, giving her an opportunity to apply her mind to an existential threat, and Johnnie fought each day for England's survival. She remembered the constant shrilling of urgent telephones, and the clattering of teleprinters, the roaring of the loud but ineffectual air filtering system, the hubbub of the voices of the controllers, the bustling, efficient WAAFs at the map table below. Now she sat alone in a silent office in an echoing building an ocean from the conflict, and she and Johnnie were both engaged in exercises of futility. Froggie Potter and Harry Pound, and many, many more, might have died for nothing.

Bridges responded within a day. She should stay the course. Nothing could be more important. Indeed, the prime minister wished her to attend a conference at which both he and Roosevelt would be present. In fact, her inclusion had been suggested by Hopkins, who had written to say that her views were both helpful and refreshing. In the meantime, the MAUD committee had produced its second report, and the prime minster wished her to consider its implications immediately.

Q: The MAUD committee?

A: It was the follow-up to the Frisch–Peierls memorandum. It confirmed that one needed only twenty-five pounds of uranium 235 to make a bomb. That gave rise to a follow-up project named Tube Alloys on the British side and the Manhattan Project on the American side. The two projects were merged in 1943. I found the MAUD report to be very upsetting . . .

Eleanor stared at the document, unwilling to believe it but knowing it must be true. In the next few months or years, the scientists would unlock the secret of the energy that powered the sun. The sun burned virtually forever, she thought, because of nuclear fusion; the scientists on earth, using fission, would unleash the full energy of a tiny sun in the blink of an eye. And such a transient sun—a nova of unthinkable power—could be unleashed in the center of a city.

If the Americans decided to develop a bomb, she had no doubt they would get there long before the British, even though it was British science (with a strong displaced person boost) that was currently leading the way. America, she now realized, as she took another stroll around the Washington Monument—it was becoming a daily habit, in part as an antidote to the opportunity to overeat in ration-free America—was simply too big, too rich, too industrialized, too peaceful, too "can do," as Americans said, for Britain to keep up. America could devote thousands of people and millions of dollars to such a project, while in England, the project would be limited to a few obscure scientists skulking around in decaying country houses and grim basements hoping their laboratories wouldn't get bombed by the Luftwaffe that night.

Upon returning to her hotel, she found she had been invited to the White House by Harry Hopkins. He later served her tea in a charmingly quaint, old-fashioned manner.

"I understand you will be attending the conference next month, Mrs. Shaux," he said.

"Yes, sir, but I have no idea what it's about."

He poured her more tea, then opened a drawer in his desk and pulled out a copy of the MAUD report.

"What do you think of this?" he asked.

"I . . . I think the project has the wrong name, sir," she said slowly. "I think it should be called Pandora's Box."

"It's that bad?"

"Worse. Lord Acton said, although I'm not sure if this is an exact quote: 'All power corrupts; absolute power corrupts absolutely.'"

"Interesting," Hopkins said. "I hadn't heard that. Who is Acton?"

"Lord Acton was a nineteenth-century historian. Historians spend their lives studying men with power."

Hopkins grunted and glanced away to his left, and Eleanor had an intuition he was glancing in the direction of President Roosevelt, a man who would doubtless be the subject of many history books and weighed on Acton's scales for centuries to come.

"If we assume that such a bomb is feasible, sir, and we cannot assume it is not, it is essential, vital, that we get it first," she said. "We must develop it before Tojo, before Hitler, before Stalin."

Hopkins still seemed lost in reflection.

"That report is the most important and most dangerous document in the world, sir, without hyperbole," she pressed on.

He placed it back in his desk and wiped his hands with a handkerchief, as if the report was poisonous.

Q: Where was the conference? In Washington?

A: In Newfoundland. It was extremely cold.

Eleanor waddled onto the deck of the United States Navy cruiser *USS Augusta* wearing every stitch of clothing she possessed. She was just in time for the formal opening of the conference. A chill wind gusted across Placentia Bay, in Newfoundland, Canada, creating whitecaps on the waves and sending shivers down Eleanor's back. This is August, she thought; God only knows what it's like in January.

Churchill was there in one of the rakish, theatrical uniforms he loved to wear—this one was some sort of naval garb. Perhaps he was hoping that the captain of the battleship *HMS Prince of Wales* would let him steer the ship on the way back to England. And standing beside Churchill was Roosevelt. She had seen him a thousand times in newspaper photographs, but something seemed odd. He was tallish, with small pince-nez eyeglasses and a broad smile above a big, slab-like chin—her first impressions—and a long cigarette holder jutting from his teeth. Then she realized what was unexpected—he was standing or, rather, leaning against the rail behind him. He was being held upright by a young officer who was his son, as she discovered later.

How strong can America be, she found herself wondering, if both its president and his right-hand man have terminal illnesses? The moment that the formal introductions and greetings were over and the official photographs were taken, the president was assisted to a chair, and Churchill sat down beside him, perhaps so that any additional photographs would not show that only Roosevelt was sitting.

This was the start of the Riviera conference, which was planned to call for the defeat of Nazi Germany and the start of a new world order based on peace and democracy. Eleanor was extremely dubious about the second objective: the League of Nations, put in place to ensure peace and democracy after the Great War, had been an utter failure, so why would a new world order fare any better? Churchill might get Roosevelt to commit to the war effort at least on a practical level, although she doubted that Roosevelt would do it.

There were two or three dozen conference attendees waiting to be introduced, one by one, and Eleanor, by far the most junior, was at the end of the line. She was also, she realized, the only woman for many miles; the crews of the *Augusta* and the *Prince of Wales* must have amounted to close to three thousand men, not counting all the attendant ships surrounding them. She had her own cabin aboard the *Prince of Wales*, displacing a commander, who in turn displaced two lieutenant-commanders, and so on down through the ranks. No wonder she had a reputation for causing trouble in naval circles!

She wondered what the Red Tape model would say about this meeting and what it would say about the MAUD report and Churchill's decision to give it to Roosevelt. Cassius would have to give the model a major refit. She watched the two leaders sitting together: the president at ease, chain-smoking through his long cigarette holder, laughing often, gesturing expansively, and Churchill sitting next to him like a fat garden gnome, the keening wind shredding his cigar smoke.

Churchill, she knew, was *desperate* to get Roosevelt to commit to fight Hitler, but Roosevelt, bound by popular American political opinion as well as his own judgment, did not wish to fight another painful European war for no good reason. He had proclaimed sympathy for Britain's struggles, and he had muscled the Lend-Lease Act through Congress, but he had not moved beyond sympathetic support to active engagement in the conflict.

Churchill, according to the popular press, was the "last lion," the embodiment of the British Empire, the unwavering defender of all things British, the embodiment of its imperial reach, a man utterly devoted to its glorious past, a relentless defender of its grim present, and the key to its uncertain future.

As she waited for her turn to meet Roosevelt, she began to formulate how she might express the purpose of this conference, this relationship between Roosevelt and Churchill, in zero-sum terms. Suppose the power of the United States and that of Britain were to be expressed as two arcs moving in time, with . . .

Then it struck her like a blow: Churchill realized that the days of imperial Britannia were past. America would be the future leader of the world. No more "Rule, Britannia!" Churchill, she realized in shock, was trying to cement a partnership with Roosevelt not to lead but to be led. He was handing on the baton of global supremacy. Churchill, the idealist, was also the pragmatist! And thus he had handed the future leader of the world the key to its most powerful weapon: the MAUD report.

The next three or four days passed in a whirl. Eleanor knew she was right—Roosevelt, Averell Harriman, and Hopkins—the Americans—were clearly in charge of the proceedings. The central document, the Atlantic Charter, was their document, their vision, at which Churchill could only huff and puff and to which he could only submit.

Q: Churchill didn't get what he wanted?

A: Yes and no. He got a joint declaration, a declaration that, among other things, called for the destruction of Nazi tyranny, but it contained no American declaration of war. It was a statement no longer than a single page of text that described a vast vision of the future of the world.

Q: This was the Atlantic Charter? They signed it together?

A: Yes—the Atlantic Charter was the founding document of the United Nations and many other pillars of the modern world, the basis of modern international law and international institutions, but it was never signed. In fact, there was no actual piece of paper. All we have are the radio messages sent from the Augusta and the Prince of Wales containing the text.

Q: Was Churchill pleased?

Churchill was reclining on the bunkbed in his stateroom aboard the *Prince of Wales* as they returned across the Atlantic.

"Well, Wing Officer, did I win?"

"You didn't get a declaration of war, sir, nor did you get more ships or aircraft or tanks," she said. "But I think you prevented him from slipping away. You hooked him, sir, but you did not land him."

"Then I have won." He smiled, and lay back on his pillows. "I think I'll take a nap."

She considered telling him he hadn't won and simply had not lost, but a soft snore prevented her from saying anything more.

THIRTY-SEVEN

Q: When was the Riviera conference?

A: In August. As soon as we got back, we started updating the model for the German advance in Russia. I knew that the result of that conflict would be pivotal.

"You are certain, Wing Officer?" Churchill asked. "You are certain Moscow will hold?"

Churchill sat in his private office with only Lord Beaverbrook and Sir Edward Bridges in attendance.

"We have a projection of eighty percent, sir," Eleanor said. "The odds are four to one in favor."

Churchill frowned.

"The stakes are very high; indeed the entire future course of the war is in the balance. If we send help and succor to the Russians and they fail, we will have paid a terrible price for nothing."

Churchill's frown deepened. Eleanor said nothing. This is the essence of leadership, she thought, as she watched him weighing the situation and reaching a decision. She found she was holding her breath.

"Very few people agree with you, Wing Officer, on either side of the Atlantic."

"I know, sir."

He paused again. His cigar had gone out, and he took a little while to get it going to his satisfaction. Eleanor sat on the edge of her chair, still holding her breath.

"Very well," Churchill said at last. "We will assume the Russians will hold. We will proceed on that basis."

He sat back, as if exhausted, but then an impish grin appeared.

"If they do not hold, Wing Officer, I shall hold you personally to blame."

"I don't doubt it, sir."

Q: Meanwhile, your husband was . . .

A: He was flying almost every day. I continued to believe that the rhubarbs over France were unnecessary, futile, and far, far too dangerous.

Shaux checked the skies above him for the thousandth time. So far, so good. They were flying what they had come to call the southern loop, a low-level patrol from Cherbourg to Boulogne, just a mile off the coast of France, designed to suppress E-boat activity. Somewhere above them, lost high in the dazzling haze, was a shadowing squadron of Spitfires.

The Spits were 339, now commanded by Diggers. If he miraculously survived the war, Shaux wondered, would he always think of 339 as his favorite squadron? He admired and respected the American volunteers he was flying with in 188, and he was even growing fond of Whirlwinds, but somehow it just wasn't quite the same. Diggers had created a new squadron badge for 339, Shaux had heard, with a flying frog as its centerpiece.

It was roughly a hundred miles from Cherbourg northeastward to Boulogne, about twenty minutes at 300 miles per hour. Twenty minutes was not much time for the Luftwaffe to put up 109s or 190s to intercept them, and they would have to put up aircraft ahead of 188, in the Calais region, because aircraft coming from any other direction would never be able to catch up.

For a couple of months, 188 had been operational, and Shaux felt they had become an efficient, cohesive unit. The key, he felt, was staying at low levels, below one thousand feet, below Freya radar detection height. A typical sortie involved a dash across the Channel, not far above the wave tops, and then a surprise visit to a harbor in the hopes of catching an E-boat or two. Occasionally they'd go inland to shoot up an airfield or a railway yard.

At these altitudes Whirlwinds were just about fast enough, and agile enough, to defend themselves against 109s and 190s, and the Whirlwinds had the advantage of surprise: few Luftwaffe pilots had encountered them before and assumed that they would be no more maneuverable or quicker than Beaufighters. Occasionally a 109 was even foolish enough to stray into the range of a Whirlwind's four cannons.

The Peregrines still failed but far less frequently. Shaux felt they had made sufficient progress to inform Rolls-Royce and invite their engineers to visit. But he had received a reply from Bald Head declining to come down and reminding them that all modifications had to be preapproved by Rolls-Royce and that the Peregrines should therefore be reset to their factory specifications immediately.

Shaux checked the skies and the horizons for the thousand-and-first time; there was nothing to see except the Channel breakers rolling in and the low hills of France just off to their right. They must be just past Dieppe. In another minute he'd nudge over to the coast to get an exact fix; they'd soon be coming up on Le Touquet and Étaples. There was a small airfield at Le Touquet where they might see some aircraft on the ground, and the small yacht basin at Étaples, just across the river to the north, might be holding an E-boat.

Still, this all seemed a bit of a sideshow. Flying rhubarbs armed with cannons against targets of opportunity in occupied France was like sticking pins in the side of an elephant. If Fighter Command was going to stick with Whirlwinds, they should be given light bombs or, better yet, torpedoes, so that they could inflict more damage. In fact, it would be interesting to come up with an aerial version of the three-inch rockets he had seen in the antiaircraft Z Batteries—now that would be something! He'd speak to the ground crew riggers and armorers and see what they thought.

Eleanor agreed with him. She was cooking up a plan to get him transferred to MI6-3b, which would be the functional equivalent of being transferred to the Garden of Eden, but that would have to wait until she got back from Moscow—not that he knew she was in Moscow, of course.

"Follow me, Baseball," Shaux said, changing course slightly to cross the coast. The coast was turning due north; there was an estuary coming up: yes, it was the Somme. Le Touquet would be directly ahead. A minute to go. Shaux wondered if anyone had warned Le Touquet's antiaircraft defenses.

"On your marks, Baseball," he said. Glancing back he could see that 188 was in excellent formation. They really were good, even if Leigh-Mallory didn't take them seriously.

Overhead Berck-Plage, everyone tucked in nicely. Overhead Merlimont, three miles to go. Overhead Stella, two miles, twenty-five seconds. Safety catch off. Down a hair. Over a golf course. Le Touquet in sight. Last check above: nothing to see. White airfield buildings in sight, with the airstrip beyond. No 109s or 190s on the ground. But off to the right, at the far end of the field, tucked almost round a corner, what was that? Could that be a Junkers Ju 52? Too late to see but definitely worth a second look.

They flashed overhead Étaples—nothing noteworthy—and Shaux led them into a sharp left turn that would take them out to sea and bring them back to the airfield but this time flying the length of the field, northeast to southwest, rather than flashing across it.

Ju 52s were workhorses, light bombers or transport aircraft. They were rugged and reliable, with three engines like the American Ford Trimotors. Catching a stray 52 on the ground would make the trip worthwhile.

"Baseball, bandits to your north at angels zero-five," said the controller in Shaux's headset. "Shadow is engaging."

Diggers and 339 had spotted 109s or 190s and were jumping on them. There was no need to be concerned. Now out over the Channel, 188 was coming around for their second pass over Le Touquet.

"Baseball," Shaux said in acknowledgment.

"Bandits now overhead Le Touquet at angels zero-five," the controller said.

Shaux didn't know if these were the same bandits that 339 was chasing or another group. Unfortunately there were no clouds, and it would be easy for the bandits to spot 188 above the waves, but this was no time to cut and run. It was infuriating that the controller could hear both squadrons, but the squadrons could not hear each other.

"Baseball, follow me," Shaux said, completing the turn.

Less than a minute to Le Touquet. Diggers was close by, somewhere above them. Hopefully 339 had the new bandits in their sights. Thirty seconds. The field was in sight, directly ahead. Flak antiaircraft fire erupted from both sides of the field, sending tracer flashing through 188. Somebody just behind him—Red Two, Shaux thought—staggered but stayed in formation. Twenty seconds. Shaux saw muzzle flashes from one of the batteries, some sort of makeshift sandbagged revetment with 20-millimeter cannon barrels sticking out, but it was too late to do anything.

Pursued by flak, 188 swept the length of the field at twenty feet. Now he could see the Ju 52—no, there were three Ju 52s at the far end. Except these weren't 52s. These aircraft had gun turrets behind their cockpits. Well, they were enemy aircraft, whatever they were.

"Tallyho," he said, and opened fire.

They flashed above the enemy aircraft. Two burst into flames, and the third exploded as he crossed over it. What had they been carrying?

"Eyes wide open," he said, beginning another turn towards the sea. "Follow me."

A Spitfire appeared just ahead of him, trailing smoke and crossing his field of vision from left to right at no more than two hundred feet. Almost immediately two 190s appeared in pursuit.

It was not a good idea for Whirlwinds to turn into a stream of 190s—anything could happen in this kind of random melee. There were very probably more 190s around. Catching the 190s would require all the supercharger boost the Peregrines could muster, well above the safety levels he had calculated. It would be ridiculous to chase the 190s only to have the Peregrines overheat. He must, unfortunately, abandon the Spit to the 190s. The decision was obvious.

"Baseball turn right," Shaux said, and turned sharply after the 190s, standing his Whirlwind on its wingtip and opening the throttles wide. "Follow me."

Q: And you went to Moscow, even as the Germans were advancing towards it?

A: I did.

Q: Wasn't that dangerous?

A: It was.

She stood on the outskirts of a gathering in the Kremlin, watching Stalin and sipping a glass of vodka. Stalin seemed remarkably courteous, she thought, considering he was the greatest mass murderer in the recorded history of the world. She had been introduced to him a few minutes earlier. He had been polite and wreathed in smiles, with a gruff, rumbling voice that dispensed platitudes through an interpreter.

"Try tossing it back, if you can," Harry Hopkins advised her, pointing to her vodka. "That way you can't taste it."

"I'm just edging over to that potted plant so that I can discreetly dump it."

Russia required everything from aircraft to pickaxes to reinforce its desperate defense against the Germans, and everything would have to be carried to them through a hideously dangerous Arctic convoy route from Iceland and all around Norway to Murmansk and Archangel. She shuddered. How many men would die so that Russia could survive? How many men would die because she insisted that Moscow would hold?

The purpose of this "Caviar" conference—not much of a code name, she thought—was to agree on the details of this support. The British delegation was being led by Lord Beaverbrook, not Eden, the foreign secretary. She remembered Eden asserting that Hitler would never invade Russia.

"Now, Mr. Eden, guess what?" she thought to herself with a silent burst of spite.

Harry Hopkins led the Americans and effectively the combined American-British mission.

Over the past few days, her job had turned out to be to play the contrarian once more. The American ambassador, Laurence Steinhardt, and General Marshall, back in Washington, were convinced that Stalin would soon be defeated and that sending aid to Stalin was nothing but a waste. Stalin was running out of tanks, aircraft, and soldiers, while

German losses had been insignificant. Stafford Cripps, the British ambassador to the Kremlin, agreed with Steinhardt: an epic Russian defeat was imminent.

Eleanor had disagreed.

"Why?" Steinhardt demanded.

"Well, sir, Hitler's supply lines are already extended and subject to bad weather. Most of his supplies are dependent on horse-drawn vehicles."

"Why does that matter?"

"It is a mathematical impossibility for six hundred thousand horses to support three million men at a distance of one thousand miles. Hitler will lose because he doesn't have enough horses."

"Are you serious, Mrs. Shaux? It all comes down to horses, not tanks, not artillery, not aircraft?"

"Deadly serious, sir," she said. "If you wish, we can do the calculations."

"Gentlemen, this is nonsense," Steinhardt said, turning to Hopkins and the others.

Stafford Cripps offered a supporting snort of derision.

"Actually, Mr. Ambassador, I think she's right," Hopkins said.

"I fear she's wrong, Mr. Hopkins," Cripps said, shaking his head emphatically. "I know Russia. I know the Russian people."

"I do not, sir," Eleanor said. "But I do know mathematics. Mathematics transcend national borders."

Now, three days later, all the delegations were toasting each other in the Kremlin at the conclusion of the conference, and Eleanor was watching Stalin and trying to decide if it was a breach of diplomatic protocol to pour her vodka into a nearby potted plant. Stalin had a thick head of hair and luxuriant eyebrows and a bushy mustache and broad, stubby hands; he's a peasant in a gilded palace, she thought. He disconcertingly reminded her of her favorite uncle, Eddie, a benign man who had given her a pony. The rocklike soldier standing beside him like a statue was Marshal Zhukov—square jawed, heavyset, seemingly unstoppable, like a human battering ram. He was the man who would have to stop Hitler, if her prediction was to prove true. These are men without mercy, she thought; could they outweigh even Hitler in cruelty?

She half-noticed someone handing a telegram to Stafford Cripps, who glanced at it and frowned. He hesitated for a moment and then handed it to Eleanor.

"I'm sorry, Mrs. Shaux. We've just been informed that your husband went down in France. His aircraft was on fire and he parachuted. They don't know if he survived or not."

THIRTY-EIGHT

Q: Now, I think it's true that you heard your husband had gone down in France while you were in Moscow?

A: Yes, it was completely ghastly. We knew he'd gone down on fire and had parachuted out, but we knew nothing more. It took about a month for the news to filter back through the Red Cross in Switzerland that he was alive. Injured but alive: that was still all we knew.

Shaux reclined awkwardly in an antique wheelchair. It had spoked bicycle wheels and a basket weave seat. He found he was rearranging himself every thirty seconds out of frustration as much as discomfort. Every time he rearranged himself, the basketwork squeaked in protest. His right leg was sticking out in front of him, balanced on an ancient carved wood–and–wrought iron support at exactly the right angle to cause passersby to bump into it and jolt his leg.

His ankle had been badly twisted and would bear no weight; he would have to hobble around on crutches or be wheeled around in this contraption for a couple of weeks or more. A doctor visited him daily and assured him, via an interpreter, that nothing was broken or seriously damaged, and he would recover fully; in the meantime he would just have to be patient.

The doctor chuckled to himself at this witty double entendre, but somehow the humor got lost in translation, particularly after several repetitions. Pain medicines were, unfortunately, in short supply, at least for prisoners of war.

Shaux was in no hurry, of course. As soon as he was able to travel, he would be shipped off to a POW camp in Germany.

It would all try the perseverance of the most phlegmatic soul. His starboard engine had burst into flames as he was closing in on an unwary Focke-Wulf 190. The 190 seemed oblivious to his presence; the rest of its swarm was in disarray. The whole encounter was a mess: a chaotic, aimless, running battle between Spits, 190s, and Whirlwinds. But it might be the rare occasion in which Whirlwinds could get the better of 190s. It would be a huge boost for 188's morale to knock one down.

Then, exactly as he had reported to Rolls-Royce time and time and time again, the Peregrine overheated and experienced catastrophic failure. It was not over-revving, the coolant system and the oil pump were working, and the radiator flaps were correctly adjusted; it just succumbed to some combination of its many, many ways of overheating. He had fired at the 190 anyway to try to show 188 it was possible for Whirlwinds to win. The 190 had staggered, but he didn't know the end result—he was much more concerned about his own aircraft.

He was overhead Rouen with no chance of getting home on one engine. If he continued to fly, he would certainly be shot down. If he managed an emergency landing, he'd just be giving the Whirlwind to the Luftwaffe. If he dithered in indecision, the flames might spread and engulf him.

"This is Baseball Leader, on fire, bailing out. Baseball, re-form on Red Leader, re-form on Red Leader. Good luck."

Now 188 would be in Grady's good hands—they'd be fine. He trusted Grady's instincts, just as he had always trusted Diggers's instincts.

Without waiting for a reply or acknowledgment, he turned the Whirlwind south, away from the town so that it would probably crash in open countryside, released the canopy, and jumped. The tall tail flashed past him uncomfortably close, but then he was clear and staring down, searching for a clear spot to land. His parachute opened with a bone-jarring jerk.

The gusting winds pushed him inexorably towards the serried ranks of Rouen's roofs and towers, as jagged as teeth in a shark's open jaws with the massive stone edifice of the gothic cathedral of Notre Dame at their center. He was drifting northward over the Seine towards the heart of the medieval city. There were no parks or open spaces that he could see, just spiky rooftops and gables. The wind wouldn't let him try to ditch in the river. The cathedral had an enormous spire—it must be close to five hundred feet high, and he was already below the pinnacle. He was being blown into the cathedral; it was simply too big to avoid, and the wind was too strong to resist. He tugged at the parachute control lines and just managed to evade one of the tall towers at the west end, but he was swept onward and downward into the statue-encrusted west facade.

A carved stone saint, or possibly an angel, snagged his parachute canopy, swinging him around with another bone-jarring thump into the arms of a bearded apostle some twenty feet below. His right foot came to a sudden stop in a neighboring apostle's lap. A flock of pigeons erupted from their resting places in the statuary and flew noisily away. The bearded apostle seemed unmoved by Shaux's abrupt arrival, as if pilots fell out of the sky and into his lap on a frequent basis and such events did not disturb his endless contemplation of eternity.

There Shaux hung helplessly for an hour or so, perhaps thirty feet above the cobblestones. He decided that the trimotors they'd seen at Le Touquet were probably Italian SM.81s—Pipistrellos, as they were called—although it seemed irrelevant now.

Eventually the *pompiers* arrived with a tall ladder and cut him down, and the gendarmes arrested him.

Now he was in the town hospital, guarded by a sympathetic gendarme with an extravagant mustache. At night he slept in a locked prison ward; his ward mate, a man recovering from an appendectomy, had been charged with murdering his wife's lover with a hatchet. The man had a tendency to mutter, and Shaux avoided making eye contact with him. Shaux wished he had Charlie to protect him—poor Charlie, he would be bereft, betrayed once more. He knew that 188 would take good care of him, but even so, Charlie must believe that he was fated to serial abandonment.

After a few days of increasing boredom, a Luftwaffe officer came to see him. Shaux was not sure what rank he was, but he wore the Iron Cross dangling from a ribbon around his neck. He drew himself up, saluted, and clicked his heels.

"Ah, you are the famous Squadron Leader Johnnie Shaux," he said, in accented but clear idiomatic English. "Otto Borman at your service. I am major, the same rank, I think, as yours."

Shaux had no idea of the appropriate etiquette, but the man seemed friendly, and Shaux returned his salute as best he could.

"Good morning, Major," he said, not knowing what else to say.

"I am pleased to meet you," Borman said, holding out his hand.

"Good morning," Shaux said again, and took his hand. Borman's uniform was much grander than Shaux's own, he thought a little wildly, with impressive rank badges on the collars and a rakish cap loaded with silver braid.

"I think you must have upset your superiors!" Borman said. "You are in the doghouse back in England, no? Perhaps you seduced an air marshal's daughter? No? I am certain of it!"

"Why do you say that?"

"Why else would you be flying such a piece of crap?" Borman laughed. "The Whirlwind! You are a superior pilot, a Spitfire pilot. The best, not the worst! That is why I conclude that you are being punished."

Johnnie found himself automatically jumping to the Whirlwind's defense.

"It's a good aircraft."

"Yes, perhaps, better than the Messerschmitt 110, I grant you," Borman said. "But with crappy engines."

"The Peregrines—"

"The Kestrels were good, but the Peregrines are not so good. You see? I know Rolls-Royce. Very superior! I studied there one summer. Derby. Terrible beer but pretty girls! Foreign apprentice!"

Shaux had always thought of Germans as rigid and formal martinets—well, that was the way they were usually portrayed in books and films—but Borman was anything but: he was a human dynamo as his words poured out.

"Well, I think . . . ," Shaux tried again.

"I know, I know; Kestrels powered the first Junkers Stuka, yes, other Heinkels and Dorniers, even early Messerschmitt 109s, all true. But the Merlin is better, much, much better. Better than even the Daimler-Benz 602, even though I will be shot for saying it!"

He looked over his shoulder theatrically, laughing at his own joke, and Shaux found himself laughing too.

"Well . . ."

"But the BMW 801, fourteen cylinders, forty-two liters, air-cooled radial, is the finest of all, which is why the Focke-Wulf 190 is the finest of all."

"Well . . ."

"I saw you! I saw your engine on fire without fighting! That is why I say the Peregrine is crap! Overheating!"

"Well . . ."

"You plan your attack very good, and you jump us fair and square, an excellent maneuver. You completely surprise us, you are about to attack my good friend Adolf Mannheim, and then—poof! Engine on fire! That is why you are a prisoner, Johnnie Shaux, even though you are a good pilot. Because I fly a 190, and you fly a piece of crap. I rest my case."

He threw his arms out wide and laughed in delight at his analysis, and Shaux found himself laughing back.

"You fire on Adolf, just for a moment, even though your shitty Peregrine is on fire, and hit his tail. Adolf had to jump, so a victory to you. Adolf is very embarrassed—whoever heard of a fine 190 being shot down by a piece-of-shit Whirlwind? Come, I take you to the Luftwaffe officers' mess for lunch. Adolf owes you a glass of schnapps for beating him. We are based at Boos. Not far. A complete dump, but it has a hard runway. With your leg you literally can't run away, no?"

"True, but I'll try anyway."

"Ha, Johnnie Shaux." Borman laughed.

He helped Shaux rearrange himself in his wheelchair and started for the door. "By God, this thing is heavy! Hard to move! What a piece of crap! It must be powered by a Rolls-Royce Peregrine! Be careful—it may catch on fire!"

The days crawled by. Shaux divided his time between wondering what Eleanor was doing in America, wondering how 188 was getting along without him, and improving his French as best he could. He had spent a few weeks in France in May and June, before Dunkirk and the collapse of French resistance, and he had acquired a basic smattering of the language. Borman burst in upon him at periodic intervals to carry him off for an alcohol-fueled meal.

Shaux advanced from the wheelchair to two crutches to one crutch to a walking stick. He began a covert survey of the hospital and the movements of the staff, wondering how it might be possible to escape as soon as he could manage to walk a hundred yards. The gendarmes seemed both sloppy and bored and probably not overly concerned if an Englishman should slip away.

On sunny days he was permitted to sit on a balcony twenty feet above a public street below. Shaux calculated how many bedsheets would be necessary to make a rope twenty feet long. If he secured the sheets to his wheelchair and more or less jumped off or slid off the corner of the balcony, and landed without jarring his ankle, he could hobble away up an alleyway and round a corner before anyone noticed.

There could be a real opportunity. He began hiding extra sheets under his mattress. He redoubled his efforts to learn French so that he could communicate with the Resistance if he was able to escape. *"Je suis un aviateur anglais, aidez moi . . ."* or should it be just *"m'aidez?"*

Borman came to see him again.

"You have been pronounced well, Johnnie Shaux. You will be transferred from the custody of the Gendarmerie National to the Luftwaffe. It will now take a few days or a week or so for your transportation to be arranged. You will be taken to Germany to be put in a POW camp run by the Luftwaffe. The Stalag Luft camps are very superior, the best. In the meantime you can be housed in our guardhouse at the airfield. The food is better than the city jail."

THIRTY-NINE

Q: Now, remind me of the time line in 1941. Barbarossa was when?

A: Barbarossa, the German invasion of Russia, was at the end of June. I was sent to Washington at the beginning of July, and the MAUD report came out while I was there. The Riviera conference in Canada was in August, and the Caviar conference was in September.

Q: In Moscow?

A: Correct. All through this period, everyone was focused on the German advance. They were approaching Moscow—they got within ten miles. Most people, including the Americans, thought they would capture the city.

Q: But you did not, because of Hitler's horses!

A: The horses and the snow. It began to snow at the beginning of October, and the German advance, known as Operation Typhoon, got bogged down—quite literally. Belarus and Estonia turned into a sea of mud. It took the Germans until the beginning of December to get to the outskirts of Moscow, but by then it was too late. Marshal Zhukov counterattacked, and the undefeatable German army was defeated.

Q: And the horses? Why the horses?

A: A horse can pull, order of magnitude, 150 pounds for twenty miles in a day. Hitler had six hundred thousand horses in Russia, a staggering number, so he could move almost a million tons of materiel a mile every day. Now, it is almost exactly one thousand miles from Berlin, in eastern Germany, to Moscow. So a horse can move 150 pounds from Berlin to Moscow, on average, in twenty days. But a horse eats about 15 pounds of hay a day.

Q: So?

A: So . . . a horse can only haul its own food half the distance from Berlin to Moscow, not all the way. Hitler should have stopped in Minsk.

Q: You're joking, aren't you, Dame Eleanor?

A: Fortunately for the world, I am not. Given the values I have indicated, for how much a horse eats every day, how much it can pull, and so on, "x" is indisputably the distance that Hitler's supply lines could stretch. Solve for "x."

"Wing Officer, you have upset Stafford Cripps," Churchill said, wreathed, as ever, in his own unique penumbra.

It was becoming a pattern, Eleanor thought, that she would upset some high-ranking person or other on one side of the Atlantic or the other and, in due course, Churchill would hear of it.

"I'm sorry, sir."

Churchill stared at her for a long moment. Was that a twinkle in his eye? It was hard to tell.

"Do not be," he grunted. "Update your mathematical model to reflect the full potential of the MAUD report, and do so with all deliberate speed."

He picked up a fountain pen and started to write notes on a typewritten page.

"The House of Commons awaits, Wing Officer," he said, in explanation and dismissal.

Q: This was before the Germans were stopped in Russia, or after?

A: Oh, long before, while Stafford Cripps was still predicting Moscow's fall. I spent October redoing the model. It helped to keep my mind off Johnnie.

MI6-3b, Eleanor discovered, had now subdivided itself into a series of parallel projects that were becoming progressively more competitive.

"It's possible I'm not the ideal leader for this group," Bramble confessed. "Everyone seems to be working independently. It's been getting worse ever since Jayne had to resign."

Jayne, who was now Mrs. Jayne Bramble, was due in November. Without her iron fist in control of MI6-3b, the technical research officers were breaking in rival fiefdoms, and the model was producing different and even opposite predictions.

"No one seems to do what I ask them to do," Bramble told her.

"Let me help you solve that problem," Eleanor said, and called a meeting of all the TROs. She was shocked to realize there were now more than twenty of them. God alone knew how many WAAFs supported them, as well as Crenshaw's army of form fillers and report writers.

"I regret to inform you, gentlemen, that, for budgetary reasons and conflicting war priorities, we have been told to reduce our staff of TRO mathematicians on this project," she told the assembled throng. "I have therefore asked Mr. Bramble to select ten of you to continue. I regret that the remainder will have to be transferred to the Shetlands for security reasons. Unfortunately it's getting very cold up there, and it's still only October."

The room was silent.

"You will be notified shortly if you are on Mr. Bramble's list. In the interim, we will have only one version of the model and only one set of results. Are there any questions?"

There were none.

Commander Crenshaw, the administrative officer, seemed to be emboldened by Jayne's departure and was attempting to make inroads into what had been her undisputed territory. He was proposing, in the name of efficiency and economy, that Malvern House should have a centralized filing system, including all the TROs' files and papers, all under his general management. He cited security concerns and told her that two suspected enemy spies had been detained for questioning. They had been snooping around Aldeburgh, he said, attempting to collect information about herself and the TROs. It had never occurred to Eleanor that the enemy would be remotely interested in her, but as soon as Crenshaw told her, it became blindingly obvious.

Eleanor told Crenshaw she would consider his filing proposal. As soon as he had left her, she sent an urgent message to Sir Edward Bridges and had it carried by a Wren dispatch rider. Later that same evening Crenshaw was posted to a naval facility in Holyhead in Wales, effective immediately.

It occurred to her for a fleeting second that if the enemy intelligence services were interested in her, they might also be interested in Johnnie, but Cassius and MAUD demanded her immediate attention and she set that thought aside.

Cassius was working more obsessively than ever. Eleanor wavered back and forth in her mind but decided to give him the MAUD report and responsibility for developing the analyses Churchill had requested. That meant giving him knowledge of the possibility of atomic fission bombs, with all that it implied. He came to see her the day after she handed him the report. His eyes were glowing with excitement.

"There is a God!" he said. "The Third Reich can be incinerated!"

She knew he would apply all his skills, fueled by his consuming hatred of Hitler, to modeling and analyzing the consequences of such a weapon. His endeavors would be intensified by the possibility of not just cremating Hitler and his henchmen but also reducing the entire Nazi capital to ashes.

This was work for which Johnnie was far better suited, intellectually and emotionally, but, alas, he was now far beyond her reach.

She had a growing fear, a sort of ugly feeling gnawing at the corners of her brain, that she was becoming party to the greatest sin that mankind could ever commit. She was enabling destruction on an unimaginable scale. She was helping to unlock Pandora's Box.

Q: And then?

A: Then I was sent back to America at the end of October. Churchill wanted discussions about naval cooperation in the Pacific, just as we were cooperating in the Atlantic, and with the new Russian convoy system, and he wanted me to go to Pearl Harbor for that purpose. Hong Kong and Singapore were very poorly defended.

And he wanted me to see what the Americans were doing with the MAUD report. All in all, I was spending a lot of time on transport aircraft. I was becoming an informal diplomat, although I am far from diplomatic.

Q: Why you, if I may ask?

A: Well, I suppose I knew everyone; Harry Hopkins on the American side and Churchill on our side trusted me; I wasn't threatening to anyone because I could always be dismissed as just a girl, so I was a convenient go-between, I suppose.

Q: And why you, from your perspective?

A: I felt we had fought the Battle of Britain and survived, but we were still vulnerable. I know it sounds silly, but I felt I had to keep doing what I was doing to preserve the chance that 11 Group had given us, so all those lives wouldn't have been thrown away in a losing cause. Only the Americans could rescue us. Only the Americans could invade France and rescue my husband.

Shaux was back to square one on his escape plans. The guardhouse was built of concrete blocks, and the cell windows were barred. Occasionally he shared his quarters with a Luftwaffe airman arrested for being drunk and disorderly or petty theft.

Borman brought him, under guard, to the officers' mess on several occasions. The other officers treated him politely, as an interesting curiosity. Borman's friend Adolf insisted on buying him a glass of schnapps on every occasion. Shaux was struck at how much they had in common with their 11 Group opponents—the same stories, the same drinking, the same strange combination of restless energy and utter exhaustion, even the same jokes. All these, Shaux thought, were the result of the same acute stress, the same uncertainty as to whether they would be alive tomorrow.

"I have shot down RAF aircraft, it is true, Hurricanes and Defiants," Borman said one evening, as they shared a drink. "Also four Spitfires. It is necessary. I bear no ill will. I think you understand?"

"I understand."

"Have you been shot down?"

"Twice," Shaux said. "Once in a Defiant overhead Dunkirk and once in a Spit above Kent last year, last September."

"I have shot down Spitfires over Kent last September. If it was me, I apologize!"

"Oh, I'm certain it wasn't you."

"Why? You think I'm not good enough? Ha?"

"No, no, I'm sure you are!" Shaux laughed. "No, the chap who shot me down tried to shoot me up when I was coming down on my parachute. He himself got shot down immediately by my own chaps."

Shaux reflected, with surprise, that his English was deteriorating. Well, he was surrounded by German and French voices . . .

"Ah, yes, the famous 339 Squadron," said Borman, tossing back his drink. "You see—I study 11 Group closely. Forewarned is forearmed."

He gestured to a steward for more drinks.

"I was shot down once by a Spitfire, but I landed in the Channel and managed to get picked up by an S-boat and was rescued within ten minutes. Amazing luck! Perhaps it was you who shot me down. Did you ever shoot down a 109 off Calais at the end of August last year?"

Shaux knew Borman meant it as a joke, but it actually triggered a memory of attacking a 109 and seeing the pilot bail out and land in the sea near an E-boat. Obviously there had been many such incidents, but somehow it did ring a bell. He remembered it, he supposed, because he had decided not to attack the E-boat—getting shot up once is enough for any day.

"Yes, I think I may have done. It's possible," Shaux said. "If I did, sorry about that . . ."

"We are both survivors." Borman shrugged. "You have your medals and I have mine. Sometimes it all seems so pointless."

Back in his cell, it occurred to Shaux that Otto had become his friend—as he thought about it, his only friend. Shaux had always been something of a loner. Shaux had enjoyed the easy congeniality of the junior common rooms at Oxford and the 11 Group officers' messes, and he cared strongly about Diggers and Froggie, but he had never actually had someone that he could talk to about personal things. He could almost talk to Otto—if Otto would let him get a word in edgeways—more than to Eleanor because Otto was flesh and blood, whereas she was a miracle that had appeared, been briefly transformed into flesh and blood, and might disappear at any moment for reasons he could not fathom. If he didn't understand why she had come to him, he couldn't understand if she would stay.

Perhaps it was some kind of perverse stubbornness, some strange obtuseness, Shaux thought, that drew him to befriend his enemy. He wondered, for the fiftieth time that day, what Eleanor was doing.

FORTY

Q: You still believed, even at that late date, that America would not enter the war?

A: I did not believe they would become combatants. They would support us and, as a result of the conference in Moscow, Russia. But they would not send young American men to die in what was still an intra-European conflict.

Q: So your quest was pointless, in your own opinion?

A: Not completely pointless. The United States was, in practical terms, conducting an undeclared low-intensity war in the Atlantic, even though it was still neutral. Anyway, we were hoping for that same kind of active cooperation in the Pacific. Perhaps some marines in Hong Kong, for example, or some escort carriers . . .

When Eleanor returned to Washington—there was a nip in the air, and the uniquely American holiday of Thanksgiving was coming up—Lord Halifax's secretary reluctantly allocated her the same office in the British embassy. Clearly Eleanor was almost persona non grata, if not quite; the office was small and at the end of a confusing series of corridors. The secretary handed her a newly printed embassy dress code regulation and suggested Eleanor study it carefully.

Hopkins had arranged a preliminary conference to map out the objectives and boundaries of cooperation in the Pacific. This would be followed by a conference in Pearl Harbor to discuss the specifics.

"What is your general assessment of the Pacific theater, Mrs. Shaux?"

Eleanor groaned inwardly. Everywhere she went, it seemed, panels took turns to question her analyses; this time it was a combination of naval officers and diplomats. It was just a question of time, she thought, before one of these panels would ask her to spell "apocryphal" or "arrhythmic."

"Japan has already taken Korea, Manchuria, and now China, sir," she began. "As long as you ignore their aggression, they'll concentrate on eating up the rest of Asia—the Dutch East Indies, Malaysia, Burma, Hong Kong at some point, Singapore in order to control the Strait of Malacca, and so on."

The room was silent and Eleanor plowed on.

"India is probably too big and too populous to swallow, but they'll go for Australia if they get half a chance. War between Great Britain and Japan is inevitable, and I doubt we can stop them."

"They'll keep expanding?" one of the diplomats asked.

"The Japanese live on a string of mountainous islands with poor natural resources and no oil. They are turning Asia into a series of subordinate tributary colonies that feed them agricultural products and raw materials and thereby make them rich and powerful."

"An interesting analysis. How do you support it?"

"Britain is a series of islands with limited natural resources and no oil. We successfully turned Asia into a series of subordinate tributary colonies that feed us agricultural products and raw materials and thereby make us rich and powerful. That is how small islands become dominant hegemons."

That produced a series of grunts around the table and almost, although not quite, some hint of acknowledgment.

"Uh, Mrs. Shaux, what exactly is your position in the British government?" someone asked. "What is . . . let me see . . . what is MI6-3b?"

"We are a branch of Military Intelligence—actually just one of several—responsible for analyzing and predicting enemy activities, sir."

"Second-guessing Hitler?" It was as close an explanation as she dared give: Red Tape was still on the secret list.

"Exactly, sir."

"In that case, will the Japanese attack us?"

"Given the present balance of forces, sir, it is not in Japan's best interests to attack the United States. For that reason they will avoid the Philippines. Their limited resources are best devoted to maintaining their grip on their recent conquests and adding more."

She looked around the table. She had their attention, she saw—she was, after all, a novelty item—but not their belief.

"The United States is not an immediate threat," she continued. "You are still figuratively and literally over the horizon. They will only recalculate if something changes."

"Such as?" asked an admiral.

"Oh, something that changes the balance."

"Such as?" he asked again.

"Well, it could be almost anything that makes them think they have a decisive advantage . . . something irresistible . . . such as keeping the fleet deployed forward at Pearl Harbor, for example, sir, instead of leaving it in San Diego. That might make the Japanese risk an attack."

"I don't understand."

"If the Pacific fleet is concentrated in one spot, particularly a vulnerable forward position like Hawaii, which is a very long way from the United States and is a relatively poorly defended position Japan could readily attack, they might imagine they could deliver a knockout blow."

"That's ridiculous," another admiral broke in. "Massing the fleet is a deterrent."

"Perhaps, sir, but it also creates an opportunity for you to lose. If the fleet is in San Diego, you can't lose. Move the fleet to one forward exposed spot, and you can. I believe Admiral Richardson advanced the same point."

"Admiral Richardson was relieved of his command precisely for making that point, Mrs. Shaux; it was then, and it still remains, absurd."

It sounded as if he intended his statement as a threat.

"Are you suggesting that the entire United States naval doctrine is wrong, Mrs. Shaux?" the admiral asked. "Are you an expert in navy strategy?"

"No, sir, I am certainly no expert. I'm only suggesting that, if the fleet is in San Diego, you have no way of losing. If it is concentrated in Pearl Harbor, it creates the potential for a knockout blow against you."

"Rubbish!" the admiral snapped, just as Leigh-Mallory had done a couple of months ago. "How can you say such a thing?"

"Because it's logical," Eleanor almost said, or, "Because it makes sense," or, "Because it's obvious." But she remained silent, knowing he wouldn't listen. Logic or sense, it seemed to her, probably played no part in naval doctrine.

"Let us move on," the most senior admiral intervened. "We are very satisfied with our deployments, Mrs. Shaux, but we thank you for your concerns."

He rose to signify both the end of the meeting and his dismissal of her argument.

"However, we will welcome your thoughts on the South China Sea and the Strait of Malacca. We can take that up when we reconvene in Hawaii."

After dinner she took her favorite walk out to the Washington Memorial. Johnnie was locked away in a German POW camp, and she wouldn't see him for years, perhaps never. The fierce intensity of their love had kept her sane ever since the Battle of Britain, had acted as an antidote to Churchill's demands and the pressures of creating MI6-3b and demands of increasingly complex mathematics, and had sustained her against the withering contempt of the military and diplomatic powers that be. She was a woman in a man's world, but ever since he had gone down, she had been denied the opportunity to be a woman.

The war would last for several years, at least. Johnnie would be a captive until the end and might not survive even then. She was, in effect, a functional widow, married to someone completely beyond reach. Or a nun. Some are born chaste, some achieve chastity, and some have chastity thrust upon them.

Britain was incapable of invading Europe alone and therefore incapable of rescuing him. Only American power could do so, and she was failing to entice America into the fray.

Tears welled up unbidden, followed by heart-wrenching sobs. She was all alone and there was no one to comfort her.

Life was too difficult. Everyone hated her. She lived in a world of men who refused to treat her as an equal. They just stared at her and tried to imagine her naked. They didn't understand the MAUD report or what it meant—they couldn't even be bothered to read it. They didn't understand why it was a mistake to concentrate the fleet; they didn't understand that it was literally impossible for Hitler to support an army in front of Moscow.

She had lost control of her work. The TROs were multiplying like the sorcerer's apprentice's brooms. Bramble and Cassius and a dozen others had taken her model, her idea, and turned it into something else, she knew not what, some kind of instrument of war or perhaps many instruments of war.

She didn't understand what she was doing in America. Churchill was sending her hither and yon, always the odd woman out, always the annoying contrarian. She had been cast adrift. Soon she had to go even farther, to Hawaii on the other side of the world, where, doubtless, there were more men waiting to tell her she was wrong.

The war was consuming everything, like a cancer, like a plague.

Johnnie was locked into some barbed wire cage who knew where. He had doubtless disappeared back into an impenetrable stoic trance, an impermeable fog beyond her reach, perhaps forever. His agony would be ruthlessly suppressed but eating away at him, a cancer growing ever larger, eating his soul.

One day he would just die. They'd open him up to perform an autopsy to see what had killed him, but there'd be no Johnnie left inside. He'd been all eaten up, consumed by too much stress, too many horrors, too much pain, and too much hopelessness, all alone in his cage, infinitely lonely.

FORTY-ONE

Q: Your husband's captivity must have been hard for you.

A: It was, but harder yet for him.

Otto Borman sat brooding by the fireplace in the Luftwaffe officers' mess, staring into the embers of a dying fire, his face full of dancing shadows and his conversation more eclectic than ever.

"Do you think Winston Churchill is a good man?" he asked suddenly, apropos of nothing, as far as Shaux could tell.

"What?" Shaux said.

He had always considered Churchill to be one of those distant, godlike figures who ruled from Olympian heights, like senior-ranking RAF officers with gold braid on their hats, or the fellows of his college sitting at the high table for dinner, or the governors of the orphanage in which he had grown up. One didn't like or dislike them; they simply existed, far above evaluation by mere mortals. Eleanor knew Churchill well, but that didn't make him any more real to Shaux.

"I don't know. I don't really think about him, to tell you the truth. Why do you ask?"

"Why are you fighting, Johnnie Shaux?"

Another odd question—and not an easy one to answer. No one had asked him that before. He had never made a conscious decision to fight; fighting was simply something that had happened.

"I'm permanent RAF, not just hostilities only," Shaux said. "I joined when I was fifteen, long before the war, as a fitter."

The fates had swept him along, from the orphanage to the RAF to Oxford and finally to the war, even to this chair by the fireplace, and he had simply been carried along by the current.

"Fitter? What is this word?"

"Engine mechanic," Shaux said, and tried to raise Borman's spirits. "On Kestrels, not Peregrines, before you ask!"

Borman smiled.

"You're not fighting for king and country? For the glory of the British Empire? Rule Britannia? There'll always be an England?"

"Not really!" Shaux laughed. "Why do you ask?"

"Because I sometimes . . . never mind . . . one last drink before I put you back in the guardroom cell? Yes?" He waved towards the bar and gesticulated. "Tell me, Johnnie Shaux, are you engaged or married?"

"Married."

"You are lucky."

"Yes, very lucky," Shaux said.

"I was engaged once but no longer."

"Oh, I'm sorry to hear that. What happened, if I may ask?"

"Her grandmother was Jewish."

"I don't understand," Shaux said.

"Neither do I, but that's why I'm fighting: to prevent Aryans from marrying Jews."

"What?"

Otto stood and tossed his cigarette into the embers.

"I'm sorry, Johnnie Shaux. I'm in a bad mood tonight, that's all. Please forgive me."

He spread his arms and shrugged his shoulders in a gesture of helplessness.

"I owe you an apology for my bizarre behavior. I am a mess. I am baroque, rococo, even, no question."

"No, not at all," Shaux said automatically. Baroque? Rococo? Was Borman sober? He glanced around the room. They were alone, except for a distant waiter at the bar and an acutely bored airman waiting to escort him back to his cell.

"There are things I can't really talk about to anyone here—they wouldn't understand. I am a heroic fighter pilot, with Knight's Cross of the Iron Cross. My picture is in the *Berliner Illustrirte Zeitung*. Very dashing. I receive many letters from young ladies wishing to reward me for my services to the fatherland as only young ladies can."

Shaux remained silent, sensing that a dam was about to overflow.

"I asked you why you are fighting. Let me answer for myself. I am fighting for my father, a general in the last war. I have no choice. He is very important. He is a friend of Hermann Göring; he is very high in the Party."

Borman paused to toss back his drink before continuing.

"My father is a proud man, you must understand, and he feels the loss of the first war ruined his life. Germany should never have accepted the terms of the armistice in 1918, in his opinion. He was ruined by the financial collapses after the last war. We lost our land in Prussia. From nobleman he is made to be hotel night manager, being humble to bourgeois people below his station, in his estimation. All this he hates. We lose the house and live over the stables. He is deeply humiliated."

Borman seemed unable to sit still.

"Then he joins the National Socialist Party, and his life is for the cause. Now he is committed to reversing the Treaty of Versailles, to the rebirth of Germany. This may mean nothing to you or me, but it is everything to him—the restoration of Prussia as a great power. We will jump from 1871 until the present!"

Shaux raked his memories of ancient high school history classes for the year 1871. He seemed to remember it was the year that Germany crushed France in the Franco-Prussian War and created the German Empire.

Borman paused while the waiter served their drinks and retreated into the shadows. Shaux sensed that this was a confession that had been bottled up inside him for a long time. It was a confession he could not make to another German or a member of the Luftwaffe, Shaux guessed, but only to an enemy.

"Ha! He disapproves of me deeply, even though I have the Knight's Cross, even though I am praised by his friend Göring. You see, Johnnie Shaux, when I was in the college, I study engineering, but I wanted to be a dancer in the cinema, like Fred Astaire, the American. I am a good dancer, a very good dancer. I dance so I can get girls, many girls—it works very well. I get many girls. Then I find the one perfect girl. Life is perfect!"

He laughed.

"But no, that is not good enough for my father. Far from it! Her grandmother is a Jew so she is a Jew: that is unacceptable. God forbid his son should just be happy! His friend Göring arranges for me an officer's commission in the Luftwaffe, and here I am."

"What about the girl?"

"I don't know; I have not heard from her," Borman said.

He stared at Shaux, his eyes filled with anger, or hopelessness, or perhaps nothing at all.

Later, back in the guardhouse, Shaux wondered if it was better to have a difficult father or no father at all. Certainly Shaux's father had never done him any wrong . . .

In the meantime, on a more practical level, if he managed to escape, he could head north to Belgium, east to Switzerland, or south to Spain. Belgium was occupied, just like France, but it was much closer, and he couldn't count on walking more than twelve or fifteen miles a day. So Belgium was perhaps ten days away or less if he could find help.

The following morning Borman came to see him without any hint of his usual lighthearted chatter.

"Do you know what is the Abwehr, Johnnie Shaux?"

"No, sorry. I don't."

"Military intelligence. We have been told they are coming to take you."

"Why?"

"Transfer papers, signed by the Oberkommando der Luftwaffe, all very official. Dated today, 6 December, 1941. They are driving from Paris to collect you."

"Why?"

"They must think you have information, intelligence."

"About what?"

"I don't know. I've never heard of it before, taking RAF for questioning. The reputation is not good."

Shaux felt the hair standing up on the back of his neck, some primeval warning of danger, the feeling he sometimes got when he sensed there might a 109 or a 190 up his backside.

"Do you know anything they might be interested in?" Borman asked.

Oh God, he thought, I know Eleanor, and Eleanor's work, and . . .

"Of course not! I'm an officer," he said. "All I have to give them are my name, rank, and serial number. I don't know any secrets, and I'm not a spy."

Borman shook his head.

"I doubt the Abwehr is interested in your name, rank, and serial number, my friend Johnnie."

"I've heard of the Gestapo," Shaux said.

"The Gestapo is civilian; the Abwehr is military."

In practical terms, Johnnie thought, that could be a distinction without a difference. Would Yeats sustain him if . . . he could not bring himself to finish the thought.

"I don't know. I've never seen this before," Borman muttered. "Other RAF pilots, sure, they go off to the Stalag Luft camps in good order. As long as you are with us, the Geneva Convention applies. We treat RAF pilots fairly because you treat Luftwaffe pilots fairly. It is a matter of honor. You are a POW, in the custody of the Luftwaffe. But, if they take you, who knows?"

"You mean . . . ?"

"I mean who knows, Johnnie Shaux?"

Later that day Borman returned, still wearing his flying gear.

"The Abwehr is in Reims. It is necessary to drive you to them. I have volunteered."

"Now?" Shaux asked. Again the hair stood up on his neck. His stomach was in tight knots.

"Now," Borman said. "I regret you must be in handcuffs."

He led Shaux out to an ancient Citroën lorry repainted with Luftwaffe markings.

"We sweep back and forth across the land, we pilots," Borman said as they started. "First one side, and then the other, as the winds of war blow us. First you in France, you told me, then me. Up in our aircraft, high in the sky, a Spitfire, a 190, but they both look the same from the ground."

Shaux wondered if he could jump out of the lorry while it was moving without reinjuring his ankle. But he was in handcuffs . . .

"Perhaps you will be back again in years to come, as fate dictates," Borman said, slowing to pass a child on a bicycle. "Perhaps the tides of war will sweep us out and you in. That is, of course, assuming you avoid flying crappy Whirlwinds!"

They were approaching the outskirts of Reims. If Shaux was going to jump, it would have to be now. The door opened from the front with the hinges at the back, so he'd somehow have to avoid being hit by it.

"I am sorry to confess I shot down another of your colleagues, a Spitfire, today," Borman continued. "Why is Fighter Command doing these stupid raids? It is so pointless. Fighter Command used to be much shrewder."

Shaux scarcely heard him. He was going to have to jump, to take his chances, or face the Abwehr. He didn't really know who they were, but he definitely did not want to find out. He gauged the distance to the door handle, bearing in mind his handcuffs. Borman was busy driving, staring forward with both hands on the wheel. Shaux would count silently to three, and . . .

"I have something for you," Borman's voice broke in. "Here, take the key to your handcuffs."

"What are you doing?"

"Now brace yourself. It is necessary that I lose control of the truck on this slippery road and get injured."

Borman spun the wheel abruptly, and the lorry careened off the road and into the ditch, canted over at a ridiculous manner. Shaux and Borman landed in a heap, almost upside down against the canvas roof.

"Excellent! Ha! I think my arm is broken," Borman gasped in Shaux's ear, wincing in pain. "It is necessary that you run away immediately before another vehicle comes along. Fortunately we have crashed where there are woods to hide in, and it is growing dark. Auf Wiedersehen, Johnnie Shaux."

Shaux lay for a moment in shock, not only at what Borman had just done but also at the hideous risk he was taking.

"I don't know what to say . . . ," he started. "Won't you be in trouble?"

"No—I am a hero, don't forget. A flying ace, a champion of the Reich, an eagle of the skies. My father is high in the Party, a friend of Göring. Besides, no one shoots down a Spitfire and then lets a pilot escape. Now go immediately."

"Are you sure?"

"I am the master of my fate, Johnnie Shaux, just as you are of yours. Go!"

Shaux shook his head to clear it and started to think. The windscreen had shattered, and he climbed through it. This road ran east and west, and therefore Belgium, about 150 miles northeast, was to his right.

"Do me one favor," Borman called out.

"What?"

"No more crappy Whirlwinds, Johnnie Shaux. They're too dangerous. *Viel Glück!*"

Shaux nodded, turned abruptly, and headed for the trees.

Q: It is said, Dame Eleanor, that he escaped with the help of a sympathetic Luftwaffe officer. Can you confirm that?

A: Oh really! That silly old rumor never seems to die! What nonsense! It sounds like something in a novel, doesn't it! His POW transport lorry crashed, and he was able to get away.

FORTY-TWO

Eleanor awoke. There was a strong smell of cleaning fluid and the insistent sound of a vacuum cleaner. Someone was crooning nearby. The lights were very bright, even though her eyes were closed. The crooning was the new smash hit "Chattanooga Choo Choo." Her arm hurt. No, it was her leg. No, it was both.

Someone was singing, "Pardon me, boy. Is that the Chattanooga Choo Choo?" And someone else was making rhythmic sounds like "Wah, wah, wah." Her leg hurt a lot. She tried to move it, but it must be stuck. Now there were two people singing, "Wah, wah, wah." What did "Wah, wah, wah" mean? What language was that? Her arm hurt. That wouldn't move either.

Someone was saying, "Mrs. Shaux, are you awake?" Not the singers, someone else. There was no singing; perhaps she had dreamt it or perhaps they had left; perhaps they'd been chased away by this new voice. Oh, of course, "Wah, wah, wah" was a sound, not a word—they were pretending to be trombones in Glenn Miller's orchestra on the gramophone. She must be in America: only Americans could afford vacuum cleaners . . . it was probably one of the new Hoovers. She'd watched them vacuuming in her hotel in Washington. She'd have to get one if they made them in England.

"Mrs. Shaux, are you awake?" the voice asked again. A man's voice, not unkind but firm, with an American accent.

"Yes," she answered, but her mouth was not working.

Someone was tapping her shoulder gently, the shoulder that didn't hurt.

"Wake up, Mrs. Shaux."

She opened her eyes. A man in a white coat—a doctor—was staring at her. She was lying in a hospital bed. Her left arm was encased in plaster inside a cage by her side, and her right leg was suspended by pulleys stretching down from an overhead rack. Everything hurt.

The doctor flashed an even brighter light in her eyes, one by one, and checked her temperature.

"Let me tell what has happened, Mrs. Shaux," he said as he worked. "My name is Davis, Dr. Steven Davis. You're in the military hospital in Honolulu."

"Honolulu?" Why was she in Honolulu?

"You were injured during the attack. Do you remember that?"

"What attack?" she managed to ask.

The man was making no sense. She wished he'd stop talking nonsense and give her something to make the pain go away. Honolulu? Wasn't that in Hawaii?

"The Japanese attacked," he said, wrapping a blood pressure cuff around the arm that didn't hurt and pumping it up. "You were on an inbound flight from San Francisco, just coming in to land."

Suddenly she recalled loud noises, people screaming, a plane—a plane she was flying in—seeming to fall out of the sky.

"I remember someone shooting at us."

He was silent until he finished his measurements.

"That was a Japanese plane, Mrs. Shaux. They attacked the anchorage in Pearl Harbor and the docks and the airfield. They sank eight battleships."

"Oh God! Does Admiral Kimmel know?"

"Of course he knows," the doctor said, smiling. "President Roosevelt knows. The whole world knows. We declared war. We're at war with Japan."

"When?"

"Two days ago."

So, it had come to pass. Once again she'd anticipated the enemy, and once again she'd been ignored. Now the most powerful nation in the world, the most powerful nation the world had ever known, would enter the fray.

Thousands would die—hundreds of thousands, probably millions.

All Europe, all the British Empire, Japan, China, Russia, and now America were engaged. All Asia would be consumed. It was a world war.

America would win, of course, provided it didn't make mistakes and therefore lose. Unfortunately they had laid out a piece of bait so rich, so fine, so desirable—eight helpless battleships neatly tied up in a row—that the Japanese had been unable to resist it.

She'd have to be stronger than before. She'd have to get directly to President Roosevelt in person and make sure he understood how not to lose and therefore how to win. She'd have to make him understand the significance of the MAUD report, the most important piece of paper on the planet. She would have to convince him that he should not let Stalin defeat Hitler and continue until all of Europe was in his grasp.

Oh my God! If the Japanese had attacked Pearl Harbor, they'd almost certainly attack Singapore and Hong Kong as well! She had to warn Churchill anew.

There was no time to lose. She tried to rise, but she was imprisoned and trussed up in plaster and pulleys.

The doctor was leaning over her again.

"You have a broken arm and a broken leg, Mrs. Shaux; your left radius and your right tibia, to be exact. They're not complicated fractures—clean breaks—and you'll heal nicely. You appear to be in good health and in your early twenties, so four to six weeks, no more. You have lots of cuts and bruises, but those will heal quickly. In fact, you're very lucky not to have suffered worse; the pilot saved your life, no doubt about it."

Now she remembered everything: coming in, flying low over the anchorage with all the battleships lined up in the early light of a beautiful dawn; circling Hickam Field and approaching for landing, with the noise of the lowering wheels in the slipstream; a sudden row of bullet holes appearing in the side of the fuselage just ahead of her, as if sewn perfectly by a Singer machine; the violent rearing of the cabin as the pilot took evasive action; a fleeting glimpse of another aircraft flashing past her window; bodies and the luggage flying everywhere; a harsh crash! as the plane landed so heavily the wheels snapped off;

more perfect rows of holes, this time accompanied by loud noises and a sudden scream of pain from one of the other passengers—yes, it was the admiral who had told her he was satisfied with the forward deployment of the fleet—the agonizingly loud screeching of the metal belly of the aircraft as it careened down the runway in a cascade of sparks, as if she were riding a firework rocket or a shooting star; the sudden softness of a woolly wall of impenetrable darkness at the end of the runway that gave way, in due course, to the sounds of the "Chattanooga Choo Choo."

"I think that's more than enough for one day, Mrs. Shaux. You need as much rest as possible. I'll give you something to take the edge off."

Soon she was alone, under the unblinking lights.

Oh God! She had failed to prevent this attack. She had failed to prevent an avoidable war. She had failed the Americans she had been sent to help. Eight battleships! No one had ever lost eight battleships in a single encounter—not even the French at Trafalgar. She had failed Churchill. She had almost certainly failed the people of Hong Kong and Singapore. She had been sent to Honolulu to try to explain to the navy how dangerous it was to have all their ships in one place, all their eggs in one basket. She had not done so . . . she had arrived too late . . . she had done too little, too late.

She needed to discuss with Harry Hopkins whether or not Hitler would declare war on the United States. Roosevelt would need to know, as well as Churchill. It would be a colossal mistake by Hitler, but she still needed to calculate the probability given Japan's preemptive attack. She called out for a pencil and paper so that she could write the necessary functions, but her mouth had stopped working again.

She was alone in the middle of the Pacific, eight thousand miles from home. The lights were still too bright even though her eyes were tightly shut. She had failed everyone. She couldn't even calculate the probability that Hitler would declare war. Her thoughts careened and lost focus and blurred into a kaleidoscope as the medicine took effect.

Faces flickered through Eleanor's mist: Churchill, in a smoky haze; Stalin catching her tipping vodka into a potted plant and complaining to Churchill; Susan Smith, in despair, gripping a pair of knitting needles; an admiral demanding she spell "asymptotic"; Charlie sitting, wearing Froggie's scarf and watching the sky with his full, unwavering attention, waiting infinitely patiently for Johnnie to come home, waiting week in and week out until, one day, he died of a broken heart, just like that; and Johnnie, alone in a cage, convincing himself that she had just been a daydream after all.

SECOND EPILOGUE

Q: You began this evening's show by saying that 1941 was worse than 1940. Now I can see why.

A: Yes. The fact that we didn't lose the Battle of Britain left us able to fight on, but things went very badly for us. It was a grim struggle for survival in 1941. There was no hope of victory, just a stubborn refusal to roll over and die.

Until the moment of Pearl Harbor, I expected we would lose because I expected the Americans would not fight. They would help, certainly, even help a great deal, but they would not join the battle. I never sensed Roosevelt was looking for an excuse to declare war. I thought that public sentiment and common sense would keep America from throwing away blood and treasure on what was just the latest ruinously self-destructive European war in a series of such wars stretching back through recorded history.

Q: But they did declare—

A: Even after Pearl Harbor, when the United States declared war on Japan, it did not declare war on Germany or the Axis powers as a group. But on December 11, 1941, several days later, Hitler made a catastrophically bad mistake. He declared war on the United States.

Q: But surely the United States would have entered the European war eventually.

A: Perhaps; difficulties—grave difficulties—between Japan and the United States were simmering in the Pacific before Pearl Harbor, and there was a de facto, low-level war going on in the Atlantic—U-boats against American destroyers. But such low-grade wars can go on for decades—just look at the current Middle East.

In retrospect, it's very fortunate for us that Hitler did push America into the European war as early as 1941.

Q: Why?

A: Well, if Hitler hadn't pushed the Americans into the European war, then in 1945 Stalin would not have stopped when he met the American and British armies in Germany, because they wouldn't have been there.

Q: Why not?

A: D-Day would have not taken place when it did. Therefore Stalin would have come straight across Western Europe, and what is now the European Union would have been the Union of European Soviet Socialist Republics. There would have been nothing to stop him.

Q: You mean . . .

A: In real history, Stalin only stopped because he reached the front lines of the British and American armies. Without them, he could have continued westward until all Europe was under his control, and you and I would have been citizens of the British Soviet Socialist Republic.

Q: Surely you jest?

A: Do I? I'll leave it up to you.

Q: Dame Eleanor, I do believe you're teasing me.

A: Am I? I'll leave that up to you as well.

Q: I wish I knew . . . Well, anyway, you've brought us from the Battle of Britain, in September 1940, to Pearl Harbor in December 1941, just as you promised.

In all the battles, in all the conferences, in all the turning points, what stands out most, in your mind?

A: Oh, in looking back, I think . . . Well, I think it's all receding into the past; it's becoming a sort of dim tribal memory, like the Battle of Trafalgar or Agincourt—some sort of battle long, long ago, mentioned in school but not studied . . . And now, people see parades, and a few old men in wheelchairs with medals on their chests, and I suppose people wonder what it's all about . . .

Q: One memory, Dame Eleanor, that sums it all up?

A: Oh, without a doubt, it's Churchill asking Park how many aircraft we had in reserve, and Park replying, "None." It was so like Keith Park—the unvarnished truth.

As Churchill subsequently wrote, "The odds were great; our margins small; the stakes infinite."

Q: And, to finish our story, Dame Eleanor, or at least this part of it, what did you do after Pearl Harbor?

A: Well, let me first say that, as you know, America had its aircraft carriers out at sea when the Japanese attacked Pearl Harbor, thank God, and so were spared. That made the vital American victory at Midway the following summer possible, and it was a massive counterblow against Yamamoto.

But, to your question, the hospitals were overwhelmed, so I was sent back to America to finish my recovery—San Francisco, such a beautiful city, such wonderful food and wine—and then home, at long, long last, in February.

I landed at RAF Ringway, near Manchester. I was tentatively trying to hop my way down the stairs, trying to keep my weight off my weak leg, when someone picked me up and set me on the ground.

I said thank you automatically, without looking up, getting my balance on my crutches, and the person said: "Welcome home," in Johnnie's voice.

Q: You didn't know he'd escaped and made it back to England! What did you do?

A: I could do nothing. Charlie was so excited he had knocked me over.

AUTHOR'S NOTES

Infinite Stakes

The Battle of Britain remains one of the most dramatic and pivotal battles in recorded history. The battle occurred a year after Hitler's invasion of Poland in September 1939, which triggered World War II. That year, from September 1939 until August 1940, witnessed an astonishing series of British losses and defeats, which Winston Churchill, who became prime minister in May, aptly described as a "cataract of disaster."

The Battle of Britain began early in August of 1940, climaxed on September 15, and by the end of that month had metamorphosed into the nightly blitz on London and other major cities. The scale and intensity of the Battle of Britain, as a standalone five-week clash of two air forces, was unprecedented and has never been surpassed. More than two thousand aircraft were destroyed in a mere forty days, an average toll of fifty aircraft per day.

The Battle of Britain was fought to establish air superiority over the English Channel and southern England in order to permit a German invasion of Britain. The RAF retained control and never relinquished it, and Hitler was therefore forced to abandon the invasion; four years later, in June 1944, British and Allied air superiority made the D-Day invasion of Normandy, in the opposite direction, possible.

It is now generally agreed that on Battle of Britain Day, September 15, the RAF had approximately thirty aircraft destroyed and twenty aircraft damaged, while the Luftwaffe had approximately sixty aircraft destroyed and twenty aircraft severely damaged; the RAF had thirty pilots killed or wounded, and the Luftwaffe had approximately 150 airmen killed, wounded, or captured. These numbers are sharply lower than the contemporaneous claims but still indicate a decisive advantage to the RAF.

England prevailed in the Battle of Britain, but only barely, and the following fifteen months continued to be a cruel struggle for survival. It is fair to say that the Battle of Britain was England's only significant victory in a long series of disheartening and debilitating defeats. There were four principal battlegrounds following the Battle of Britain: the blitz, the nightly bombing of British cities against which the British initially had no defense and during which tens of thousands died; North Africa and the Eastern Mediterranean, where British and Commonwealth forces were losing ground because they were outnumbered by the combined strength of the German and Italian forces; the North Atlantic, where convoys from the United States and Canada were savaged by the highly successful Kriegsmarine U-boat (*Unterseeboot* or submarine) offensive—here again, the convoys had no effective defensive technology at that time; and Russia, where very few expected the Russians to survive Hitler's onslaught.

    Thus, at the end of 1941, Hitler's Germany was still poised for victory, and the British were still staring into the abyss.

As I did in *Breaking Point*, which was set in the midst of the Battle of Britain, I tried to keep the historical context of *Infinite Stakes* as faithful to history as possible. For example, Churchill really did spend September 15 in the Battle of Britain Bunker, he really did forget it was his wife's birthday, and the two waves of Luftwaffe attacks that day really did consist of the numbers and types of aircraft I describe.

    The events I describe in 1941—Barbarossa, the MAUD report, the Riviera and Caviar conferences, the sacking of Park, the rhubarb raids, and so on, did occur, as, of course, did Pearl Harbor.

    Roosevelt and Churchill used a small group of trusted advisors rather than entourages of diplomats and generals to undertake sensitive negotiations. This inner group, operating in great secrecy, included Lord Beaverbrook on the British side and Harry Hopkins on the American side. My fictitious Eleanor would have been one such trusted emissary.

The various officials I mention really did hold the positions that I describe, and I have included a list of these people later in these notes.

It was with great trepidation that I gave imaginary dialogue to real historical figures—Churchill, Park, Hopkins, and so on—but I tried to do so with respect and out of admiration. I struggled with giving dialogue to Leigh-Trafford because I may have been unfair to him, but the positions I depict him as taking he really did take. He, unlike the others, did not survive the war, and so he was denied the opportunity (in contrast to Churchill) to write self-exonerating and self-congratulatory memoirs.

The various aircraft, engines, and technologies I have described all existed (with the exception of Red Tape, of course) and performed approximately as I have described; thus, for example, it took a Spitfire II approximately ten minutes to reach twenty-five thousand feet.

There can be no question that Rolls-Royce produced a long series of aero engines of unmatched quality, including the superb Merlin and the mighty Griffon, the finest reciprocating piston engines ever built. But, alas, it is unfortunately true that the Peregrine and the Vulture really were rare failures in Rolls-Royce's very fine record.

There was one operational Whirlwind squadron. It's a pity that the Peregrine was unsuccessful, because the Whirlwind would have been successful if given adequate and reliable power. Over a hundred were built. As it was, the Merlin-powered Mosquito became arguably the finest twin-engined fighter-bomber of World War II.

Eleanor, her model, her team, and MI6-3b did not exist, of course, although von Neumann was very much alive and really had created the basic theory of zero-sum games (although it was never applied to World War II as I have depicted Eleanor doing—as far as I know), and he really did work on the Manhattan Project with Enrico Fermi.

Johnnie, 339 and 188, and all their pilots are similarly fictional. However, there really were three magnificent Eagle Squadrons manned by brave American volunteers—188 would have been a fourth.

WORLD WAR II
SUMMARY CHRONOLOGY

From Poland to Pearl Harbor

1939		
September	Hitler invades Poland; the start of World War II	
October	Stalin occupies Eastern Poland	Shaux starts Defiant training
November	Start of the Winter War; Russia invades Finland	
December	Phony War—no attacks in Western Europe	Eleanor joins WAAF
1940		
January	Phony War	
February	Phony War	Shaux posted to Eindhoven, Holland
March	Phony War	Eleanor posted to Air Ministry
April	Hitler invades Denmark and Norway	
May	10: Hitler invades Holland, Belgium, and France 10: Churchill becomes prime minister 26: Dunkirk evacuation starts	Shaux begins air operations

June	4: Dunkirk evacuation ends	Shaux shot down over Dunkirk
	10: Italy declares war; Mediterranean campaign begins	Shaux posted to Abbas, France
	22: Fall of France; France surrenders	Shaux escapes France
	18: Stalin occupies Estonia, Latvia, and Lithuania	Shaux starts Spitfire training
July	Hitler prepares an invasion fleet for his Operation Sea Lion	
August	12: Eagle Day—start of the Battle of Britain	Eleanor posted to 11 Group Shaux posted to 339 Squadron
September	6: Start of the London blitz **15: Battle of Britain Day**	Eleanor transferred to MI6-3b Shaux posted to A&AEE
October	Operation Sea Lion cancelled; nighttime blitz intensifies	
November	U-boat campaign intensifies	
December	U-boat campaign intensifies	
1941		
January	U-boat campaign intensifies; siege of Malta intensifies	
February	Siege of Malta intensifies	
March	Rommel attacks in Africa	
April	Siege of Malta intensifies; Greece falls Siege of Tobruk begins Lend-Lease Act signed	
May	Crete falls	
June	Hitler invades Russia in Operation Barbarossa	
July	Germany makes rapid advances in Russia	Eleanor arrives in Washington Shaux posted to 188 Squadron
August	Riviera conference, Atlantic Charter	Eleanor attends Riviera conference

September	Moscow conference, start of Arctic convoys	Eleanor attends Caviar conference Shaux becomes POW
October	German advance in Russia slows	Eleanor back at MI6-3b
November	Germans approach Moscow, Tobruk relieved	Eleanor returns to Washington
December	6: 7: Japanese attack on Pearl Harbor 11: Hitler declares war against USA Zhukov counterattacks in Russia	Shaux escapes Eleanor in Hawaii Shaux escapes

Counterfactuals

After *Breaking Point* I was often asked what would have happened if 11 Group had lost the Battle of Britain. What-if scenarios are fun, but such counterfactuals can also provide valuable insights into the consequences of actual events and decisions.

In *Infinite Stakes* Eleanor makes two counterfactual analyses in her interviews. The first addresses the question of what would have happened if Germany had won the Battle of Britain. She posits that the tactical situation would have swung in Germany's favor during 1941.

- Germany (with assistance from Italy) would have been able to gain complete control of the Mediterranean and the Suez Canal and therefore Arabian oil fields. (The Royal Navy would not have been there, and the Australians would not have remained in North Africa.) This would have obviated Hitler's need to gain control of oil fields and other sources of raw materials by striking east and invading Russia.
- All of Africa would have been available; South Africa would have been particularly tempting.
- Germany would have gained control of the Royal Navy and the North Atlantic (although some of the fleet might have been scuppered). This would have rendered an American invasion of Europe virtually impossible.

The long-term strategic situation would also have swung in Germany's favor.

- Germany would have gained control of British atomic physics, then the most advanced in the world. It is entirely reasonable to assume, therefore, a working German atomic bomb in 1944.
- Eleanor therefore suggests that German could have had the battleship *Bismarck* (which would not have been sunk in 1941) patrolling with V1 cruise missiles and V2 ballistic missiles (both of which it had successfully developed by 1944) topped with atomic warheads.
- This would have permitted Hitler to threaten the United States directly.

Her second counterfactual analysis addresses the United States remaining neutral in Europe.

- If Germany had defeated Britain in 1940, there would have been far less tension in the Atlantic, no Lend-Lease Act, no Atlantic convoys and U-boat attacks, and no real *causus belli* for American intervention.
- Even if Britain had not been defeated, it was far from clear that the United States would have declared war on Germany. Public sentiment demanded a focused response to Pearl Harbor in the Pacific. It was only when Hitler declared war on the United States, several days after Pearl Harbor, that the United States finally entered the European war as a belligerent.
- The Soviet Union advanced on Germany slowly but inexorably from 1942 to 1945, eventually overrunning Berlin and most of Germany. The Soviet armies only stopped when they met the British and American armies coming in the opposite direction. But if Britain was defeated in

1940 and/or the United States did not enter the European war, there would have been no D-Day and therefore no British and American armies in Europe. (The British could not have accomplished D-Day on their own.)

• The Soviet Union could therefore have "liberated" all of Europe and established Soviet governments in Britain, France, and so on, just as it did in Eastern Europe.

There are many other counterfactuals one can play with, but these two examples illustrate that the modern world could easily have been radically different if not for 11 Group's tenacity and Hitler's penchant for making catastrophic mistakes.

Winston Spencer Churchill

One of the oldest debates in the study of history is whether historical circumstances create great men and women or whether great men and women create history. As Shakespeare said, "[S]ome are born great, some achieve greatness, and some have greatness thrust upon 'em."

It has often struck me that the muddled, inexplicable, tendentious, and hideously wasteful World War I was presided over by men who were, in the arc of history, relative mediocrities producing a mediocre result, whereas World War II was presided over by relative giants, men of stunning drive and willpower (good or bad): Roosevelt, Churchill, de Gaulle, Stalin, Tojo, Chiang Kai-shek, and Hitler.

It seems to me that before 1940 Churchill was a man of prodigious but unfulfilled ability. Then fate called forth the monstrous Hitler and presented Churchill with a challenge that would test his abilities to their limits. To quote Shakespeare again, from a different play and context, the situation in May 1940, with the combined armies of Britain and France collapsing helplessly before Hitler's Panzers, required a man who could call upon the British to "imitate the action of the tiger, stiffen the sinews, summon up the blood" and "disguise fair nature with hard-favored rage."

And they did.

Churchill really did collect phrases and store them for future use. Just as many of us launch arias in the shower, Churchill is said to have orated in the tub. As far as I know, he did not say "bent but not broken" or "so many for so little." He did, however, write of that day in the 11 Group Operations Room: "The odds were great; our margins small; the stakes infinite." He did, also, use the phrases "pray do this" or "pray tell me that" and so on, to the point that his wartime orders became known as "Churchill's Prayers."

Churchill's self-confidence knew few boundaries. If he had encountered a mathematician like Eleanor, I am sure he would have convinced himself that he, too, could have created the Red Tape zero-sum model, except he had better things to do and so would leave the mathematics to lesser mortals. He wrote in his autobiography:

> I had a feeling once about Mathematics—that I saw it all. Depth beyond depth was revealed to me—the Byss and Abyss. I saw—as one might see the transit of Venus or even the Lord Mayor's Show—a quantity passing through infinity and changing its sign from plus to minus. I saw exactly why it happened and why the tergiversation was inevitable: and how the one step involved all the others. It was like politics. But it was after dinner and I let it go!
> —Winston S. Churchill, My Early Life

I don't know if he was serious or joking, but after such a tergiversation I'll let it go.

William Butler Yeats and William Ernest Henley

The Irish poet and Nobel Prize winner William Butler Yeats wrote this poem in commemoration of the son of a friend who had died in a freakish friendly fire accident at the end of World War I.

> *I know that I shall meet my fate*
> *Somewhere among the clouds above;*

Those that I fight I do not hate
Those that I guard I do not love;
My country is Kiltartan Cross,
My countrymen Kiltartan's poor,
No likely end could bring them loss
Or leave them happier than before.
Nor law, nor duty bade me fight,
Nor public men, nor cheering crowds,
A lonely impulse of delight
Drove to this tumult in the clouds;
I balanced all, brought all to mind,
The years to come seemed waste of breath,
A waste of breath the years behind
In balance with this life, this death.

It had always been one of my favorites—so dark, so fatalistic. When it came time to write about a pilot in the Battle of Britain facing extreme danger, it seemed to me that he might find a sense of refuge, even reassurance, in these simple words.

In sharp contrast, "Invictus," by William Ernest Henley, describes the poet's dogged determination to endure in spite of great hardship (in his case, severe health issues) and has inspired many, including Nelson Mandela during his long imprisonment.

"Invictus" (the Latin word for "unconquered") is an announcement of defiance:

Out of the night that covers me
Black as the pit from pole to pole,
I thank whatever gods may be
For my unconquerable soul.

In the fell clutch of circumstance,
I have not winced nor cried aloud.
Under the bludgeonings of chance
My head is bloody, but unbowed.

Beyond this place of wrath and tears
Looms but the Horror of the shade,
And yet the menace of the years
Finds and shall find me unafraid.

It matters not how strait the gate,
How charged with punishments the scroll,
I am the master of my fate,
I am the captain of my soul.

Churchill used the last two lines in a speech to the Commons in September 1941 during the darkest days when events in the Atlantic, the Mediterranean, and in Russia were all going badly.

My Shaux took refuge in Yeats, while my Borman of the Luftwaffe, fighting back against the cruel hand he has been dealt, quotes Henley.

Rolls-Royce Piston Engines

Rolls-Royce produced piston aero engines from 1915 to 1955. During this forty-year period, Rolls-Royce developed no less than seventeen distinct models, many of which were significant upgrades redesigned from previous models. All were named after birds of prey, and several of these models were very successful, particularly the early World War I Eagle, the interwar Kestrel, and the World War II Merlin and Griffon.

The Eagle, introduced in 1915, produced 250 horsepower from a V-12 twenty-liter design. Two Eagles powered the first-ever nonstop crossing of the Atlantic in 1919. The V-12 thirty-seven-liter Griffon developed 2,400 horsepower—an order of magnitude more powerful than the Eagle—and entered production in 1942. Griffons are still used in some applications, such as the Battle of Britain Flight, some aeroracing, hydroplanes, and even competitive tractor pulling.

It was, however, inevitable that some Rolls-Royce designs would be less successful than others, particularly as the drive for yet more horsepower at a yet greater range of heights pushed some designs beyond their limits.

My fictitious Johnnie Shaux had the misfortune to encounter two of these disappointing designs, the Peregrine and the improbable Vulture, but he also had the pleasure of flying and exalting in the superb Merlin, of which more than one hundred and fifty thousand were built.

The Whirlwind was the only aircraft to use the Peregrine, which was finally cancelled in 1942. The X-24 Vulture was used to power (or, to be precise, to underpower) the Avro Manchester bomber, another unsuccessful aircraft. But rather than throw away the airframe, four Merlins were tried instead of two Vultures, and voilà, the hugely successful Lancaster was created.

By the end of World War II, jet engines had been invented and tested and had entered the conflict, and Rolls-Royce's magnificent creations therefore became obsolescent. The company, of course, turned its attention to jets and remains one of the world's leading manufacturers. The first British jet fighter, the Gloster Meteor, was powered by two Rolls-Royce RB.23 Welland turbojet engines.

The Evolution of the Atlantic Alliance

World War II began when Hitler invaded Poland in September 1939, long before Pearl Harbor. It was not until Pearl Harbor in December 1941 that the United States finally entered the war.

In the early stages of World War II, American public sentiment was sympathetic to the British side, but the American people decidedly did not want to enter another war to save Europe from itself a second time. (The United States had entered World War I in its waning stages but still suffered grievously on the barbaric Western Front, where, at Belleau Wood in 1918, Sergeant Dan Daly of the US Marine Corps urged his men on into battle with perhaps the most noteworthy of all exhortations to advance: "Come on, you sons of bitches. Do you want to live forever?")

In 1940 and 1941, the United States faced threats across both oceans. In the Pacific, the Japanese Empire was rapidly expanding its sphere of influence and building up its military capabilities. Relationships between the United States and Japan were on a downward slope, with increasingly strained diplomatic and trade relations. In the Atlantic, the highly successful Kreigsmarine U-boat campaign was attacking supply convoys, including American as well as Canadian and British shipping. However, protected by two oceans, the United States was completely secure.

Public sympathy in the United States was pro-British and Canadian. The new Neutrality Act of 1939 permitted the United States to sell war supplies to the British but on a cash-and-carry basis. The British paid in gold and were literally running out of money by the end of 1940. Cash-and-carry was therefore replaced by the Lend-Lease Act in 1941, under which the United States could simply lend Britain and its allies the supplies they needed. Roosevelt placed Harry Hopkins in charge of Lend-Lease (as he had been similarly in charge of federal relief programs during the Depression), making him immensely powerful and influential over Soviet, British, and National Chinese policies.

In parallel, the British war effort was being seen, to an increasing extent, as a global defense of democracy against fascism. This was reflected in the Atlantic Charter, which called not only for the end of the Nazi regime but also for a broad, new world order based on democratic self-determination. This document, drafted by the United States and grudgingly supported by Churchill, laid the foundations for the United Nations and other international bodies and meant the end of European colonialism.

Eventually and only after all of this did Japan attack Pearl Harbor, precipitating the Pacific war, and Hitler declared war on the United States.

Belgian Bouviers (Bouviers des Flandres)

Bouviers are big, powerful working dogs originally used in Belgium and Holland to herd cattle and pull light carts. They have thick, short coats, large heads with longer hair, and exceptionally powerful jaws. A full-grown male can weigh eighty pounds. They are intelligent and strong enough to serve as police dogs and other types of service dogs.

It is said that Hitler hated Bouviers after meeting them in World War I, but I have no firm documentary evidence to support this.

The Tizard Mission

Henry Tizard was a radar scientist who led a mission to the United States in September 1940 to offer an exchange of scientific research information in the hope that American expertise and resources could be used to support British war efforts.

Among the scientific offerings were the following:

- Whittle's designs for a gas turbine engine led to the first successful Allied production jet engine in 1943. (The Luftwaffe won the race to produce a jet fighter.)
- The resonant cavity magnetron was the key component of viable airborne radar.
- The Frisch–Peierls memorandum was a scientific paper demonstrating the practicality of atomic weapons.
- There were other technologies and inventions, including rockets, advanced superchargers, gyroscopic gunsights (predicting where the target would be, not where it was), self-sealing fuel tanks, and plastic explosive.

Origins of the Manhattan Project

The Frisch–Peierls memorandum and its 1941 successor, the MAUD report, led directly to the British Tube Alloys and the American Manhattan Project.

During the 1930s, atomic bombs were thought to be infeasible because an explosive device, even if theoretically possible, would be far, far too big to be carried in an aircraft.

However, in 1940 two émigré nuclear scientists working at the University of Birmingham in England, Otto Frisch and Rudolf Peierls, calculated that a few kilograms of uranium 235 would be sufficient to produce an explosion equal to a thousand tons of dynamite. Their document included the farsighted observation that the only defense against such a bomb was to get one first. (Mark Oliphant, the Australian scientist, also worked with Frisch, Peierls, and Tizard.)

Their memorandum led to further analysis, resulting in the MAUD report that was completed in July 1941 and confirmed their assessment. This in turn triggered the British Tube Alloys project to begin development of a bomb, and the American Manhattan Project, which was launched in October 1941.

Hiroshima and Nagasaki were bombed in August 1945.

It should be noted that the Frisch–Peierls memorandum was an official secret, but Frisch and Peierls, as German expatriates and technically "enemy aliens," had not yet been given security clearances when they wrote it. Thus the notion that my Eleanor was not allowed to know the content of her own work is not without a real-world precedent.

Glossary and General Notes

RAF Aircraft	
Beaufighter	The Bristol Beaufighter was a versatile twin-engine heavy fighter. The Beau became a very successful night fighter once the RAF had perfected the AI Mark IV airborne radar. This is the radar Shaux was testing at RAF Martlesham Heath in the winter of 1940–41.
Defiant	The Boulton Paul Defiant was a single-engine fighter with a rotating gun turret behind the cockpit. It was too slow and had too limited a field of fire to survive against Me 109s and Bf 110s. This is the aircraft that Shaux flew in the early months of 1940 and in which Eleanor manned the turret in my prequel, *Breaking Point*.
Hurricane	The Hawker Hurricane was the workhorse of Fighter Command during the Battle of Britain, accounting for two-thirds of 11 Group's victories. Its reputation suffers from comparisons to the iconic Spitfire, but it was an extremely successful fighter.

Manchester	The Avro Manchester was an unsuccessful heavy bomber powered by two Rolls-Royce Vultures that were unequal to the task. Avro replaced the two Vultures with four Merlins and voilà, the highly successful Lancaster was born.
Mosquito	The De Havilland Mosquito was a highly successful fighter bomber powered by two Merlins and constructed from laminated plywood. It was still in the prototype stage when Shaux flew it at A&AEE.
Spitfire	The Supermarine Spitfire was an air superiority fighter that was produced throughout the war. While it was outclassed by other aircraft at various stages, its continuous and sustained improvement meant that it was still as good as any other by the time the war ended.
Whirlwind	The Westland Whirlwind was a twin-engine heavy fighter that suffered from being designed only for the Rolls-Royce Peregrine and could not be retrofitted for another engine. There was one operation squadron.
Luftwaffe Aircraft	
Dornier 17	The Do 17 was one of two primary types of Luftwaffe *Schnellbombers* (fast bombers) that flew in the Battle of Britain. These twin-engine aircraft could carry a ton of bombs. They were relatively slow, flying at a little more than 200 miles per hour, and poorly defended. The Luftwaffe would send dozens, sometimes hundreds, of these bombers in close formation for mutual protection, surrounded and covered by defending Me 109 and Bf 110 fighters. After September 15, the Luftwaffe switched to night bombing, the blitz, which was successful until the introduction of British AR4 radar.
Focke-Wulf 190	The Fw 190 was a highly successful Luftwaffe fighter introduced in 1941 as a replacement for the 109 (which, however, remained in production). It was superior in performance and maneuverability to the Spitfire Mk V and remained the dominant fighter in Europe until the arrival of the Spitfire Mk IX at the end of 1942.
Heinkel 111	The He 111 was the other *Schnellbomber,* similar to a Dornier 17.

Junkers 87 (Stuka)	The Ju 87 was a highly successful Luftwaffe dive-bomber. However, it could not survive against Spitfires and Hurricanes and played only a limited role in the Battle of Britain and no role in the blitz.
Junkers 88	The Ju 88 was a third type of *Schnellbomber*, designed to replace the 17s and 111s. Ju 88s saw limited operational activity during the Battle of Britain and the blitz.
Messerschmitt 109	The Me 109e was the principal Luftwaffe fighter during the Battle of Britain. It was superior to the Hurricane and marginally inferior to the Spitfire Mk II. Much of the strategy for the aerial battle over southern England depended on these performance differences.
Messerschmitt 110	The Bf 110 was a twin-engine heavy fighter during the Battle of Britain. It proved to be so inferior to the Spitfires and Hurricanes that it needed its own protection from 109s, and 110s were often used for nuisance raids and diversions to try to draw 11 Group into combat with 109s.
Technologies	
AI Mk IV	Airborne Interception Mark IV, RAF airborne radar. In combination with GCI, it permitted interception at night, thus curtailing the blitz.
Chain Home RDF	RAF radar system to detect Luftwaffe aircraft over France and Belgium
Freya	German GCI. *Bettfeder Freya* is a fictional variant (Bedspring GCI).
GCI	An acronym for "ground-controlled interception," an RAF radar system to detect Luftwaffe aircraft over England. (Chain Home faced the Channel and could not be turned round.)
Huff Duff	High-frequency direction finding, an RAF radio identification system to track RAF aircraft
Magic	A US program to decipher the Japanese encryption system
Pip-Squeak	IFF transponder system (identification friend or foe)
ROC	Royal Observer Corps, who performed a visual search for aircraft
R/T	Radio telephone
Ultra	British program to decipher the German Enigma encryption system; based at Bletchley Abbey

Historical Figures	
Max Aiken, Lord Beaverbrook	A Canadian-born newspaper magnate, influential conservative politician, and Churchill confidant, Beaverbrook served in various wartime ministries, including the Ministry of Aircraft Production and the Ministry of Supply. He was widely considered to have had a major positive impact on aircraft production during the Battle of Britain, thereby contributing to 11 Group's survival. His son was a distinguished fighter pilot, leading 601 Squadron in the Battle of Britain. Beaverbrook was Churchill's personal envoy, also becoming close to Roosevelt in so doing. Clement Attlee, then deputy prime minister and Churchill's successor in 1945, commented that "Churchill often listened to Beaverbrook's advice but was too sensible to take it."
Edward Bridges	Sir Edward Bridges was the most senior British civil servant throughout the war and until 1956. As cabinet secretary, he headed Churchill's professional staff and managed much of the information that flowed to and from him.
Hugh Dowding	Sir Hugh "Stuffy" Dowding was the creator of the Dowding system and AOC-in-C of Fighter Command in 1940. He was ousted following the Battle of Britain and sent to Washington.
Anthony Eden	Sir Anthony Eden was British foreign secretary from 1940 until 1945 and subsequently Churchill's successor as prime minister.
Enrico Fermi	Enrico Fermi was one of the extraordinary group of brilliant scientific minds who left Europe to escape fascism. He started to develop the antecedent technology for the atomic bomb as soon as he received news of the Frisch–Peierls memorandum and the subsequent MAUD report. He not only had a Nobel Prize but also had his own subatomic particle, the fermion, and even his very own element, fermium, with the atomic number of 100.
Wilfrid Freeman	Sir Wilfrid Freeman was vice chief of Air Staff for R&D, responsible for sponsoring the development and acquisition of the Spitfire, the Hurricane, and other key aircraft. He is also credited with sponsoring the Merlin and for installing a Merlin in a P51 Mustang, instead of an Allison, thereby creating one of the world's finest fighters.

Lord Halifax	Edward Wood, Lord Halifax, was British foreign secretary under the Chamberlain government. He was a supporter of accommodations with Hitler (appeasement). When Churchill became prime minister, he became the British ambassador to the United States.
Averell Harriman	Averell Harriman was a career US diplomat who served as US special envoy for Roosevelt during the war. He was a primary architect of the Atlantic Charter. He subsequently held numerous senior Foreign Service appointments.
Ernest Hives	Ernest Hives, later Lord Hives, had a legendary career at Rolls-Royce. He started as a mechanic in 1903, progressed to be a test driver, and later developed the Eagle aero engine. By 1936 he was general works manager. He oversaw the development of all Rolls-Royce engines, including the Merlin (and the Peregrine), and in 1941 he committed Rolls to developing Whittle's gas turbine (jet) engine. He became managing director in 1946 and chairman in 1950. Sir Wilfrid Freeman wrote of him: "That man Hives is the best man I have ever come across for many a year. God knows where the RAF would have been without him." He is said to have described himself as "just a bloody plumber." His son Edward was an RAF pilot killed in 1940.
Harry Hopkins	Harry Hopkins was a social worker who became a key architect and implementer of the New Deal during the Depression in the 1930s, heading the Works Progress Administration and other initiatives. He was diagnosed with stomach cancer and given only four weeks to live in 1939. He survived to become Roosevelt's closest foreign policy advisor, even moving into the White House. He supervised the implementation of the Lend-Lease Act and attended all the major Allied conferences. He wanted to resign after Roosevelt's death, but Harry S Truman insisted he stay. He died shortly after the war in 1946. Churchill described him as a man with "a flaming soul."

Trafford Leigh-Mallory	Sir Trafford Leigh-Mallory was 12 Group AOC during the Battle of Britain and was a fierce rival and critic of Keith Park. Part of their disagreement was professional—Leigh-Mallory favored large formations and aggressive strategies, the exact opposites of Park's tactics—and part was personal. Leigh-Mallory was ambitious and eager for promotion beyond his secondary role in the Fighter Command hierarchy. Leigh-Mallory and his supporters were successful in ousting Park and Dowding as soon as the Battle of Britain was over, and he subsequently went on to be promoted to head Fighter Command and all the Allied air forces on D-Day. He was killed in a flying accident late in 1944.
Frederick Lindemann	Frederick Lindemann was Churchill's chief scientific advisor during the war. He advocated deliberate bombing of German civilians to prevent them from working.
George Marshall	George C. Marshall was chief of staff for the US Army through-out the war. His career has been somewhat overshadowed by that of his subordinate, Dwight D. Eisenhower, but he was a brilliant organizer and a man of genuine vision. Following the war he became secretary of state and was the prime mover behind the Marshall Plan, for which he received the Nobel Prize.
John von Neumann	John von Neumann was another émigré European genius. He was a Hungarian who emigrated to the United States in 1932. His family followed him when antisemitism grew in the later 1930s. Like Fermi, he excelled in many fields, including mathematics, quantum mechanics, physics, economics, artificial intelligence (with Alan Turing), computing, and, of course, game theory. He, like Fermi, played a major role in the Manhattan Project. Fermi told a fellow scientist that von Neumann's brain worked ten times faster than his own. He developed the minimax theory in 1928, but did not publish his theory of games until 1944. Thus my fictional Eleanor was extrapolating from a limited and very early version of his game theory. One wonders what she thought when the *Theory of Games* was published in 1944!

Keith Park	Sir Keith Park was a New Zealander with a distinguished record as a fighter pilot in World War I. He was appointed 11 Group AOC two months before the Battle of Britain. It is said that Leigh-Mallory had wanted the job, another source of the enmity between the two men. Park was sent into obscurity in November 1940 but subsequently reemerged to take command of the RAF in the Mediterranean at the height of the Battle of Malta, producing another brilliant victory against the odds. Johnnie Johnson, one of Fighter Command's greatest pilots, said of Park, "He was the only man who could have lost the war in a day or even an afternoon."
James Richardson	US Navy Admiral Richardson protested the berthing of the Pacific fleet at Pearl Harbor in 1940 and 1941, for which he was relieved of his command.
Franklin Delano Roosevelt	FDR was the thirty-second president of the United States, serving four terms from 1933, in the height of the Depression, until his death in office in 1945. During the late 1930s and early 1940s, he walked a fine diplomatic line, supporting the enemies of Japan and Germany without declaring war. Following Pearl Harbor he placed the entire economy on a war footing, and American industrial production, as much as the American military, overwhelmed the Axis powers. The Atlantic Charter, an agreement made with Churchill before the United States was at war, presaged not only the American war effort and postwar world order but the end of the United Kingdom as a world power and the emergence of the United States as a superpower. FDR, who suffered from severe polio, died in April 1945, one month before the surrender of Germany in May and four months before the surrender of Japan in August.

Joseph Stalin	General secretary of the Communist Party of the Soviet Union. Joseph Stalin, a native of Georgia, became de facto dictator of Russia following the death of Lenin in 1924 and remained so until his death in 1951. It is interesting to contrast the state of Russia in 1924—impoverished, devastated, and suffering from the consequences of civil war; a vast backwater—with Russia in 1953, which was a nuclear-armed superpower controlling half of Europe. And yet, one might argue, it was impoverished, devastated, and suffering from the consequences of Stalinism. During World War II, following Barbarossa, Stalin fought back with complete disregard for the sacrifices he required of his own people and was successful in bringing Germany to its knees. It's hard to know whether Stalin was the biggest mass murderer of the twentieth century; estimates vary from ten to twenty million, and therefore Mao Zedong may have won this particular trophy.
Laurence Steinhardt	US ambassador to the Soviet Union, he was certain Russia could not stop the German invasion.
Georgy Zhukov	Zhukov was one of the great theater commanders of World War II, along with men such as Eisenhower and Rommel. He counterattacked against the German army in front of Moscow in December of 1941, pushing the Germans back—and kept pushing until he captured Berlin three years later.
Miscellanea	
John Dryden	This poem is a translation of an ode by the Roman poet Horace. This version was published in 1685. *Happy the man, and happy he alone,* *He who can call today his own.* *He who, secure within, can say,* *Tomorrow, do thy worst, for I have lived today.*
E-boats and S-boats	These fast motor torpedo boats were known as Schnellboots (S-boats) to the Germans and enemy boats (E-boats) to the British: so an E-boat to Shaux is an S-boat to Borman.

T. S. Eliot	"The Hollow Men" (1925) ends with this: *This is the way the world ends* *This is the way the world ends* *This is the way the world ends* *Not with a bang but a whimper.*	
Latin	The first two lines come from the Catholic rite of confession. The last two, I admit, I included for fun. An 11 Group controller in 1940 would never, ever have said *"Bonum dies habeas"* in any language!	
	"Mea culpa." *"Ego te absolvo a peccatis tuis"* *"Gratias tibi,* Lumba." *"Omni tempore,* Red Leader. *Bonum dies habeas."*	My fault I forgive you for your error Thank you, Lumba. Anytime, Red Leader. Have a nice day.
Shakespeare	"Alas, poor Yorick! I knew him, Horatio." Hamlet finds the skull of someone he knew: *Hamlet,* act V scene I	

AUTHOR BIO

John Rhodes was born during World War II while his father was serving at an RAF Fighter Command airfield. After the war he grew up in London, where, he says, the remnants of bombed-out buildings "served as our adventure playgrounds." A Cambridge University history graduate, he is the author of the award-winning *Breaking Point*, the prequel to *Infinite Stakes*.

Printed in Great Britain
by Amazon

58658022R00199